Elysian Fields

A NOVEL

MARK LaFLAUR

Mark LaFlaur (signature)

Mid–City Books

NEW YORK • NEW ORLEANS

Copyright © 2013 by Mark LaFlaur

Published in the United States by Mid-City Books.

Mid-City Books
Post Office Box 150005
Kew Gardens, NY 11415-0005

FIRST EDITION
Library of Congress Control Number (LCCN): 2012954187
ISBN-13: 978-0615729862
ISBN-10: 061572986X

Interior design by Beverly Butterfield, Girl of the West Productions, Petaluma, California. Cover design by Rachel Perkins, New York. Cover photograph by Derek Bridges, New Orleans. Street tile designs by Evelyn Menge, New Orleans.

marklaflaur.com
facebook.com/ElysianFieldsBook

To Janet—

lovely and graceful,
careful and discerning reader

Men are so inescapably mad that, by a twist of madness itself, it would be mad not to be mad.

Les hommes sont si nécessairement fous que ce serait être fou par un autre tour de folie de n'être pas fou.

PASCAL, *Pensées* (1670)

The past has a reality that we do not suspect, some substantial living existence. The past is lived, entered—not exactly *again*, for it is always there.

MAURICE NICOLL, *Living Time and the Integration of the Life* (1952)

CONTENTS

Elysian Fields

March 1999

TO GET TO THE END OF THE WORLD from New Orleans
you go west across the river and south on Highway 90
and when you come to Highway 1 you take that all the
way down to Grand Isle, the end of the line.

And so he drove southward, silent and determined
through the too-bright and quickly warming morning
as though cruising closer to the sun with his corpulent
younger brother snoring beside him, safely sedated in the
down-tilted passenger seat, his enormous belly nearly
even with the window ledge.

Just because he was thinking about it didn't mean he
was a murderer. Not yet.

Fratricide. Like a brand of rat poison.

He pushed his brother's face toward the window, but
nothing stopped the snoring.

He drove straight on, steady now, one hand on the
wheel, eyeing the road ahead with a dull gaze, nearly
numb with the boredom of the repetitive scenery and
the increasingly heavy saltwater air. It was too hot for

1

March, too hot for any time of year. Shouldn't a rental car's air conditioner work for longer than the first hour? The sun glared forcefully like the all-seeing eye of God, exposing everything with a vengeance: the gray road, the lavender blossoms of water hyacinths floating on the dark waves of Bayou Lafourche gradually diminishing amid the salt waters encroaching from the Gulf, the waves getting higher, choppier, and the patches of swamp grass and flatness everywhere as far as the eye could see. After Cut Off, Galliano, and down below his mother's hometown of Golden Meadow, the road along Bayou Lafourche was the highest point in the landscape, a narrow strip of pavement banked by levees to hold out the swamp water, a fraying thread of terra firma at sea level winding down to the Gulf of Mexico.

Immolation. Like one of the sacraments.

Simpson remembered the first time he'd thought of putting his brother away: in a tank of electric eels at a pet store. But even when Bartholomew was young he was ten times too heavy.

He parked along the white shell road as close as he could get to the fishing camp, a shack on stilts at the end of a pier. He dragged his gargantuan brother, still unconscious, into the cabin, left the dead weight sprawled on the floor inside, then clicked the padlock. He took a minute to catch his breath and massage the cramping muscles in his arms. The heaving and dragging part was over now. He had prepared methodically and visualized each step of what he had come here to do—it would be so easy, no witnesses—but now he was beginning to admit the misgivings he had been suppressing. Maybe it wasn't necessary after all, perhaps not the best solution. Dousing the cabin and pier with gasoline and lighting a match and leaving all his cares behind was not quite what Mother had in mind when she said take care of your brother. Yet it was because of him she had suffered so. It was Bartholomew who had just sat there nibbling his nails while she lay unconscious on the floor.

Simpson set the red gas can by the cabin door and drove away.

See if the sun does my work for me.

Bartholomew was just waking up in a suffocating heat after several hours' sedation by a barbiturate cocktail (Valiums surreptitiously slipped into his Cap'n Crunch), and only gradually came to realize he was locked inside a small, sweltering one-room shack on stilts over salt water and clumps of sea grass. He smelled gasoline. The room was eight feet by ten, its only door locked, and two side windows boarded up with plywood. The walls were made of rough, thick planks that had never been sanded or painted, and the roof and floor were split and splintered in many places. Fierce white-hot light flared in through the cracks in the ceiling and walls. The smell of salt water, sun-hot wood, and gasoline. The sun was throwing its heat down on the shack and the hot air was stifling, damp with the moisture in the air and from his own sweat that seemed to rise in a mist from his pores and hover around him. He sat on the rough plank floor, groggy, sweating profusely, and crying. He weighed over four hundred pounds, and he couldn't swim.

He had slept all the way down so he did not hear his brother talking aloud to himself with sarcastic, self-amusing explanations about going to meet Mother and Father at the Rabineauxs' old fishing camp, where they would all go looking for the legendary Mud Man of Bayou Lafourche. The camp, a shack built for storage and occasionally sleeping (not for comfort, as most of the time the fishermen were out on the boat), was now one of the last remaining cabins between Port Fourchon and Grand Isle, where Louisiana finally disintegrates into the Gulf of Mexico. Thirty years ago this was swamp- land and the Gulf was a half mile away, but the land was sinking, the salt water had moved in, and this was now the land's end.

The sweat was running off his nose, dripping down his arms, down through the half-inch cracks between the planks. He knelt down and pressed his hands together. *Whatever He allows to befall us is always for our salvation.* Hard to kneel straight up. He was weak and groggy and tired. Hard to pray when you're hungry, to concentrate when you're . . . After all his years of prayers and devo- tions, the Lord would not leave him to perish. But had not the martyrs also died in cruel filthy tortures, treated like meat, hacked apart and burned like dogs? They split you down the middle and peel back your skin, and jeer, "Let your God save you now!"

About three miles from the cabin, Simpson was lying on a bed in an air-conditioned Grand Isle motel room, exhausted from driving and overthinking, justifying, rationalizing, grieving. His tension headache, throbbing for weeks, had taken up permanent occupation, like a round-the-clock jackhammer crew. The dark curtains blocked the sunlight. The steady hum of the window air conditioning unit drowned out all external sounds and by cooling the air seemed also to dim the light to a soft gray blue, like the fading glow of an old black-and-white television set. With its pale green cinderblock walls, the room had an aged, vintage sort of atmosphere, from a time before he or his brother were born. A hospital base-ment or fallout shelter from the 1950s. It felt accom-modating in an impersonal, anonymous way, yet it also had the air of being a place where someone might have committed suicide.

Or murder.

How would he explain to the police?

Try to be practical for once. Seeing in terms of sym-bols and metaphors, hearing "sermons in stones," came naturally to him; it was grasping concrete, matter-of-fact reality—what everyone else knew as the real world—that was a constant challenge.

As he stared up at the dim gray ceiling, he asked him-self again if he was just going to scare a lesson into him, or if he was really going to go ahead and get it over with. If you're going to do it, now's the time. You've come this far. No one would ever know. No one except . . .

Tell me why I shouldn't. What's he ever done for me?

He was never really my brother.

Whatever he decided, however things turned out, he wanted to make sure he would feel the right way after-ward. One day when he looked back he would feel good to know he'd been decisive for once in his life. Or twice.

For months before she was hospitalized Mother had assured him, "I'm fine. It's just a little shortness of breath." But then at Charity she was begging him to pull the plug. "It's up to you, the eldest son."

He recalled having read somewhere about ancient cultures that would sacrifice the old ones. Infantocracies, ruled by the young. An appointed day each year, like a harvest festival, when everyone over a certain age is herded into the village square and stoned or burned for the common good. A leveling, a clearing, like burning the fields after the sugar cane harvest. Let new life flourish. And why shouldn't it be the young who decide when the old ones have outlived their usefulness? But his plan wasn't like that; it was an act of mercy.

"Take care of your brother. After me, he's all you have."

I'll take care of him, all right.

Who else was to blame, after all?

He just sat there. How could he just sit there?

During his father's visitation at the funeral home more than a decade before, while Gasper's friends and customers from the taxidermy shop were paying their last respects, Mother had pressed his hands between hers and said, "Promise me, Simpson, promise you'll stay and help with Bartholomew. Please don't ever move away. We need you here." Then she began sobbing, dabbing at her eyes with a tissue, then another. "He loves you more than you realize." She squeezed his hands, and he saw himself held to the ground, like Gulliver pinioned by the Lilliputians, immobilized beneath piles of wet Kleenexes.

"Let me go now," she pleaded. "Let me rest in peace."

"Ssshhh. You don't mean that. Get some sleep, now."

"That's what I'm axin' you for. I have prayed to the Lord for mercy. Now do as your mother tells you."

After an hour or so at the motel he drove back to the shack. The sun had not ignited the gasoline, even though the solar force was not only pressing down but felt like it was twisting from side to side, rubbing it in as though with cruel intent. He parked the car and walked, whistling and jingling his keys in his pocket, nearly bouncing along the pier to the cabin.

He removed his baseball cap and mirror-eyed sunglasses to peek in through a knothole in the door just below the padlock. Bartholomew was kneeling in a sweating fever trance, mumbling to himself and bobbing up and down.

Simpson sat down on the step to think about it some more. Time to pull the trigger? If he had really meant to do it he would not have waited this long. Should have done this years ago. Or maybe he wanted to make him suffer first. Sometimes decisiveness is a gradual process.

He was dressed like a man prepared for physical labor. His thin cotton shirt was wet down the middle of the back and his sleeves were rolled up high on his thin biceps. With his black New Orleans Saints cap emblazoned with a gold fleur de lis and the words I BELIEVE, he could have been a man engaged in spiritual work of some kind.

What if this is a mistake?

He squinted out across the choppy waves of dark water surrounding the last remaining tufts of sea grass and the gnarled husks of long-dead oaks. This place was earthy, somewhat fertile, and yet the scene felt desolate under the blinding-bright sky that looked oppressively wide open. The salt water was burning away the green. End-of-land sadness. Though this was a place where the land meets the sea, it was not dramatic or picturesque, but just where the exhausted earth fell apart and the salt water took over, a little more each day.

A white pelican, a rare sight around here, passed from left to right about a hundred yards ahead, a noble deep-billed bird with strong wings beating slow and even across the flat horizon. He had never seen a pelican so bright a white.

Weems, are you insane? You can't do this to him.

But art, poetry is worth any number of idiot brothers.

A pioneer must clear his own path.

Quick, before the millennium.

He's not an idiot. He's just . . . What was the diagnosis, the clinical term?

And if I go ahead with this, it's going to help me finish a poem?

"O God," Bartholomew moaned quietly. "Mother, help me." Now he was lying on his side like a bloated hog, panting, the sweat pouring off his face in sheets. He crawled over to peer through the knothole. He spied

8

his brother's sweat-darkened shirt as Simpson sat there striking matches one at a time and whistling pieces of one of Dad's old tunes.

"You're doing it wrong," Bartholomew said. "You keep hitting the wrong notes."

No reply.

"I can't believe God's letting you do this to me. He doesn't usually allow this kind of thing."

Simpson turned and frowned at the blue eye in the knothole. "God allows everything, obviously. You think he's up there watching over each one of six billion little human—"

"No, me in particular, 'cause I send him so many prayers."

"Send more. Make it quick."

"Aren't we still brothers?"

"We never were."

Silence. A slight breeze, water slapping against the pier, waves upon the clumps of earth and sea grass. Now the wind seemed to be rising. A pair of brown pelicans glided past, flapping calm and steady on the breeze, then seagulls passed from left to right, swooping down occasionally to the water, diving at fish.

"If you hurt me I'll still go to heaven—"

"Shut up."

"—'cause I'm asking God to forgive you."

"Shut up. Shut up!"

Bartholomew knew this could not be the end because the Lord was going to come again during his lifetime, as Mother had promised, though sometimes he worried

9

about what he would be in the middle of doing at the instant of the Second Coming. The trumpets would sound and the power and the glory would shine forth as the heavens opened to the full radiance of the Lord's return. Now, in his ears, all through his head he heard a great roar swelling up from the Gulf of Mexico as though warning of a mountainous wave surging toward the land. He squeezed his eyes shut and pressed his hands over his ears.

When he released his hands the roaring had stopped and all he heard was a hollow distant rushing sound like the wind you can hear in a seashell. Someone whistling, the sound of splashing. His nose twitched at the scent of gasoline, and he stiffened with terror. He peeked again through the knothole.

Simpson was still sitting there, flicking wooden matches across the box, watching them flare and hiss out in the water. A few splashes of gasoline, a little spark, and he'd be free at last, free at last. No one would ever know. And yet . . . Maybe this isn't the solution. Dr. Finestein would notice him missing. And the police? Voices sounded in his head, echoes of Mother and Father, counseling tolerance and forgiveness.

After me, he's all you have.

Everything is forgiven.

He was reaching for the gasoline can when his brother screamed.

"No!"

Bartholomew howled and pounded furiously on the door, hurled himself wildly at the walls in a panic-tantrum, throwing four-hundred-pound full-body slams that shook the cabin and rocked the pier's pilings.

"Damn!" The impact knocked Simpson forward, his hands smacking flat against the rough pier planks, splinters piercing deep into his palms, and he just barely caught himself from falling over into the brown salt water and sea grass.

Bartholomew was bouncing around the sweatbox in a rage, crashing against the walls like a mad bull in a crate.

Simpson was just getting to his feet when the door crashed down on him like a drawbridge and Bartholomew came charging out, trampling him under the boards.

1

Pursuit of
Carnal Knowledge

Early February 1999

MOTHER WAS ON HER KNEES and Brother had a knife in his hand when Simpson walked in the house.

His laundry basket fell to the floor.

"What the—. What in God's name are y'all doing?"

Melba was down on the living room floor with a screwdriver, tearing open a stuffed mallard, one of Father's proudest mountings, and Bartholomew was sitting hunched over the pink Formica breakfast bar with a steak knife, sawing intently at the belly of a yellowfin tuna.

They looked up and said in a single anxious voice, "We're looking for money!"

"In Dad's taxidermy animals?"

"We were hopin' maybe he'd hid some away for a rainy day, like for Bartholomew to live on after I'm dead."

"But you're alive."

"Well, you never know." Melba touched her silver cat's-eye glasses to straighten them, but only tilted them at a different angle. "I wonder sometimes."

"You've completely destroyed his collection."

Simpson scratched at his longish red hair and looked around the room at the formerly stuffed bobcat, gutted carcasses of a half dozen mallards, and a little three-foot-long alligator that had been one of his father's favorites. Out of each animal streamed the dried dust of old filler material, spilling out on the sofa, the floor, the breakfast bar. Tiny particles hovered and glinted in the air.

"Rampage" was the only word for it.

"I think y'all can stop now. Mother, have you run out of money? Is that what this is about?"

She cleared her throat. It was hard to admit outright. "Social Security and my pittance used to cover it all, but . . ."

"It'll be all right. We'll figure something out."

He turned to his brother, who was breathing heavy from his exertions as he picked the stuffing out of the two-foot-long yellowfin. Simpson walked to the breakfast bar and watched his large-bodied sibling quietly for a few moments, but Bartholomew would not look at him. He tried to read the words printed across the chest of the Xtra-Xtra-large T-shirt that did not quite cover his brother's full wide belly, but some of the letters were lost in the wrinkles.

"Bartholomew," he said gently. Simpson paused for a moment, sensing the name still vibrating in his throat and chest, a solid resonance. There was a feeling like déjà vu, like two different times present at once.

"Barto, would you please come over to the sofa for a minute? Let's have a little talk."

He stopped picking at the fish for a moment and stared straight down at the gold specks in the old pink Formica. Then, still not looking at Simpson, not acknowledging his brother's presence, he rose from the stool and waddled over to sit in the middle of the sofa. The old springs groaned, and they could hear the further splintering of a plywood plank Simpson had set beneath the cushions long ago to reinforce the seat.

Now the T-shirt's message was visible: 2 BLESSED 2 B STRESSED.

Simpson shuddered at the sight of his mother sitting on the floor with her glasses askew and her white wig off-center. At once he felt pity and something like nausea.

He held out his hands and said in a soothing voice, "Here, Mom, why don't you have a seat. Make yourself comfortable."

"Not a bad idea," she replied agreeably. She reached for his hands and held tight as he helped her up. She groaned and winced at a sharp pinch in her lower back as she stood, and held on to Simpson's wrist to steady herself as she moved to sit in her easy chair.

"Mom, I can lend you some money."

"Why don't *you* sit down now?" Bartholomew burst out in a loud voice, smoldering with irritation at Simpson's infuriating habit of always standing, *lording* over them from six and a half feet. Simpson was thirty-six years old and he should know better. Bartholomew was thirty-three and he didn't have to prove his maturity to anyone.

"You know, Bartholomew, you and Mom shouldn't have to be running out of money. Barto, you need to once and for all *go* to a psychiatrist and get yourself certified so you can start getting disability checks. We've talked about this for years. You're eligible for Supplemental Security. You're certifiable. And you can't put it off any longer."

"Mmm-hmmm." Melba was nodding her head. "That is so right."

"Sit down," Bartholomew said again.

"Y'all are missing out on hundreds of dollars a month, brother. You're eating her out of house and home—"

"Foul! Personal attack!" Bartholomew yelled. "Anyway, it's her money, and she loves feeding me."

"And those two air conditioners in your bedroom— the utility bills must be ungodly."

"They are definitely ungodly," Melba confirmed.

Bartholomew pouted, then put his hands to his face and pretended to cry. "You wish I was never born, both of you!"

"Oh, Pumpkin—"

"Mother, please. He cries that line every time a shrink is mentioned."

Simpson turned to his brother and held out his hands in earnest. "Bartholomew, please, I'm not attacking or criticizing you, but if y'all are at the stage where you're panicking and rippin' open the taxidermy collection— which is irreplaceable, you realize, and I loved that little alligator—looking for hidden treasure, then maybe something's not right. Mom, I'll lend you the money— I'll give you the money, or get some out of your mutual fund. But you, Bartholomew, you've got to make an appointment with Dr. Norkel, or whoever can see you, and just ask him, politely, respectfully, Bartholomew, to walk you through whatever steps you need to take—"

"Cease! I know what to do!"

"Then why haven't you goddamn done it?! You kill me, Barto. I swear to God, one of these days—."

Simpson caught himself at the brink of a tirade that would surely have stressed what a fine thing Tiny had done for the family years before when he saved them all from the sin money of the Louisiana Lottery. The flame that torched that check had left burn scars of permanent embittered resentment, not to mention the chronic financial stresses that could have been avoided.

"Well pardon me, Lord Mandeville," Bartholomew huffed, "for existing on *your* planet."

Simpson took a few deep breaths, counting to ten, letting his shaking subside.

He had never known the precise psychiatric diagnosis the doctors presumably decided upon when Bartholomew was at the state children's mental hospital for a year when the other kids his age were in second grade. The disturbances were said to be partly chemical and neurological. Some form of autism or Asperger's laced with idiot savantism? Who really knew? Simpson had been a child himself at the time, and all his parents would say was that Bartholomew was sent to Mandeville "to get better." He did not know how the doctors there had tamed him (pharmaceutically? surgically?), but after a year his brother had come back with enough self-control (usually) that he was able to resume his schooling with the other children. In later years, whenever Simpson had tried to pry some explanation out of his parents, all they could give him were the same old simplistic euphemisms that made him wonder whether they themselves had understood anything the doctors said. He had tried to ask Dr. Norkel, but the information was protected by patients' rights restrictions. Questions about Bartholomew's condition seemed only to agitate Mother. She insisted that he was "all better now," and the most she would concede was that he was healing, perpetually healing.

"Mind if I breathe?" Bartholomew asked.

"Sure, knock yourself out."

"Don't be too hard on him, now, Simpson."

"Mom—. I'm sorry I yelled at you, Barto. Please, now, for Mom's sake—for your own sake—we're asking you, please go see the doctor. You won't have to get any shots. Nobody's going to trick you. We won't let anybody lock you up."

"Liar, liar." Bartholomew pressed his hands to his ears.

"Will you, Bartholomew, please?" Simpson pressed on in a softer voice. "Will you promise Mom and me you'll call the doctor tomorrow and make an appointment? Wouldn't it make Dad happy?"

"Maybe. Maybe I'll promise *her*, if—"

"If?"

They leaned closer.

"If you'll *sit down* and stop *lording over* us!"

"Yes sir, with pleasure." Simpson grinned and flopped down in his father's old easy chair. There actually were times when you could sit and talk with Barto and you'd think you were talking to a normal adult. If someone who had never met him were to walk into the room, he might think at first that Bartholomew was a regular, ordinary person.

For a short while, the Weems family was at peace.

Simpson leaned back in the La-Z-Boy and looked at the worn armrests. It would look better upholstered in leopard skin, or panda, like the booths at the Saturn Bar.

"Simpson, honey, I am thankful to the Lord you're here to help, as you promised."

He gulped, something turned in his stomach, and a guilty look must have shown on his face, but her eyes were closed.

She was reclining in her own easy chair, her hands folded neatly in her lap, her face composed. Usually her sons' arguments distressed her—even their conversations could make her uneasy—but the possibility that Simpson might actually manage this time to sweet-talk Bartholomew, who suspected every word out of his brother's mouth, into going to see the doctor . . . it just might be the answer to a prayer. *Please, Lord Jesus, let it be.*

Alas, a mother could hope and pray, but she had just about given up any real expectation that Bartholomew would ever see a doctor again, and had stopped trying to talk him into it. But Simpson was welcome to try, and more power to him. It was for this kind of help that she had asked him years ago to never abandon her the way so many sons left their mothers. The two things that would most gladden her heart as a mother were the very hopes she had least confidence of ever seeing fulfilled: Simpson marrying a nice girl and raising a family, and Bartholomew having the financial security of disability insurance, at least until the government cut everyone off. Melba was resigned, but not complacent. With both of her sons she had said and done about all a mother could think to do, short of losing her mind over it, to see that they would not be lost without her after she was gone. Bartholomew and Simpson knew very well that she was in her mid-seventies—there were no secrets in this house—and that she wasn't in the freshest pink of health. But boys will be boys. They seemed to prefer chaos and catastrophe to common sense and taking precautions.

Drained by the panic that had sent her tearing through the animals, relieved and gratified by Simpson's offer, soothed by Bartholomew's promise, and slightly drowsy from her medicine, Melba felt such peace of mind that she slipped into a tranquil rest. Her glasses slipped down her nose, and her mouth drooped open.

Simpson shuddered and felt that sick sensation again. *She'll look like this when she's dead.* Eyes closed, mouth agape, not knowing anyone's seeing her like this. It will be a day just like today.

Father had died more than a decade before, and after college Simpson had moved into an apartment three blocks away. Melba and Bartholomew lived as ever on Invalides Street, carrying on their life together as though the peeling-off of Gasper and Simpson had only refined the family to its core, the indispensable primary elements of Melba and her Bartholomew. They were complete unto themselves, like a couple, self-sufficient and entirely satisfied with their arrangement. *He has replaced Dad.* It was disturbing to realize, though for many years the fact had been there for anyone to see.

Simpson often wished his father were still here, yet he liked playing the role of paterfamilias. It suited him and brought out some of his best qualities: good judgment, patience, and consideration for others. He felt proud knowing the steady hand on the helm was his own. His mother had said on more than one occasion, "Thank God you're here, Simpson. You're my rock." What would they ever do without him? Mother had told him he should feel free to live his own life, even if that meant moving to another state with a better economy. But then in the next breath she would say it warmed her heart that he was so faithful to his family. When Simpson later reminded her she had said he was free to go, she acted surprised. "Why would I ever say such a thing? We need you here."

He pried himself from the old recliner and began separating his laundry into piles outside the washer-and-dryer closet between the living room and the kitchen. Whites in the left pile, colors on the right.

Bartholomew was staring intently at his fingers picking at themselves, fidgeting. *Norkel, Norkel, Norkel.* He shivered with a sudden chill from the cold white walls of Mandeville on the other side of Lake Pontchartrain where he'd been sent after disrupting too many classrooms with his screaming tantrums. Madnessville, the other patients called it. Hours of group counseling and therapy every day. After a year he was released and began second grade again with a note to the teacher: "HANDLE WITH CARE. HIGH I.Q. FRAGILE." Mandeville. The whole place had the hard chill of a cold steel water tank. It didn't help that Mandeville was also his brother's middle name. Then the big storm howled and threw tree limbs at the windows. You could hear it through the layers of glass and concrete and pale green tiles. Then the lights went out.

Without looking, Simpson tossed a pair of blue jeans into the pile on the right.

Bartholomew's eyes were caught by a book of matches falling from the pants pocket and landing silently on the rug a few feet away, behind Simpson.

He heaved himself up from the sofa and moved quietly like an elephant on tiptoe to the breakfast bar, only a few feet behind his brother. "You want some iced tea?"

Simpson turned around, looking surprised, then smiled a little and said no, thank you, and turned back to his sorting.

Bartholomew bent down and in a silent sweeping motion snatched the matchbook from the floor, then moved near the refrigerator. He held the matches up to the light and gasped. The red and black matchbook showed a naked, large-breasted woman tilted back in an oversize champagne glass, a drink in one hand, and her legs dangling over the rim, a high-heeled shoe hanging loose.

BOURBON BATH • 341 RUE BOURBON
Warm Baths with Hot, Slippery Wet-Dream Girls!
X X X • Lust Heaven Enterprises • X X X

"*Bourbon Bath?*" exclaimed Bartholomew, loud enough to wake his mother, and possibly the neighbors. "What's a wet-dream girl?"

Simpson spun around with a look of alarm, glanced over at his sleeping mother, and with a nervous laugh said "What?" He held his finger to his lips, then fanned his hands downward in a quieting motion.

Bartholomew stood nearly as tall as his brother, though now he was tilted back, and his eyebrows were arched high with suspicion. He always knew Simpson did bad things when he was away from them, but now there was evidence.

"Lust Heaven?"

"What—? Where'd you hear that name?" Simpson asked in a near-whisper, glancing again toward Mother.

"*Here!*" Bartholomew flashed the matchbook and held it high out of reach. "This fell out of your blue jeans. *You* didn't notice, but I did. Bourbon Bath?" Then his voice boomed, "Are there *naked women?*"

"Ssshhh! How should I know?"

"They were in *your* pants."

"So you say. I've never seen 'em before. Maybe I have. Let me see."

Simpson snatched the matches from Bartholomew and frowned at the crude black and red cover. He laughed with strained casualness. "I don't know what this is about. Looks like a health spa or something."

"You go there and take *baths* with *girls*?"

"No!" Simpson shot a nervous glance toward the living room. "No, don't be ridiculous, Barto, my God," he forced a laugh, thinking what an *idiot* he was to forget to check his pockets before wash day. No telling what might fall out.

"What do the triple X's mean?"

"Barto, please, lower your voice, for God's sake. You'll wake Mom."

Bartholomew frowned and clapped his hands over his ears. They recorded all dialogue, whether he liked it or not.

A few hours later, Bartholomew was spying discreetly from behind a pine tree as his tall gangly brother boarded a city bus at the corner of Invalides and Elysian Fields. The door hissed shut and the bus rumbled on toward the French Quarter. Lust Heaven. He stepped away from the tree and shuffled massively to the bus stop to wait for the next 55 Elysian Fields or a taxi passing by. Across the road in the neutral ground, a light breeze blew through the grove of white cypress and white poplar, rustling the brown and golden leaves on the ground around the two water fountains near the curb, one broken, the other nearly so.

Bartholomew stood six feet and three, but as to his weight, he had given up counting when it passed four hundred. His complexion was smooth as porcelain, his skin a light pink as though he'd been bathed in milk under fluorescent lights as a youth and kept indoors all his life. His reddish blond hair grew thick and unruly, and the contrast with his dark eyebrows gave the impression that there had been some mistake. His eyes were a curious robin's-egg blue, and a thin line of red circled his irises, suggesting a deficiency in some nutrient or hormone. After more than three decades, people in the neighborhood still had not gotten used to the sight of him.

By his watch, the next bus arrived precisely seventeen minutes and fifty-two seconds later. For the 55 Elysian Fields that was not bad, especially around nine on a Saturday night. The driver lowered the bus by pneumatic decompression to help the large-bodied passenger step aboard. The dozen or so riders watched as a tall round pink man with a boy's face and scattered blond hair paid his fare. He stood awkwardly, with hunched shoulders and a slumpy posture, and his long pants were low on his hips, bunched around his ankles, almost covering his large brown shoes. He moved a few steps forward, gripping the handrails and scowling at the garish parti-colored upholstery, before settling down across two front seats reserved for the elderly and handicapped.

The vibrations rattled in Bartholomew's ears as the bus passed white-columned houses with lighted upstairs windows yellowing the trees in the front yards. He didn't notice his reflection because he was looking *out there*.

On the downriver, back-of-town side of the old city of New Orleans, away from downtown and the Garden District, Elysian Fields Avenue was a broad three-lane boulevard stretching from the Mississippi River toward Lake Pontchartrain five miles away, the only street in the city to run straight from the river to the lake. The boulevard's mix of grand and simple wooden houses faced each other across a wide neutral ground that once held two railroads and a canal running along Champs Elysées, beginning at the base of the old Marigny plantation where Esplanade meets the levee. Gasper Weems had claimed there actually used to be two canals, "each going a different direction," though he may have been thinking of the railroads that used to run on opposite sides of the one canal. Beginning in the 1830s, most travelers from along the Gulf Coast or the eastern seaboard approached New Orleans through the back door by crossing Lake Pontchartrain and catching a train at Milneburg for the half-hour ride through the backswamp into the city; this way was usually faster than winding up or down the Mississippi River to the front-door entrance along the wharves. For as long as anyone could remember, though, the neutral ground had simply been a wide lawn planted with live oaks, magnolias, cypresses and palm trees separating the in- and outbound lanes.

Bartholomew had studied the map, so he knew where to go. He liked to pore over city maps and bus routes as a pastime, the way he memorized baseball statistics and *TV Guide* listings: He knew the streets' names, their angles, destinations, and intersections, but he never went to any of these places. He ventured forth only to church (till he renounced churchgoing as idolatrous), the grocery store, the local branch of the public library, and to nearby Dillard University's community service radio station to read news items for the blind. That was enough. With maps, he was like someone who can read a language but never speaks it.

The bus passed Pleasure Street and stopped at Humanity, just before the interstate. The door opened and a well-dressed couple in their thirties stepped onboard, leaning on each other, tipsy and tired, laughing. They paid their fare and sat down, still giggling, two seats from Bartholomew.

"Oh," the woman groaned, her laughter subsiding, and raised her hands to her head. "I got nothin' but a headache so bad."

"Poor baby." The man leaned close and rubbed the back of her neck.

When he looked up he saw the large pink white man gazing at him with sad calflike eyes.

"Thirteen years is a long time to be dead," Bartholomew said, loud enough for half the passengers to hear. "My father fell off a ladder. He was putting up a bird feeder. He died."

The man's eyebrows rose, and the woman burst out laughing, then covered her mouth. "'Scuse me, I'm sorry," she said, wiping her eyes. She moaned and muttered softly, "Oh, this ain't helpin' my headache."

"I'm sorry to hear that about your daddy," the man said.

Bartholomew nodded solemnly and looked away as the bus passed under Interstate 610 and approached Abundance. The street names often seemed to say something funny about the places or the people who lived there. For example, Simpson lived on Dormition Street.

As they came closer to town, the neighborhoods looked older and poorer, though some must once have been grand. Many of the houses were dark and looked uninhabited. Vine-covered bungalows, dilapidated Victorian shotguns, two-story Greek Revival houses tilting to one side, broad-limbed live oaks, rusted cast-iron and white picket fences along many front yards, and thin pale dogs nosing through the scraps among the overturned garbage cans.

Bartholomew pulled the cord to get off at Dauphine Street near the park, a few blocks downriver from the Vieux Carré. He stepped down from the front of the bus, moving laboriously, gripping the railings on each side, and nearly tumbling over the half dozen customers clustering too close to the door.

"Out of my way! Out of my way!" he said in a high bellow, waving and fluttering his hands impatiently.

"You're supposed to get off in back," a clean-cut, stern-faced man informed him.

Bartholomew paid him no mind. He had no time to quibble over proper doorways.

He was at Washington Square Park on Elysian Fields where the Desire streetcar line used to run, outbound on Dauphine and in on Royal. He had seen it on an old map. Through the dark cast-iron fence he saw a couple of light-colored roses in bloom. The night air felt peculiar, too warm for this time of year, though the weatherman said in a few days it would be turning cool again.

He knew how to get there—through the Marigny triangle across Frenchmen and Esplanade into the Quarter—but he had never actually been on Bourbon Street itself, and could only imagine what he would see there. He walked past the fence along the park, tapping his fingers upon the flaking paint of the iron bars, and the leaves on the sidewalk crunched underfoot. The scents of palm and banana trees mingled with odors of auto exhaust and cigarette smoke from the bars. As he passed a corner on Frenchmen Street he could hear several bands playing at once; the Afro-funk beat sounded suggestive, sinful, and the smells of alcohol and tobacco confirmed every suspicion. He knew before he left the house (Mother was asleep) he would be walking into the valley of the shadow; he had prayed for courage and protection. But had not the martyrs likewise passed unscathed through snares of temptation and wickedness? Therefore he had faith. *My strength is as the strength of ten.*

Bartholomew had honestly not been to this part of town in about twenty-five years. He had certainly never come to the French Quarter alone; the only time he could remember being here was with Father and Simpson, when he was about eight or nine, shortly after Mandeville. They had stayed on the safe outer edges, walking from busy Canal Street along well-traveled North Peters and Decatur, on the river side, to the Café du Monde across from Jackson Square. Gasper had told the boys all about the delicious sugar-powdered beignets—golden deep-fried dough sprinkled with confectioners sugar—and the thick strong café au lait. Bartholomew ate three servings of three beignets, while Gasper urged him on. "Eat, boy. These are world-famous." He patted Bartholomew on the back. "Get 'em while they're hot."

He had no idea what really went on deep inside the Quarter, but he had heard stories, and he could imagine. He was not surprised that his brother was going there. Mother had better appreciate the trouble he was putting himself to for her sake. Meanwhile, Father was looking down on all of this with a heart of grief. He had always been a good father to his sons, and now look what the firstborn was doing in the flesh bars of the Vieux Carré.

In the Wet Dream room, he stripped down to his Fruit-of-the-Loom jockey shorts and hung his clothes on hooks along the wall. Mignon was one of the special girls at Bourbon Bath, available by appointment. The black curtains parted and there she stood, petite and demure in a transparent negligee loosely tied at the breast. Short blonde hair fell in bangs above her brown eyes and curled near her ears, almost touching the corners of her full pink lips.

"Hey, big spender. Haven't seen you in a while." She smiled and twirled the drawstrings of her negligee.

He was lying back in a large acrylic champagne-glass tub, the water lit from below by a lighted color wheel of red and green and blue and violet. Like bathing in a lava lamp, oozing slow and easy.

"Missed you, too. I've been out in San Francisco."

"Again? Takin' baths with them cold Pacific nymphs? You make me jealous."

"Come get wet."

Her negligee fell to the floor.

As she climbed in and straddled him, he sighed and murmured, pulled her close, and kissed the skin between her breasts. The touch of her flesh was like warm silk of infinite softness; her supple young body was smooth as oiled glass and tight and trim as a Greek sculpture of a nymph or naiad, soap-slippery and firm. As she rubbed herself avidly on him, belly to belly, her thighs squeezing his, the sensation of her unbelievably smooth skin seemed to penetrate and suffuse his being with a sweet silken intimacy he had only felt in the rarest of dreams. Wet dreams of Mignon. She smiled, stroked his hair, kissed his cheeks and throat, and whispered hot words in his ear. In the water with Mignon, he felt clean and wholesome. She made him feel more *himself*, the person he ought to be. After their first few baths together, she had gently asked if he wanted someone else, or if she was doing something wrong, because he didn't seem to be as excited, if he knew what she meant, as her visitors usually were. She believed him when he said his minimal response resulted from an old injury, and she didn't take it as an affront to her beauty and womanliness. "It's hard to be soft," he joked, but somehow with her he still felt potent and manly.

"Close your eyes." He reached behind his back and pulled out a Ziploc baggie. "Keep 'em closed." From the dripping clear plastic bag he withdrew a little gift and said, "Okay, you can look."

She was surprised: A delicate gold chain necklace with a champagne glass charm.

A dozen responses came to mind, but all she could say was, "For me?"

"Here, let me put it on you."

She hesitated, then leaned forward. "That's so sweet. You shouldn't have."

"I didn't mean to embarrass you. I've been wanting to give you something nice. I think I love you."

Her eyes widened briefly, then closed. She licked his throat and breathed hotly in his ear. "Silly," she whispered. Men said this to her at least three times a week. "You're sweet, but I'm not supposed to accept gifts."

"My brother knows about us."

"Your brother?" She looked amused, then concerned.

"About Bourbon Bath, I mean. A pack of matches fell out of my pocket. Stupid of me."

She pressed her forefinger gently upon his lips. "Don't worry. Nobody knows about us except us."

Bartholomew paused at a corner to catch his breath. *I will fear no evil: for thou art with me.* It would have been difficult even for a thin person to walk with any speed or grace through the crowds in Bourbon Street. Carnival season was under way, and the masses were even thicker than usual, all drunk and disorderly, it seemed to him. He moved on, his arms hanging limp at his sides, or sometimes extended before him as though to clear obstacles from his path. "Excuse me. *Excuse* me!" There was really no need to be polite to these people. He was relieved that no one seemed to recognize him (not that he knew anybody), yet he was offended that they all assumed he fit in, that he was one of them. He tried to inhale as little as possible, because of the smells, but a four-hundred-plus-pounder huffing through milling crowds on a warm night needs to breathe some. Lights winked and flickered at him from up and down the two- and three-story corridor of buildings like a narrow gaslit Gomorrah with wrought-iron balconies and ferns up above red and purple neon signs flashing COLD BEER and HOT PLEASURES. *My brother is on this street somewhere.* Music clanged and blasted from the open doors of rock and zydeco clubs, blues halls and jazz joints with spinning mirror balls and red-lit stages. Lights were bright and swirling, countless kinds of music were pulsing at once and merging into casual cacophony; a thousand voices laughing and shouting, tap-dancing boys clacking on the sidewalks for well-fed tourists smiling and tossing dimes. *Who are all these people?* Pale-faced teenagers in dark cloaks, businessmen and women clutching plastic cups of beer and hurricanes and juleps and jungle juice and pussy sugar. "Move, you fat white meat!" Somebody poked Bartholomew in the side as a group of black boys too young to be teenagers pushed past him in a rush. Bartholomew yelled after them, "You should be in bed!" A couple in matching salmon-colored satins giggled and said they should be, too. Two mounted policemen on chestnut stallions at a street corner talked calmly to each other, laughed at a joke, just letting it all happen.

From a distance Bartholomew saw a large white-painted cross towering above the crowded street. Over the moving heads the cross looked like a grave marker in a field of grass. Then he saw the sign flashing LUST HEAVEN . . . LUST HEAVEN. Under the blinking red and gold neon was a baroque painting of St. Sebastian roped and chained to a Roman column, his head thrown back in agony or rapture as smiling, full-breasted nymphs and mermaids fingered the neon arrows piercing his chest and loincloth. The painting was outlined with small white marquee lightbulbs blinking in an endless moving sequence.

Glancing over his shoulder at a bearded, white-robed man holding up the cross, Bartholomew took a deep breath and stepped up to the door. A heavy-browed doorman gave him a dubious glance and shrugged. "Step on in, the girls'll take care of you."

34

I can take care of myself. His heart was pounding as he entered the bar. A friendly dark-eyed young woman wearing only a fleshtone negligee appeared at his side, smiling. "Whatcha thirsty for, sugar?" She pressed herself shamelessly on his arm, and her long dark hair tickled him.

He emitted a nervous squeak and backed away.

"Nothing, thank you," he said in what was meant to be an upright tone, but came out as a series of peeps. "I'm just looking for my brother."

"Uh-huh." She smiled. "Never heard that one before. What can I get you to drink, baby? You just want a Coke?"

He nodded but could say nothing. He was trembling and sweating profusely.

"I'll get you a Coke." She patted his arm and turned to the bar. He watched her walk away, then clapped his palms to his eyes.

Bartholomew slouched there in a loud strobe-lighted showroom of whirling mirror balls reflecting colored laser lights streaking across a young woman—actually a girl, possibly underage—loosely dressed in a nurse's uniform strutting and posing provocatively on the little stage. Sitting nearby at small round-topped tables were about twenty men and a few women, sipping, smoking, watching. The hard-beat music pulsed bone-deep—he could actually feel his flesh wobble—as the nurse with a stethoscope listened closely to various parts of her freckled body. Her blouse was held in place by a single red button, and her skirt was short and sheer. When he realized he was actually seeing through her skirt, he averted his eyes in horror.

He stood there lost, helpless, too big to hide. He could not believe what he was seeing.

Nor could he believe the price of a Coke.

"Well," the girl explained, "you're not exactly payin' for the drink. I'm Felicity. Like me to do a special dance for you?" she nodded toward the side tables. "I'll make you happy."

"I'm already happy!" he snapped. He wiped his forehead with the drink napkin and glanced around with anxious suspicion. "I'm looking for my brother. He's tall and skinny and has a hooked nose and messy-looking red hair. I have to find him. Mother doesn't know he's here."

"Mother?!" she laughed. "And you came to take him home. Aren't you sweet."

"Don't distress me! Where's Bourbon Bath? Is this it?"

"Ssshhh." She pressed lightly against his arm. "Come on back this way. It's okay. Mama don't need to worry."

She led him back through a narrow curtained corridor lined with slender Asian showgirls with inviting eyes and soft hands touching him like butterfly wings.

"Hey, sugar loaf."

"Give us a kiss."

"Y'all hush," said Felicity, "he's with me." She pulled him by the hand to a room whose arched entrance was lit by a purple neon cursive script, *Lust Heaven*, flanked by flashing red pitchfork-like arrows pointing down and in, down and in. The room was filled with plush sofas and divans, ottomans, easy chairs, with tasseled lamps and a floor of imitation Persian carpets, standing ashtrays, and drinking glasses made of real glass. A half dozen handsome men in dark suits and loosened ties sprawled dazed and rapt on the sofas were being actively entertained, each by his own buoyant girl whose state of undress and aggressive thrusting movements made Felicity in her negligee appear modest and chaste.

"Come on in here." She pulled him into a small room and sat him down on the dark velvet sofa. She parted a black curtain that revealed a one-way mirror window, then sat beside him, her hip and leg against his ample thigh. Bartholomew hardly noticed Felicity pressing against him as he leaned closer to spy on his brother's exploits.

He was shocked. Simpson, undressed, was lying back in a large glass bowl, a bubble bath, talking with a naked girl on his lap. She sat facing him with her legs around his waist, elbows on his shoulders. They appeared to be conversing.

"They just sit there?" he asked, disappointed. "Talking?"

"That's about it. That's your brother? Yeah, he does have a hooked nose. You think she's prettier'n me?"

Bartholomew blushed. "I don't know," he blurted irritably.

"I don't see what's so special about Mignon, either."

Bartholomew was watching Simpson's hands on the woman's behind when he felt Felicity lean over and breathe warmly on his cheek.

"Eeek!" He shivered and shrugged her away.

"I need to get back up front. The boss'll be wonderin' where I ran off to."

She stood before him, hesitated, then gently pulled his face to her breasts. She held him there a moment. She wanted to give him something. He blinked his eyes once or twice, but his head held motionless, his neck rigid.

She released him.

"Okay, show's over. Your brother's all right."

Bartholomew followed her obediently. He is *not* all right.

Felicity gave him a light pat on the rear. "Be careful gettin' home."

When he stepped out into the street he half expected everyone to stop and point at him with shock and moral outrage, but no one paid him any mind. They're so numbed by it all.

How long had he been in there? Walking out onto Bourbon Street at night was like emerging from a movie theater in midday. Images of them flashed in his eyes, as though they were still touching him and whispering invitations. If Mother asked where on earth he had gone and why so late, he would have to tell the truth. Simpson was bad. He would have to be punished, banished. There could be fluids on his clothing. He could be bringing diseases into their house each time he came over with his laundry basket—his *plague* basket.

Bartholomew shuddered. Simpson was in trouble. *Don't get God started.* But this . . . this was not the kind of trouble to bother the Almighty about; he would have to handle this himself. *The Lord don't like crybabies.* And Father, looking down from his place in heaven, was becoming very angry.

Go see Rev. Bud. He'll know what to do.

Then came the worst part of a bad night.

Four young men with short clean-cut hair and white T-shirts stood near a corner holding picket signs about sin and salvation. The T-shirts were printed with a bold black cross and the words BODY PIERCING SAVED MY LIFE.

He scowled with disdain. What did they expect to accomplish here?

One of them caught his eye and approached with a smile. "Do you get it?"

Bartholomew walked faster, impatient to leave the street behind.

"Do you get what it means?" the fellow asked again, smiling with perfect white teeth and bouncing along at Bartholomew's elbow, pushing a brochure at him. "For God so loved the world—"

"Cease!" cried Bartholomew. He reared back in all his massive towering height and indignation, raised his forefinger like a prophet of old and with wide furious eyes commanded, "Cease, in the name of Jesus!"

The proselytizer was stricken dumb. His jaw fell slack.

"I already *am* a believer!" Bartholomew roared, then huffed away, ashamed at himself.

The young man did not follow, but when he caught his breath he yelled out a verse of scripture, throwing the words at Bartholomew's back.

Bartholomew shuffled out of the French Quarter feeling soiled and defiled.

"I'm moving to San Francisco. I'm getting out of here. I've been meaning to go there for years. *Years*," he emphasized, looking deep into Mignon's receptive brown eyes. Probably since you were in nursery school. "I've been saving my money—what I haven't spent here—and, and I decided tonight I'd like you to come with me."

Now she had to say something: "You're real sweet to ask, but be realistic. I'm just a girl in your dreams. And thanks, but I shouldn't keep this lovely necklace."

"Come with me. You could change your name to Mignonette—"

"*You* already have." She rubbed a bar of soap in light circles around his hairless chest. The soap film and bubbles glistened in the blue and violet light. She cupped her hands and poured water down the front of him.

"And you're goin' there to do what? Write poetry?"

"Right. I've got it all planned out. Come on with me, M. You'd love it. We could live in North Beach and you could dance and bathe just like you do here—"

Her thigh muscles tensed. "Oh, right, that's what I'd want to go to California for: more of this."

"Okay, but, I mean, you'd have this to fall back on, just in case, like I could get a job at a copy shop if I needed to."

"I get suspicious whenever a guy says he's got it all planned out. Meanwhile you've been going to poetry readings and workshops and all that?"

He clucked his tongue and waved his hand dismissively. "I'm ready."

"*Really* ready?"

She cupped his cheeks in her palms and pulled him close, to taste her. "Are you gonna want to take off your jockey shorts this time, or keep 'em on like usual?"

"I think I'll prob'ly keep 'em on for now."

"For now," she echoed dryly. "And you want me to come to California with you."

He glanced away, not sure what she meant.

"Are you the kind of man who comes inside, who *enters*, or are you the kind that just kind of skulks around the edges and watches?"

"Oh definitely the latter," he replied at once, in all candor.

She smiled, and leaned close to kiss his cheek. They slithered and splashed around the bath for a while, soaping and rinsing, and he tickled her and she squealed and splashed him, laughing, and they were very happy together.

"I love you," he said again.

Mignon became still and looked at him. "No, honey."

She cupped her hand behind his neck and pulled him close. Their foreheads were touching. "You like me," she said softly, "and you may think you love me, but you are definitely not *in love with* me."

41

He frowned. How did she know that? How did she know what he felt?

"You're funny," she continued, "but I don't think you're that crazy."

He smiled.

"How much do you spend a month comin' here to Bourbon Bath, anyway?"

"If I told you," he murmured in a suave, manlike tone as he played with her nipples, "then you'd believe I love you."

"You love parts of me. You don't know me well enough to really love me. Anyway, you wouldn't love me all the time."

He didn't know how to reply.

"But that's okay." She closed her eyes as she rubbed her slippery thighs on his and soaped his chest with her tight smooth belly.

"Hmmm, San Francisco, California." She lay her head on his shoulder. "I don't know, Samson. I think that might be too out there for this blond pink-lipped virgin."

He laughed and glided his hands down her back and squeezed her rhythmically. Only then did it occur to him that if she had said yes, he'd have to tell her his real name.

2

House of Weems

IT WAS MORNING. Bartholomew sat at the edge of his mother's bed, observing closely as she put on her makeup at her little soft-lighted vanity mirror. Breathing heavy while she hummed to herself, he gaped at the elastic distorted mirror image of her plump fair cheeks as she applied powder, rouge, and the same red lipstick she'd always worn.

"A little more there. Right there."

"Bartholomew, thank you, I believe I know how."

It made him feel part of something to have this time with Mother as she started her day. It was a time of peace they had together. She was his mother, and if he wasn't there to watch her as she put on her makeup then what kind of son was he?

He watched intently. "You haven't brushed your wig yet."

"I'm getting to that. First I've got to put my face on."

"You should get a new mirror. Half your bulbs are burned out."

"There's always my birthday."

Every morning she made sure she woke first so she could put on her wig before he came out of his room. She couldn't help it that her hair had gone baby-thin, but the sight of his mother without the wig was liable to agitate him. Or not: it was unpredictable. Once when he was about five she had colored her hair from straw blonde to brown just to try something new, but he had thrown a screaming tantrum, and she had to go right straight back to the beauty parlor. The last time he saw her without the wig—it was an accident; it was a day when she was sick—he made a terrible high-pitched sound and drummed his feet on the floor till she began to think something was seriously wrong with him.

"Too much rouge on the right cheek," he pointed out. "You should put more care into your makeup. You spent more time on those dead people than you do on yourself."

Years had passed since her retirement as a funeral home's cosmetician, but she could still feel the sensation of resting her right elbow on a corpse's chest while brushing on face powder and rouge, touching the cold forehead to steady her touch with the eyeliner pen.

"That's sweet of you to say. I guess I should. I just figured it was their last dressing, whereas for myself, I could always touch up later."

"But you never do. You just rush through it even though you know it gives me pleasure to watch you."

"I know it does, baby. Every morning."

"Did you just sigh?"

"No, I—"

He leaned over and looked at her face. "You need more rouge on the left cheek. Here, let me—"

"No, honey, I can—"

"*Mother!*" he shouted in her left ear.

She clapped her hands to her ears and sighed to heaven. "Bartholomew, really."

She let go of the powder puff and let him dab the rouge on her cheek. His touch was gentle and steady, almost professional.

"You know, if you ever need a job—and you definitely do—maybe you could take my old job at Lourdes. You already know everybody there."

He said nothing. He touched up the right cheek to balance the color, then pulled her chin. "Turn this way." He bent over and studied her face closely. His breathing was heavy, labored.

"You need to work somewhere, anyhow," she said. She looked up at him, but he would not meet her eyes.

The house at 973 Invalides Street was still listed under the name of Gasper Weems, though the master of the house had gone the way of the angels many years before. Invalides (pronounced IN-va-leeds) was one of the entry streets off Elysian Fields Avenue into the neighborhood known as Dangers Park. It was said to have been named after a nice respectable street in downtown Paris, France, but the Invalides of New Orleans, with its tombs of St. Perpetua's and the wooded park across the street from

the sun-bleached clapboard houses surrounded by rag-
ged, moss-draped oaks and unkempt weed-lawns, looked
less like a cosmopolitan avenue than a lane through a
cemetery on the edge of a rain forest.

Situated in a little-known, rarely traveled part of
Gentilly, Dangers Park proper was a small two-block
square of wooded park grounds and a little bayou, but the
name extended to the neighborhood of about a dozen
square blocks off Elysian Fields that surrounded the
park and the adjacent cemetery of whitewashed tombs
and statues. (Gasper said the name had nothing to do
with perilous dangers, but came from an old landowner
named D'Angers, though Gasper's facts of history, such
as his claim that the park's bayou was once a tributary
of Bayou St. John, were sometimes not verifiable.) The
park did have its perils, though; a team of tree doctors
had determined that half the live oaks in the neighborhood were being eaten from within by the voracious
Formosan termites that had been gutting the city's trees
and houses since they arrived on a navy ship around the
end of World War II. During a recent storm, all around
town high winds had toppled big old oaks that had been
hollowed out, devoured from within. No one knew for
sure how far the insects had spread, but for about a week
every May they swarmed thick at night for an hour, and
everyone had to dim their lights or stay inside. Perhaps a
third or more of the city's million trees were thought to
be infected, slowly dying on the inside.

Most of the families in Dangers Park had lived in
the neighborhood for at least a generation, and some

for three or four. Melba and Gasper had moved in soon after they were married; he said they'd lived there forever, though she distinctly remembered they had settled there in the nineteen-fifties.

The houses and yards never lacked for greenery, though lawn mowers and fresh paint were not in evidence. The entire neighborhood was heavily overgrown, as though the city grass-cutters had not come near in decades. In some empty lots, trees had grown thick since the weeds were last cut. Indeed, the story was that long ago one of the original landowners had somehow crossed or embarrassed the mayor of New Orleans, a hot-tempered autocrat with a long-burning memory. In return, the mayor had ruled that not a penny of the taxpayers' money was to be wasted on keeping up what used to be that scoundrel's property. Some said (though this was a matter of some dispute) that there had actually been a city ordinance forbidding "expropriation" of municipal funds for use on the land later known as Dangers Park, but anyhow by the simple inertia of tradition the area had become a sort of no-man's-land among the city workers. The mail was often late. Phone service was erratic, though wrong-number calls seemed to gravitate there, and even television and radio signals sometimes wavered. But there was more than municipal neglect pervading the neighborhood. Gasper repeated as fact what he'd heard from his taxidermy partner, Roscoe, who lived nearby, or from old Suff, the can and bottle collector: the land, near the old Gentilly ridge, had once been an Indian or slave burial ground.

"That explains why the ground around here's so God-blessèd *fertile*," Gasper would say proudly, gesturing with a sweep of his hand at the banana trees and palms, pink-flowered azaleas and crape myrtle, and elephant ears and monkey grass all growing wild and high. "This whole area's bones piled on bones."

"And because it rains every other day," Melba added.

"That's right, dahlin'."

Simpson was skeptical about the burial ground story—the only bones he was sure of were in St. Perpetua's. About all that was piled up out here was the track bed of the old Pontchartrain Railroad, now the neutral ground of Elysian Fields Avenue, that had stretched for miles through a swamp and cypress forest out to the lake. In the old French maps, this backswamp beyond the city of La Nouvelle-Orléans was vaguely designated as *terres vacantes*. The swamp was drained beginning around 1900, and the cypresses lived on in the form of hardwood floors and door and window jambs in the local houses built up in the following decades.

The houses on Invalides, constructed just before and after what Gasper liked to call the Great War, or the World War, were mostly clapboard bungalows and shotguns made of wood and set up on brick pilings several feet off the ground. The houses all looked more or less alike—gentle on the eyes in material and design—yet no house was quite the duplicate of any other. Most were painted white or shades of faded yellow and gray, with dark trims, green shutters and occasional awnings, and the houses were set close together, six or eight feet apart, except for the few with driveways or carports. Between the houses ran narrow brick or flagstone walkways, often separated by a chain-link fence. Window-unit air conditioners dripped down on the bricks, where green and brown moss grew thick and slippery.

The Weemses's floors had settled and tilted at various odd slants and curves because the pilings had never been balanced in all the years since the house was built, or at least for as long as they had lived there, though Gasper could have called any of a dozen or more contractors in town to shore up the house's foundation. (There was no bedrock beneath the city, so in periods of low rainfall the water table dropped and the drying subsoil contracted and sucked the pilings down.) The floors were built of strong cypress planks, but, sturdy though they were, the walls and floorboards shook and groaned when Bartholomew crossed the room. Like most of the city's homes, the Weemses's was wooden, thin-walled, without insulation, built to allow breezes to pass through the many windows and the main hallway in the hot season, eight or nine months long. In the crawl space between the floorboards and the ground lay no insulation but three feet of shadows and cooler air. In addition to cooling the house, the elevation gave some protection from flooding, a periodic consequence of living near sea level. Sometimes the rain would fall thick and hard for hours, and water would rise in the streets as the pumping stations all over town could not work fast enough. During a recent flash flood, over in Mid-City a floating corpse had drifted by and settled on a man's front porch. He wrapped the body in sheets and sat out on the porch with it, sipping beer, smoking cigarettes, waiting for the coroner's office to send out a boat to pick it up.

The house of Weems was partly painted several different colors. The front and one side retained the dull beige that had been painted over the entire house about forty years ago. On the other side, a later pair of painters had covered the wood slats with coats of plum-colored enamel that looked wet even to this day. All the other walls on the outside of the house had been brushed with other color schemes, and likewise abandoned. A little statue of the Virgin Mary in the front yard was half-obscured by a red and white sign warning that the house was guarded by Superior Security and Protection, though that had only been true for a few months several decades ago, amid rumors of a crime wave, when Gasper thought their home could use a little extra protection, until he and Melba decided money couldn't buy the kind of security that prayer could provide. The painted, faded statue had been left by the house's previous occupants from the early 1950s, and even if Melba had ever thought to remove it, she would have refrained for fear of bringing on bad luck.

Gasper Weems was a model of fiscal prudence and tended not to throw his money after passing fads, so it was not until the late 1960s that he began buying air conditioners. In the nineteen-twenties and thirties, air conditioning was found only in movie theaters and the finer hotels and restaurants downtown, and window units appeared in the fifties. Simpson grew up with a rotating fan in his room to keep the humid air moving in the summer nights, and he slept under a single sheet or with no covers at all. When Bartholomew was only a few years old, Gasper decided it was time for the family to have an air conditioner in the living room. Then he bought another for the master bedroom. As other neighbors bought cars, the Weemses bought air conditioners, based on Gasper's conviction that a cool home is a comfortable home, and a comfortable home brings up good children, etc.

The house was full of windows, either thickly curtained to shut out the bright sun, or, as in Bartholomew's room, plugged with air conditioners. At least until the evisceration witnessed by Simpson, the walls and shelves were populated by lifelike stuffed animals Gasper had brought home from the taxidermy shop over the years—mostly the mountings never claimed by customers. Once a week Melba dusted the mallards and trout, the foxes and squirrels, whose mountings trembled on the walls when the air conditioners were humming. Picture frames over the sofa were unevenly spaced and tilted at odd angles. In the center, an anniversary photograph of Melba and Gasper, mounted under a circular mat, had slipped in its frame; their eyes peered from a porthole. The brothers' head shots, set on opposite sides of the parents and positioned asymmetrically, looked off in opposite directions. Simpson's high school graduation picture, not well focused and showing his long hair fashionably coiffed, hung askew, and a surly, unflattering portrait of Bartholomew in his late teens, with unkempt long blond hair and dark bushy eyebrows, frowned half-hidden from behind the edge of an oval mat. Even if the frames had been mounted straight, the vibrations in the walls would have kept them perpetually off center.

At random times the television's volume would slowly increase; you never noticed until it had been escalating for some time, and suddenly it was deafening. Because their TV was old, built before the days of remote controls, Melba would have to get up, walk over and turn it off, tap her fingers a few times on the dark wooden cabinet, then turn it on again. She thought it was curious that the runaway volume did not seem to bother Bartholomew, even though his hearing was so acute he could hear a Bible page turn on the other side of Elysian Fields. Not only did the volume slip, but the TV's color receptivity fluctuated, so that a show might begin in full color, fade to black-and-white halfway through, then possibly return to color by the end; or the color could vanish for weeks at a time. Melba and Bartholomew had grown so accustomed to the chromatic variance that they hardly noticed: color programming was muted into a vaguely sepia tone, and when it was black-and-white they simply filled in the colors.

The banging and clattering and grinding sound outside was Bartholomew dragging Mrs. Gagliano's old steel garbage can up from the curb after the trash collectors passed through. He did not mind helping an elderly neighbor, but mainly he was annoyed by the sight of the can lying out in the street, the lid tilted up against the curb. It was disorderly and negligent; it made the neighborhood look bad. To think that those garbage men were getting *paid* to throw people's property around like that. He had written letters to City Hall but nothing ever changed. Mother said they were lucky to have trash pickup at all; half the time the trucks seemed to rumble right on by.

Bartholomew dragged the trash can to its spot on the concrete slab along Mrs. Gagliano's driveway. Drops of sweat spattered onto the gray steel lid as he clanged it into place just so, with the handle aligned with the driveway, and he was breathing heavy from his exertions. Under the strong morning sun the sweat had evaporated before he let the screen door slam behind him.

"That was awful sweet of you," said Melba as he lumbered irritably through the living room, causing some of the pictures on the walls to tilt further off center. "Grace always says what a helpful neighbor you are."

He ignored her and went back to the bathroom to wash his face and hands. He could feel it coming: She was going to prod him again about getting a job. If he could do helpful little things for the neighbors, naturally he could also get a paying job. If he could volunteer at Dillard's radio station, then surely—

"Mother!" he shouted, though she was not in the room, and had not said anything. He peered over the edge of the towel and saw himself in the mirror, his face red, the sweat beading on his forehead.

Watch therefore; for ye know not what hour your Lord doth come.

"You all right in there?" Melba called from the living room. "Bartholomew?"

He went in his room, turned up the air conditioners from medium to high, and knelt to pray.

About an hour later Melba pulled her broom from behind the refrigerator and said, "You know, Bartholomew, if we lived in a house next to somebody—"

"We *do* live in a house next to somebody!" he shouted.

"—I mean in the same house like in a double, or apartments—then we couldn't be bangin' around all the time like we do, yellin' and all. Ever thought of that?"

"We don't yell," he hollered. "Anyway, we're ten feet from next door so it doesn't matter."

It was a clear February morning. Feeling the sun on her arms, it seemed this was the first true sun-warmth she had felt since the year turned. Spring was coming. The birds' chirping in the backyard trees like they were happy about something made Melba picture her grandmother, Big Mama Cremiere, out sweeping the porch in the early light when the birds are singing good morning and the first delivery trucks are passing on Grand Route 1. And the damp smell of the shrimp nets, the waters of Bayou Lafourche lapping up against the sidewalls. That would be a long time ago, when Mama was growing up in Golden Meadow. But the birds all still sounded the same.

"I don't know, Bartholomew. Sometimes these walls ain't as thick as we think."

"Simpson complaining again?"

"No, don't get upset, now. I was just thinkin', that's all."

She stood on the back steps and gave her broom a good shake. She could see her grandmother's stout hips wiggling as she swept, Big Mama in a faded flower-print dress pulling tight on her filled-out body like she hadn't changed out of it since she was seventeen. That's where Mama got her work-work-work ethic: from her own mother always carrying a broom or passing the mop and wiping up with the dish towel she looped around her apron string, frowning at specks of dust and cracking that towel like a whip.

If your father would wake up earlier on a regular basis, Verna would say, taking the words right off Big Mama's lips, he'd see all the dust on the floor 'cause the early side-ways sun lights up things you don't see later in the day, and maybe then he'd get up on his hind legs and sweep a little, too. That's just one reason why he oughta get his ass up earlier and don't keep God waitin'. But try tellin' him that. He gotta stay up late, listenin' to that damn radio at the kitchen table and smokin' till all hours. And what's he thinks he gonna hear in all that static? When we was first married he used to know it's best to be up *before* the alarm goes off, but he's forgot that. Early hours, the holy hours. Him, he sleeps right on through.

Did all the women in her family marry lazy idle men, Melba wondered, or was it just that the Cremiere women were such conscientious, industrious types by nature that no husband could reasonably be expected to measure up? All she knew for sure was that she had done a little better with Gasper than her mother or grandmother had done with their men. Anyway, there always seemed to be more to do around the house than any one soul could keep up with. What would Mama or Big Mama say about those tired-looking drapes—*Why don't you iron them, girl?*—or that smell of dust in the living room rug?

And what would they have thought about the way her boys turned out? She probably didn't want to know, yet somehow her foremothers' judgments trickled through, anyhow, like voices through the walls—*You should make that boy mind you!*—or like the radio signals Gramp used to tune in to late at night. It was like they all lived in one big house and their voices all carried through the walls, yelling about the red beans and rice burning or a home run on the TV. In her mind Melba could hear Gramp and Bartholomew chattering away for hours about the New Orleans Pelicans or the New York Yankees, though in fact Gramp had pretty much slipped out of the picture frame by the time Bartholomew was old enough to follow sports. They would have loved watching games together.

It was nice the way they all stayed in the house with you and kept their conversations going—nice as long as you didn't think about some of them being dead. She heard Gasper *all the time*, and talked to him, too, usually

56

about the boys. Melba was not crazy, hearing these voices; they were really there. She had given it some thought, as to whether she was turning nutty in the head, which she figured a woman of her age and experience probably had every right and reason to do, but it wasn't that at all. You hear what you hear, and some families are just closer knit than others.

"What, Bartholomew?" she shouted. "I can't hear you out here."

He appeared at the back door. The door frame seemed to vanish as he filled the space. "I said: Is Simpson coming by tomorrow after work?"

"I reckon so. He said he would."

Bartholomew fidgeted with his belt loops, which he couldn't quite see under the curve of his belly.

"Why, Pumpkin, you got other plans?"

"There's an outer space program I really, really want to watch, but you know how sniffy he gets about the TV being on when he's gracing us with his presence."

"It's not the TV being *on* so much as the volume, I think. Of course you can watch your show. Simpson and I can come out here and talk, as long as you keep the volume low enough so we can hear each other."

"All right," he said cheerlessly.

"He always has been the quiet, sensitive type, you know," Melba added, but he had gone back inside.

As long as she didn't think about them being dead it didn't hurt so bad to remember them. But, like this morning, seeing the sunlight on his bed, and then knowing he'd never warm it again with his body . . . It hurt her heart to think of it, that he was never coming back. So many years had passed since his funeral that sometimes it seemed he had been dead much longer than they were ever married. Most of the time, though, if she didn't think about certain things, Gasper didn't feel far away at all. As a matter of fact, he felt closer in her heart than in her mind. Maybe that was the kind of man Gasper was. It was something to think about . . . as long as she didn't dwell on the deadness.

Bartholomew returned to fill the doorway. "Maybe I'll play him a song on my new harmonica."

"Oh, did you learn a song?" Melba leaned on the broom and rubbed her back.

"Not really. But maybe I'll know one by tomorrow. 'Amazing Grace' or something."

"I'm sure he'd like that." Discreetly she pressed her hand to her chest and rubbed in circles. "Remember when you sang nice to him when he came back from the hospital after those ugly boys kicked him?"

"That was a long time ago. Aren't you done sweeping yet?"

"Almost. You want to finish up for me?"

"I want you to come listen to me practice."

"I can hear you just fine out here."

"All right. Just don't tell me if I hit a wrong note."

Simpson was not here—he only appeared to be standing behind a cash register at CopyQwik, a photocopy and computer center downtown on Baronne Street, shortly after dark on a slow night. His notebook was open before him, his pen poised, almost erect, but instead of writing he was gazing out the window to a lighted upstairs dance studio across the street where a couple were going through the steps of a duet. They too could probably hear and feel the muffled pulse of a Carnival parade's marching bands on St. Charles two blocks away. In about a week things would quiet down for a while. Although he loved Carnival, and even though this would probably be his last before he moved, Simpson had decided this year's Mardi Gras would have to roll without him. Too much to do. He lived on the other side of town from where most of the parades passed, anyway, and he tended not to be anywhere near the action unless he was working the late shift or was invited to a friend's party. In recent years late shifts were more common than invitations. In the studio across the street a woman in a blue blouse and a man in a red shirt were rehearsing a ballroom dance, coming together, turning, spinning apart and stopping. She pointed to his feet and said something. He didn't seem to understand. She repeated the gesture, then they tried the moves again and again. Like watching fish in an aquarium, colors moving in a silent world.

Something about this scene was familiar.

So sweet being with Mignon, so pretty and kind. And so practical. He tensed as he recalled Bartholomew's discovery of the matchbook, then relaxed as he considered that although his frequenting a water-pleasure house in the Vieux Carré was not the kind of habit a mother needs to know about, Melba might be somewhat relieved that, while he wasn't marrying or siring children, he was at least occasionally seeking the company of women, like a normal person. Meanwhile, in the spaces between baths with Mignon and visits with Mother—in that vast chasm—lay his usual routine of longing, promises, and inertia.

Tonight I'm writing, he had been telling himself all day. Work of the imagination. Maybe revise a rough draft. Try to get past the first line.

Simpson Weems, his biographers would one day note, was not handsome in any conventional sense—he felt he wasn't handsome in any sense, nor the least bit conventional—but women tended to find him attractive in a charming, boyish way, though his fair, freckled complexion made him look incomplete, not quite grown up. There was a kindness about him that people tended to trust, accentuated by his sensitive-looking hazel-green eyes, and a perpetual air of mystery, a heightened sense of wonder . . . or was it disorientation. He was a naturally attractive man, in the raw genetic material he was born with, but he did not dress or groom himself to his best advantage. His fire-orange hair, about four or five inches long, grew in shaggy tangles; it was not the kind of style about which someone might say, "My, that's a very *combed* head of hair"—it wasn't any kind of style at all. Although he felt he had a weak chin, that and his freckled nose gave him a distinguished profile—a bust or silhouette might suggest a profound thinker of the Enlightenment—but under fluorescent lights, in his

Thrift City clothing, Simpson looked more like someone who was in a band. He did not actually play an instrument, though there was a musician he likened himself to. Fellow workers had grown accustomed to seeing a picture pin of George Harrison on his blue CopyQwik apron: Harrison long-haired and full-bearded on the cover of *All Things Must Pass*. Simpson, known around the shop as a photocopy artist extraordinaire, had made the three-square-inch photo-pin on a high-resolution copier, laminated it, and affixed a safety pin with Krazy Glue. Every day he wore the little icon as a subtle way of projecting into other people's minds the truest picture of his real inner self. (Isn't all jewelry but an outward show of the gold within?) The long hair and beard, if he wore it, would be an expression of his inner freedom, his private wildness. The greatest part of any man, he had written in a notebook, is the part he never shows to others, but suggests. The wildest part of Simpson Weems was a secret, inner beard he never shaved, hair never barbered. Inwardly he was free, free to not comb his hair. If anyone asked about the pin, he simply said he liked Harrison's music, and let the picture subtly speak the thousand words it would take to explain that his ideal self-image was precisely that kind of "bearded bard" look of a cool mind and a cool head, of George Harrison circa 1970, or Alfred, Lord Tennyson, and clad in some brown or gray medieval cloak, dreaming timeless dreams.

He was dreaming now of the city of his fondest wishes, as he had done since college days with his artist friend Button. Although physically he was in New Orleans, in his heart his primary residence was San Francisco: its cool Pacific breezes scented with eucalyptus, cappuccino and marijuana were the air he breathed. He looked to California as a prisoner peers from his cage and dreams of blue skies not crossed by bars of iron. That his future lay in the charmed and scenic Bay Area was as certain as the dawn's following the night. Only San Francisco would do; he had never seriously considered moving anywhere else, just as he had never intended to let his roots sink in or his heart find love in the fertile grounds of New Orleans. A day not lived in California was a day wasted. Once he was *out there*, his real life would begin.

Like a man struggling to breathe he yearned to thrive in the place where the Beats had flourished, the poets of spontaneous free verse whose language flowed like jazz. Allen Ginsberg had shifted the San Francisco Renaissance into high gear in 1955 with his legendary performance of "Howl" at the Six Poets at the Six Gallery reading on Fillmore Street with Rexroth, Snyder, McClure, and others, and with Kerouac and Ferlinghetti among the electrified audience. Simpson had read all about it in *Literary San Francisco*. He wanted it to still be *then*, in that time, with him in the middle of it. He belonged there—in his mind he *was* there—just as he belonged at the first Human Be-in in Golden Gate Park in '67, the year of the Summer of Love, amid the psychedelic rock of the San Francisco Sound. More people claimed later to have attended those famous, iconic gatherings than the sites could have accommodated, so why couldn't he join in retroactively, too?

Although he supposed San Francisco must have changed some since then, he knew he too would prosper in a city so congenial to poets, dreamers, subterraneans. The Golden State to him was a dimension all its own where new realities were invented all the time. In his imagination the cool invigorating city by the bay was a land of the lotus-eaters (in a good way), a perpetual present under blue skies amid iridescent flowers in a paradise beyond the mountains and seas, west of where the sun goes down, far from the crowded exhausted exploited continents, beyond the wars and oppressions of man. Maybe he was idealizing a little, but he could dream, couldn't he? There he would meet others like himself, and he could breathe free while they walked about the city and its sunlit parks talking endlessly of art and the imagination and eternity . . .

The first exploratory visit to the Bay Area he had planned, to last two weeks, would have taken him to the city, to Berkeley, Oakland, and maybe Muir Woods, but at the last minute he'd had to cancel the trip to help arrange his father's funeral. Other interruptions followed, breeding insecurity, paranoia: it seemed that the surest way to bring on a family calamity was to plan an itinerary and book a flight.

He had actually succeeded in visiting San Francisco once, but thanks to his brother he had had to cut the trip short, only to return home and find . . . it made his blood boil even to think about it. He still felt like strangling Bartholomew over that little stunt, or treating him to the business end of a meat ax. That was two years ago.

Even if he wasn't writing much poetry lately, revenge fantasies kept his imagination busy. Mother and Brother did not know he had been in California; he let them believe he had gone to Austin with one college buddy to visit another. Anticipating that he would be moving soon after that exploratory visit, he had prematurely sold his old car to cover the travel expenses and add to his San Francisco savings account. He still had not bought a replacement. He kept telling himself he was going to move soon, so why spend the money when he could just take the bus to work and read while the city transit authority did the driving? The interruption of that trip had made him more determined than ever to establish himself out West, and yet he lived in fear that he would never actually see California again. Would someone in his family have to die before he could live and breathe in the promised land?

"I love my sweet Jesus . . ." Bartholomew sang as he pushed back and forth on the reinforced porch swing, his hands resting on his lap, head tilting slowly from side to side, a placid smile on his wide face and a dreamy, faraway look in his pale blue eyes. "Dear sweet Jesus . . ." If the day wasn't too hot, he would sing his song all morning long, blending with the sounds of blue jays and mockingbirds *craaaking* at each other, the drone of distant lawnmowers, a propeller plane passing overhead a mile away, and the uneven, rising-falling yells of

J.J. the vegetable man calling out from the side of his truck, "Good tomaters. Good peach," pausing to light a cigarette and scratch behind his ear, "Good satsumas, nice Plaquemines orange." Weaving in and out of all these sounds, Bartholomew's off-key monotone sang the same words over and over, the same melody, with the same feeling. Every morning, and sometimes in the evenings, too, he sat on the swing and sang of his love.

Indoors, Melba could hear him as she thumbed through her *Reader's Digest*. After a few hours, his singing could grow a little wearisome, but after all he was praising the Lord, and it kept him on the other side of a wall, and happy, the same way his food and prayers and after-lunch naps pacified him, so she dared not ask him to stop.

Simpson walked in one day looking alarmed. "Doesn't he embarrass you, Mother? Don't the neighbors complain? I heard him from a block away, resounding through the oaks like the death groans of the last dinosaur."

Melba looked surprised. Why on earth would anybody object to a nice boy singing Sunday school songs on his front porch?

"You know very well Bartholomew has always sung to himself. He has such a pretty voice. And anyway," she peered at him over her eyeglasses, "you didn't seem to mind him singin' when you were in the hospital after that awful boy kicked you you-know-where."

"I don't remember that."

"Oh yes, he sang to you, and read to you, and—"

"I don't remember. I don't remember!"

"Mercy!"

Tender-hearted Melba was easily distressed by strife, particularly of the brotherly kind. Jesus said whatsoever ye do unto the least of these my brethren, so ye do also unto me. "Y'all hush. Y'all givin' me the grandes douleurs." She would stop them if she could, but boys will be boys. She was not the worrying type, but she could not help but live in a state of perpetual concern about Bartholomew. At any moment, any little thing might cause him to explode. Everyone had heard stories of high-strung delicate-nerved individuals suddenly snapping and grabbing a knife off the counter and going after the whole family. Melba could picture him bursting into flames, screaming out of the house and running in front of a city bus on Elysian Fields, or huffing madly up the narrow sidewalk along the Mississippi River Bridge till he was bumped over the railing by a carload of intoxicated delinquents. There was just no telling.

And Simpson! A mother tries not to worry but that young man was too serious for his own good. Always skulking around by himself, frowning like he's thinking deep thoughts. He had always been a solitary type. He should find a nice girl and settle down. But at the gentlest suggestion he would bristle as though she'd told him to join a church or eat raw turnips. "I don't *care* what's good for me." What kind of talk was that? Once or twice she had almost confided to her good friend Buzz that she sometimes worried whether he might rather settle down with someone other than a nice girl. Anything would be better than seeing him in sour moods all the time, though, irritable and hypersensitive. Simpson had to know she wasn't being critical; she spoke only out of motherly concern. And there is no such thing as an overly concerned mother.

Melba laid aside her magazine and went in to the kitchen. She pulled a blue Tupperware bowl and a bag of pecans from the cupboard, then went out to the back patio and sat on one of the padded chaises longues.

Several minutes later Bartholomew appeared, book in hand. He stood frowning at the pecans and wincing at the cracking sounds.

"Oh, there you are. You gonna read awhile?"

He sat down with a great whooosh on the chaise longue beside her. He opened his large picture book and frowned with exaggerated concentration.

She cracked pecans meditatively, crunching every minute or so. Each time she cracked a pecan between the metal pliers, he winced and sighed irritably.

"If it's that painful, you could go read somewhere else. What's gonna happen to you when I'm gone, I wonder, Bartholomew?"

"I'll take care of myself, the way I always have," he grumbled. "Is that going to be a pecan pie for me?"

"Maybe, if you're nice. Whatcha reading?"

"*Lives of the Bloody Martyrs*. I haven't gotten to the part about me yet."

"Martyrs? When did you get interested in them?"

"From Reverend Bud. Since his own church kicked him out, he identifies with the martyrs. So do I. No one knows how I suffer."

"I'd just as soon you didn't go near that nasty strange old thing. He's two inches from a welfare case himself, and no kind of role model for a nice young man."

"Don't talk about him like that. He's my friend. He's a man of faith. You said I could try other churches, and I found his. It's not his fault they defrocked him."

She popped a pecan into her mouth and chewed thoughtfully. It wasn't worth arguing about. "Anyhow, we gotta be thinkin' about this. You remember how unprepared we were when Daddy died. We had to borrow a casket for the visitation."

"You're still digging at me about the lottery money. That's what this is about, isn't it?" Not once had anyone in his family ever thanked him. How sharper than a serpent's tooth.

"I just want you and Simpson to be provided for."

"It's *me* you're worried about." He slapped his book shut against his thigh. "Why do you always couch your worries in terms of 'us'? You think I don't know what you're doing? Of course Simp's gonna be okay 'cause he's got a job and went to college and everything. I'm the helpless indigent you're worried about."

"All right, then."

Bartholomew's jaw dropped slightly.

"You're right. It is mainly you I'm worried about. What are you gonna do?"

"Maybe I'm gonna scream."

"Knock yourself out."

Melba cracked several more pecans and tossed the meat into the Tupperware bowl. Her obstinate sons *wanted* bad luck. They preferred disasters to good sense and precaution.

"The Lord helps them who help themselves," she added.

"I'm *quite* aware of *that*," he said with some heat, "but I am not going to have my head shrink-rapped. I've had enough psycho-babble to last a lifetime."

She knew very well what happened last time he went to a doctor. He was healthy and strong as a buffalo, and there was no need for him to get a checkup.

"Bartholomew, I'm trying to be practical and you're just sitting over there being clever. I hope you're still clever when I'm no longer here."

He was not going to the mind cage. Doctor Norkel and his kind just loved intriguing cases like his. They stroked their beards and tapped their clipboards and uttered professionally considered opinions, all backed by medical science, yet they knew nothing of what was inside him. Not the speckliest inkling. He was surprised his family had only committed him once. Why didn't they just put an end to it? There were so many ways they could make it look like an accident. But they were willing to suffer some just to make him suffer more: a life sentence cuts deeper than execution. It was their way of getting back at him, to make him stay in his life.

He could think of no reply, except to say: "*For unto me it is given in the behalf of Christ, not only to believe on him, but also to suffer for his sake.* Philippians One twenty-nine."

"You changed a word."

He sighed irritably and opened his book again. Only the martyrs and their biographers could know his torments and tribulations.

When the crowd caught up with Bartholomew they tied him to a stake in the town square. One of the marshals, or a military priest, took a tanner's knife used to cut the skins of sheep and cattle, and held the blade to a fire of flaming coals. Bartholomew raised his eyes to heaven and to our savior on the cross as the chief inserted the blade a quarter-inch into his throat and began slicing straight down the front of Bartholomew's chest. Blood spurted in brave bursts that turned to flame as the blade passed over the sacred heart of Jesus alive within him as our savior joined Bartholomew in his agony, Christ who will never abandon us.

"I'm going inside," he announced abruptly, though it took several attempts to heave himself up from the chaise longue. "I have to say my prayers and do my warm-water gargling before I go to the recording studio."

"Oh that's right, I forgot it's today. See if they can start payin' you."

When he prayed he closed his bedroom door and knelt before the old sofa, leaned forward on the cushions with his head bowed, his nose against the cushions, and uttered the name *Jesus Lord Jesus* over and over. He bowed to welcome the presence, the healing touch. It is in humbling ourselves that we open the door. As he made his petitions for Mother's health and the repose

of his father's soul and for peace in the world, he envisioned himself petting and stroking the Lord, comb-
ing his beard. He reached up to the gaunt tortured
body on the cross and pressed his hands to the suffering victim's stomach, ran his hands down the rippling
hard-muscled abdomen, across the torn loincloth and
down his whipped and bleeding thighs, exhausted in
his travails. *Righteousness shall be the girdle of his loins.*

Bartholomew's favorite images of Jesus were those of
the Savior sitting with the animals and the little children, smiling into their eyes, holding them, hearing their
prayers. With gentle Jesus he felt safe, forgiven; he could
lay his head on Jesus' lap and the Lord would stroke his
hair with mercy. But he was also drawn to the pictures
of Christ on the cross with his head tilted back, his eyes
aghast, grieving for the sins of man, forsaken by his own
father.

After his prayers he felt content, filled with love for
Jesus, and suffused with peace. How it vexed him, then,
whenever he emerged from his air-conditioned chamber of prayer to find Simpson the invader sitting at the
breakfast bar, his hungry-cat eyes flickering as he tried to
think of something nasty to say. "Praying for chocolate
fudge ice cream again?" (He had only done that once!)
It was a soul-test: God was trying him. If thou canst
go in peace and be vexed not by the haughty visage of
thy heathen brother, then mayst thou sit near the right
hand of the Lord thy God. Only the Father knew how
he struggled to hold his temper. Bartholomew heaved
with wrath, yet he must forbear because he knew not

71

the day or the hour when the Lord would come again. Would his hand or voice be raised to smite his brother when the Son of Man returned? It would be just his luck to be in the middle of an unbrotherly act when the Lord appeared in all his glory, and Christ would have to interrupt his Second Coming to say, "What doest thou, Brother Bartholomew?" All the angels would turn and witness his hand upraised in the act of smiting—for shame!—and his soul would be burned onto the red walls of hell for ever and ever. Not even his close personal relationship with Jesus would save him; it would be out of His hands. To think that he could lose his temper and in a blind instant destroy the closeness with the Lord he'd prayed so long to attain—it was terrifying, like looking into the screaming furnaces of hell. He prayed for patience to forgive his brother for wishing him unborn, though he feared the Lord would never believe him.

"Seems fitting that he's behind glass in a padded cell," grumbled the sound engineer as he adjusted the volume and tone. "Right where he belongs."

"He's good," said the producer. "Be nice to him."

"He's a nut and completely annoying. You haven't seen him when he's proselytizing the hell out of me. A few days after Christmas he's pushing his baby Jesus cake on me, saying 'Eat, eat,' like he's my mother. Or I ask him for a sound check and he gets all huffy and starts channeling the prophet Jeremiah. You may be spoiling him a little too much, Boss. He thinks he's little prince Edward R. Murrow, or some televangelist."

"I didn't say he's not annoying, I just said he's good. Listen to that rich baritone, that pronunciation. How is it that he doesn't have more of an accent?"

"Mastering all those Old Testament names, maybe?"

"He's a natural."

The engineer looked at his boss with amazement. "You really envy him."

"If I had a voice like that, you think I'd be sittin' here? Okay, that's good, Bartholomew," he said into the intercom. "One more, and then it's a wrap."

It was true that Bartholomew took pride in recording a high-quality broadcast, in much the same way that he was exact about his prayers and other priorities. He was prized by the station producer for his precision, intonation, and the way he paused for effect. He had a natural sense of timing. He came in on Tuesdays and Fridays, and the sound engineer or an assistant would give him an intro script and a handful of clippings to read for the visually impaired. He practiced in a spare sound room equipped with acoustical tiles and a mock microphone and speaker. The engineer thought it was funny seeing the disheveled, red-faced Gargantua with his sweat-damp hair mussed, shirt half-untucked, frowning in intense concentration with the handful of newspaper clippings clutched in his fist.

It was through the producer that the pro bono job had come about. Rich Levine was a sport fisherman in the Gulf when he could get the time, and had long been a customer of Rabineaux & Weems. He and Gasper used to have long "sportsman's paradise" conversations about fish and game that annoyed Roscoe Rabineaux, in part because he envied his partner's knack for customer relations. At Gasper's funeral service Levine had heard Bartholomew read a passage from Isaiah that gave him goose bumps and spine chills. With a cultured-sounding voice that projected well—Gasper's youngest evidently had experience in speaking up—and his almost faultless enunciation of uncommon multisyllabic words . . . he was a born announcer. Visually he might not be right for television—not even for a community cable channel— but for radio it didn't matter what he looked like. Rich Levine had been in the business long enough to know that sometimes the talent you're looking for appears in unlikely wrappings. With a voice like that he could show up in his bathrobe and scuba fins.

At the funeral Levine approached Bartholomew as he was standing with his mother. After giving his condolences for the family's loss—Mr. Weems was a friend, a kind man and the best at his craft—he complimented Bartholomew's sensitive, reverent reading of Isaiah. Would he ever consider reading news stories for the blind for Dillard University's community radio station? He was careful not to praise too much, however, but rather to emphasize the Christian goodness such a practical and pleasing use of Bartholomew's God-given talent would bring to those whose blessings from the Creator did not include the sense of sight.

74

"Oh, that's a *lovely* idea, Bartholomew," Melba said. She left it at that after a subtle wink from Levine suggested that any more encouragement might backfire.

"I could read Scripture, too. That's better for 'em."

"Well, maybe. Let's see how it goes with the *Times-Picayune* first."

As it turned out, once he agreed to do something, Bartholomew also had a talent for turning up on time.

Adjusting the treble and midrange settings for the next recording, the engineer was thinking *Just don't offer him a job*, but said nothing for fear of giving his boss ideas.

Shortly before dinnertime a few days after the shredding of the taxidermy collection, Simpson brought his mother an envelope of several hundred-, fifty-, and twenty-dollar bills. He felt a little guilty that she should be running short of money, for he had pushed her to let him help manage her assets. Several years before, when Melba said she would like to buy a twenty-five- or fifty-dollar U.S. Treasury bond from time to time, whenever she had a little extra left over at the end of the month from Social Security and her pension from the funeral home, he pointed out that she could make a quicker and probably higher return by investing in a mutual fund. Treasury bonds take so long to mature, and for someone her age . . .

Melba was reluctant at first, but her doubts were allayed as he explained and re-explained that it was all legitimate and fiscally responsible. There was very little risk and much likelihood of profit, as the investments were protected by regulations, market value was only going up, and, besides, everyone was doing it. He had been educated about the practice by one of his CopyQwik customers, a financial adviser at a brokerage on Poydras Street.

Simpson had come over one night equipped with some mutual fund brochures and a calculator and notepad, but waited until Bartholomew went back to his room for his after-dinner prayers, for Mother didn't need the distraction of the fatling's moralistic objections to usury and gross profiteering. At length, she came to see that her money really could work better for her if deposited in a more aggressive investment sector. Simpson's clinching argument was that Father would approve. He sweetened the temptation by offering to put up the entire $500 initial investment. She could add her own deposits when possible and observe the total account value growing in each monthly statement.

She agreed to try it if he would take care of the deposits. "And put it in your name, honey. Those monthly statements are just too complicated, and it's prob'ly best if I just forget the money's there." By the deposit schedule they agreed upon, at the first of each month, provided she had a little extra to put in savings, she gave Simpson a certain amount in cash, which he duly deposited for her. It was also on the first of each month that he deposited a portion of his wages into a California savings account, and had been doing so since college, though he considerately spared her from this knowledge.

For the first several months, whenever he came home to wash his laundry he would unfold the latest statement to show her by how much her account value had grown. "My, my," was all she could say. Something about the whole idea smelled of bad magic. "Okay, I've seen enough." She averted her eyes.

One week it happened that before the cash was deposited in the mutual fund, an unexpected car repair left him temporarily short of money. Because of a bad experience with debt some years before, he preferred not to charge the repair to his credit card. He meant to tell her about the temporary loan from the cash envelope, but never got around to it, and quietly repaid her account a few weeks later. After that, other emergency spending needs began to sprout new heads. The first time Mother had said she didn't need to see the statements, he had noticed a dark thought twitch in a corner of his mind. But after all, hadn't he put $500 into starting her account? How many sons would do as much? And wasn't it on account of her and Bartholomew that Simpson had been stuck in New Orleans all these years? He would repay her when he was rich and famous. He'd send a check from California.

The time to repay her came sooner than that. After the taxidermy rampage, he withdrew several hundred dollars from his San Francisco savings account.

"Oh, Simpson, you're so good to your mother," she said when he handed her the envelope. She reached up to him so he would lean over and give her a kiss. "This is from the mutual fund?"

"No, that takes so long, and you have to jump through all these hoops and they kill you with fees and taxes, it's just not worth the trouble. This is just a little something to get by on till Bartholomew gets a job. Any day now, right, Barto?"

Bartholomew was sitting on the sofa, smoldering with vexation, irritable with hunger. Simpson's visit was making dinner later than usual.

"By the way, did you call Dr. Norkel?"

"Who? About what?"

"Bartholomew!" Emotionally no different from the 150-pound second-grader sent to Mandeville. Volcanoes of temper, torrents of unhappiness, whirlpools of selfishness and dependency. Some kids, you just wished you could erase it all for them and start from scratch.

"Adolphus Norkel died. I outlived him, just like I said I would. It's Dr. Finestein now, and he's on vacation."

"Till when?"

Bartholomew clapped his hands to his ears, then over his mouth, then his eyes, round and round in a circle of evasion.

Melba frowned. "You look foolish as three monkeys. Answer your brother."

"I don't remember. I left a message. He's supposed to call me."

"Barto, you can make an appointment without speaking directly with the doctor himself. Please try again, okay? Call tomorrow. Phone lines are open."

He turned to his mother, who raised her eyebrows in approval, and her heart was so full of gratitude and optimism she had to sigh.

"That sounds like a good plan, Simpson, don't you think so, Bartholomew? Just give it another try."

"I suppose I can manage," Bartholomew moaned wearily, as though the effort really might be the end of him. "Isn't dinner ready yet?"

After dinner Bartholomew felt full, content, pacified by two helpings of his mother's rich spaghetti, and sat longer than usual at the dinner table while she washed the dishes, clacking the Melmac dinnerware loudly in the sudsy tub splashing with running water.

Simpson observed him sitting there almost tranquilized. "Mom, this was a great spaghetti. You should cook this more often."

"Thank you. Come by more often and I'll be glad to."

"Seen your friend Buzz lately?" he asked. "What's the old girl up to these days?"

"Not lately, but I'll probably be seeing her soon when I go get some ingredients for your brother's birthday cake. It's coming up, you know."

"That's right, it is," Simpson said with cheer that sounded almost genuine.

After a moment, he asked softly, "Bartholomew, tell me again about when Jesus died."

"The first time?"

"Yes." There he goes again, blending the father figures. He leaned forward on his elbows across the dining table. "How did they do it, the Roman soldiers?"

"With rusted nails."

"Did he feel the pain?" Simpson asked gently.

"Yes," Bartholomew whispered. "It hurt bad."

"I wasn't sure how much it really hurt him, you know, because you know if he's the son of God then he could control the level of pain . . ."

"It hurt him *more* because he's the son of God. He agonized for every soul that was alive then and every soul to come. The pain went through him in all directions."

"Wow. That must have really hurt." It was hard to keep a straight face. Simpson wanted to keep him going, to see where this could lead. When he wasn't being suspicious and hypersensitive, Bartholomew could sometimes be frighteningly pliable.

"But he was wounded for our transgressions, and with his stripes we are healed."

"How long was he dead?"

"Three days." Bartholomew stared straight ahead. "It seemed like a lifetime."

Growing up, Simpson had heard Mother and Bartholomew talking about Jesus every night at bedtime. When they were young the boys had shared a room, so through the years they both heard the same stories over and over. Simpson lay there while Mother sat on the edge of Bartholomew's bed (even though there was more room on Simpson's) and told Bible stories to put them to sleep. She told them about Jesus' tender never-ending love for all the little ones, always holding them in his arms, close to his heart. Suffer the little children . . . And a fatling shall lead them. "He watches over you in your sleep," she'd say, then lead them in reciting,

> *Now I lay me down to sleep.*
> *I pray the Lord my soul to keep.*
> *And should I die before I wake,*
> *I pray the Lord my soul to take.*

After the Bible stories Bartholomew seemed always to drift sweetly off to sleep, but Simpson was kept awake by the intensity of Jesus' eyes. *He watches over you.* Everywhere he was being watched, every act recorded, remembered infinitely. Jesus loves me when I'm bad, though it makes Him very sad. The space on the wall above the television occupied by a portrait of Jesus was a place where Simpson's eyes never ventured.

"Did everybody just cry and walk away?" he asked. "Did they just figure it was all over?"

Bartholomew's eyes fluttered. "Some of us stayed. We took him down and bathed him, anointed his many wounds, then dressed him and lay him in the tomb."

He was silent a moment, staring into space, his fingers idly stroking the table top. "He had promised eternal life, and then he went and died, and his wounds and suffering were so terrible. He was gone."

Simpson shifted uncomfortably. He glanced at Mother, humming to herself as she dried the pots and pans. Sometimes she would chime in with her own memories of Jesus. She would be sitting in Father's La-Z-Boy, working a crossword puzzle under the 60-watt glow of the standing lamp, and Bartholomew would be talking to himself or to Mother or Simpson—or to no one in particular—and she would speak as though the miracle had been performed or the parable told only yesterday in Jackson Square. She would peer over her eyeglasses sliding down her nose, adding, "Yes, and he told Lazarus to rise and walk, and Lazarus walked as he was bid." Bartholomew would nod in confirmation, as though he had witnessed it too, and it had happened just as she described it.

"Did the Lord suffer while he was dead?"

"He was *dead*." Bartholomew gave him a strange look.

They were silent.

"Bartholomew, do you ever get the feeling you live in a different world from everyone else?"

Bartholomew frowned and closed his eyes.

Simpson looked at him, waiting.

He was about to answer for him when Bartholomew replied at last, "The world I live in is the only world there is."

3

Every Day, in Every Way

THE FOLLOWING MORNING, Simpson had just finished placing a new roll of receipt paper in the cash register when a haggard, possibly homeless middle-aged man in a denim shirt and a worn red baseball cap limped to the counter to pay for copies of his resume, a list of warehouse and construction jobs. The man's eyes were hidden under the bill of his cap, but his cheeks were lined and sunken, his lips dry and cracked, like the face of an old cigarette-smoking heroin addict. His hands, too, were worn and scarred, the veins prominent, the fingers callused and nails chipped as he tapped impatiently on the counter. Simpson was ringing up the sale when he glanced at the name at the top of the resume. Nicholas C. Kline. 129 South Rocheblave Street. Suddenly near panic, wishing there were some way he could cover the name tag that trembled over his racing heart, he slipped the resumes into a CopyQwik folder, handed the man his change and receipt, then turned to help the next customer. As the man limped toward the door, Simpson felt a sick sensation squirming in his guts. His breakfast was about to erupt.

He asked the next customer to excuse him, then directed a younger assistant to come take the front counter for a few minutes. After vomiting as discreetly as possible in the employees' restroom and rinsing his mouth, he asked his coworker Latoya for a cigarette. He never smoked tobacco, not since trying a cigarette or two in college. He went down Baronne and around the corner to a dim, smoky bar mostly patronized by off-duty security guards, parking lot attendants, and occasionally a *Times-Picayune* reporter meeting with a confidential source. He ordered a quick shot of Early Times on the rocks and a glass of cold spring water. The bartender sympathetically lit the cigarette for him after watching the customer's shaking hands fumble with the matches. Simpson coughed out the first few puffs, then as the bourbon took effect his trembling gradually subsided and his throat became somewhat numbed to the smoke's sharp sting. The dreaded Cutter. Surprised we haven't crossed paths before now. Didn't know if he was even still alive. Heard he was brain-damaged; someone must have typed that resume for him. After the cigarette and another demi-shot, his nerves were settled enough that he could go back to the copy shop and pretend to function as a calm and normal person.

The four-unit apartment house where Simpson lived at the corner of Dormition and Invalides was built of brick that had been stuccoed and whitewashed long ago, and over the years mold and mildew had mottled the walls and coated the lower parts of the building with layers of green that gave it the seasoned, distinguished look of an establishment with presence and gravitas. He had chosen the apartment not because he liked it, particularly, but because it was within a few blocks of his mother's house and it had a vacancy. That was all. The rent was low, which let him save for his relocation and justify his residence in what was really, he had to admit, just a few cracks shy of a shambles. You get what you pay for, he reminded himself each time a doorknob came loose in his hand or a faucet dripped, dripped, and cockroaches boldly crossed the kitchen floor, and the oven's burned-out heating element went unreplaced for months even after he complained to the landlord's management company. But every home has its imperfections.

He had moved in to the apartment only temporarily; when he signed the lease he expected he would be there no more than a year—just long enough to save some money. He had never thought about moving anywhere else in New Orleans—when he moved it would be to the West Coast—except once when he was looking at a newer and fresher one-room house on a sunny lot with pine trees about five blocks away, on the other side of Elysian Fields. But Mother had pleaded with him not to move so far away. "Three blocks is too far already."

His father had died during Simpson's third year at the state university, where he was pursuing a degree in creative writing, with a minor in liberal studies, and developing a liking for Buddhism and Hinduism. When

Gasper first died (imperfectly, as it turned out) in the early eighties, Simpson had returned to New Orleans to comfort his mother and settle the estate. The settlement of Gasper's financial affairs, when the time came, was disappointingly simpler than the family had anticipated, though the shock of the simplicity caused complications of its own, as there turned out to be no secret savings account set aside for Bartholomew's uncertain future.

Simpson had not needed to withdraw from the university, yet he had done it, and that was that. Perhaps he had had enough of college life. Maybe he had just been waiting for an excuse to drop out, some event on which to blame his inevitable shortcomings, for he assumed that whatever paying occupation he set himself to, his heart would not be in it, and his mind would not be present, either, because Simpson Weems, whose aim was for something higher, had never really been of this world, and felt no particular obligation to involve himself in its affairs. But maybe it wasn't exactly that he anticipated failure, but preferred passive resistance to the corporate, consumer economy. Perhaps. But one did not need a degree from an institution of higher learning in order to practice noninvolvement, and as for renunciation of works, it was not doing much for his poetry career.

Although it would one day be a given among his biographers and literary historians, his immediate family had no idea that within Simpson lived the soul of a poet—potentially the most promising in America in the twenty-first century (he had dawdled too long to make it happen in the twentieth). Mother and Brother knew nothing of his plans to move to San Francisco to self-actualize. There he would become the writer he had been *in potentia* for more than a decade, perhaps several decades, for who can say when a poet's promise is first engendered? Simpson's closet shelves were stacked with rough drafts and poems written long ago. During his golden years of productivity he had enjoyed some distinction among his creative writing peers, with several poems published in his high school and college literary magazines. On his last day of high school his senior English teacher Mrs. Frazier touched his shoulder and said warmly, "We expect big things from you, Simpson." Then again, an earlier teacher had noted on a report card, "high aptitude, but daydreams, wastes time." Most of his poems concerned suffocation or escape from quicksand and other forms of entrapment. Bondage without discipline. Since leaving college his engines had stalled, but still his head and notebooks were stuffed with first lines of poems he would complete one day, pregnant phrases scrawled on envelopes and matchbooks and po-boy wrappers ... He knew that to fulfill his promise he must move to a place where he could work without distraction. He owed it to himself—to his destiny—to establish a new life, his own personal *vita nuova* in the most favorable surroundings conducive to free expression. For what does it profit a man or his country if he have a gift but keep it hid, or silent?

All things come to pass in their appointed time, and a natural born artist can no more avoid his destiny than an acorn can resist the nurturing influences of rain and sun.

It was regrettable that family obligations had compelled him to stay so long, stagnating, decaying, in his hometown. But could not genius find ways to transmute decay into fertilizer? That his family never suspected the talent within him was no discouragement, nor did he mind that the only verses they ever read were in the Psalms and Proverbs. One thing in that old black book of theirs was true: A prophet is not without honor, save in his own country, hometown, neighborhood, and local bar.

All glory and honor is thine, O mighty poet.

When he grew intoxicated by the fumes of his potential, he would try to pull his thoughts back down to the contemplation of practical matters. Drive a U-Haul? Simply pack a suitcase and go Greyhound? Rent a car and drive nonstop through the desert at night listening to the austere sounds of early Dylan? He liked the idea of living simply, modestly, in a one-room apartment, with a desk and a bed, perhaps a sofa and a reading chair with a standing lamp, and maybe a good Persian carpet for those chilly San Francisco nights and mornings. (He had been envisioning his apartment in such minute detail for so many years that he sensed he must owe back-rent to someone.) There would be a view of Coit Tower on Telegraph Hill, the great spire of the Transamerica pyramid, and perhaps the bold red towers of the Golden Gate Bridge. Fragrant scents of eucalyptus would drift in through the windows, perhaps borne in on the evening's fog. Through the windows too would clang the bells of the cable cars as they whirred by on their gleaming rails, and perhaps the foghorns of tugboats in the bay, while in from the cafés of North Beach would waft the sharp aromas of roasted coffee ...

But back to practical matters—for it was only through his talents for planning and preparation that he was actually going to plant himself in that idealized, aroma-rich apartment—he had to figure out the smoothest, gentlest manner of escape; Mother deserved to be left in the most considerate possible way. Brother deserved only to be left. In all the years he'd been planning this move, he had never quite arrived at the perfect scheme; it always seemed the way would suggest itself when the time was right. Was it already too late? *Just go.* Don't explain, don't ask permission, and, above all, do not feel guilty. He had already given his best and brightest years to satisfying his mother's request. Melba and Bartholomew had each other. And Simpson's escape would only bring them closer, which should make them all the happier. His departure would please Bartholomew, whose felicity, as ever, was Melba's joy.

O Poesy! for thee I hold my pen,
That am not yet a glorious denizen
Of thy wide heaven—

He clicked his ballpoint and leaned intently over the blank sheet of resume bond stationery borrowed from the copy shop. On the way home from work, while the bus was rerouted to make way for another parade, he had thought of a good first line, a phrase that would lead somewhere, he could feel it.

> *She shows me something:*
> *the wind that blows the veil . . .*

Then what? Who is "she"? Try to be concrete, specific. Mignon?

The phone rang. He tried to ignore the first few rings.

"Hello? Oh, hi, Mom." He cleared his throat. "What's up?"

"I just wanted to thank you again for bringing over that money."

"Oh, sure, you're welcome. Just a little something to tide you over till we get Bartholomew situated somewhere."

"Yes." She sounded hesitant, or distracted.

"Something wrong?"

"Everything's fine. Everything's . . ."

"Good."

He waited. "Was there something else?"

He could hear Bartholomew in the background.

"Oh, your brother wants me to get off the phone. When are you coming over next?"

He suppressed a sigh of impatience. "I don't know, Mom. Sometime soon, I'm sure."

"Good. Okay. Just wanted to say thank you."

"You're very welcome, Mom."

"So you think maybe in a few days, then?"

"Very likely."

Bartholomew's voice was rising, expanding.

"Okay, better go. Sweet dreams."

He went to the kitchen sink and splashed cool water on his face, then stood out on the back porch for some breaths of fresh air to clear his head. It never failed. Anytime he tried to write, the phone rang. He would unplug it, but that would invite an emergency.

He sat down again and clicked his pen a few times as he stared at the line he had written, then reached to the fruit bowl for a peach. He closed his eyes and inhaled the fresh clean fragrance, sweetening as it ripened. The sweet taste of Mignon. He drew the peach smell into himself, savoring the aroma, pure as the very breath of virtue. The ancient Chinese believed the peach tree confers longevity, so why not its fruit?

He looked up to his hand-lettered affirmation sign of the week, tacked up on the wall to remind him:

EVERY DAY, IN EVERY WAY

I AM BECOMING

MORE AND MORE ~~POTENTIAL~~ NORMAL

He stared at the words scrawled on the fine paper. *She shows me something . . .* Then what? Something that rhymes with *veil.* Doesn't have to rhyme. Just write something. Anything.

First word, best word.

A drop of sweat spoiled the page. He crumpled the crisp paper and threw it across the room. It landed near several other tossed rejects and sweat-damp paper towels.

He pulled out a clean sheet.

Suddenly it was dark
and I couldn't see what was happening

When are you coming over?

How about never again? Can we schedule that?

He wiped his forehead and bowed his head in his hands, a familiar position.

Why did he have to be so cold and mean to her? She meant well, deserved better. Even if he wasn't mean, he felt stiff and overly formal. Impossible to relax around them. Were they really his family?

It was hopeless. He couldn't possibly concentrate in this damned chaotic city—the family vibrations were intolerable! How was he supposed to focus when Mother kept calling and Bartholomew was only three blocks away, singing "I love my sweet Jesus" while his powerful gravitational force like a black hole sucked everything toward him, him, himself? Simpson would be leaving soon, just as he'd told Mignon. By April he could be living in San Francisco, and there, in springtime in the fertile fields of Bohemia, he could finally concentrate and *produce* in a way he had never been able to do at home.

Every day I'm not writing is a day wasted, subtracted.

He nuzzled the skin of a peach, took a breath of sweet fertility, then reached for his dream notebook, a treasury of poetic images. The last entry was from several years ago. He turned the pages, frowning at familiar, overly literary entries he'd passed by many times before, then stopped at one from around the time he'd left college:

There's a baby being born from a baby born in order to deliver the new baby. Yellow fluid around the edges. It's coming now.

It felt like something he could work with, but after several false starts that involved graphic obstetric imagery, blood and fluids, torn membranes, and wailing newborns, he crumpled the page and tossed it against the wall.

He watched the ball of paper roll to a stop, then opened his well-worn copy of *Howl and Other Poems* and began copying the first lines of "America."

When he could not concentrate past the first line of a new poem of his own, he kept busy by rereading and emulating the potent, seminal works of Ginsberg, Whitman, and other models of excellence. If the juices were flowing he might write an imitation of "Sunflower Sutra" or "Song of Myself"; if not, he would copy page after page of their words in his handwriting, seeking to absorb and assimilate the voice and style of the masters, just as young painters in the Uffizi and the Louvre copied masterpieces onto their own canvases. What he loved in these poets was their wide-openness, the free-flowing, long-running lines that seemed to embrace and carry everything imaginable in their current, above and below the surface, like a great overflowing all-fertilizing Mississippi River of language, life, possibility. Yet he worried he had relied too long on imitation. Where's the originality?

He knew well that a poet's talent, like that of a musician or mathematician, may only flourish early in life, if it blossoms at all. Maybe his best years were already behind him. Already a decade older than Keats was when he died. By the time he got to California, would he be only half the artist he could have been, with half the creative energy?

"America" was a long poem, several pages of long lines. He kept at it for a few minutes, then abruptly—it was like someone else was inside him—he grabbed the pages and flung them in the air.

"This is pointless!" he shouted.

It's always been pointless.

He bowed his head in his hands. A bead of sweat trickled down his wrist. How many times have I been through this? What would Allen think? He'd be horrified. He'd feel sorry for me. He would weep. This was fifty years ago.

Get a grip. No tears. Self-pity is weakness.

Nothing Ginsberg ever did is as important as what I might write tonight.

When he was in San Francisco he had been able to write quite freely at the Caffé Trieste. For a half hour the words just came pouring out naturally, easy as breathing. A half hour in heaven. If it happened once, it could happen again. Maybe even here at home.

He bit into the peach and chewed pensively, letting the juice drip down his chin, then reached for a broad-tipped marker to make a new sign. But the pen was almost dry, so he spent thirty minutes walking down the avenue to a 24-hour convenience store and back. He sat down again at his desk, pulled the extension-arm lamp closer, leaned over the white poster and wrote in bold dark letters, the marker squeaking across the paper with potent chemical fumes:

I AM A POET

He leaned back and studied the balance and proportion of the letters. Then he brought out his colored pens and leaned over his work, shading in carefully along the outlines of the letters. Simpson had made dozens of these confidence-building affirmation posters over the years. Many were straightforward and factual, like the one above. Some were inspirational: IT IS NEVER TOO LATE TO BE WHAT YOU MIGHT HAVE BEEN (George Eliot) and WRITE TODAY, PROCRASTINATE TOMORROW. Others were urgent, verging on desperate, in their exhortations. IF NOT NOW, WHEN?

He picked up the phone and dialed the 1-800 number for reservations at American Airlines. After two minutes on hold he hung up. Better to use a travel agent.

He pulled his well-thumbed copy of *Tales of Beatnik Glory* from the shelf, but instead of reading he sat there thinking, staring out the window.

If not now . . . But there was time. He would go to San Francisco and everything would work out for the best. Genius can't be hurried. True talent flowers in its own time. But when he read that Dylan was only nineteen when he came from Minnesota to the heart of the Greenwich Village folk scene, and Martin Luther King was only thirty-nine when he died—only three years older than Simpson was now!—heat prickles of an anxious urgency broke out on his forehead. Of course, King had been driven by the hot whips of historical necessity, "the fierce urgency of now." He could not have bided his time, for too many depended on him, whereas the development of Weems's poetic art, though arguably of comparable significance in the long run of history, was perhaps of a more gradual nature. Nevertheless, Simpson saw enough similarities between their works and destinies that he felt he had better sharpen his pencil and move it.

"What happens if the levees break?"

Simpson and his coworker looked at each other, then back to the customer. Her sale had been rung up and she had the bag in her hand, but she was not yet ready to leave. She looked worried.

"They won't," said Simpson with a reassuring smile. "They're built to last. It's okay."

He and Latoya Giselle the computer geek had been looking over a monthly sales report when this customer, an attractive young woman in a Guatemalan vest, came to the front counter.

"On the way in from the airport we passed by these canals. I asked what they were and the taxi driver said they carry rainwater out to the lake. But what if the water gets too high and the walls break?"

Simpson watched her hands as she folded and re-folded her paper bag of manila folders and colored pencils. Specks of paint on her fingers.

"They won't. They were built by the Corps of Engineers. Made to last."

"But what about in a hurricane? That's a lot of water, isn't it, and high winds?"

"The city could flood, parts of it," said Latoya. "It's happened before. They tell us we're safe, but keep a hammer in the attic in case the water rises and you need to break out."

She meant the last part as dark humor, but the customer was not smiling.

Just a few days earlier a German tourist had asked Mr. Dumond the same question. What if a hurricane struck during Mardi Gras?

"I just moved here," the woman continued, "and now I'm reading all these things about flood risk."

"Where do you live? What part of town?"

"Just off Magazine."

"You should be okay there."

"But what about everyone else?"

"They should keep a hammer in the attic too."

"Hurricane season's been pretty calm the last few decades, overall."

"And anyway, the season's only from June to November."

The customer glanced behind them. "Well, thanks. I feel better now."

Simpson was about to ask Latoya if she had been getting this kind of question more often lately when behind them the store's owner said, "Latoya, Weems, can y'all come in here with me for a minute?"

Chet Dumond motioned them into his office. He shut the door and, with a heavy heart, informed them that a national photocopy chain was making an aggressive, lucrative offer to buy the two CopyQwik of New Orleans, Inc., stores. Representatives of the national firm had indicated that they were also considering simply opening a new store in the vacant space across the street below the dance studio and letting CopyQwik be driven out of business. Either method would suffice. If the sale went through, there might be job cuts.

"I just felt I should let y'all know, and I'll be tellin' the others too. These national firms like to bring in their own managers when they buy out a company 'cause they want to make sure things are done their way."

Simpson and Latoya looked at each other.

"But of course they'll need and me and Latoya," said Simpson, exuding confidence. "And I'm sure we'll fit right in to their corporate scheme."

Dumond scratched his rounded chin as he squinted at the George Harrison identity badge clipped to Simpson's blue CopyQwik apron.

"Something wrong?" Simpson looked down anxiously, afraid the thumping of his heart was trembling the badge.

"Don't I pay you enough to get your watch fixed?" said Dumond, pointing to the cracked crystal of Simpson's drugstore Timex.

"The pay's fine, sir."

Although the store's name sounded contemporary and its machinery was the state-of-the-art, CopyQwik was an old family-run business with a musty, stagnant feel to it; you expected all the coins in the old gray cash register to have been minted around the Great Depression or World War II. The Baronne Street store in the Central Business District had been a going concern on the same corner since the early 1940s when it was founded by the original Old Man Dumond, and the store out on Veterans Boulevard in Metairie also had a vintage feel, though not cool or hip vintage so much as left behind, out of date. Chester Jack Dumond's business style was as old-fashioned as the day he was born. For instance, however cutting-edge the new computers and copiers—and to his credit he did invest in excellent equipment—he maintained a business staffed by an Assistant Superintendent of Reproduction (Simpson), and, in Latoya's case, a Mistress of Computing Services.

"Anyway, Latoya and Weems, y'all have been so dependable for me all these years now, and I'll try hard to make sure they keep you. But maybe y'all were thinking about movin' on somewheres else, anyways."

"Thanks for the heads-up," said Latoya.

"Mr. Dumond," Simpson cleared his throat roughly, "you know, I've been with CopyQwik a long time—"

"Now, don't y'all leave yet, please. As long as it's my store you're safe, but if you were thinking of movin' on, or looking around . . ."

"All right," said Latoya.

She sighed, and they looked at her, feeling it too.

"They're makin' me an offer I may never see again, and—." The boss looked away, sniffling loudly. "But hell, who knows, it may not go through, anyways."

Would his biographers later note that it was at this critical juncture that Weems with newfound decisiveness boldly actualized the long-planned move to San Francisco? But the buyout wasn't a done deal yet. Anything could happen. That was what scared him. Only last week he'd asked himself, How am I paralyzed? Let me count the ways. For one thing, he hesitated to leave his job because he had been with CopyQwik for so long it would be impossible to earn the same salary at a comparable position anywhere else. How much is a good superintendent of reproduction services worth? He was stricken, too, by not knowing how he would go about selling himself (an unsettling, distasteful notion) to prospective employers in San Francisco. Well, Mr. Weems, they would say, if he could even get in the door, your résumé shows impressive loyalty to this one single company since you left college without a degree. And you did get a couple of promotions over the course of your fifteen years there. They must have valued your ... (here he would anticipate the word "inertia") ... your dedication.

He was thirty-six and didn't know what else he could do for money. He probably shouldn't expect to make a good living as a poet right away. It was somewhat assuring to know that San Francisco would have no shortage of copy shops, but wasn't fifteen years in this line of work long enough? What else can I do? he whimpered. Oh for God's sake, Weems, he scolded himself, stop cringing. You can't crawl to California timid about what the master race might permit you to do. It's a place for pioneers, not moles, you worm. He figured he should probably work on building up a little confidence. Working eight to ten hours a day at CopyQwik was not conducive to raising self-esteem. The job bred self-contempt, which seemed to thrive, even metastasize, under the cold white fluorescent lights.

Back in his place behind the counter, he opened a note-pad to sketch out a to-do list for his move, but instead of writing he gazed without focusing at the traffic passing by on the street outside. Everyone else was going some-where. He assured himself once again that the day was coming soon when he would live in that Better Place that awaited him, but the promise felt hollow, unreal. It was as though inside him there was a growing, restive populace that no longer believed the Great Pretender. Wimpson Seems. How long was he going to sit around waiting for someone to hand him a ticket? He had long known that to move prematurely could ruin everything, so he had thought it best to wait until the moment was ripe so he would do it the right way. He had trusted that he would recognize the opportunity when it showed itself, but was it possible he had missed the signs?

In college he had known a guy who lived in a Ford Econoline van stalled with flat tires in a dormitory parking lot. This studious ascetic, who read at the li-brary and showered after swimming at the Huey P.

Long Field House, claimed he would move into a dorm or apartment once he improved his grade point average to where he deserved more comfortable lodgings. Until then . . .

Simpson heard the searing roar of a jet passing overhead, airborne to far horizons. That could be me up there. But no genie with a magic carpet, no sprinkling of fairy dust was going to make it happen for him.

But something, or somebody, might give him a shove.

Okay, okay. One day at a time. He was planning the groundwork now, in 1999, so that he could begin the new millennium in the right place. Breathing those rarefied airs of eucalyptus and roasted coffee, a creative type like him could not help but thrive. And now, ready or not, that beautiful shimmering city on the hills was a great deal closer than it had been only a few days ago.

> *Whoever has no house now, will never have one.*
> *Whoever is alone now will stay alone,*
> *will sit, read, write long letters through the evening,*
> *and wander on the boulevards, up and down,*
> *restlessly, while the dry leaves are blowing.*

Simpson could feel his future biographers waiting with pens poised to record the signal events of his life. They watched for him to make his move, *the* move; waited for him to start writing again. Something. Anything.

When he moved back to New Orleans after college it had not taken him long to find a job and get settled in an apartment of his own—after three years away there was no way he could have fit back into the confines of his parents' house—but after the transition he never quite resumed the daily practice of writing poetry. Something told him he might benefit from taking a temporary break from the regular practice of daily composition and instead reading intensively to make up for his aborted university studies, though this "something" was only an inkling. Fifteen years later he had nothing on paper to show for having heeded that inkling.

Poetry required concentration, yet focus eluded him, focus and the energy for persistence. One distraction of course was the vexing proximity of a particular loud, overgrown crybaby, but another worry—more like a paralyzing dread—was that he had been permanently disabled by an injury in junior high school, just at the threshold of adolescence. The ancients believed creative and sexual energy are two aspects of the same inner current. The stream that flows up and down, like a fountain, always rising while falling, or like the circulation of a tree's vascular system of phloem upward and xylem down. Had that bully's black boot like a battering ram between his legs crushed his root chakra and ruptured forever his creative wellsprings?

Whether chakras were real or not, he had a problem.

There was a tree in Dangers Park, a tall pin oak or elm that had been blasted by lightning some years ago, its trunk split open. The black tree of Dangers Park:

scorched stumps that once were limbs. Springtime came and went, but no leaves sprouted. Like looking in a mirror, every time he passed it.

And then there was the recurrent, crippling anxiety that a certain obnoxious creative writing classmate at LSU had been right when he said, "You're a pretender. You don't belong here." Was that the real reason why he'd never gone back, and let himself go slack?

Over the years he had developed intricately reasoned excuses for his rather limited productivity. His powers of justification had built a fully staffed Department of Anesthetic Rationalization that worked overtime to shield him from certain sensitive questions, such as why he was not already in San Francisco, crowned with laurels, or at least published, or why he had not managed to complete a single stanza since college. But, after all, sequoias don't reach their heights in a year, and poetry is a gradual, cultivated art whose practitioner needs experience, the enrichment of sensibility through study, and time to ponder, time to heal, daydream, time to loaf and watch the clouds go by . . .

The lightness of his portfolio suggested an artistic intention to streamline and simplify. The stillness of minimalism. A green square on a blue background, like a painting by Rothko. A song composed of a single chord, struck once and sustained. There was an eloquence in silence, a poetry in nothingness—it was a Zen thing—from which he began to formulate an aesthetics of understatement or nullity that sounded impressive when first conceived but offered little consolation when he felt himself mired in inertia, trying nothing, going nowhere.

He knew why the words didn't come easy. Familiar though he was with the Beat maxim of "first word, best word" that allowed for relaxed improvisation, his high expectations for himself strangled spontaneity. He was under such strict self-imposed demand to produce refined and deathless verse with every stroke of the pen that he stuttered, choked, scratched out lines, and over time became a ruthlessly efficient self-cancellation machine that rejected as unworthy each little idea and would not accept a rough draft. Perfection or nothing. He felt the biographer-critics reading over his shoulder and opining that the line he was about to write was not one of his best, perhaps a rather unfortunate choice of words, and, come to think of it, not an especially original thought, really not worth writing down at all.

O me! O life! of the questions of these recurring . . .
The question, O me! so sad, recurring—What good
amid these, O me, O life?

He was guilty of being poorly educated because he had never finished college, so on lunch breaks he would go around the corner to deVille Books or to the public library on Loyola, and on weekends he haunted the secondhand bookshops that seemed to sprout on every street in the Quarter. To fill the gaps in his education—a never-ending project—he read the ancients and the moderns and everything in between, but especially the Beats, Surrealists, and the Romantics.

It wasn't that he was intimidated by his predecessors (well, maybe a little), but in his conscientious studies he was perhaps overly concerned with the preparatory stage, maybe too humble in estimating his readiness. The more he read, the less capable, the less worthy he felt to take his place among the great ones, or even the good. They intimidate you. They *want* to intimidate you.

Was it possible that he had only dreamed up a future in poetry to justify the reclusive, marginal quality of his existence, to excuse himself from living directly in the everyday human world that came so naturally to others? In moments of honest reflection he did sometimes ask whether his reading were not an evasion of the real work to be done: the achievement of something that might make the dead poets, there in the shadow realm from which they can see us, sit up and take notice. But no, fail not, brave heart, for the way is the preparation, and the study and the work are one. *The lyf so short, the craft so long to lerne.* It seemed he must be forever preparing for a test he didn't deserve to take.

It was Friday night around nine-thirty after a long day at CopyQwik. He had long felt drawn to San Francisco, but now he was beginning to feel pushed there, too. After years of idly drifting, things were happening a little too quickly. Seeking solace, a calm safe harbor, he turned naturally to the comforts of a bath with Mignon.

The man at the door said she was no longer at Bourbon Bath.

"But she was here just last week. Where is she?"

"Slipped away. No forwarding information."

"What? Just like that? Why—"

"When we say we got some slipp'ry girls here we ain't kiddin'. Maybe I can interest you in a sponge-bath with Plushette—she's a lot to love—or maybe a tubful of these new Filipino cuties we just got in—"

"No, no," Simpson said, backing away. "I liked Mignon. I guess I'll check back later. If you see her, tell her Samson needs a good shampoo."

He turned next to Temps Perdu, his favorite watering hole, for a drink on the way home. He couldn't stop worrying. *Mignonette, my tender, tasty morsel . . .* He had frightened her away with that necklace. She had discovered he wasn't really a poet. And now he was being pushed out, *propelled* to San Francisco. This was not quite how he had envisioned his move. How could he face his mother and tell her he was leaving? After all these years, that was one part he had never quite figured out.

Built in the 1920s, Temps Perdu looked like a frosted ice cube of white stucco, an art deco box with neon-lighted porthole windows under the palms and live oaks across Esplanade from the Quarter, in the direction of Elysian Fields. The bar was old, dimly lit, a place where there was only one time, one atmosphere, a single TV baseball game playing endlessly in black and white. A loosely dressed grandmother sat at the end of the bar, nursing her third Budweiser, and several seats away an off-duty fireman was playing checkers with a part-time astrologer. The walls were papered with yellowed, curling calendars, vintage Pontchartrain Beach advertisements, and political campaign posters printed decades ago. It was easy-going and anonymous if you just wanted a quiet drink. You never knew who might pass through— a half-forgotten classmate from third grade, or a famous musician or actor slumming in the underworld.

Simpson sat at the bar in a tense, hunched posture, sipping on a glass of cold spring water and a "nitro fizz" cocktail, one of the specialties of the house, nibbling his fingernails, and glancing at an attractive woman in a black turtleneck and a pleated gray skirt sitting alone, several stools away, with short dark hair flecked with silver, cut in a 1920s flapper-style bob, like Louise Brooks. She looked familiar. An actress? No, someone he once knew. Her nose, the curve of her eyebrows. Her name began with an I. It was a foreign, exotic-sounding name like Indra. Inge? Isadora?

He went to the men's room and was staring at the graffiti-scrawled tiles above the urinal ("Why look up here when the joke's in your hand?") when it came to him that he remembered her from LSU, though still her name eluded him. Her hair used to be longer. Only a few weeks ago a glimpse of a magazine cover had made him wonder what ever became of her. It was in the early 1980s when she had placed a couple of stories in the most prestigious literary magazine of all, sending a delicious frisson of envy and vicarious celebrity through the English Department. The creative writing students were electrified. In a department not given to hyperbole she was regularly spoken of as a genius. Everyone on campus had expected the books would naturally pour out of her like rabbits, and the top prizes would follow. Her competitors hoped for some kind of reflected glory, and even those without high expectations for themselves looked forward to saying they had gone to school with her. That was more than fifteen years ago.

Why couldn't he remember her name?

He moved one stool closer and said hello. She gave a guarded smile and was cautiously friendly, willing to talk but reserved, till after a minute or two she slapped the bar and said "I remember you!" though he could tell she did not remember his name, either. She recalled that he'd once made a very clever and well-phrased remark, a line that had stuck in her mind, though she could no longer recall precisely what it was.

They were both disappointed.

"That's all I've ever wanted. To make a lasting impression."

"Sorry. It was quotable, though; I used to use it myself. Without attribution, I confess. I probably have it in a notebook somewhere."

"I can't remember either. That's the sad part. Oh! Mimi!" He slapped his forehead and laughed. "Of course. I'm Simpson. Simpson Weems."

"Right! Okay, now I remember."

They both laughed off the tension and took a sip, looking at each other over their drinks.

He wasn't surprised she'd forgotten his name, but hers . . . he should have remembered instantly. She had been famous around the College of Arts and Sciences as the student most likely to be internationally renowned. All the writing students wanted to be like her, revolved around her, wanting to be her friend, her protégé, despite the comments some made behind her back. A few quit the creative writing classes in disgust; she was so over-qualified that they would never be able to compete. Better get out now. She had everything: imagination, style, versatility, sophisticated allusions, the black tur-tlenecks . . . She was even, some of the male students allowed, not bad looking.

"So, Mimi, how many books have you published so far?"

"Please, let's not talk about that." She groaned and lay her head down on the bar and rolled it slowly back and forth. The forward-curving points of her bob covered her eyes, and the black-and-white television light reflected in the streaks of silver.

"Sorry." He bit his lower lip. "None of my business, really." What a crass, impertinent question. The quantity of her output wasn't exactly the most important thing to ask about.

"How about you?" she asked. "You writing?"

"A little."

He had often envisioned titles and jacket designs for his first book of poetry. *Sleeping Till Noon* (or *Fresh*

Graves) would be a slim, elegantly bound volume of his best work. On the back cover, perhaps above a portrait of the author in a contemplative pose, would appear endorsements from established poets whose expressions of admiration would scarcely conceal their envy.

He cleared his throat and sat up straighter. "I seem to be best at coming up with opening lines. I've been compiling a Poet's Compendium of First Lines, you know, seeds of future poems. Some good stuff. Maybe I can sell it one day as a starter kit and someone else can actually write the poems."

Mimi made a hesitant laugh-like sound, not sure if he was serious. All she had written lately, she admitted, were two clever slogans for some local-humor bumper stickers he'd seen around town, along the lines of a popular one-liner, IT'S NOT THE HEAT, IT'S THE STUPIDITY. She had earned a few hundred dollars off the T-shirt licensing sales. Just a few catchy phrases, she said.

"That's not bad, though. I mean, if you've got the kernel of truth there, it's like haiku, and you don't need some long drawn-out exposition, you know?"

She looked at him with wary gratitude and unbelief. "You're very kind."

"I'm serious. Sometimes the best poems are only one line long."

"In what culture?"

"Anyway, who says the bumper sticker isn't a literary form? Who has time for anything longer? I saw a good one recently in San Francisco: IT'S NEVER TOO LATE TO HAVE A HAPPY CHILDHOOD."

111

She snorted. "Cute, but . . . Once the damage is done, you know . . ."

He gave a wry laugh and squeezed his knees together involuntarily.

Mimi saw his mouth tighten at the mention of damage, a brief wince in his eye lit by the television's blue-white glow.

"Wait, I remember now: You're the guy who smacked . . . what was his name, Will . . . Willyum Asher?"

"Something that began with 'As-'. Yeah, I'd pretty much forgotten about old Willyum yum yum."

"Yeah, right in the kisser."

It was not long before Simpson left college, which was also around the last time he'd been published. Asher was a close-clinging adherent in the informal school of Mimi, a hanger-on of Velcro-like tenacity. In the solar system that formed around her he would be Mercury or Venus. Some of the students called him "Willyum yum yum" because he was a remarkably pretty boy—growing up in Uptown New Orleans he had been a child model for D. H. Holmes and Godchaux's—and always neatly groomed, too neatly for college, and attired in crisply pressed slacks and dress shirts. The nickname might not have stuck but for his evident self-admiration; it was said that the mirror was his closest friend.

Mimi did not appear to welcome the cult, or even to notice that it existed—her indifference augmented its mystique among the participants—but fellow students naturally sensed that their own careers would benefit from proximity to the star, so they orbited around her, shining by reflected glory, quoting her, absorbing energy from a glance. Their closeness to a classmate whose stories had appeared in *The New Yorker* and *The Atlantic* naturally boosted their self-esteem. With confidence came productivity, which in turn generated further confidence, and so on. Some of the satellites fancied they were stars themselves.

Willyum Asher was one follower who elevated himself less by literary effort than by demotion of his competitors. Only a week earlier he had humiliated a talented and earnest young woman with a lacerating critique; she dropped the class. When a poem of Simpson's was selected for publication in the university's literary magazine and Willyum's were rejected, the former model was indignant. There must have been some quid pro quo between the *Manchac* editors and Simpson. Bribery? Sexual favors?

For days Asher went around informing any classmate who would listen that as a matter of historical fact Bayou Manchac once led from the Mississippi to the Gulf of Mexico but now was merely a cut-off backwater that led nowhere. *Nowhere.*

Before a poetry workshop one afternoon, he waited until Mimi arrived to tell Simpson, in front of a dozen other classmates, "They just felt sorry for you, Simply. That poem is shit. You may as well quit now. Save your ink and your daddy's money."

"Yum Yum, you look frazzled," said Simpson coolly. "Compose yourself."

A few classmates snickered.

It was true: the former model's brown hair was in disarray, that is, some hairs were out of place, sweat-damp and dangling on his forehead. His chiseled, perfectly symmetrical features were discolored by a reddish glow, and the left collar tab of his shirt was unbuttoned, flying loose.

"You're a pretender, Wimpson Seems. You don't even belong here. How'd you pay 'em off on the *Manchac*, with a hand job? A full blowjob?"

"It was picked because it's a good poem. If I'm published it's because of my work; you're not published because you're lazy. So shut the fuck up." To punctuate his point, Simpson smacked Willyum upside the head with the flat surface of his hardcover notebook.

Asher's cheek and ear flamed bright red. He was so stunned he could only sputter a few lame, inarticulate insults, his hair further disarranged and his cleft chin trembling. He was not accustomed to victims fighting back.

"Get a thesaurus," said Simpson. "You've got the vocabulary of a sixth-grader."

When Willyum made a sudden move as if to swing, Simpson's right fist busted his lip and loosened two front teeth.

"That's for Denise last week. What a prize pig you are. You're not fit to sharpen her pencil, and there's no telling what damage you may have done to her forever."

Asher wiped the blood from his lip and looked at his wet red fingertips.

"One more thing: The last guy who called me Wimpson was a high school bully who's now brain-damaged and walks with a limp."

This happened the day before Willyum was to headline a well-publicized group poetry reading at a bookstore on Chimes Street, just off campus. His friends advised him to sit this one out, but he insisted on reading in order to show he was undaunted. With a broken front tooth and a swollen upper lip, he lisped and mumbled through two poems before he took the audience's hints and sat down.

"Remember how he *lithped* at the reading?"

Mimi laughed. "I didn't go; I heard about it. What a jerk. That guy was obnoxious."

"I didn't go either, actually. Heard about it. He sure liked you, though."

"Well, you know how people are nice to you for reasons of their own. I guess we were all pretty insecure."

"Anyway, congratulations on the bumper stickers. It's more than I've gotten published lately."

"Well, I would just say—not that you asked my advice—but I'd say write what you want, be all you can be, but beware of self-delusion."

He gulped. He nodded. "Good advice."

"I don't know what happened," she said glumly. "I thought by this point I'd be living in Paris or Tuscany with a few short-story collections to my name, an agent in New York, and writing to my heart's content. They kept telling me, write more like 'Still Life,' do more like

'No Way Home.' But they stopped liking what I was sending, and I started doubting I had anything to say, and started to drink for inspiration, and . . . it all kind of unraveled. Now I'm in the human resources department at Hibernia. It's sort of an H.R./P.R. hybrid position they created for me. The people are nice, and the money's not bad. Steady income. Don't tell anyone I told you this. Burn this letter."

"That would be a good title."

"You use it, then. Put it in your compendium, for others to complete."

She sipped her drink in silence, and as he looked at her reflection in the bar mirror, she seemed to be receding, and the mirror coming closer.

"I'm moving to San Francisco," he said, hoping to lighten the atmosphere. "I'm getting my ticket in a few days for an exploratory trip."

"That's fantastic! Good luck."

He expected one of them might say something more on that subject, but it fell flat.

"How's Button?" she asked, looking up brightly. "Menendez. Seen her lately? What's her ass up to? Still teaching art at Delgado?"

"Oh yeah, right," Simpson smiled with fond recall. He'd forgotten they knew each other. "I believe she is. I've been meaning to give her a call, so I'll tell her you were askin'."

"If you're going to San Francisco you might check with her, 'cause there was a guy we knew, a poet, she'll probably remember his name, and he may still be out there. Maybe he could show you around a little, you know, as a friend of a friend, and maybe introduce you to some other poets."

"That's a good idea. Thanks, I'll ask her."

They both looked away, sipped on their drinks.

"Yeah, it's been too long since I've seen Button."

She lay her head down on the bar again and rolled it from side to side.

"You keep doing that. What's wrong?"

She shook her head but said nothing.

There wasn't much more for them to talk about.

Simpson wanted to ask again about her writing, but he didn't want to cause more pain. Mimi was in a state of gloom and apprehension for the next few minutes, until he said good night, thanks, and wished her the best.

As he walked away, and for days afterward, he felt acutely uneasy. The bar's mirror, or some mirror, was still before him, everywhere he looked. *The past is never dead. Not even past.* This meeting was no accident. It was a message, possibly a summons. The omens were every-where. It occurred to him that the signs had been visible for some time, but only now was he beginning to see: He would be moving soon. It was happening, ready or not.

4

The Reverend Bud Rex

BARTHOLOMEW WAS STILL FUMING, even after yelling at her till his throat hurt. It was her fault his throat was raw. She had interrupted his prayers to remind him to look for a job. While he was *on his knees* praying! She knocked on the door, opened it, and from the hallway she said, "Nice weather. Good day for a job hunt." Then quietly closed the door. "Melba! I'm talking to Jesus!" She broke his concentration, shattered his composure, and in his rage he was unable to communicate with the Lord. He screamed at her till she cowered in a corner with her hands over her ears. "This is no way to bring in money!" he berated her. "It's because of *my prayers* that this household's so well provided for!" Then he said something that really hurt her. "Why don't *you* get up off your retired butt and get a job?" Under the onslaught of unreason Melba dared not argue or even try to bring the conversation back to basics: We need money. Social Security and the pension from Lourdes aren't enough anymore to keep up with the rising costs of medicine and utility bills for the multiple air conditioners, plus all the ice cream and cakes and cookies. All who can work,

119

should. And it would please his father if he would help his mother.

Eventually she got him to agree to try. She was at the breakfast bar, wiping a plastic plant with a damp sponge, and he was standing a few feet away, slouching, gazing at nothing.

"Say, Bartholomew, you know, that nice Mr. Levine at Dillard might have something for you. He sure likes you a lot."

"They don't have any money. They just cut his salary."

"I'm sorry to hear that, but talk to him anyway. Maybe somebody he knows . . . Or Mr. Tong could prob'ly use some help baggin' his groceries again. Or you could water the petunias at the French Market, or fold towels down at the Lee Circle Y. All kinds of useful jobs you could do, you know," she softened plaintively, " 'cause we sure could use a little—"

"Melba!" He stamped his foot on the floor, and the pictures on the wall trembled. "I'm *already* useful! You're sending me out there so they'll laugh at me again."

"No, honey, that was just that one time. They were just kids and didn't know any better."

Now she was wiping off her breakfast bar stools, making the vinyl squeak. Melba was proud of her red vinyl seats, like from a ritzy diner.

"Something else you might try: You could go talk to Mr. Krebs at Lourdes and see about maybe being a chaplain or something. You're so good at prayin', and so compassionate, I bet you'd be a big comfort to the families. There's a real need for that, you know. It could be like a ministry, kind of."

"Depressing!"

"And you'd be so good sitting with the families in the chapel or the viewing room, prayin' with 'em . . . How'd you like that? Gettin' paid to pray? That'd be the natural-lest thing in the world for you. I bet it'd be real rewarding. And even in hard times, you know, the funeral business always keeps on rollin'."

"Too sad, and too stressful. I did ask Mr. Levine one time if I could read Scripture for the blind, but all they want is news from the *Picayune* and *Newsweek*."

"Or, Bartholomew," Melba purred, "you could do home visits, or be a prayer partner at one of the nursing homes. You know, like social work. A mercy ministry."

"My burdens are already unbearable," he moaned.

"But whatsoever ye do unto the least of these my little ones, so ye do also unto me."

"Well," he allowed, "if you put it that way."

"Good, then it's settled. Now let's fix breakfast."

She could call it settled, but still he was seething.

He was halfway through his oatmeal when the electricity failed and the lights went out.

"Oh no! The air-conditioning!"

Melba told him to remain calm and keep eating while she went out to check the fuse box. Several neighbors were out doing the same. There was nothing they could do but wait for the power company to restore service.

He began to fidget.

"Oh, hush now. You're not even feelin' warm yet."

"But I will!"

He slurped his oatmeal sullenly, pushed the bowl away, and sat sulking in the gloom.

"Bartholomew, after you brush your teeth, go put on some nice clean clothes and go catch a ride on an air-conditioned city bus and get yourself a job in a nice air-conditioned place. You need to help your mother out."

He suddenly lurched forward and clanked his spoon on the bowl. "You talk like 'my mother' is someone other than you."

"Go on, do what I say."

He looked down at the sweat darkening his shirt. "See! I told you!" He clapped his palms to his glistening forehead. "The heat is intolerable!"

"I know it is, baby. Go take a shower and cool off a little, then get dressed up nice. How's that sound?"

He was in the shower frothed with soap bubbles when he looked up in alarm: he had seen a white flash out of the corner of his eye . . . *Hold yourself ready, therefore, because the Son of Man will come at the time you least expect him.* But it wasn't the Coming. Not this time. Some new light was shining unto him in that flash, however. Perhaps the answer to a prayer. He turned off the water and stepped out to dry off with the large sea-turtle beach towel Mother had given him several Christmases ago.

While he was showering, she picked out his clothes for him and laid them on the bed: long brown pants and a plaid short-sleeve shirt, size XXXL. Then she sat at the kitchen counter licking the point of a pencil and thinking of additional places he could try, such as the public library. It was rather warm. She patted her face with a paper towel. She put down the pencil and pressed her palm to her chest and rubbed in circles, trying not to panic. *Dear Jesus God in Heaven, not before he gets a job* . . . But it passed. The pressure that sometimes followed a shortness-of-breath episode. Like a hippo's hoof on her breastbone. The tension had been worrying her for several months. For over a year, actually. It never really went away, but only intensified from time to time. She pictured a rope knot being pulled tighter and tighter. She had hesitated to say anything to the boys because she didn't want them to worry. Whenever a sharp pain jabbed her she rubbed her chest and patted her breastbone to ease the constriction, and asked Bartholomew to please lower his voice. What else could she do? Once when she had told him the reason why she kept nudging him to get a job was that she needed expensive heart medication but they couldn't afford it, he replied, "And if I get a minimum-wage job at the library we'll be able to keep up with the rise in prescription drugs?" She implored him with pain in her eyes, "Please, son, in the name of the Father." He held up his hands. "All right. All *right!*"

He kicked his way into the brown pants and shrugged irritably into his shirt. He combed his hair haphazardly and tossed the comb in the sink.

"Okay, honey, here's a little list. Oh, don't you look handsome!" she said, admiring his fresh tidy appearance.

"It seems a sin to have to wear my nice church clothes just to get a job."

"I know it does, sugar, but man does not live by the Word alone, but by the sweat of his brow. Here's a quarter. Call if you get lost."

Bartholomew stood at the corner on Elysian Fields where he had caught the bus the night he followed Simpson to that bad place. The sun was warm in the grass and oaks along the boulevard where white and yellow butterflies were flittering by, and people were out walking and riding bicycles. A heavy truck passed, and he felt a slow wavelike shudder in the ground. He sighed and gripped the handle of the rose-colored parasol Mother had given him to protect him from the sun. Behind his black plastic dime-store sunglasses he was frowning. The bus was making him wait, he was growing quite cross, and he was not going to tolerate this much longer. Her Social Security and pension checks should be enough. What did she do with all that money, anyway?

He gazed at the tall dark telephone poles lining the boulevard, one after the other. Crosses whereon our Lord hath given his life.

Maybe the bus drivers were on strike.

It was entirely too warm for February. "Stop it!" he screamed at the sun. "Cease!" He reached in his back pocket, but—and she would hear about this—Mother had neglected to supply him with a handkerchief.

That was absolutely the last straw!

On the other side of Elysian Fields was a nice little shrine where he liked to stop sometimes on his way to see his friend the Reverend Bud Rex. In a green and shaded spot beside a white clapboard house was a cool trickling fountain and the statue of a saint and his dog, surrounded by flowers and a dogwood tree. Bud Rex lived just two blocks from there.

The traffic was clear. Even if a bus had been in sight, it was too late.

With an abrupt impatient huff, Bartholomew stepped down off the curb and crossed the city-bound lane of Elysian Fields to the neutral ground, passed the public water fountains near the grove of white cypress and poplar, then crossed the other lane. The traffic unnerved him—they'd just as soon run over you as change lanes—and he was huffing from walking so fast.

At the corner was a large shade tree, the first along an oak-lined street. Safe now, he walked from the broad boulevard and the bright sun to the cool shaded shrine of the saint and his dog in a spacious yard on the side of a white house. He entered the yard unself-consciously. Beside the concrete statue was a fountain fitted with a greenish copper life-size head of a bearded pagan god from whose open smile cool waters trickled, splashing and gurgling in a black iron bowl. The statue was of St. Roch, a gaunt medieval holy man lifting his robe to show a wound in his leg, and at his feet a small dog sitting loyal and attentive, looking upward, holding in its mouth a bread roll as though offering it to the saint. The statue was old and speckled with moss and lichens, and, with the cool trickling sounds of the fountain beside a dogwood tree, conveyed a calming presence. Mockingbirds chirped and sang on a live oak branch about twenty feet overhead.

Bartholomew dropped the parasol and knelt to pray. *O Lord, O St. Roch, help us have enough money without me having to get a job! Keep the Norkels away, and take care of Mother and bless Father's soul in heaven, and take care of Rev. Bud too. And do not make me have to get a job!*

The owner of the house peered through her curtains at a massive figure on his knees in the yard between her house and the neighbors', with his head bowed, making the sign of the cross. She came back a few minutes later and he was still there.

Then her husband appeared over her shoulder. "What's he doin', prayin'?"

Before she could answer he threw open the front door. He stood there in his sleeveless undershirt, glaring, and a breeze ruffled the gray hairs on his chest. "Hey! What's the matter with you?!" he barked. "You got no respect for the private property of decent people?"

The Reverend Bud Rex was a sightless white-bearded former preacher who lived alone in a broken-backed shotgun single squeezed between two enormous live oaks and falling apart inside. The grayish brown cypress planks had never been painted, and, though sheltered somewhat from fifty or a hundred summers' suns and heavy rains, they looked weathered and exuded an air of grim endurance, an aura of matured vitality that painted wood cannot express. Live oaks grew so close to the house—rather, it had been built into such a narrow space already tight with trees—that their large above-ground roots had unsettled the columns of bricks the house was resting on. Although the elongated shack looked steady—if it hadn't fallen yet, perhaps it never would—when the high winds blew it groaned and listed, and might topple either way. The slanted and fallen brick pilings had caused some of the rooms to crack and split; the walls and floors were twisted askew and awry. Through the floorboards mice and other vermin came and went, depending on the food supply. Beneath the bedroom a brick piling had fallen sideways, so the floor slanted sharply. The plaster wall was cracked with a jagged scar, and wisteria and a few thin branches of a sweet olive tree grew through the hole in the wall. Rev just shut the door and never went in that room. He meant to get around to having someone fix it one of these days, before it got too bad.

Bartholomew crossed the spongy compost of a front yard thick with fallen leaves and rust-colored camellia blossoms and newspaper pages blown in from the street. He could hear the television booming inside. He inched his way carefully up the splintering wooden steps on the right side; the one time he'd tried stepping up the middle, he felt a sickening crunch of dry-rotted wood and cut his shin. The rough-planked porch was covered with trash, cardboard boxes, and an old gray sweater rotting amid the leaves and paper wrappers.

He pounded on the front door to be heard over the television. The one little window in the door was nearly opaque with yellow pollen dust and an orange mold of some kind. He knocked again. An object struck the door from the inside—a shoe, perhaps—Bud Rex's way of saying come on in.

Bartholomew opened the door and peered into the dark room that smelled of dust and stale urine, lit only by the television and dim light through the curtains. He could just make out the form of the old man in his chair. The side windows were tinted with mildew, half-shrouded in dust-laden drapes, and several were darkened by cardboard taped over broken panes.

Bartholomew yelled, "Can I turn the TV down a little?" He was bursting to tell Rev what awful things were happening.

The elder made an impatient, vaguely affirmative gesture with his hand. He was not able to see the television, which had lost its sharpness anyway, but he liked to listen to praise-the-Lord broadcasts and nature documentaries. His hearing wasn't what it used to be, so he turned the sound up high.

Bartholomew lowered the volume. "That okay?"

"It was okay before. Sure, I don't mind. Have a seat. Glad you stopped by."

Bud Rex's voice was deep and craggy, as though he had been a heavy smoker for decades. He did not so much speak as croak. Bartholomew could have imagined he was a great stout bullfrog, except that the Reverend was a very thin old man. His pale figure rested in an easy chair near the sealed-off fireplace that now held a small gas heater. He wore a long white beard to mask burn scars and reconstructive surgery from a mugging (stabbed in the eyes). On the rare occasions when he left the house, he wore dark glasses to hide the scars. He was wrapped in an old wool blanket and sitting on a nest of old pages from the *Times-Picayune*. He sometimes had problems with a condition he didn't like to talk about.

Bartholomew sat down on a plain wooden chair that fit him like a stool. It creaked and groaned as he shifted back and forth. He could no longer contain the anxieties churning and tumbling about in his mind. "Oh Rev, I have to tell you these terrible things that have happened—"

"Sssshhhh." The Reverend raised his hand to calm the troubled waters.

Bartholomew moaned plaintively as he waited for the master to speak. Rev's white beard, like his hair, was long and disheveled, but in the dim light he looked majestic. Bartholomew revered him like one of the prophets of old.

The Reverend Bud Rex had been a first-rate preacher until, halfway through his life, he went and got himself married. Miss Lila Frankie from Mobile appeared in the congregation one day, a lively eager red-haired gal dead-set on marrying herself a minister man. She heard Bud's sermons and her soul caught fire. What this dusty old preacher needed was a revival meeting under the big tent. But life was much simpler when he preached about love from the pulpit. After they were married he decided Lila asked too many questions and chattered like a tree full of blue jays. Sometimes she flat-out told him he was wrong about this, didn't understand about that. He didn't need such back talk. He took to drinking, a man who had never had a thirst for alcohol. He started forgetting his sermons, repeating last week's lines, falling asleep and having accidents. Bud got to smelling so rank and urinating on himself so bad Lila made him sleep out in a tent in the backyard. One night he fell asleep too close to the Coleman lantern.

I am the man that hath seen affliction by the rod of his wrath.

A pair of black-suited church elders came to see him in the burn unit at Charity Hospital. "This here's a tolerant city," they explained patiently. "And it takes a lot to make folks around here think you're strange. But a preacher's in an unusual position. *You're* in an unusual position. Just lie low for a while, maybe up in Mississippi. Make yourself scarce till this blows over. Then, maybe, once the dust settles . . ."

"What the *hell* are y'all tryin' to tell me?" he gasped, and fainted.

While he was at Charity he lost his wife and his congregation. During the divorce proceedings Lila shared conjugal intimacies and the lawyers elicited allegations and admissions disturbing enough to darken his name. No one wanted a man with such strange habits and tastes preaching to them anymore.

He hath set me in dark places, as they that be dead of old.

Bud Rex never left New Orleans. How could he even think of living in Mississippi or anywhere else? It's a crazy world out there. He made himself scarce by staying home, collecting his meager pension, eating from his weekly food basket, praying for forgiveness, and trying to piece together what went wrong. For months he sat indoors in the summer heat with the windows closed, without even a fan blowing, drenching himself in sweat and repenting for his wrongdoing, whatever it might have been. To have loved? *My sighs are many, and my heart is faint.* Sweat dripped through his beard, soaked his shirt and ran down his legs under the Sears khaki trousers. He lost twenty-five pounds, thirty, thirty-five. They made him feel like a leper, unclean, outcast. There was only one who still believed in him. Bud rarely went outdoors, except at night to water his garden or dip his cup in the rain barrel. Once a week someone from the church came by with a basket of food collected by the congregation. And that was it, after all his years there: one weekly basket of rice and grits, Vienna sausages, Fritos, Wonder Bread, and Spam. Some thanks.

Also when I cry and shout, he shutteth out my prayer.

Bartholomew blurted out all at once, "Oh Rev! I have to talk to you. It's really critical and I don't know what to do! My brother's doing something very bad, and—"

"Calm down, now, son. The Lord is thy shepherd."

"Yes sir." Bartholomew paused briefly, then launched back in. "Mother's making me get a job—oh, it's just intolerable!—and they're pushing me to go see a psychiatrist and then I'll get sent away again but they don't care—"

"Bartholomew," the elder interrupted. "Slow down. The Lord is with thee."

"Oh, it's hot in here," he panted. "I'm sweating and she forgot to give me a—"

"Here," said Rev, tossing him a roll of toilet paper that unspooled in flight across the room.

"Oh, thank you." Bartholomew dabbed anxiously at his face and throat. Damp shreds of tissue stuck to his cheeks.

"I dreamed about caves again last night," the Reverend began. During Bartholomew's last visit, Bud Rex had taught him that some of the ancients believed Jesus was born not in a manger but in a cave, like Zeus and certain other pagan gods. "Some folks may not think so, but that says something about the Lord. He could've been born anywhere, and he chose a cave. Think about that. I dreamed last night about the cave where John the Baptist's followers were cleansed in the purification rituals, and then I was in the catacombs where the early believers sought shelter during the persecutions." He could still see the high chapel-like hollow in a dimly lighted cavern, a pale orange glow and dripping sounds of water trickling down the moist membranes deep inside the living body of the earth.

"But anyway, Reverend Bud—"

"The heart of man—"

"Simpson's doing something naughty and sinful that would just *slay* our mother if she ever found out. And he's always wanted to get rid of me, you know. He never wanted me."

His voice caught, then he cried piteously, "It's so unfair!"

"Oh hush. Crybaby."

"Thank you."

"The Lord don't like crybabies."

"Rev, I have to tell you what I saw."

"*My son, despise not the chastening of the Lord; neither be weary of his correction; For whom the Lord loveth he correcteth; even as a father the son in whom he delighteth.*"

"Yes sir. But Simpson, my brother, he's three years older and—"

"Yeah, yeah, you told me."

"He goes to a place on Bourbon Street and takes baths with a naked girl!"

Bud stroked his beard.

"I followed him there and saw it with my own eyes. What will Mother think? You said yourself a man's every action soothes or pains his parents' heart, and my father's getting angry. He doesn't like what Simpson's doing to us, and all I can think is, 'Don't get God started.' I have to do something, but I don't . . . I can't—." He clapped his palms to his eyes and wailed.

The elder was moved by the anguish in his voice.

"Come here, son." He reached out his pale hands.

Bartholomew came and knelt, sobbing and blubbering, and lay his head down in the Reverend's lap. He wept. There was a comfort in laying his head on Rev's lap that was different from the solace in Mother's.

Rev rubbed his hands affectionately across Bartholomew's thick hair. "Ssshhh," he said. "Ssshhh." He shifted in his chair and pulled Bartholomew a little closer. He had always wanted a boy. The peace that others can give us. On various private occasions he had been comforted by members of his flock.

Bud Rex stroked Bartholomew's head and recited in a sepulchral voice, like a bullfrog in a concrete pipe, "*Let not your heart be troubled: ye believe in God, believe also in me. In my Father's house there are many mansions: if it were not so, I would have told you. I go to prepare a place for you. And if I go and prepare a place for you, I will come again, and receive you unto myself; that where I am, there ye may be also.*"

Bartholomew sighed contentedly.

"Don't trouble your mother with this," said the elder in a deep croaking admonition. "And don't concern yourself overmuch with the mote that is in thy brother's eye. Rather, pray that he will feel the forgiving love that is always there, it's free, because Jesus gave his life for us. Let the light come to Simpson from above, within, and not by an anxious brother's burning torch. Do you hear me, son?"

Rev lifted up Bartholomew's head from his lap and lightly cupped his chin. "Understood?"

"Yes sir. Okay. I believe."

"It's not for you to worry about. Righteousness is mine, saith the Lord, or something like that."

"And if thine enemy hunger," continued Bartholomew, "feed him; if he thirst, give him drink: for in so doing thou shalt heap coals of fire on his head. That's nice."

"And remember, God don't sleep. You can always come talk to me, but don't trouble others with what you've seen. Of them that have understanding, much is expected. Okay, get up now, my leg's asleep."

Bartholomew returned to his chair. Feeling hot again, he remembered his grievances and burst out, "She interrupted my prayers! Pushed me out the door and said, 'Call if you get lost'."

"So help God answer her prayers."

"No! False!" he shouted, forgetting for a moment where he was.

"Honor thy mother and father. She isn't askin' much. Think of all they've done for you. It'll comfort her to know you're working. You know she worries what'll happen when she's no longer here to look after you. You've been indoors long enough, dozing like the Seven Sleepers in the cave for a hundred years. How're you gonna serve the Lord like that? Go forth and do your mother's bidding. And wouldn't it please your daddy, too? Look not on your brother's affairs, but on what you can do for your mama 'n' them."

Bartholomew had been told countless times about the seven youths of Ephesus slumbering until the Day of Judgment—Rev. Bud loved the cave-and-martyr stories—but today he was not moved.

"It would take a miracle, all right."

"I believe in miracles."

"I had a job, once. The stockroom boys called me names. One day I bent over to pick something up and my pants split open down the middle and they laughed at me, and I commanded them to cease. Like this: 'Cease!' "

Rev smiled. "Sometimes I dream my sight's been restored. I'm outside the town of Bethsaida and the Lord he toucheth mine eyes, and asks what I see, and I see men as trees, walking, roots and branches. Again he toucheth mine eyes, and I see all clearly. Come back soon and read me some more Scripture. Let's make it old Ezekiel."

"I bet you wish you could have your eyes back."

"Sure, but I reckon I'm all right." Rev was silent a long time. "I see what the Lord shows me. The holy catacombs, and the caves where Jesus was born and where his body was laid. The heart of man is full of caves, you know."

"I wish you could see me," Bartholomew said sadly.

Rev again took a long time to answer. "There's always heaven. Like you, I believe."

5

Mariage Blanc

EVEN AS SIMPSON FELT HIMSELF gravitating westward, his hopes were dampened at times by a fine mist of sorrow at the prospect of leaving New Orleans. In unexpected moments, as when he realized this may be the last time I ever see this golden late afternoon sunlight on these oaks along Esplanade *as a resident of New Orleans*, he would find himself enveloped in a kind of melancholy, anticipatory nostalgia for the city where he had lived for so many years—the only home he had ever known, except for the university in Baton Rouge. Someday I will look back and wonder why I thought I had to leave. He hadn't even managed to extricate himself yet, and already he was homesick.

It was still dark when the alarm sounded. As he loaded the filter for a cup of coffee, spilling some grains of dark roast on the kitchen counter, he recalled having read somewhere that you can tell what is sacred to a man by what he chooses to do on the Sabbath, by how he uses the free time that is his alone. Before the sun rose over the West Bank of the north-flowing Mississippi—that was just the way New Orleans was situated—Simpson

137

dressed in his pine green trousers, a blue cotton work shirt, and comfortable Timberland walking shoes for treading over concrete and cinderblocks, white shell, brick paths and railroad ties, through weeds and broken glass, wherever his curiosity might take him. The forecast for this Sunday in early February was for an overcast sky and slightly cool breezes. Grabbing his Swiss Army knife and throwing on his windbreaker, he set out on a long walk, one of a series of parting glances at ordinary, nonscenic, unromantic areas of the city that only he seemed to care about. Who knows when I will see these places again?

The morning air was cool and damp after last night's rain. The only sounds were of water dripping from the live oaks to their brown fallen leaves on the ground, the cooing of an early-rising mourning dove, and an occasional delivery truck hissing by on the wet pavement of Elysian Fields Avenue. Then a city bus carrying a few early weekend laborers and dawn service church-goers caused the nearly liquid ground to shudder in slow wavelike ripples, as though several feet below the street's surface the ground was still swampland.

He was a young boy when his father introduced him to the pleasures of exploratory walks around the city. It was something they liked to do together on weekend mornings before the day got too hot, sometimes on Sundays while Mother and Bartholomew were at church. Gasper had been an avid fisherman and squirrel hunter in his youth, but as the children came along Melba needed him closer to home, so he passed on to his eldest son an appreciation for his hometown's history and heritage. "Know your city, son. Get to know the streets and buildings. Stay curious." On foot and on maps, he had shown Simpson that in the neighborhood of Bywater, for example, one could go down Burgundy from Piety to Desire. In nearby Faubourg Marigny, one or two hundred years before, one could turn from Rue des Bons Enfants (now Good Children) onto Rue Mystérieuse, or plan a rendezvous at the corner of Rue D'Amour and Rue des Poètes. And then around Coliseum Square there were the nine muses: Polymnia intersecting with Prytania, and Terpsichore crossing Annunciation ... Just saying the streets' names felt like casting a spell. Was he seriously going to move away?

Simpson believed he would have come to it naturally even if his father had not taught him to appreciate a good walkabout. A mysterious something deep inside called him to take solitary walks through the shadows of the city's infrastructure, expeditions at early hours through desolate, little-traveled parts of town—the remoter, the better: among the nineteenth-century redbrick buildings of the warehouse district, beneath the massive pillars of the Mississippi River Bridge, and along the London Avenue and Seventeenth Street outflow canals that carried excess rainwater out to Lake Pontchartrain. It was a rare calling, he knew, to be an habitual perambulator of public works and desolate streets, taking in impressions, breathing in the spirits of the city's unexamined life. Like a rolling stone. There was a line in "Howl" about wandering around at midnight in the railroad yard. He felt a kind of affection for these parts of town in part *because* no one else seemed to pay them any mind. Who will love a drainage canal? I will. Who will appreciate its sturdy walls? *What if they break?* He knew he wasn't good for much, but perhaps he, who had cultivated a sincere fondness for the forgotten places and felt at home among the dead zones, *les allées des pas perdus*, could become a bard of unsung spaces.

One of his favorite haunts was the warehouse district, a formerly derelict area near the river with redbrick storage houses for cotton, fruit, and coffee built on land that had been part of the Jesuits' vast plantation in the 1700s. He had long enjoyed walking among the old brick streets and warehouses, some dating back to the early 1800s, and railroad loading docks. Although much of the area had been renovated for the 1984 World's Fair, including the new Convention Center, other parts had not been improved, and it was there he felt most at home. It was quiet and peaceful on Sunday mornings, with the cries of pigeons and sometimes seagulls in the moist heavy air, and horns of ships and tugboats out on the river. Walking these streets in the dawn's soft light, and sometimes at night, he felt the presence of stevedores and warehousemen of times past and even present, as when he rounded a corner and saw three workmen in gray overalls on a truck loading dock playing checkers on the top of a fifty-five-gallon drum. The damp air seemed to pass right through the redbrick walls along Tchoupitoulas and Julia streets, Poeyfarre and Gaiennie.

Although some of the old buildings had been renovated and converted to music halls, galleries, artists' lofts and condominiums, and hotels near the Convention Center, many remained neglected as they had been for decades, and were either razed for parking lots or allowed to fall into disrepair, to collapse of their own weight, as though the humidity-sodden bricks were returning to mud.

Meanwhile, back in Gentilly, he passed Pleasure Street and stopped at the corner of Elysian Fields and Humanity. By the names alone it felt like a setting for something special. On the other side of a wide clearing were Benefit Street, Treasure, and Abundance, but in between stood the great elevated superstructure of Interstate 610—a short auxiliary route of I-10 that bypassed downtown New Orleans—like an ancient Roman aqueduct that instead of water carried humans enclosed in sealed steel-and-glass vehicles moving at high velocity, an incessant circulatory system humming and roaring through the hardened gray channels, the sounds of tires *thwop-thwopping* through the expansion spaces between the concrete sections. He could still remember, though dimly, when this road was not here; it was built when he was in junior high school. Between shortly before his birth and when he learned to drive, the great crisscrossing national interstate system grew out of President Eisenhower's insistent pushing of Congress to build a high-speed road network for transporting troops and evacuating cities in case of atomic attack. The area had been safe so far from nuclear assault, but everyone was grateful for the big roads during hurricane season.

A passing dump truck loaded with white shell sent shudders through the ground that he could feel in his kneecaps. Father used to talk about the elevated ridges along Bayou St. John and Gentilly, and believed there were Indian burial grounds around here that the settlers had built upon. In geologic time, the land under New Orleans was recent, freshly laid sediment from the Mississippi's annual springtime floods as it changed course over the past seven thousand years or so, until the big river levees were built after the great flood of 1927. Each year now instead of laying down new land upon the layers below, the levee-channeled river flushed hundreds of millions of tons of silt out into the Gulf of Mexico. A CopyQwik customer who was a researcher at the Historic New Orleans Collection had told him that in the 1920s, work crews digging the Industrial Canal between the river and the lake had found a human skull thirty-seven feet below the ground surface. The skull was sent to the American Museum of Natural History in New York, which confirmed that it was of "a mature male of a quite modern type" characteristic of the Native Americans who had lived in these parts for millennia. While digging deep foundations for buildings in the Central Business District, workers had found two distinct layers of cypress stumps that had been cut by human hands, some only a few feet belowground and a deeper layer of forest at twenty to thirty feet down, and beds of seashells fifty feet underground. Many of the stumps were of trees that were four or more feet in diameter when cut—by whom, the workers wondered, and when? During construction of the new Charity Hospital in the 1930s, workers found a cypress stump with a colonial-era ax blade still stuck in the wood that had subsided to about fifty feet below ground level.

And then, would there come a time when the black tree of Dangers Park, too, lay beneath the depths?

He could envision what might have been here before, but when he looked up at the superstructures of Interstate 10 or the bridges over the Mississippi, it was difficult to imagine their ever being replaced by anything larger. More likely a big hurricane would shred and topple and drown the city before that happened. The land, unreplenished, was sinking, the seawater coming closer, and, although few could bear to think about it, some could foresee the day when New Orleans would be surrounded like the city of Venice—gondoliers on Canal Street—and finally would be inundated like Atlantis. Eventually the man-made structures would collapse and sink beneath the salt water, and once again the Gulf of Mexico's waves would wash up against the bluffs at Baton Rouge, as Mark Twain in *Life on the Mississippi* said they used to do. In time to come, legends would tell of the enchanting river city that subsided, submerged—sunk beneath the weight of sin and corruption, some would say—and centuries from now they would wonder whether such a place had ever really existed.

Bartholomew was stretched out on the pink Formica counter like a toad on a tongue depressor when Simpson walked in the house. With his pants pulled down to his knees, Bartholomew was lying flat on his belly on the breakfast bar, his head turned the other way, his breathing strained, agitated.

Simpson's mouth opened, but no words came out.

Melba came into the room, pulling on a pair of rubber surgical gloves.

"Mother," he strained to sound calm, "what . . . ?"

She squeezed some salve from a tube and rubbed the ointment around her fingertip, then cleared her throat and said in a hesitant voice, "Bartholomew, honey, I need you to spread a little wider. That's good. Hold steady, now."

She looked queasy as she spread the salve around, trying not to look at what she was doing.

"Mother! What are you *doing*?"

Bartholomew made a whining squirming sound.

"Oh, it's just some pinworm cream. It's a little nasty, but it's got to be done. He can't reach, himself, you see."

"Should I come back later?"

"There now, baby," she patted Bartholomew's behind, broad as sofa cushions. "You can get dressed now."

He laboriously climbed down from the counter, ignoring Simpson, and shuffled away to his room. A minute later he came back out and left the house.

Melba threw away the rubber gloves and washed her hands several times. "Poor baby, this infection's been bothering him. It causes these blisters—"

"Too much information, Mom. I really don't need to know this."

"Oh. All right." She looked surprised, possibly a little hurt. "Well, you and me can visit while he runs down to the K&B for more pinworm cream and shortness-of-breath pills. He shouldn't be long."

He scrubbed the breakfast bar with a sponge and Bon Ami powder cleanser, then wiped it with paper towels and lemon-scented antibacterial Fantastik all-purpose cleaner. He couldn't get the image out of his mind.

"Thank you, Simpson. Say, why don't we have some tuna-fish sandwiches, then you can take a look at my old typewriter for me and see what needs fixin'?"

"Shortness of breath?"

"I just feel kind of broken-winded all the time."

"Barto's suckin' up all the oxygen. Have you seen a doctor?"

"Oh, they're prob'ly busy enough with people in worse shape. I'm worried he'll tell me I need some heart medications, and they're so expensive we couldn't afford 'em even if you and Daddy and I together were all working full-time."

"Well, go see Dr. Garcia anyway and let's see what he says. Don't wait too long. I can help you pay for the drugs. And Mom, it's Rite-Aid now, remember? K&B sold out a year or two ago."

"Can't I just call it K&B and you'll know what I mean? I can't keep up with all these name changes."

The typewriter was heavy, so he carried it for her and set it down on the breakfast bar so he could work under the lights. He tried the keys, peered under the lid and poked around dubiously.

"It's just the keys are sticking," she explained. "I figured you could turn some screw and everything'd be all right."

He smiled at her. "Everything will be all right."

"And I put out some sheets of paper so you can test it."

"I see that. Thank you."

"Bartholomew should be back by now, don't you think?"

"You know where he probably is."

The only question was whose yard he was kneeling in. Every other house in Dangers Park had some kind of shrine or statue of the Virgin, or an angel, St. Francis holding a lamb, or sometimes little molded concrete animal figures and garden gnomes. Bartholomew was tolerated around the neighborhood for his sudden swerves into people's yards, unself-conscious and regardless of private property or the eyes of the world, kneeling and praying before whatever object of devotion attracted him.

"I hate to discourage his prayers," Melba said, "but sometimes I do need him to come straight home."

"He's like a dog with fire hydrants."

"Maybe Bartholomew's not the one I should send to the pharmacy when it's really critical."

Simpson's smirk vanished. "Is it critical now?"

"I'm all right, I think." She touched her chest. "For now."

"Well, if you ever need someone to go for you, you know, like, if it's important or something," he made a vague gesture with his hand. "You could call me if you want." Somehow it was hard to get the words out.

"I hate to be a burden."

"It's no trouble at all. Don't be so considerate that you end up dead."

"Thank you. You're good to your mother."

Simpson waved the compliment aside. "No big deal."

"Have you thought of anything for his birthday?"

Simpson loosened a screw with a butter knife, turned a lever, then tightened it.

"His birthday to me is like Christmas: an event to be endured from a distance. Sorry, but that's how I feel. He's about to turn thirty-four, and every year he insists on having that cake and singing 'Happy Birthday Jesus' on *his own* birthday. It's just too weird. On his special day, Bartholomew's all yours."

"I appreciate that."

He patted his mother's hand. "I need a screwdriver. I'll be right back."

In a damp dim corner of the carport near the tarpaulin-covered Buick was an old gray steel fishing tackle box that used to be Gasper's toolbox. The latch was rusted, and he had to use an old putty knife to scrape away the rust and force the box open. He found the pliers orange with rust, crusted shut, the rubber grip on the hammer cracked and rotted, the screwdrivers and wrenches rusted too. He sniffled and wiped his eyes on his sleeve, then glanced over his shoulder. How many years ago was it he used to beg his father to teach him how to use the tools, how to hold a saw, how to hammer a nail and drive a screw. Gasper answered every request with a cheerful promise to show him after dinner, or next weekend, but he forgot, or he was tired, or he slipped away to the taxidermy shop on the Saturday morning Simpson had waited for. Cornered one day, Gasper finally admitted, "I don't know how to use them, son. They were all given to me and I just keep 'em to let neighbors use when they fix things for me." Simpson never asked again, just as he had never asked what it was like to be designated 4-F, turned down by the army for poor eyesight and flat feet.

When he came back inside, he could feel the change in the room. "Hello again, Barto."

Bartholomew did not reply, but came over to the counter, breathing heavy. He picked up a loose Phillips-head screw from the countertop and stared at the cross slot in the screw's head, then put it down without a word. He loaded a big bowl with chocolate ice cream and carried it to the living room and turned on the television.

It was happening again: the volume was slowly going up. It never seemed to slip in the other direction. Simpson walked over and slapped the side of the set, turned it off, then turned it back on. "There."

Bartholomew continued eating, his eyes never leaving the screen.

Simpson told his mother about the news at CopyQwik. "We'll all be out of a job."

She wouldn't hear of it. "Don't you worry," she said, "they could never run that place without you."

"That's true."

"You're there forever and they know it."

His stomach sank with a sick feeling.

She reminded him once again that despite its limitations, CopyQwik was a job and it paid the rent, so in that respect it met the basic requirements of labor. Yes, he agreed, but what he wanted to add was that he would not be stuck in this quicksand if it were not for that plump little brother of his, His Grossness whose weight no scale could measure, the grand fatling sitting over there watching re-runs of *Lassie* and *My Friend Flicka* and eating chocolate ice cream by the carton.

"Why don't you just raise the bowl to your face, Bartholomew? Why bother with a spoon?"

"Manners, Simpson," Melba reminded him with a pinch on the arm. "Be glad of your good position with a respected company and just hold on to what you got. You don't need to be like all these other young people nowadays swingin' from job to job like monkeys through the jungle. Stability has its rewards. Just remember that. Constancy is a virtue."

"Yes ma'am." He couldn't look at her. Those were the same words she used to say to Gasper about the taxidermy shop. But Rabineaux & Weems had never been bought out by a national chain.

"Excuse me just minute." She picked up the drugstore bag and went back to the bathroom.

Bartholomew clanked his bowl and spoon down in the sink and came to stand over Simpson and the type-writer, scowling and breathing loudly.

"Do you really think you can fix it, or are you just fiddling cluelessly?"

"Just fiddling cluelessly. Barto, when did you stop going to church? Around the time you did that little Jesus Jesus touch-up job on Dad's car?"

"I did no such thing. No, it was more recent."

"So why did you stop going? They weren't devout enough for you?"

Bartholomew appeared to be as fervent in his devo-tions as ever, or more so, with his long private prayer sessions behind closed doors and his frequent kneeling at shrines in neighbors' yards.

"Churches are idolatrous. I only go there for the rum-mage sales anymore."

"Idolatrous." Simpson swallowed. "And how, I mean why—"

"All that matters is your personal relationship with Jesus. Everything else is a sideshow, like Christmas and Easter, fixating on the birth and death when we should be receiving the Word."

"And Mardi Gras?"

"Pagan foolishness. We've discussed this. I have noth-ing more to say."

Bartholomew was drumming his fists on the counter, his arms and shoulders tight with coiled tension, and sweat was dripping down his full pink cheeks.

"It's hot in here. We need another air conditioner in this room. Mother!"

"You could give up one of yours. I think she's in the bathroom."

"Doing what? *Doing what?!*" Bartholomew grabbed the roll of paper towels and wiped the sweat from his face.

"Sorry, boys," she said, straightening her housedress as she walked back into the kitchen. "Everything's all right."

As Simpson returned to probing and picking at the typewriter, Bartholomew stood close by. "Aren't there repair shops for these things? Why does he have to stay here when he doesn't know what he's doing?"

"Sorry, Ma, I can't get these keys to move. I think we should just forget it. What did you want a typewriter for, anyway?"

"I just thought it'd be handy like if I wanted to write a letter or something sometime. Or a will."

Simpson looked skeptical. "I don't know. I'd say if it turns out you do need to write a letter, then get it fixed. Don't they have one at Lourdes you could use?"

"Why walk all that way to the funeral home when we got one right here?"

"I see your point." He tapped his hands on the worn edges of the typewriter case.

"Wait, did you just say 'a will'?" He gulped. "Write down what you want it to say, and I can show it to one of our lawyer customers at work."

"That would be nice, thank you."

"And I'll ask around and see if anybody knows of a repair shop or a good typewriter for sale."

He looked at her. "Really, you're thinking about a will? Shortness of breath?"

"Now I don't want y'all to worry. I'm just trying to think ahead, that's all."

Bartholomew stood in the middle of the kitchen, repeatedly dropping the red plastic cap of a spice jar on the floor, bending over to pick it up, and dropping it again.

"I was asking Bartholomew if he would take me to see Dad's tomb sometime, wasn't I, brother?"

Melba looked surprised, and Bartholomew paused.

"Why, son? What ever for?"

"Well, he's kind of my father, see, and—."

An uneasy look passed across her face.

"It's been a long time, and I'd just like to know where my father's buried. Pay my respects."

"Thirteen years," said Bartholomew.

"Don't you think it's strange, Mom, that in all this time neither you or I have ever been to his grave? Only Bartholomew visits him."

Melba pressed her lips together, choosing her words carefully.

"We went there on the day of his funeral. I guess there's nothing *wrong* with visiting the tomb, Simpson,

I just don't see the need. We know he's right across the street. It's not like he's going anywhere."

"Bartholomew, would you show me, please? It would really mean a lot to me, and you're the only one who knows where he is. I think it's good that you visit him."

"I'll see if I can fit it into my schedule." He left the room.

"I used to have the vault number around here somewhere," said Melba.

"Mother, did y'all . . . Was I adopted, by any chance? No, I'm serious. Was I? Sometimes I feel so alien and different from the rest of y'all—especially you and Tiny. I don't even look like y'all, except I have red hair like Dad."

"Oh, honey, of course not. You were my one and only for *years*, my little prize and joy. You know that."

"What was that strange look on your face when I said 'He's kind of my father'?"

"I don't recall you saying that," she said vaguely, avoiding his eyes.

"Just now, when you asked why would I want to go see his tomb, and I replied sarcastically that 'he's kind of my father.' You looked like I'd said something I wasn't supposed to. What was it?"

She avoided direct answers until at last, blushing and stammering, she heatedly denied ever having *that kind of contact* with Gasper or any other man. All she would say, and she would say no more, was that she had her babies her own private way.

"You're joking, right?"

He leaned against the kitchen counter, feeling faint, almost sick.

"Honey," she said in a half-soothing, half-exasperated voice, "sometimes God just gives a woman a baby, and that's how it happens. She wakes up one mornin' and realizes they're soon gonna have another mouth to feed."

"Mother, this is . . . this is just not possible! There's no virgin births anymore. I took biology and it doesn't happen that way."

Just how naïve was she?

Melba sighed and raised her hands in resignation. Who was she to question what the good Lord had provided?

He didn't believe her—how could he? Was it that Catholic school she'd gone to in Golden Meadow? Better modest and chaste than informed? He had to satisfy himself by concluding that he had underestimated his mother's naïveté or powers of denial, and that his parents, though kind and decent people, were simple, little educated, and didn't understand the workings of nature.

Who were his parents, really?

No husband was ever more proudly his wife's admirer, nor any as loyal a helpmate and obedient a servant as Gasper was to his Melba. But, although he prized his good wife and praised her often, it could not be said that he ever *thought* about her, exactly. It did not occur to him, for example, to wonder why she had wanted to marry him, or ask what marital adjustments if any might make her happier, or how she seemed to think she had managed to conceive their two sons without intussusception of his manly seed.

When he first met Melba—actually he stumbled into her—in the Schwegmann's supermarket one evening in the mid 1950s, Gasper Weems was a young assistant manager at Woolworth's and taking taxidermy classes at night. On this particular evening, Melba Cremiere, a pretty blonde counter girl at McKenzie's Pastry Shoppe, came in for a carton of eggs (McPeckins Farms) because her daddy wanted his scrambled, and Gasper stopped in after work for a can of chicken soup for his ailing mother. Melba always said it was a sign of the Lord that on the night they met, she was shopping for her daddy and he was making groceries for his mama.

With thick unruly straw blonde hair and ruddy cheeks, Melba Flo Cremiere, a robust and cheerful young woman of five and twenty, buxom of breast and stout of hip, was only trying to pick a good tomato sauce, not a husband, on the night a young man bumped into her in aisle nine. A carton of eggs tumbled into her shopping cart, splattering all over her groceries.

"Oh no!" piped a thin nervous fellow with curly orange hair. He gripped the sides of his skull, not knowing what to do first, and clasped his hands together as though praying for a clue.

"I'm sorry, Miss. I'm so clumsy."

Gasper grabbed at Melba's fruits and meats, dabbing anxiously with his handkerchief to brush the egg splatter from her shopping items, but he only spread the mess around.

"It's okay, never mind," she said. "I'll just start over. It was just a few things."

Gasper felt responsible. He pulled her through the aisles, insisting on personally replacing each item in her cart. But instead of a 14-ounce box of Cream of Wheat he grabbed a 32-ounce box, and rather than Arm & Hammer baking soda he picked Head 'n' Shoulders shampoo.

"Well," he explained in apology, "I knew it was 'somethin' *and* somethin'.'"

Although Melba Cremiere grew up being called "Creamer" by her schoolmates, girls and boys alike, she remained innocent of any embarrassment about the meaning of her name until she began to fill out, and a classmate in French found her name in the dictionary. She prayed that she wouldn't be as big as her mother. She turned out even bigger. The boys, always so clever at inventing amusing nicknames, called her Milk-Jug, then shortened the name. For years after she married Gasper and took the name Weems, Melba renounced her maiden name, would not hear it spoken. But later, after her mother died, she became more sentimental and allowed herself little indulgences, like her buxom porcelain creamer from a risqué ceramics shop on Toulouse Street in the Quarter.

Verna Flora Cremiere had given her daughter half her middle name and a complete teaching, from an early age, that the center of a girl-child's duty is to consider first the needs of others. Parents first, then husband. And, provided she was blessed, she would see first to the needs of her children. Females, Verna explained, had been chosen by the Creator at the beginning of time to be the nurturing protectors. They had to watch constantly to ensure that everyone is clothed and fed, all things run smoothly, the rent is paid and the car has gas in the tank, and practical things like that.

"Isn't that for the boys to do?" Melba asked.

"Ideally, yes, but sometimes they get distracted."

"Sounds like girls got to do all the work. What do the boys do?"

"Oh, you know, they play sports, drive trucks, run businesses, that kind of thing."

Verna's training assured Melba of superiority by simple virtue of being female, and, it seemed, relegated her to perpetual subservience. "You'll be needed to hold everything together, which involves lettin' him think he's the decision maker. It's simpler that way. And don't ever contradict him in public; he don't like that. A kick under the table's usually enough. Better yet, get him to see things right before you go out."

Frizzy orange–topped Gasper was the first man Melba dated, and the only man she ever needed. They enjoyed the same simple pleasures: looking at pictures in the weekly magazines and going to the movies and church together—and they looked forward to the same things: a family and a little house they could call their own (or at least one they could call home). They married in the neighborhood church at a time when all was stable and always would be, all wars had been fought and won, all treaties signed, and all markets were prosperous and confident.

On the eve of the wedding, Verna gave Melba a list of rules penciled on the back of a recipe card for ambrosia. Melba kept the list in her top dresser drawer with her underwear.

HELPFUL HINTS FOR A BLESSED MARRIAGE

Always shine with good cheer and optimism.

Never complain. Others have it worse.

You can sleep when you're dead.

There is no such thing as an overprotective parent.

There is no such thing as a too-loving wife.

God rewards those who comfort others.

There is no such thing as a remote or undemonstrative husband; he's probably just preoccupied with important concerns.

Do not reproach your husband for sleeping late on weekends (even to the point of missing church, if necessary), for he has worken hard all week and needs his rest.

Have his coffee ready for him.

Whip him only as a last resort.

Lay up riches for yourself in heaven, etc.

From their wedding night onward, husband and wife slept in separate beds—that was their understanding of conjugal arrangements. Late on the night of their wedding, a few of the guests at the reception laughed and wondered aloud whether the bride and groom might not be wanting to leave soon "and get to consummatin' things," but it was unclear whether that ever happened.

Melba was a woman who did not mind being touched, but, at least with her husband, within limits. Bartholomew could hug her for several minutes at a time, if she let him. Simpson, before he grew into an aloof and chilly adult, used to hug and kiss her as freely as any child ever loved his mama. Gasper's hugs and touches, however, were so frequent that they needed restraint. A straightjacket might do, she sometimes thought, or a belt with handcuffs. After enough rubbing and squeezing she would say in a hard clear voice, "All *right*, Gasper, I think that's enough now," and he would obediently shrink back for a few minutes. Thus admonished, he would stand still, arms stiff by his side, but soon his hands and arms were moving again in fidgety frustrated pantomimes of affection, as though stroking her aura or receiving a charge from her energy field.

"Gasper, *please*. You're makin' me nervous as a hamster. I'm trying to roast this chicken for you and the boys, and I can't concentrate with you flappin' around me like a flock of pigeons."

"I'll go read the paper, darlin', that's what I'll do, I'll go . . ."

Usually he had to be set in motion by someone else. If they were sitting outside in lawn chairs and raindrops began to fall from the sky, he might continue sitting there indefinitely, humming to himself and tapping his fingers on the aluminum armrest, if she did not say, "Okay, honey, it's raining, let's go on inside now." He would jump to his feet and rub his hands, as though she had just proposed the most sensible suggestion and he couldn't agree more. "All right, darlin', let's go on inside. Good idea."

He was a man of subdued extremes. His sons had never known him to be anything but cheerful and awkwardly gregarious, or indrawn and passive as though the world were ending and nothing could be done. He was inclined to speak with his hands and touch people on the arm while talking or listening sympathetically, and was always quick to shake hands. At the taxidermy shop he took care of the customers up at the front desk, listening with attentive concern to their hunting tales and mounting needs while his partner, Roscoe Rabineaux, kept working silently in the back. Upon meeting someone for the first time Gasper would sometimes forget and shake hands two or three times and say, "Glad to know you," as if each handshake were the first.

But although conversation with him might suggest otherwise, Gasper brought uncommon judgment and sureness of hand to his work. When he concentrated on the mounting of a good trout or bobcat, his eyes and hands coordinated with a surgical precision that was the admiration of his trade. He was known throughout Greater New

Orleans, or at least in greater Gentilly, as a near-master taxidermist. Rabineaux took on jobs he couldn't do himself because he always knew Weems could.

Gasper was just as methodical in getting ready for bed. He wore long cotton pajamas with the top buttoned at the collar, and used earplugs to mute the sounds of his wife's robust snoring. Neither lightning nor moonlight through the windows troubled his rest because he used a padded eyeshade. He also liked to sleep with a pillow laid across his feet at the foot of the bed; he claimed the weight of the pillow helped him feel anchored, secure. Melba woke him by lifting the pillow from his feet: that sensation alone was enough to bring him back to the surface. Gasper pulled the plugs from his ears and slowly removed the sleep visor, a little at a time, making a gradual entry into the light of day, and smiled at an amusing fragment of a dream he was just emerging from, as Melba lay out his clothes for the day, dark green pants and a white shirt, black socks and boxer shorts.

He had been wanting a child or two, and often said so, pacing about the bedroom or living room with his hands clasped in front of him. "What we need is babies, Melba. We're a family now. We need to do something about that." When he said "we're a family" he included both of them, but as for doing something about it, he meant *we* as in "we sure cooked a good dinner, didn't we?" There was no question of his including her; it was himself he sometimes left out.

One afternoon in the early 1960s she was passing through Dangers Park on her way home from visiting a neighbor when the dizzy queasy sensation that had troubled her all day now forced her to stop and lean against a wooden railing on the bridge over the bayou. She gripped the rail and leaned over and before she knew what was happening—thank mercy no one was nearby—she threw up the beef stew she'd eaten for lunch. Melba wiped her mouth with an eyeglass cleaning cloth from her purse, then lay her head down on the wood. Why was she crying? She felt fine, except for the upset stomach and dizziness. Her mood was okay. Or maybe not. Her belly felt calmer now, but her face was streaming with tears. She was sad and she hadn't realized it until now. What an odd peculiar feeling. She glanced at the railing where her fingertips were tracing the lines of a vulgar word carved in the old gray wood, then averted her eyes. She looked down at the gold and blue light sparkling on the water beneath the bridge, the scattered pieces of her reflection. *There is a baby.* It was as though a voice had spoken from inside, echoing in her head and belly. *I am going to have a baby.* Melba put her palms to her cheeks, then quickly felt her stomach. She was with child. She knew it by feeling, as sure as she was breathing.

Her doctor confirmed it several days later.

When Gasper returned from the taxidermy shop at six precisely he said, "Hel-lo, dahlin'," and kissed her on the cheek as he did every day at this time. He stood at the kitchen sink with a bar of Lava soap and a hand brush, whistling a merry tune as he washed the clay and particulate matter off his hands.

"When you're finished with that, Gasper, I got some news for you."

"Oh!" He dried his hands rapidly on the dish towel on the refrigerator door handle. The towel fell to the floor but he didn't notice; his hands were twisting with excitement. "Tell me, tell me, what is it?"

"Well," Melba said, bending over to pick up the towel, "I got some good news today."

"Tell me, baby. I'm about to wet my pants."

"You just might." She smiled, giving him a chance to guess.

Gasper rubbed his fingers nervously. "What is it, sugar? Tomatoes on the vine? You won a new vacuum cleaner?"

"The first guess was closer."

Melba leaned close, her yellow wisps mingling with his orange tufts, and whispered in his ear.

"Oh my!" he gulped. "Goodness gracious almighty!" He paused to catch his breath. "We've been blessed with child!"

He clapped his hands and whooped, turning back and forth in circles and half circles. Then he remembered to hug her and congratulate her.

"We have to pray that everything goes well," she cautioned, stepping back a little from his breath, "but I believe it will. I am a woman of faith and my heart is strong."

"I know that for sure, dahlin'."

"I was thinking we could name him Simpson—if it's a boy—after your daddy. Or, if it's a girl, we'll name her Gloria, the name my mama wished she'd had."

"You're the mother, you can name that baby any name you like. We're a family now, Melber. We can go to the park and the zoo and . . . O happy day!"

"Right. So what we'll need you to do is just hold that job steady with Rabineaux. I don't know how many hours I can expect from the funeral home."

"I'll hold that job steady, don't you worry. I'll hold on to it like a, like a suckerfish, like a lamprey eel."

"That's my man."

Melba's discovery of her pregnancy with Bartholomew came in a similar way. She was sitting in the cemetery across the street on a gray Sunday afternoon, the anniversary of her mother's death, thinking tenderly of Verna, and dear old Big Mama down in Golden Meadow, buried along Bayou Lafourche. They had passed on, but she had her little boy Simpson, a comfort to her heart. *So why seek ye the living among the dead?*

He always knew just the right thing to say.

She was turning to go home when a voice spoke again, saying, *Rejoice, for there is life and joy within ye in abundance.* At the phrase "within ye in abundance" she tightened, feeling again the mysterious certainty. She envisioned a large white egg in a basket, big as an ostrich egg, and she knew.

She went home to tell Gasper the good news.

And his name shall be Bartholomew.

For three years Simpson had been the only child, and everything was peaches and Shangri-La till his mother started swelling up and said there was something growing. She didn't say it was a baby, or let on in any way that it was a natural thing that was happening. But, after all, Melba was a modest woman. She would no more have described herself as pregnant than she would have uttered the words "vagina" or "uterus."

Gasper, too, was vague and obscure about what was happening. He seemed torn between trying to tell it like a fairy tale, with all sorts of fantastical and illusory evasions, or dismissing it altogether. Each day he came up with a new story. One day he giggled and said, "You know how I said Mama swallowed a beehive? Well, she went to the doctor and it turns out she et too much cotton candy at the state fair. Remember that?"

Cotton candy?

"But why's it keep gettin' bigger every week, then?"

Gasper scratched his head. "Uh, because cotton candy expands on itself sometimes. Like, like that salt factory that fell off the ship to the bottom of the ocean and keeps crankin', making the sea water salty. Remember I told you about that?"

"Gasper, please," Melba cut in. "You're just confusin' the boy. You're amusing yourself and gettin' him all mixed up."

She didn't mind that he was telling stories—he liked to make up tales of local fauna, such as The Crawfish's Pinch and Legends of the Pelican—but a different explanation of her condition every day seemed only to worry the child.

"Then you tell one, darlin'. You tell us a story."

"All I know's about the Mud Man of Bayou Lafourche."

Simpson perked up.

"Yeah, he was the wicked stepchild of that wolf-man Loup Garou. They said he looked like a cross between an alligator and the Creature from the Black Lagoon all covered in mud-caked Spanish moss. I better not go into the gory details tonight or you'll never get to sleep, but all the grown-ups used to warn us about the Mud Man. Nobody ever actually saw him that we could be sure of, but everybody knew he'd grab children swimmin' in the bayou and pull 'em under. They'd never be seen again."

"What happened to them?" Simpson asked, his eyes wide with belief.

"He ate 'em up, bones and all, and he was constantly prowlin' for more. He made all kinds of trouble for the shrimpers, too, but that's another story."

She patted Simpson's head and poked his dimples for a smile. "It won't be much longer, I don't think, honey. Then my belly'll go back to normal, such as it is."

When Simpson thought back on the stories his father had made up to explain how the new baby had come into being, it seemed as though Gasper was not just protecting his child's innocence or telling tales for the fun of it, but that he frankly did not know, himself, any more than he would later understand Bartholomew's psychiatric condition. There had always been an air of childlike naïveté about his father—Simpson had sensed this even in grade school—so for all he ever knew, Gasper believed that Melba had become pregnant simply because they were husband and wife: that is what happens when a couple is married and sleeps in the same room. After a few years or so, a baby comes along, and then maybe another and another . . . Because Gasper's parochial schooling did not include instruction in human sexual reproduction, and his own parents had avoided the subject, he had never known for sure whether the male's participation was absolutely required, or it was optional. It was his vague understanding that the female was the one indispensable agent in the process, and the male's involvement was negotiable, possibly negligible. He thought of Melba's pregnancy as an achievement wholly her own, almost as he might regard her invention of a new recipe, a dressmaking pattern, or a game for Simpson as something that did not involve him at all, except as a loving, admiring bystander. Melba was truly amazing. He could hardly wait to see her nursing the baby.

6

A Visit with
Button Menendez

IN THE DAYS SINCE MR. DUMOND'S surprise announcement, Simpson had tried several times to pry loose any
news of further developments, but the old man seemed
to think it would jinx the sale if he spoke too soon, so it
was hard to know what was becoming of CopyQwik. He
asked Latoya if she wanted to meet for coffee or a drink,
but after work she needed to go straight to her second,
part-time job at an Internet start-up; she was not worried about life after CopyQwik. The news had stunned
him into a temporary paralysis until he realized that
there was no reason why his own plans should depend
on the copy shop: he was leaving it anyway, wasn't he?

When he was in San Francisco two years before,
he had stood outside the windows of the famous City
Lights Bookstore on the sloping sidewalk of Columbus
Avenue as pedestrians and buses passed by. He gazed
in at the customers browsing among the shelves full of
published works—none yet by him—and then at his own
thin reflection. His shadow on the sidewalk, too, looked
insubstantial, even translucent, as though the sun were
passing straight through him. Where was everybody?

Was the San Francisco Renaissance over and no one told him? He had envisioned himself here in North Beach with Ferlinghetti, Corso, and Kerouac, and in Golden Gate Park with Ginsberg and Snyder and McClure, if not yet as one of their peers then as a young practitioner in their milieu, a worthy apprentice welcome among the masters. He had told himself he was prolonging the anticipation, saving the delicacy of City Lights to enjoy later, but was it because he knew he was not an authentic, functioning poet that he had hesitated to enter the legendary bookshop when he had a chance, and went across Kerouac Alley for a beer at Vesuvio instead? Always outside looking in.

He remembered feeling happy and yet overwhelmed by the biggest city he had ever seen. Everyone must have known at a glance he was a hick, a swamp-crawler with Spanish moss in his hair. They smiled at his accent, and several times he was asked to repeat what he'd said. As he walked down Market Street toward the white tower of the Ferry Building, he gazed up at the tall office buildings, smelled cappuccino and car exhaust. On his right, the streets intersected with Market at right angles, but to the left they veered off diagonally. Grant, Kearny, Montgomery . . . Car horns honking, office workers lined up along the neutral ground—they called it a median here—waiting for the electric buses that ran up and down the center of the street, others queuing along the sidewalks for bigger, longer buses with flexible accordion-like hinges in the middle. He walked in a sort of daze along the wide Market Street sidewalk, momentarily disoriented as he thought he was back home on Canal Street. He could feel the density of history here, and yearned to know this city, its people, customs, and neighborhoods. Amid masses of concrete and stone and marble and plate glass windows, a thousand vibrations shuddered in his bones and he trembled with a sudden fear that this city was too big and busy for him to ever live here. He would be crushed and no one would notice. But how calm they all looked, how cool and professional. Aside from the grunge-punk bike messengers whizzing by, even those without suits and dresses wore stylish clothes that must have cost hundreds of dollars at least, while he moseyed along invisible, marginal, nondescript in his drab chinos and dove gray windbreaker from Thrift City.

The chance meeting with Mimi at Temps Perdu, which he might have expected would be an energizing inspiration, had instead left him with a queasy distress such as he sometimes felt after a bad dream of judgment and guilt. If even as accomplished a talent as Mimi could go limp, wrung dry like a dishrag, then what would become of an idling dreamer like him whose only achievement since college was a Compendium of First Lines? And why did she say beware of self-delusion? For days afterward he had sensed a sort of reflecting surface out there in front of him, even when he walked (as he often did) with his head turned at an oblique angle. It felt like a shadow, but to his eyes it appeared as a wavelike and variable looking-glass shimmering before him. He knew the picture was only in his head, an optical illusion, yet he felt it was out there, like a mirage of accusation, pointing at him. *Seems.* His heart pumped harder and a hot mist of sweat broke out on his face.

Somewhere, someone he once knew was dead.

However dispiriting, the encounter with Mimi did have the happy result of prompting him to call his old friend Button. It took several attempts to reach her; apparently her answering machine was not always reliable. She said she would be delighted to see him if he wanted to come over on Saturday or Sunday. Maybe by then she would be able to dig up the address of the guy she knew in San Francisco.

It was early Saturday afternoon, with a mild coolish temperature, overcast sky, and dampness in the air after the morning's rain. He did not want to be seen by his mother or brother while waiting for the 55 Elysian Fields, so he walked a few blocks down the avenue to the next bus stop. Along the way he passed by Lourdes Funeral Home, a mustard stucco building in the Spanish mission revival style with a red tile roof set back from the avenue across a wide landscaped lawn. Perhaps it was the stillness, the quiet in the air that reminded him, for the first time in many years, of a room in the back where he used to go to be alone, away from Bartholomew, when they would go to Lourdes after school to wait for Mother to get off work. It was safe there, and it felt like a laboratory. While she worked on the corpses with her brushes and powders, "prettying up the dear departed," the boys sat quietly and read their schoolbooks or drew pictures, perfectly accustomed to the presence of the still, sheet-draped bodies on which an I.D. tag was tied to each right toe. There was something calming about them. Nearby was an empty, unused room where he liked to go, with pale green–tiled walls, soft outdoor light coming in quietly through the frosted glass, reflecting on the white tiles near the floor drains beneath the slanting porcelain-topped table. He liked this room because it was quiet and secure, an inner sanctum, and it felt as though no one had breathed here in many years. It comforted him somehow to know that people used to work in this place long before he was born. It was not until many years later that he learned that there were drains in the floor of his favorite room because it had formerly been used for embalming.

A few minutes later he was on the bus toward Button's house in Faubourg Marigny near the Quarter, recalling an odd thing she had said one night in college when they were drinking beer and fantasizing about art careers in the big city: "New York or L.A. would be a great place for someone as sexually ambiguous or unannounced as you. Or San Francisco."

"What do you mean, 'unannounced'?" he had laughed nervously. "What a strange remark. 'Sexually ambiguous'? Why do you say that?"

"'Cause we're together all the time but you never make a pass at me. I don't mean to be vain, but you've got to admit, this here's a pretty juicy body, and you haven't made a move even to make it look like you're *accidentally* touching me. What is it, Simpson? Is there a problem? Never mind. It's okay. We can live in New York or California and you can take your pick and I'll be a frustrated painter and aspiring actress till the day I die."

"Take my pick?" He scratched his head with both hands. "I don't know why I haven't made a move. Sorry, I guess I really never thought about it."

"Don't be sorry, Simp, but really, tell me honest, haven't you ever just wanted to get your hands on these soft, supple, voluptuous . . . ?" She cupped her palms under and raised invitingly.

"Well, sure, I guess, but you don't just reach out and grab 'em."

"That's true. There's more subtle approaches."

He wasn't sure what she meant by subtler approaches, but he didn't ask, and the moment passed. Many moments passed. *It just doesn't occur to me.* Years later, when he recalled those college days with Button, he could see quite sharply that if she had never raised the question they would probably never have spent a night together, or part of a night.

It was not as if she wasn't attractive. Indeed, she was lovely, with shiny thick black hair and olive complexion, warm dark eyes, a slightly Roman nose, and full pink lips that always looked wet. But she was his best friend. It wouldn't be right, somehow, in a way that he sensed dimly but never quite questioned at the time. When he was writing every day for his poetry classes and she was working on a double major in fine arts and theater, they had fantasized about moving to California or New York together to launch their careers in the arts. While she talked about theaters and acting companies, he envisioned himself as a poet in Greenwich Village or in San Francisco with a view of the Golden Gate Bridge, having a simple day job in a bookstore and writing all night while she painted or rehearsed. Maybe he could draw inspiration by watching while she painted female nudes in their studio apartment, and then, before the model dressed, and while the canvas dried . . .

Button acted in a dozen or so plays, mostly modern classics, along with a few pieces of experimental and absurdist, surrealist theater in which, invariably, everyone involved seemed to have wildly divergent understandings of the theme, or disputed whether there was a theme. She often spoke about the fine pure intensity of live drama, "strutting and fretting my hour upon the stage," leaving your old self in the dressing room as you become another 'I'. "When the character comes alive in me, that's when life feels most real. The rest of the time I'm just my usual dumpy old self."

He knew that feeling.

His yearning, his "bohemian dreamin'," already active in high school, was fueled further by a movie he had chosen and watched repeatedly when he was on the LSU student union's film committee, a rough-cut black-and-white from the late fifties shot in North Beach and the Village: Grant Street intersecting with Bleecker. Scenes of inner Bohemia: young artistic types of all complexions writing, reading, and drinking at the Co-Existence Bagel Shop, Caffé Trieste, the Gas Light Café . . . The film was mostly silent, with occasional jazz in the background, and the lighting rather murky. The characters wore black, smiled mysteriously behind dark glasses, scribbled intently, smoked incessantly, and played guitar in a park near KEEP OFF THE GRASS signs. The women, some short-haired and all casually stylish in their dark slacks and turtlenecks, exuded intelligence, independence, ready for anything.

But was it strange that he kept his dream mainly to himself? He acted as if his yearnings were too precious, too fragile to put into words, even with his best friend. Was he afraid the creative energy would leak out of him if he talked about it, and then he would never get anything done? Button was excited enough about her own plans that he could sit back and listen without having to disclose much about his. He considered later, with some resentment, that everything might have been different if she had shown more interest and drawn him out, though he knew that wasn't fair. It wasn't her responsibility. At the time she was focused on her own dreams and simply assumed he would go with her and be some kind of writer or deep thinker.

"Think how romantic it would be, Simpson." Her eyes twinkled as she sang, "*Let us be lovers, we'll marry our fortunes together . . .*"

What did she mean, "sexually ambiguous"?

Their paths rarely intersected anymore, and they had slipped out of close acquaintance, though never out of memory or fond regard. On those rare occasions when

Simpson felt vaguely sexual stirrings of desire for union of some kind, he sometimes thought of Button, her fine body and always her generous heart and spirit. She would make a good mother.

A close embrace and a kiss near the lips showed she was happy to see him again.

"I found Foster's address. I went ahead and wrote him a postcard to give him a heads-up he might be hearing from you."

"Great, thanks, Button. How thoughtful."

"And if you're nice, I'll show you my latest painting. But let's talk first. Goin' to Endymion tonight, or Lucia's party after Bacchus tomorrow?"

"Not this year. I'm kind of busy getting ready for my trip. Things are in motion."

"Well, come on by Lucia's if you feel like it. She said she hasn't seen you in a long time."

Two years ago he had deliberately scheduled his San Francisco trip to coincide with Mardi Gras so he would avoid the madness. To him there was something kind of scary about that day. Random, unpredictable. He told himself he wanted some distance from Carnival until he was actually living in California, and then he could come back and appreciate Mardi Gras more. He did not mention this to Button. It made sense when he'd decided it, but now it felt like the kind of notion that, if explained aloud to another person, would sound stubborn and perverse, and possibly deranged, too.

She handed him a cup of herbal tea and pulled him by the forelock out to the back patio deck where the smooth wood planks were still damp and cool from the morning's rain. He brushed back his hair and watched her as she walked. Raindrops were still glistening on the leaves of the aspidistra and elephant ears, sparkling in the red geraniums and orange marigolds, and, beyond the trickling fountain, little rain pools on the redbrick patio reflected a light gray sky.

"You're still not married, Simpson?" she said as if with good-natured surprise. "I figured for sure some gal would've snatched you up by now."

How long had it been since they had seen each other? Still nice-looking, but his face looked thinner. A smile dimple on his left cheek that had once looked cute was turning to a scar-like furrow, and worry lines creased his forehead.

He shrugged and made a vague sound in his throat. He didn't believe she was genuinely surprised.

"It's okay, honey," she said gently. "Coupling's not for everybody."

He sat beside her on the cool damp bench and leaned back against a wall. He kicked off his sandals, blew on his hot tea, and stared at the red geraniums, the rain dripping off the elephant ears, and the water in the fountain's black cast-iron bowl. He half expected to see a small statue of the Buddha in the garden somewhere.

"It was weird seeing Mimi at Temps Perdu. I recognized her as someone I used to know, but it took me a while to place her or remember her name."

"How is she? How does she look?"

"All right, I guess. Silver in her hair. She axed about you. She says hey. Actually she seemed kind of depressed. I don't think she's writing anymore."

"She was so talented."

"Scary, isn't it?"

For a few minutes he had thought he heard occasional whimpering sounds in the background, but now there could be no doubt: a baby was crying.

He looked at her with alarm.

She shrugged and laughed lightly. "Be right back!"

He sat stunned, almost breathless. Button with a baby?

While she was gone he went to the fountain and cupped his hand for a quick sip of cool water.

She came back with a five-month-old in her arms, bouncing the infant in a light blue blanket. "Say hi to Mr. Simpson, Angelle."

Simpson dried his hands on his pants and straightened his clothes self-consciously. He expressed surprise and congratulated her, but declined her invitation to hold the infant. "Wow, that's really a pretty baby you've got there." He cleared his throat roughly. "Didn't know you had a baby," he said, not knowing what else to say and sensing with acute embarrassment that a clumsier remark could hardly be imagined.

"You okay?" she frowned. "You look completely undone. She's just a baby."

"No, I'm fine. Let's, let's sit down."

He gripped the seat and felt the cool dampness on his palms.

"Oh, look, she's drifting off again already. Just wanted her mama."

With a long skeptical face Simpson regarded the infant in her arms. He shifted uncomfortably on the bench and rubbed his bare feet along the cool slippery porch planks.

"Didn't realize you were afraid of children," she said. "Look at you. You're shakin' all over."

"I am not," he insisted, tensing tighter. "I'm fine, really."

He jerked nervously as a four-year-old boy burst out of the back door and ran up to them and aimed a rubber-band gun at his mother, then at the baby. "Put that down," Simpson ordered sternly, surprising himself. The rubber band stung him just below the eye. The dark-haired child shrieked with delight and fled into the house.

"Sorry about Orlando," said Button. "You know how boys are."

"You've got *two* children. My God, how things have changed."

"Well, you know, time passes."

She glanced at his Timex. The broken crystal reminded her of something. A recent dream.

"Two children," he said again. "Wow."

They talked for a while about kids, colds, diapers, skinned knees. He nodded, feigning interest, wondering if he could ever be a parent.

Gradually his nerves settled and his breathing returned to normal.

"So, guess where your old pal Simpson is moving soon."

"Moving?" Her eyes opened wide. "Where? When?"

"I'll be going out there next week to scout around for places to live, probably around North Beach, if I can afford it."

"The hippie section?"

"Sort of. Not exactly. You're thinking of Haight-Ashbury. Things at work have gotten . . . it looks like we're being bought out. My position's uncertain. I've been meaning to move out there for ages, anyway—like we used to talk about—so this time I'm really gonna do it. I go out there all the time, you know."

"Wow, this is wild. I didn't realize. I thought you were just taking a trip."

So many times he had almost moved there, he said, but always something—usually something fat and loud and infantile—held him back.

"I still don't know if I can really do it, you know. Leave Mom. I'm afraid of what it might do to her, but not going is killing me. I can't decide: Have I stayed because I'm weak, or is staying here the stronger thing to do? And my brother's such a drain on her, like a gluttonous vampire. Meanwhile I can't write here. Can't concentrate with their gravitational force pulling on me and all their radio static in the air. So I'm in a fix."

"So you came to see your old friend Button."

"Help."

He smiled, though in his eyes she saw pools of sorrow.

"I mean, I'm about ready to bolt, family be damned—that could be a good title—but I can just see myself getting out there and being paralyzed, unable to write about anything but my guilt at being a despicable break-promise and leaving my mother to do all the heavy lifting. That's some rich material to work with, right?"

"But did you pledge a blood oath you'd stay here forever, till the bitter end?"

"Not in those exact words, but that's what she seems to expect. A few years ago I was thinking of moving to a nicer apartment a few blocks farther away, but she complained that I was already too distant. Three blocks from her house."

Button sighed and adjusted the blanket around the baby's face.

"Yeah, sounds like you've got some material to draw from, whether you're here or there. That can be good for an artist, though, if you know how to use it."

"Let me count the raw materials: bitter frustration, resentment, dread of impotence and dissolution, dwindling energy, lack-love and lonely . . . It's all there."

"So you've been mining that trove while you're still here, right, before you go to San Francisco, or even if you never do? Be an artist where'er you be, as they say?"

"Sometimes I wonder if it's okay if I'm not really an artist after all."

"Of course it's okay. The sun will still come up to-morrow."

"Like I said, I can't concentrate. I tried for a while one night last week. Got a few lines down. Felt good for a few minutes. Sometimes I think I may have to do something to get him out of the way."

"No. You mean like—?"

"I'm just venting. Anyway, they're deinstitutionalizing all the mental patients. And now Mom's not well. Just as I'm gearing up to go—without her knowing it, of course—she's been complaining of fatigue and shortness of breath, and she's usually not a complainer. I'm trying to help her, paying for medicine and doctor's visits. This is coming out of the money I've been saving for California for years now. I don't know what I'm gonna do, but something's got to give. We're pushing Bartholomew to get a job or at least go see a doctor and get certified for Supplemental Security Income so he won't keep draining all her Social Security and pension money. He needs to be independent."

He paused and let out a sigh that turned to a groan.

"Actually I lied, Button. I don't go to San Francisco all the time. I wish. I just made it out there once, just for a short time till my brother tricked me into cutting it short and coming back home early. I swear, sometimes I could just—. Maybe I'll just be totally irresponsible and bolt out of here. I'm sick of being responsible to them and not to myself. So tell me about this friend of yours, the poet, what's his name?"

"Well, Foster's more an acquaintance I met at a party or two back in college. All I really know is he was at

Tulane and he's a poet, or was, and he always struck me as very intelligent, and nice in a reserved, don't-touch-me kind of way. Hang on a sec and I'll get his info. Here, hold Angelle while I be right back."

The baby was in his hands before he could say no. His voice froze in his throat as he watched Button walk away. His torso tightened, and he held Angelle with iron-rigid arms as though she were a fragile china vase—or a time bomb. *Just relax. Breathe.* She was already very pretty, in an exotic way, and would surely grow up to be a beauty.

Button came back with a slip of paper on which she had written the name Foster DeBris and his address on Filbert Street, San Francisco, fountain-penned in a fine, graceful hand.

"Here you go," said Simpson, returning Angelle to her mother.

"I'm not sure if he's still at this address. Somebody I knew, maybe Annette Moore, or Lil or Pepper Landry, gave it to me ages ago when I was thinkin' of visiting there. But give him a try. Maybe he can show you around some."

"Thanks. I'll write to him this weekend. Think maybe he could introduce me to some real live San Francisco poets?"

Button frowned.

"You'll have to ask him. I have no idea what kind of lifestyle he's into out there. As I recall he didn't like people to touch him, so if you meet him don't try to shake his hand. Tell him I asked about him, though. He left here kind of abruptly. Never said 'bye to nobody. I've heard that from several different people. Annette didn't seem to want to talk about him, which was surprising, but I felt I shouldn't pry. I heard he cut off all contact with his family, not that they seem to notice."

He nodded, looking at the slip of paper, then glancing at the baby.

"So, you're gonna move out there and fall in love with some cool West Coast chick and next thing we know, wedding bells'll be ringin', right?"

"Oh, I don't know about that part yet," he shrugged with a mirthless laugh. "It's pretty hard to imagine living with another person. I've kind of gotten set in my ways, you know."

"People can change. It gets easier after you've actually been in a relationship or two."

He thought about that. "Guess that makes sense. But I've lived solitaire so many years, it's kind of hard to conceive of any other way of life."

She laughed and slapped his leg. "Well, bucko, you'd better start conceivin' if you're moving to California!"

The baby began to whimper and squirm. Simpson watched as Button opened her blouse and unsnapped her nursing bra. It was crass to gawk, but he couldn't keep his eyes away. Awesome, yet somehow unsettling. Yes, beautiful. Mother and child looked complete, self-sufficient, a perfect unity.

He was reminded of a weekend morning many years before when he had come to her apartment offering a bit of drug-tasting, and Button had answered the door wearing only a crimson blanket wrapped around her. Her

185

long thick hair was tousled, sexy. She had not changed into clothes, but sat on the floor Indian-style, loosely cloaked in the blanket as they passed a pipe back and forth.

"Thirty-six seems kinda late to be moving out West to start over," she said, noticing that he was watching, "but I guess it won't matter, bein' single and all."

He nodded, gazing at the infant's lips sucking eagerly at Button's bright pink nipple. Was he supposed to be sexually aroused? Her full, milk-white breasts were lovely to behold, but somehow not erotic. They seemed too large, too . . . *mammalian*. He felt nothing between his legs, and worried that he really ought to be turned on.

"Yeah, I may be thirty-six, but in some ways I feel . . . I tell myself all the time I'm growing younger. Becoming new."

"Yeah, you tell yourself that. I hear it's way different out West, Weems. There's, what, thirty million people in California? Or more? That's something to think about."

"But you see, Button, what I'm going there for is very specific. Not many people know this, but I'm . . . actually, I'm a poet—"

"Get out of here. Really? Since when?"

Narrow-focused, he didn't notice she was being facetious.

"And sure, there's lots of poets and writers out there, which is great, I welcome that, but . . . The population doesn't scare me. I can handle thirty million people."

"I can handle thirty million," she echoed in a deep male voice.

Simpson was looking at the complexion of Angelle's face pressed to Button's white breast. The boy's skin, too, was darker. And that name: Orlando?

He glanced at her ringless fingers.

"Button, is the father of these children—or the fathers . . ." He looked at her awkwardly and glanced away. "Is he—or they—by any chance . . ." He cleared his throat. His tone seemed to apologize for asking what surely could not be the case, except that appearances seemed to suggest . . . "You know, partly, um . . . you know . . . ?"

"Why? What difference would it make, Mister White Man with a White Penis? You're really ready for San Francisco, aren't you, you cosmopolitan thing, you?"

"I'm sorry." He pressed his palms to his eyes, feeling his face flushing.

He looked down into the calm, meaty face of the suckling infant. "She sure is pretty, though."

Button eyed him coolly. "Thanks."

"Sorry, it's just hard to get used to the idea of you with kids. And it makes me mad that you have to raise them all by yourself."

So many women left to raise children alone, he thought, abandoned by the impregnators who at this very moment were doubtless playing around with some new fertile nubiles and not committing to them, either, nor mentioning the children they had already brought about, or, if they spoke of them at all, called them "my kids."

"Well, you may not like it, but you could have done something a long time ago."

"I know. I know."

In hara-kiri, or seppuku, he had read, the dagger cuts across the abdomen from left to right. In his case the blade was felt from the guts up to the heart.

"I remember your favorite song by the Beatles was 'I'm Happy Just to Dance with You'."

"That was only for a while. The all-time favorite is 'I'm Only Sleeping'."

She looked at him, not amused.

"It's just a joke, Button."

Strange to realize, to feel the fact that they had once sort of dated, and there were moments when she had subtly pressed herself warmly against him, offering her body, her friendship, her *self*, but yet he had not reached for her. Why not? It was as though branches laden with delicate luscious fruits had dangled before his face, succulent peaches, cherries, and nice pears ripe for plucking, tasting; juices bursting from the skins . . . and he had only smiled and said, "Lovely fruits, very fragrant." *He* could have been the father of children with her, instead of some—. They could be wearing each other's rings. But no, if it were ever to happen it would have happened long ago in that time when he had declined to taste the proffered fruits, or failed to even reach for them. Perhaps they hadn't really known each other very well, after all.

She pulled her blouse closed and patted the baby's lips with a corner of the blanket. She looked at him.

"What got into you that night after the R.E.M. show?"

"Oh, Button, that was so long ago."

He shifted and frowned at the baby, then at his bare feet sliding anxiously back and forth on the damp cool deck.

One October night in Baton Rouge many years before, they had gone to hear a little-known, one-album band from Athens, Georgia, at a half-empty bar near LSU. The air was cool and crisp on Chimes Street, with a pleasant scent of sweet olive. Inside, the Bayou was smoky and stale-beer-rank as ever, and half the customers were sitting at the bar or playing pool while R.E.M. played songs from *Chronic Town* and their forthcoming second album. As Simpson and Button stood near each other, listening, swaying, half dancing, he occasionally felt the warmth of her arm and breast against him, but he was mostly captivated by the chiming, arpeggiated guitar and the curious delicate expressive face of the singer.

"West of the fields, west of the fields . . ."

Later, as they walked along the edge of the campus to her apartment on Azalea Street, their hands bumped several times, and her forearm brushed against his. *She wants to hold hands.* His heart was thumping. *She's going to ask me in.* He would fail again. Rupture is forever. Button would shrug and laugh good-naturedly, patient, confident. But it was impossible. He couldn't let things get that far. And he mustn't let himself get tied down: he had to protect his poetry career.

As they went up the flight of stairs outside her apartment, his throat tightened and his heart was thrashing like a cat being stuffed in a box.

"I have to go," he squeaked.

"What's wrong?" She looked up, surprised, as she felt around in her purse for her keys. "God, you're all sweaty."

"Can't stay, sorry," he said, starting to back away.

"Simpson, baby, what's the matter? You don't look well." She felt his forehead. "Come in. Let me get you a drink of water."

He let her pull him in, for he did want to come inside, except . . . He did want to be with her, really he did. She poured him a shot of bourbon on the rocks to settle his nerves, then, for further relaxation, she rolled something for them to smoke.

"Feel better now?"

"Mmm-hmmm." He did feel good, and felt even better when she leaned over to kiss him with a light, moist touch of tongue. *Mmmm*, he murmured, thinking he might be all right, anticipating a night at Button's amid the mimosas and sweet olive, visible and fragrant through every window, a night in full nakedness on and under her red satin sheets. Gently she covered him, kissed and licked him, her soft hands hungrily searching every inch of him, her creamy skin smooth and soothing like the diaphanous veils of the virgins, an abundance of sensual pleasures, all given freely, but without any firm result.

"Maybe you need to get yourself checked on?"

He agreed he probably should. He was somewhat alarmed, a bit humiliated, slightly emasculated. It was like feeling guilty for not mourning a death more acutely.

He sat up in bed, crossing his legs Indian style.

"I don't . . ." he began.

"What, honey?" she put her hand on his knee.

It felt good there, her hand, squeezing with friendly assurance, and her eyes so warm and caring.

He had had his first chance about a year before with his friend Pepper Landry, after dancing to the B-52's at a short-lived downtown disco called Homo Erectus. A chance to have sex, make love, whatever they called it. Pepper was brainy, saucy, and physically gifted, a brunette with blue eyes and curvaceous, kissable lips as red as her '62 Comet. When the time came, and she was moaning, panting, telling him to do it . . . "Come on! Now!" . . . he sort of faltered. "It's supposed to be hard first before you put it in, right?" he asked, half-joking. "*Duh*," she scorned. She tried to help him, manually, orally, but nothing happened. "Sure you're not queer?" she asked impatiently, a question that would echo for years afterward, "because this has never happened to me before." He squeaked, "No, of course not!" Since that night, Simpson had accepted the rupture's doom of permanent incapacitation, because if he could not get hard with someone of Pepper Landry's high-voltage allure, it must be hopeless. Unitesticular, half a man.

And now again with Button on her red satin sheets.

Her hand was squeezing him warmly.

"I don't seem to have the normal drive, you know, that men have. Are supposed to have. It's strange."

He was not only anguished but baffled, too, viewing the predicament almost as though it were someone else's.

She saw that maybe it wasn't that he was unannounced, but that there was nothing to announce.

She stroked his hand, his arm, leaned close to kiss him consolingly, when suddenly—he could not have explained what came over him; he was as surprised as she was—he recoiled, rolled off the bed, grabbed his clothes and half-dressed in a blind panic, his stomach roiling and his nerves crackling like a tree on fire.

"Simpson!"

"I'm fine, really. Have to go. Don't feel well. 'Bye."

And suddenly he was gone, down the steps, two at a time, leaving her appalled, abandoned abruptly by a pale and panic-shaken *stranger*. That was no Simpson Weems she had ever seen before.

He managed to stumble and slide a half block before the convulsions in his guts erupted and he veered from the lighted street into the dark ligustrum and azaleas where he vomited in the shadows between houses. He knelt there groaning, shivering, wishing the ground would open and swallow him. He was certain there were neighbors watching. Wishing like hell he could be invisible, all the way back to his apartment on Carlotta Street he wept and spit and wiped his mouth and howled inside *What is wrong with you, you queer? I am not a queer!* Back and forth, accusing and defending, just wanting to not have to choose. *Must* it be one or the other? He should turn around and go back to her. Even if he was sweating and blathering like an idiot Button would take him in, and he could try to assure her *It's not you it's me I don't know what's wrong* and she would hold him (by this time he would be a shapeless white mass quivering on the floor) and she'd say *Ssshhh, it's okay*, even though she'd be bewildered and frightened and probably offended too. She would let him in, it wasn't too late, but he couldn't turn himself around.

It would have been a good night for a razor blade.

Later he would make a clever joke about what had come over him. He would tell her he'd panicked when he realized he hadn't brought a condom, or . . .

Button could not imagine what had gotten into him, and never did get a proper explanation. It was frightening to realize how abruptly someone you thought you knew well could turn inside out and be someone else entirely. The person you were just with suddenly wasn't there anymore.

"So, Simpson?" she asked again. "What got into you that night?"

He felt hot needles prickling his scalp. "We talked about that, remember? Well, it's like I said . . ." He shrugged and waved his hands limply. There was no need to elaborate on the account he'd given before.

She did not take her eyes off him. She was not asking *whether* they'd ever discussed it before.

"Did you ever figure out what was the matter?"

He cleared his throat with a strange honking sound, quickly followed by an exaggeratedly masculine authoritative corrected version, and said, "Yeah. I just panicked, that's all."

"Was it about more than the, the softness issue?"

He wiped his forehead with his sleeve. "It's always been a problem for me since, well, since puberty, I guess." He paused, remembering that fateful afternoon's walk home from school, with Bartholomew trailing behind. It had been a beautiful spring day . . . "I got kicked in the balls and lost one of my testes. Functionally it's not supposed to make any difference for producing, you know, sperm and hormones and whatever—the remaining one compensates—but somehow I knew I'd never be normal again. If I ever was. Like I went from twelve to seventy-five in one afternoon. Some vital ingredient's always been missing, if not testosterone then something else. I'm not very religious, but I've prayed that whatever hormone or mojo it is I'm lacking, that it's not too late to develop in me. Maybe I should be taking some vitamins or something."

He paused and touched her leg reassuringly. He was no longer sweating.

"It's definitely women I'm attracted to, Button—it's not a question of orientation—but the drive is lacking. The response. Desire, libido, whatever. And sex seems like, well, even when you and I kissed it felt good, but it was like I was getting sucked into this other world and I guess I was afraid I'd never come out again."

"I'm really sorry that happened to you, honey, but, I mean, 'sucked into this other world'? We're only talkin' about a kiss or somethin'." After a moment she added, "And anyway, why would you *want* to come out again?"

"Like falling into a vortex," he said with a faraway look, his vision diminishing like sand down an hourglass.

"So you pulled yourself back from the precipice. You guys and your self-doubt attacks." Button poked his leg. "And your timing."

"I know," he said with regret. "Was it a bad time for you?"

"You *freaked* me out, Simpson! I had to check myself in the mirror to see if I had snakes in my hair."

"It wasn't you, Button, I swear. You're beautiful. You always will be. It was totally visceral and involuntary. Sexual vertigo. Scared me, too."

"Sexual vertigo," she echoed. "So . . . well, how'd you resolve it?"

"Not much to resolve," he explained calmly. "I just don't get close to people."

Her mouth dropped open. "Simpson, baby, you can't be serious. That can't be good for you."

"It works," he said grimly. "Don't question it."

"You'll explode."

"Haven't yet." He gritted his teeth.

Finally he snapped, "Anyway, why should how I get along with women be the all-defining measurement of my psychic health?"

Her mouth, already agape, dropped lower.

"Well," she conceded diplomatically, after regaining her breath, "I don't suppose it has to be. But getting along with women wasn't exactly the issue."

"Seriously, though," he said, embarrassed by his outburst, "it sounds crazy but I haven't let myself get involved because I was afraid a relationship would distract me from my writing, even though my inkwell's been dry since LSU. And I worried it would hold me back from going to California, as if family obligations haven't been doing a fine job of that already. But I've got to do something, something different."

He frowned and waved his hands as though clearing away obstructions.

"I mean," he said with some impatience, some desperation, "I'm a poet."

Her eyes lighted up, and the baby stirred and sighed.

"A poet," she whispered.

"It used to be this wonderful world I could go into that's hard to explain. I have to get back in there somehow. And you, Button, you never did move to the big city."

"Never did." She shook her head. "I think I knew deep down if I moved back here after college I'd probably never go at all. I guess that would have been the time. So now you can do it for both of us."

"That I can do for you."

He looked in her eyes, his heart stretched full, aching with regret as he admired her beauty and goodness. My kind, dear friend.

"Have you ever been in love?" he asked, watching Angelle's moist little lips move as she slept.

As Button nodded yes, his hazel-green eyes bore in on her for a moment, then flickered away.

"I have, yeah, sure," she said softly. "It's very nice."

"Love is good."

She nodded automatically. Then she wasn't sure whether he was telling or asking.

But he was looking out at the garden, his attention moving lightly around, without a question in his eyes.

"Why do you ask?"

"Just curious."

"You are curious, aren't you? What's gonna happen to you out in San Francisco, Weems?"

"Guess I'll be a famous poet or something." He stood up and stretched his legs.

"You're really serious about this."

"Always have been." As he swallowed he felt a lump in his throat.

"Come on, let's see if we can pull Orlando's head out of the TV. I gotta fix these chirren supper. You stayin'?"

"No, I'd better go."

"You're doing it again."

"Doing what?"

Button held his sleeve. "Stay. Eat. Live a little."

"Better go."

She looked at his feet. She no longer wanted to feed him. "Don't forget your sandals. And fix your damn broken watch. It bugs me."

"Oh, you were gonna show me your new painting."

"I said, 'if you're nice'."

As the screen door closed behind her, it occurred to Simpson he must have insulted her by not staying for supper, but it seemed too late now to change his mind.

... It is ordained that good weather shall prevail, and the City of Flowers in its Festive array promises abundant pleasure to all within her gates.

Proclamation by the King of the Carnival (1934)

Carnival

THERE ONCE WAS A TIME when he took part in the Carnival season like everyone else, going to friends' king cake parties and the great super-krewe parades of Endymion, Bacchus, and Orpheus, and then to Zulu and Rex on Mardi Gras morning. Everyone gathered at Button's apartment in Marigny before the Krewe du Vieux parade, Pepper Landry hosted a few Saturday afternoon Iris blowouts—one year she hung bananas and bunches of grapes from the ceiling and asked each guest to bring a goldfish for her aquarium—and everyone warmed up for Bacchus at Lucia Tomasino's on Prytania. Friends came in from all over, and everyone was in fine spirits. Those parties were fun in their time, but now they all felt long ago, far away, another lifetime . . .

This year Simpson decided he would observe Mardi Gras from a distance by staying home where it was quiet, far from the madding crowd, where there were no eighteen-wheeler-size floats with masked and costumed revelers tossing glittery beads and doubloons and gaudy plastic cups to the happy, hollering, arm-waving multitudes. Not this year. He was already happy, anyway, thinking of where he was going to be next week, and he had work to do, preparing the way to the Best Coast. CopyQwik like most other businesses downtown was closed for the holiday, so after a leisurely breakfast he sat down at his plain pine writing desk and rolled up his sleeves.

He began by writing a brief letter to Button's poet friend Foster. He went through several drafts, all of them self-conscious, overly polite, explaining too much and apologizing for the lateness of the request. Soon the floor was littered with rejects. A recurring dream of wading through rooms piled waist-high and rising with crumpled sheets of paper, the ink running, blurring, blood-spotted Kleenexes, a swamp of balled-up paper that turns to quicksand up to his chest, his neck . . . He should have written to Foster as soon as he got home from Button's; the post office being closed today would make the delivery even later. There was always Priority Mail. Or would that make him look desperate? This, he realized, dabbing at his forehead with a paper towel, *this* was why he was not already out in California: rather than just doing it, whatever it was, he procrastinated and exhausted himself by overthinking every imaginable consideration. What if I do this? Or maybe that? By the time he realized he did not need to anticipate all possible eventualities, the moment had passed, the sun had set.

Feb. 16, 1999
Mardi Gras Day

Dear Foster:

Happy Mardi Gras. I'm an old LSU friend of Button Menendez, who I believe has written to you about my upcoming visit to your fair city.

I will be in S.F. next Thurs. 25th through Sat. March 6. I'll be staying at the Hotel Bohème on Columbus near Broadway. This is an exploratory visit for when I move out there in a few months, I hope, maybe in April or May.

Could I ask a favor? Don't worry, I'm not asking for a place to stay. If it's not an inconvenience, would it be possible to give me a kind of "poet's tour" around North Beach and other Beat and bohemian haunts? I'm interested in the San Francisco Renaissance through the early Haight-Ashbury counterculture scene, the intersection of Beat and hippie. I'd be much obliged. Maybe you'll let me treat you to dinner. Also, if you feel like it, maybe we could go hear some jazz or something.

I hope we'll have a chance to meet.

Thanks, and best wishes,

Simpson Weems

797 DORMITION STREET
NEW ORLEANS, LA 70122

After he sealed the envelope and affixed a new thirty-three-cent stamp, Simpson wrote in his notebook a thought that had come to him while drafting the letter. *I am a man of many weaknesses. If I am yet a man at all.* It felt important to be able to admit it to himself, to commit the recognition to paper. Know thyself, even if it hurts. His usual tendency was to go the other way and comfort himself, whether there was any truth in the assurance or not. He read the words aloud, then closed the notebook.

He had meant to spend some of the afternoon reading through his dream journal in hopes of mining some useful images, but the main project of the day turned out to be reading and revising an account of a strange Mardi Gras experience from shortly after college that had left him sated with an excellent sufficiency of Carnival revelry, and a little spooked, too. He had forgotten about this untitled little narrative until reminded by something Button said. It took him a while to locate the manuscript in a dusty old cardboard typing paper box up in a closet. Rust from the steel paperclip had stained the first and last pages of onionskin. Who were those men he was with, those odd beings? Who was "Dion"? Although the prose style made him wince, reading the sketch gave him some assurance that he was not entirely incapable of completing a piece of writing when he set himself to it. He had forgotten that he'd actually written something since college.

As he reentered that weird, half-forgotten day, he vaguely recalled that he had wandered off with these masked strangers because he thought he'd heard them say they were headed to a party at the house of some semi-famous poet where he understood there would be interesting women, poetesses and lady painters and suchlike. Mardi Gras is normally abnormal, inherently unreal and fantastical, but this experience was even more so, as though he had passed through the looking-glass into a midsummer night's dream in wonderland. They say God looks out for fools, drunks, and little children—but not always. You never know what might happen when you're drunk and wander off with strangers. It was also possible that someone had slipped something into his drink, or there were granules of hallucination powder in something he smoked. He could no longer remember how much of this story had actually happened, an uncertainty compounded by the distancing third-person point of view. At the time he had typed it out, he had probably assumed he would later be able to distinguish the actual from the fictional, but after the passage of years, that turned out to be not so easy.

"Without, roared the Iron Age, the angry waves of American traffic; within, one heard only the murmur of the languid fountain, the sound of deeply musical voices conversing in the languages of Paris and Madrid . . ."

LAFCADIO HEARN
"A Creole Courtyard" (1879)

It is another kind of time, not horizontal or linear but more like a spiral staircase on a mad carousel. He loves costuming on Mardi Gras day, swigging bourbon or chilled vodka from a silver hip flask and running loose and anonymous through the Quarter, veiled by mask and cape and whatever else he's found at Thrift City or St. Vincent de Paul, dancing with strangers, flirting with who knows whom. At balcony parties on Royal or Dauphine he and his friends toss beads and flash enough skin to tease or alarm the revelers in the streets. Invisible in his costume he can be anyone, or no one, a creature of the moment blending invisibly amid the revelry all around, free to say anything and not have to explain, the purest freedom. For this one day, especially if you're masking, identity is fluid, permeable, transitory.

You're dancing with abandon in wild loopy flamboyant undulations with fellow revelers male and female and whatever. The music too is happy and jumping, funk and Afrobeat pulsing with zydeco accordions, Professor Longhair and Tuts Washington and Monk Boudreaux blasting out of bars along the street and from speakers set out on balconies. Your hips are shaking and your feet are down there somewhere and everyone is dancing, singing along, waving arms in the air and nothing is still but the buildings, and today even the brick walls seem less solid than usual . . .

The Rex and Zulu parades passed long ago, it's late in the day, near dusk, and for hours they have been wandering the streets of the Quarter, stopping in for refreshment at Fahy's and Molly's and again and again at Déjà Vu and who remembers where else. *Partying like there's no tomorrow (for tomorrow we die), he spins and twirls amid the sparkly and garish costumes of Louis XIV courtiers, bird people, and the nearly nude satyrs outside Homo-Rama and In the Buff. Now he turns to the bright friendly eyes of several young women in flowing gowns pressed tight to their nipples and thighs then waving free like sheer curtains in a breeze. Three, then five, then seven—their number seems to multiply and diminish again as they swirl around him. They smile and sway like belly dancers, alluring Hawaiian aloha girls in slow motion, beckoning him closer, caressing his face and neck with scarves of silk and satin, but gradually the women fade, transforming into the vague then sharper outlines of skeletons and skull-faced men circling around him, now prancing in a stiff pogo-stick-like insect dance, a hopping ritual of praying mantises . . . No, this must have been a dream.*

Now they are drinking in the brick-walled courtyard behind Lafitte's Blacksmith Shop, standing lightly, almost effortlessly, as though floating upright in a fluid medium of zero gravity. The friends he was with earlier have wandered off, and now he is with three strangers who seem almost familiar, like friends of friends he may have met once at a party, but they're all wearing masks, so who knows? His new companions do not know or seem to care who he is or what he looks like behind his feathered mask. He introduced himself as Dion, the first name that popped into his head, and now it seems not just a little late but unnecessary to tell them the name he usually goes by.

If something was slipped into his drink, this could be where it happened. As he listens, their voices sound strangely interior, as though not entering through his ears but simply being there in his head, in his mind, the way aliens are said to communicate with abductees. Their accents sound vaguely European, maybe from previous centuries or from countries no longer on the map. He thinks he hears them say they're going to a party at some poet's house.

The shorter of the three, who wears a long black robe trimmed in gold, says that each year, at the end of Mardi Gras night, at midnight, he burns his costume. "I just take off whatever I'm wearing and lay it in the street and toss a match on it. Shouldn't drag the same old skin into the next year."

They set out for a house on Esplanade where there is a party that one of them says has been going on "for a long, long time." He makes it sound like generations. Is this where the women are? The farther they walk, the quieter his companions become, and a heavy atmosphere seems to settle over them, as though specks of coal dust and ash are filtering down through the air. Other sounds seem to grow fainter . . .

It is a mild night in early March, and the weather is soft, slightly cool, but through the air passes a breeze of autumn, like a draft from the other side of the year, Halloween or All Souls breathing through a Mardi Gras mask. It feels strange, this wrong-time-of-the-year chill in the air, as though something in nature or time were coming to an end, instead of the fertile, fresh-start feeling natural to spring.

"Y'all, is it still Mardi Gras?"

As they walk along Esplanade he recognizes Temps Perdu across the street. More people than usual are standing around outside, drinking and smoking.

They come to a large house that fronts Esplanade, with its back to the Quarter: a balconied, three-story Creole mansion with a façade of beige terra-cotta that in the moonlight appears chiseled out of bone. The house, set snugly amid the palms in the front yard and the dark craggy branches of live oaks reaching across from the boulevard's neutral ground, appears excessively ornate even for the Quarter, with filigreed columns and iron lace grillwork balconies on the second and third stories crawling with wisteria and hung with baskets of lush ferns.

"Is this the poet's house? Are we there yet?"

They pass through the tilting wrought-iron gate and enter the mansion through a tall heavy door that groans on its rusted hinges like a coffin lid. They pause in the foyer. It smells of dust and captured air, ancient papers and fabric, a house where there has never been an electrical wire or outlet, only candles and oil lamps. On the walls he sees the murky outlines of oil paintings in heavy gilded frames—the faces in the portraits appear different each time he looks, though in the dim light it's hard to be sure—and from somewhere he hears faint voices, perhaps upstairs, or under the floorboards.

He follows them up a creaking carpeted staircase to a spacious high-ceilinged room whose floor is strewn with pillows of crimson and royal blue, furnished with bowls of grapes and candles in red glass jars, and from beyond the velvet curtains a sound of voices, wineglasses clinking, and faintly off-tune violins. Familiar notes, a melody he's heard before.

Have they finally arrived, Dion asks, at the party that's been going on a long time? Where are the girls? We're getting there, the tallest one says. He pulls a bottle from his purple cloak, uncorks it and drinks. He passes the bottle to the short one, who drinks and passes it to the third masked figure. "Drink up. You'll feel strong again." Dion accepts the bottle—it's surprisingly heavy—and tilts it back. As he sips the wine, sweet and thick as port, he smells a familiar fragrant burning herblike odor, as of cannabis or opium.

It is near midnight and they are outdoors again. They wait while the short one undresses at the intersection of Dauphine and Ursulines, stripping off every thread, and piles his costume in the street and sets it on fire. The naked one now walks beside Dion and the others toward a nearby bar on Burgundy. Without his clothes he has the trim, athletic body of an eighteen-year-old gymnast. From behind a mask it's okay to look.

The last part of the evening he remembers: They are in a dark, dungeon-like grotto bar without a sign or name. He doesn't remember entering, but it feels deep underground. He asks what time it is, but his companions just smile as though that's a silly question. He doesn't know what they are drinking, but it tastes like the port they drank from the heavy bottle. What he would really like is a drink of fresh cold water. A rock band is playing somewhere in the bar—pounding drums and out-of-tune guitars, like Ziggy Stardust filtered through industrial grunge metal. Whatever the source of the sound, it is playing at maximum volume, but on the only stage Dion can see, across the crowded smoky room of red candle-lit tables, *two slender naked young humans of indeterminate or unfixed gender coupling in a yin-and-yang 69 are rolling on a purple satin water bed in paroxysms of intensive fellatio and advanced cunnilingus, oozing like a human lava lamp, just at the edge of orgasm. But no one seems to be watching them, or at least the sexing dyad are but one attraction among many.*

It seems late enough that midnight must have passed long ago and technically Mardi Gras should be over, closed down by the police, but this year, or at this hour, in this precinct, there are no authorities. No one seems to be paying for the drinks; no money can be seen changing hands. Tobacco is not the only smoke in the air; the aromas of opium and hashish and something more acrid waft through the room. In one corner several guests sit on pillows around a Turkish water pipe, puffing meditatively, their faces obscured in the shadows.

"Is this the Cave?" Dion asks, thinking he might be in the legendary nightclub said to be underground, accessible only through a series of subterranean passageways. Even if it is, they might not tell him; legend has it that anyone who has actually been to the Cave is sworn to secrecy. You're admitted by invitation only—you have to know someone—and to go and tell anyone that you have been there, or how you arrived, would be an indiscretion of unspeakable indecency. Some say that if anyone tells non-initiates about having been to the Cave, it will disappear. There could be other cavern-taverns like this around town, subterranean grottoes once occupied by private clubs until some garrulous fool spoiled the secret for everyone.

Dion repeats his question.

"It's a cave," one of his companions replies ambiguously. "A genizah."

"A what?" Are they still speaking English?

"It used to be, anyway, before they made a club out of it. It's an old Hebrew or Arabic word for 'hiding place' or 'storage room' or something. It was where they kept religious relics, heretical texts, usually next to the synagogue, maybe during the exterminations. They used to have them in Jerusalem, Alexandria, Cairo."

"I've never heard of a synagogue in the French Quarter."

The fellow explains that there were ancient storage places pocketed around the Quarter that have mostly slipped from memory, underground rooms of forgotten, forbidden lore. Some of them may date from before the fires of the 1700s. Who knows where they are anymore. Secret vaults of historical records, maps and pictures of what the old city used to look like, neighborhoods, canals, names of streets, locations of slave pens, Indian cemeteries, dueling oaks, hanging trees . . .

"If you know where to look, here and over in Treme and under the Superdome, you can probably find remnants of nightclubs for other kinds of music no one remembers once passed through here. Jazz was just one of many styles, and it happened to catch on."

"Well?" asks Dion. "Where is it? Where are we?"

His companion smiles patiently as though waiting for him to understand. "I'm just saying these spaces exist. Pockets of history, old time. Sometimes they are physical places, sometimes they're . . . Memories, like. If you want to find 'em, you'll have to look for yourself. But they exist."

He is about to ask again his long-ignored question when he feels a warm moist pleasurable sensation under the folds of his robe, rhythmic and tender, affectionate, concentrated on him. This is all for you, and it never ends. *Maybe the girls have found him. No one else seems to notice what is happening, and he dares not look under the table for fear the sensation will stop. Someone gently lays a hand on his shoulder and leans over to blow a fragrant illicit smoke into his mouth, and he tilts back into her soft tresses and inhales infinitely. His blood vessels expand, his vision extends far beyond his skull, and dimensions unfold in layers and colors he has never seen before, luminous and iridescent. He feels as though he is being transported on a magic carpet, propelled by the moist tender pleasures under his clothing. All he wants is for the smooth ride, and the memory of it, to go on forever.*

Next thing he knows, he is outside, alone in the dark, and the bar or cave is nowhere to be seen. Scrawny dogs and thin black cats creep among broken bottles, and rats rustle through the trash in the gutters. He searches for his car or bicycle in the dark and empty streets.

Can't remember if he drove here or walked.

7

How Many Dead Fathers

DON'T PARENTS USUALLY DIE ONLY ONCE? Whenever Simpson remembers Gasper's demise, there are always multiple deaths, all blurring together, never one simple and conclusive ending, but only successive waves of decease. He dreams repeatedly of a black-draped visitation scene that keeps happening over and over. The mourners are circling round a spiral staircase overlooking a white-tiled foyer where the open casket is displayed amid ever-fresh bouquets of lilies and white roses. The child-size figure in the coffin does not look like his father, not Gasper, too young to be dead, too small to be a man, too frail to be anyone's father. The corpse takes a breath, but remains still. Earlier it lifted a finger, then yawned. An elegant woman in a black hat and veil, slim, sophisticated, looks at her watch and shakes her head. She is tired of having to come to the same man's funeral over and over. No, says Simpson, this is the first time. I'm sure this is the only time he's died. I would remember. He sees her watch: thirteen zodiac signs and no hands to tell the time. No, she insists, it's always him. It's him every time, a thousand little deaths, none of them quite adding up. She sighs impatiently. He can't even die properly. He can't do a single thing all the way through.

"Your father means well," Melba often said. The excuse came to sound terribly insufficient, like saying of someone, "He's at his best when everything's going well." It seemed beneath the minimum level of dignity a person would be expected to maintain. Imagine having a father about whom more could be said. He designs admirable buildings. Even something simple. He sings nicely, or rides horses well. Poor Father. In the end, they couldn't even say he changed rolls of toilet paper well.

Except for Bartholomew's gloomily mumbling, "Remember that you are dust, and unto dust you shall return," over and over, like a chant or a threat, the brothers did not speak as they crossed the street to the cemetery. Bartholomew very decidedly did *not* want to take Simpson to Father's tomb on a damp cool day in February, or any other day, and he wouldn't have, except Simpson kept asking politely, repeatedly, and Mother gave them some pretty artificial flowers from one of her front-yard flower pots to bring to the grave, so he felt obligated, even though Simpson didn't love Father as much as he should—he never had—and really didn't deserve to be taken there. But he could hear Rev. Bud Rex counseling him that, as for deserving and being worthy, that was the sort of judgment best left to the mercy of the Maker. Anyway, as Mother remarked, it was Ash Wednesday, after all. Bartholomew understood that to mean maybe

Simpson was repenting, as he should, for not being a good son, not a good brother.

It was a gray afternoon, and there was a chill in the black iron gate of St. Perpetua's clanking shut behind them. Rows of tombs, walls of vaults, lanes of white shell between the beds of grass with headstones and statues, and cypresses and magnolias here and there. Gasper was interred in a numbered vault in one of the long walls of whitewashed concrete crypts four high and forty or more across that formed the cemetery's perimeter. Names and dates were carved into the front panels whose outer facings were of granite or soft white marble like soap bars veined with light gray. Some of the names were so old they were illegible, and a few of the older facings were worn through by the rain, like marble steps in an ancient stairwell smoothed and bowed low in the center. Sprigs of fern grew from cracks in the marble, small trees from the brick and mortar crevices.

Bartholomew carried the plastic flowers in one hand and a roll of duct tape in the other. He stopped and pointed.

GASPER MONTELEON PLAISANCE WEEMS

1925 + 1986

LOVING HUSBAND, DEVOTED FATHER

Simpson reached out with both hands and his fingers hungrily traced along the letters of his father's name.

They were silent for some time, staring at the marble panel as through a window.

"I never realized he was only sixty-one when he died."

Bartholomew did not reply.

"Barto, you suppose Dad saw heaven the first two times he died?"

"Rev. Bud says he was probably in a cave outside the pearly gates."

Simpson looked at him. "That old preacher friend of yours?" He thought about that. "You think he's right? A cave?"

"I don't know. I just know I miss him."

Simpson wished he had been the one to say that.

Bartholomew was looking down at the orange and pink plastic flowers as though he could smell them.

"Well," said Simpson, "if you're gonna do it . . ."

One by one, a pink and then an orange, alternating, with seven strips of duct tape, Bartholomew attached the flowers to the marble vault beside his father's graven name. Thirteen years was a long time. There had to be a way to see him again without having to wait to see him in heaven.

He turned halfway toward his brother and, without looking directly at him, said irritably, "Well, aren't you going to say a prayer for him?"

While it is well known that cats are endowed by their creator with nine lives, humans are generally understood to be granted but one, so naturally it came as quite a surprise to everyone when, after Gasper struck his head and died from a fall off the toilet seat, he came blinking and yawning back to life. For about an hour, he lay quite dead.

"No one can doubt it," said Dr. Garcia. "Gasper's life has left him. I'm so sorry."

The ambulance's red emergency lights were flashing through the front window, lighting the faces of Melba and Hector Garcia, M.D. Bartholomew was hiding in his room. A small EMT team was standing by as the family physician comforted the widow.

She looked down at her husband's calm, composed face, his head turned awry, snapped in his fall, and his limbs aligned in more or less the same deathlike stillness in which he normally slept. He looked every bit as deceased as the bodies whose hair and faces she dressed daily at Lourdes. And yet, and yet she felt . . . Anyone else could look at him, check his pulse, listen through Dr. Garcia's stethoscope to the absence of breath and heartbeat, and by any other vital signs determine that the body in question was a corpse. (May his soul rest in peace.) But Melba, who loved Gasper and knew him as no other had ever known him, felt in her heart that he had only gone away for a spell and would soon return.

"Leave him here."

"Pardon? Say again?" said Garcia. For a moment he thought she said—

"He just needs to collect himself. Leave him here with me."

"Madam, I have seen great faith before, but this . . ."

Melba shrugged modestly. It was simple, really. Gasper just needed a little time to recover, and he'd be back to his old self.

"He was only changing a roll of toilet paper, Dr. Garcia, sittin' on the seat with the lid down when he lost his balance somehow and hit his head on the edge of the sink and fell right smack on that hard tile floor. He didn't mean to die. I'm sure I'd've known if his time had come."

Garcia said he understood completely, but unfortunately the cemeteries were full of people who never meant to die in quite the way or the time they did. It was a regrettable fact, but—

When at just that instant—

Melba later said that if the trusted family physician had not been sitting right beside her she might not have believed it herself: Suddenly there was Gasper sitting up and stretching, looking a little disoriented, rubbing his eyes like he was rising from a nap that had left him with a headache and a knot on the side of his head.

"Glory hallelujah."

"Well I'll be . . ." Garcia kept saying. "I never . . ." Other than that, he was speechless. Never in all his years of medicine—no, not even in New Orleans—had he ever seen anything quite like this.

Hector Garcia was not the only one to utter the word "zombie." No one could quite believe it, let alone begin to explain it. As he later reported the resuscitation to a roomful of his white-coated fellow physicians seated around a conference table, a man who had clearly been dead—as methodically ascertained by the standard checkpoints and vital signs (here they all nodded)—after about an hour without breath or heartbeat, and well long enough for the onset of permanent brain death and the first stiffenings of rigor mortis, he suddenly opened his eyes! The patient blinked and sniffled and began to move, and then he was sitting up, scratching his head, and wondering what happened.

Had the wife and son been praying over the body? one doctor asked.

Had Garcia checked the vital signs every fifteen minutes even after pronouncing the patient dead?

Had this, had that . . . ?

"The mother's hands were clasped, and she was surely praying hard. The younger son was hiding in his bedroom, in the initial stages of acute denial, and very likely praying like the devil. The older son was on his way home from LSU."

Upon hearing from Mother that Father had died (with her apologies for telling him over the phone, but, after all, he *was* up in Baton Rouge), Simpson instantly called a friend for a ride to the Greyhound station, but before leaving he went to Thomas Boyd Hall and formally withdrew from the university. He acted without thinking, yet he knew exactly what he was doing. When the father dies, the eldest son withdraws from college. Halfway home, gazing out the bus's tinted windows at the cypress and water oak swamps around Gramercy, Simpson calculated with satisfaction that with one stroke of filial sacrifice he would both honor his father's

221

memory and assure Mother that she could rely on him to step in as the man of the house.

When he walked in the front door and saw his father sitting in his La-Z-Boy and laughing (giggling, actually), Simpson was shocked at first, then disappointed and even slightly offended. Then he was indignant. Only after an instant's silent fury did he feel relieved and joyous— the lost father hath returned!—and he joined his mother and brother in anxious grateful weeping.

Gasper laughed heartily at the sight of all his family crying at once—for him! It was just too funny.

"Y'all just goin' nuts, all of y'all, thinking a man like me 'd bump his head and die," he giggled, covering his mouth. "I think I just got a little disconnected there for a while."

"Disconnected!" Bartholomew boomed. "You were so disconnected you were dead! Dr. Garcia said your life had fled, but we never lost faith, did we, Mommy?"

"Can't let go of my Gasper." She motioned to Bartholomew to hand her the Kleenex box.

Gasper was ready to turn on the television to watch the Braves and the Red Sox, but Melba couldn't have the TV on during such a momentous reunion. What a day to have no film in her camera!

It was beginning to dawn on Simpson that he was no longer a college student. He stood in the middle of the living room, shifting from foot to foot, tensely clutching his backpack's shoulder strap. Gasper lounged contentedly in his easy chair and Melba relaxed in hers, and Bartholomew slouched massively in the middle of the sofa, his shoulders oddly hunched and his hands in his lap, palms pressed together, and his dark eyebrows frowning in some kind of concentration.

Since going away to college Simpson always found it strange to come home, to breathe again the distinctive smell of his family's little house on Invalides. They had never seen him in his new world—they were not curious and knew nothing of his college life, the bigger outside world he was discovering, his friends, teachers, new ideas and experiences. Baton Rouge was just over an hour's drive away, yet they had never visited, and he hadn't thought to invite them. It just happened that way. And so they all carried on, the happy household of Melba and Gasper and Bartholomew, and life on Invalides passed by as it always had and always would.

And now he had pulled out of college for nothing.

"Well, Simpson," Bartholomew almost shouted, "are you gonna rush off now, now that Daddy's okay?"

"May I sit down a minute, first?"

Bartholomew ducked his head down and frowned at his fingers fiddling in his lap.

"You can stay as long as you want, Simpson," Gasper said. "You're home now."

"Amen." Melba nodded gratefully.

"You're home again, too, Dad."

"Listen how sweet Simpson's talking."

"You hush. Don't make fun of your brother."

"It's almost like he's sincere."

223

"Oh God, I'm going back to Baton Rouge right this instant."

He still hadn't put down his backpack.

Melba interceded. "Simpson, honey, you're welcome to have a seat. Bartholomew, you are being *ugly*. Don't talk about your brother's sincerity like that."

Bartholomew glared at his knuckles rapping together with fidgety aggression. He would never forget, never forgive Simpson's look of disappointment when he walked in and saw Father was alive. Mother and Father were too trusting to see their eldest son as he really was. Simpson never meant thank you, he just said it. He rarely gave birthday presents and never wrote "Love, Simpson" on anything Bartholomew had ever seen. They deserved better.

"Well, I'm sure glad to be here, anyway," Gasper exclaimed cheerfully. He patted his right hand on the armchair. "Now if we could just turn on the TV, Mama."

"Lord, man, you were dead and now you're risen, and you want to watch a baseball game?"

"Melber, if you loved baseball like we do you'd understand."

"He's right, Mommy. Please let's turn it on. *Please*?"

Bartholomew began rocking forward on the sofa, trying to raise himself up from the deep-sunken cushions. On his fifth failed attempt Simpson clucked his tongue with exasperation and switched on the game for him.

The Braves were ahead by two.

Bartholomew settled back with a sigh, Gasper clapped his hands, and Melba turned her chair a few degrees closer to the television.

Simpson could go now. It was not that they didn't want him, nor did he ever doubt that, in their way, they loved him, but the parents and brother were so completely sufficient unto themselves that the family foursome he had almost grown used to was no longer symmetrical, if indeed it ever had been. He was the first-born son, yet he did not belong in this house with them, these almost-strangers. He seemed to lack something, perhaps some essential chemical property that would be necessary to bond with this compound. He was welcome to stay, or he could go. Simpson felt himself detaching, distancing, wintry and impersonal, like an iceberg breaking loose from Greenland.

"Yes! Beautiful swing!" Gasper exclaimed, pumping his fists. "Oh this is a wondrous day."

"Wondrous strange," Simpson added, and turned to find Bartholomew frowning at him with a low rumbling growl.

Though much was unexplained, it was beyond question that Gasper Weems was again among the living.

From that terrifying, mystifying afternoon until Gasper's next fatal fall, from an even higher altitude, the man of the house carried on as though he had never lost consciousness, had not been pronounced dead by a physician, and hadn't caused (or provided an occasion for) his eldest son to withdraw from the state university. The neighbors found his return more charming than weird, and took it all in stride. When Thelma Dupuy next door said one day, "Gasper, I heard you died," Grace Gagliano laughed, "Yeah, but he got over it."

The light in the high-ceilinged hallway had been out for weeks. Melba had asked Simpson several times to change the bulb, but he had been busy settling into a new job and apartment and hadn't gotten around to it. One afternoon while she was out shopping, Gasper, whistling a happy tune, climbed up five steps on the ladder and unscrewed the dead bulb. Bartholomew held the ladder steady with one hand and aimed the dim flashlight up at the light socket. He noticed a red and white warning sticker on the step between his father's feet. "Dad! Stop! Listen. It says here, 'DANGER: Do not stand on or above this step. You may lose your balance'." Gasper chuckled, "Can't lose what I never had, son. Kinda like the lottery. Now take hold of this bulb—" But with one hand on the ladder and a flashlight in the other, Bartholomew froze, flustered at being presented with a third object to hold. "I can't!" Gasper put the bulb in his pants pocket, and he was just giving the new bulb its first twist when—and Bartholomew would never forget, never stop seeing it happening and rehappening in slow motion—his father lost his balance and fell upside down, striking the hardwood floor headfirst. As he slumped to the floor the lightbulb burst in his pocket with a hollow pop.

A dark wet stain appeared on Bartholomew's pants.

226

He left him crumpled on the floor. On the TV shows, the characters always bark, "Don't move the victim!" Wait till help arrives. Mother would be back soon. He didn't think to telephone Simpson at work. He sat still, or nearly still, for half an hour. It was a quiet time of day. The clock ticked evenly, water dripped in the kitchen sink, an airplane passed high overhead, and the rotating floor fan kept up its even sweeps of breeze as though no one were home and nothing had happened.

Melba walked in with her arms full of grocery bags and her sunglasses slipping down her nose.

"I think he died again."

The groceries hit the floor. A jar of olives rolled across the linoleum and came to a stop at the foot of the refrigerator.

"Lord have mercy, where is he?" She stepped over the spilled groceries toward Bartholomew, who had not moved a muscle since her key turned in the lock. "Where *is* he?"

"In the hall. He fell again. He was on the ladder."

The springs creaked as Bartholomew heaved himself up off the sofa. He followed her into the hall.

Melba folded the ladder so she could get around it and knelt over her husband's crumpled body. "Oh, Gasper, baby." She cradled his head in her arms and patted his lukewarm forehead.

Bartholomew stood behind her, his arms crossed awkwardly over his chest.

"What happened, Bartholomew? How long has he been like this?"

"He was on the ladder replacing the bulb you kept asking Simpson to change, remember, but he's been so preoccupied with his new job—"

"Tell me what happened to your father."

"He fell."

She looked up at him. "*How* did he fall? How long ago?"

"A half hour. And I was holding the ladder," he added quickly, "it wasn't my fault. He just lost his balance and fell. It's Simpson's fault. He—"

"Never mind about that. Here, help me pull him into the living room. Good Lord-a-mercy! What's all this glass?"

"Oh, the lightbulb busted in his pocket when he fell."

Melba changed his clothes for him—fortunately he wasn't cut—and after a lot of heaving and bumping, they managed to drag the body up onto the sofa. She straightened his clothes and brushed his hair.

They sat down for a moment to catch their breath.

"Think he's dead for good this time?"

Melba looked at her husband on the sofa, composed and dignified as an Egyptian king. It was too soon to tell. She patted her chest lightly. Gradually her breathing calmed.

"I s'pose we'd better call Dr. Garcia. Then let Simpson know. Hope he don't quit his job this time."

"No, don't call the doctor yet," said Bartholomew.

"Good thinkin'."

Gasper lay dead still for hours and hours. It felt like an entire day.

He's just resting, Melba prayed over and over. Please, Lord. He just bumped his head.

She had to call Roscoe at the taxidermy shop and say Gasper might not be in the next day; he wasn't feeling too well.

"He ain't dead again, is he?" Rabineaux joked. "Don't let him get away from me, now."

Melba laughed with a heavy heart and said he'd soon be good as new.

She was in the middle of cooking jambalaya when she saw Gasper sitting up and stretching, yawning, blinking and rubbing the bump on his head.

"Mmm-mmmm," he murmured, savoring the lively aromas of chicken and andouille sausage frying in the skillet with the chopped celery and garlic and onions.

"Mommy had faith," said Bartholomew, pointing to the three plates on the table.

"I knew your cookin' was extra special," he said the next day, praising Melba to their neighbors.

"Good enough to wake the dead, it looks like," Mrs. Dupuy observed.

"Careful with that recipe, Melba," said Grace Gagliano, glancing across the street at St. Perpetua's.

Gasper was never the same after his head-bumping falls—he would laugh and say he was never the same *before* he bumped his head—but Simpson suspected his father might also have suffered some mini-strokes or other hard-to-trace neurological damage resulting from countless jolts of sheer frustration with Bartholomew.

Who wouldn't blow a few fuses at his antics? One, concerning the Louisiana Lottery, was a serious act that would set the family back for years to come, while another was a more short-term irritation that could be painted over, more or less.

Bartholomew had seen a car in a body shop's parking lot marked with red X's to indicate needed repair spots before a repainting. But where others saw X's, he saw crosses, crosses whereon His only begotten Son gave His life for us, and the light of a new idea shone unto him. He had seen countless religious bumper stickers, and phrases like PRAISE JESUS and JESUS MIRACLE POWER painted or decal-lettered on the sides of cars and trucks around town, but not until now had he thought of volunteering his father's car for evangelical service, to spread the Word of the Redeemer throughout the city. *Go ye therefore, and teach all nations.* With a can of blood red spray paint from the local hardware store he wrote the name of the Savior in uneven, two-foot-high letters on the sides of his father's white Skylark. He moved the spray can slowly to get the letters the right shape and size; the excess paint dripped red down the sides.

Gasper was a devout believer, but his Christian forbearance was sorely tested by his son's embellishments.

"But I improved it!" Bartholomew protested. "Jesus Is Lord. John three-sixteen. And this way you won't need car insurance because no one will run into you. You're protected. Think of all the money I've saved you."

Gasper shook his head. "Traffic don't work that way, son. Not on this earth. You bought the spray paint, and you'll pay for the repaint job."

"Dad, no! Think of Jesus!"

This incident prompted the one occasion when Bartholomew held a paying job—bagging groceries at Sammy Tong's grocery and loading the customers' cars—though only long enough to earn the money to pay to have his father's car repainted. Simpson learned later that Mr. Tong, knowing how much Bartholomew needed to earn, had paid him a higher hourly wage just to bring his employment to an early conclusion. But even after the new coat of white paint, and then another, the name of the Lord still showed through.

Gasper stayed off ladders for about a year, and all was well until the day before Christmas. It was an oddly warm day with a flavor of early spring, so the decorations around the house had the look of belonging to another season, as though left in place since the Christmas before. It isn't this time of year at all, Melba thought as she brushed her wig and fixed her face at the vanity mirror. Before starting breakfast she woke her husband as usual by lifting the pillow from his feet, and while he took a shower she made his bed and laid out his underwear, a yellow short-sleeve shirt, and gray pants. Gasper's pants were always solid: brown, gray, or dark green. He had once wanted a smart-looking pair of plaid golf pants he saw in a catalog, but Melba shook her head. Too flashy, and not befitting a man of his age and dignity.

She was already busy in the kitchen. As Bartholomew would doubtless remind her, before he even said good morning, Christmas Eve was the day she baked the baby Jesus cake, a childhood treat that even in his twenties and thirties he continued to demand with undiminished zeal. There would be no peace in the season of giving if Melba dared even suggest that the cake was only for children.

"False! Sacrilege!"

It was common in families with little ones to bake a round cake, usually solid but sometimes a ring, with white icing and sprinkled with green and red sugar and a birthday candle for each of the twelve days of Christmas, and embedded within was a tiny plastic baby, pink, brown, or gold. The baby Jesus cake was a yuletide complement to the king cake that is first baked for Twelfth Night, the beginning of the Carnival season. Normally a child outgrows the custom after a few years, but for Bartholomew Christmas would not be complete—it could not even be—until they all sat around the dinner table and sang happy birthday and made a wish for the divine infant, and then he blew out the candles. After he passed twelve he insisted there be a candle for each year of his own life. Then he began expecting the same cake on his own birthday, too. On the few occasions when Melba had tried to let the tradition quietly drop, he screamed and rampaged as though he were being eviscerated with white-hot tongs. "It's okay, honey," she said soothingly. "Ssshhh. Jesus is still born this day in a manger. Settle down, Boo. I'll get started on that cake right now."

Melba set the dough in the oven and adjusted the temperature, then pulled out the vacuum cleaner while Gasper smoked his pipe out on the back patio. He had been itching to hang his new bird feeder. It was the first clear day after two days of rain. The sun was shining, and mockingbirds and sparrows were singing happily all through the neighborhood. The ground and bark smelled damp and rich, and in the cleansed and freshened air there was a sense of relief after the long rainfall.

He pulled out the ladder and the bird feeder, still fresh from the lawn and garden center. The red and white plastic smelled irresistible, and the bird feed looked wholesome as wheat and barley.

Bartholomew stormed out the back door and slammed it shut. "I'm in there studying my numbers," he said indignantly, jabbing at the sports section's scores, "and she starts vacuuming!"

"Come help me here, son." Gasper carried the ladder out in the yard and stopped under a live oak limb.

"No, Father. I am not climbing up on that—"

"Just hold it still while I put up my new bird feeder. It's my Christmas ornament. Ain't she pretty?"

Bartholomew eyed it suspiciously. "No. Too risky. Let Simpson do it. The ground's too wet. You're going to fall again and die on us, and then where will we be? You *keep doing* this! The last time you stayed dead for *hours*." He said this with hot resentment, as though Gasper had deliberately held out on them to vex and distress him personally.

"Gee, son. Didn't realize you felt that way."

He turned the stainless steel hook screw around in his hand. Shaped like a question mark.

"Go ask Mom, and if she says it's okay, then I'll help you. But she's gonna say no. I'll go get the door mats from the car so you can lay 'em under the ladder so you don't fall and break your neck."

With that, Bartholomew turned toward the front yard.

Gasper didn't know what had gotten into the boy, but he wasn't sure a son should be talking to his father that way.

It was really a simple operation. With the hook in his right hand, he steadied the ladder legs on the ground and started climbing up the ladder. He gripped the leg-thick limb with his left hand, and with his right he pushed the screw up into the rough bark and twisted.

"Dad!" Bartholomew shrieked at the same moment Melba burst out the back door screaming "Gasper!"

The ladder flipped sideways and he grabbed the limb with both hands. He kept his head and didn't shout or scream, though his legs were kicking frantically six feet off the ground.

They came running and placed the ladder approximately within reach.

"Here! Here!"

Each of them clutched one of his feet to guide him to the ladder. Finally he was safe. All at once he slipped or the ladder tilted and his jaw struck the top step as he fell and his head smacked the mud and the ladder crashed down on him, striking his right temple.

Melba screamed, and Bartholomew fainted.

She dragged her husband inside to the sofa, then roused her son with a bottle of ammonia from under the kitchen sink.

He stood by, rubbing his eyes and whimpering as she removed Gasper's muddy clothes and washed him, then wrapped him in his bathrobe.

The body lay still on the sofa.

They sat down and looked at him.

Melba turned to Bartholomew. "My strength is as the strength of ten . . ."

She waited for him to complete the line, but his nose wrinkled and twitched.

"My cake!"

She ran to the kitchen.

He was crying and everything blurred as he knelt down in front of his father's body. He bowed his head and prayed. *Come back. Bring him back.* He did not touch the body for fear it would be cold.

That night, after many prayers, Melba and Bartholomew carried Gasper back to his bed. They lay him under the covers, settled his pillows the way he liked them, and said good night.

"We'll have to have Christmas without him."

"You hush, O ye of little faith."

"He's dead, Mother. He won't wake up this time."

Bartholomew went in his room and turned the lock.

Melba banged on his door. "You don't know that for a fact!"

Why didn't Simpson answer the phone? She tried the copy shop, but they said he was off. Where was he, volunteering again at the Rampart Street soup kitchen?

After three days of checking the body for any vital signs, with hope diminishing, then vanishing, Melba finally called Dr. Garcia. He was horrified. "*Three nights* you slept with the body there in the room with you?" He implored her to never again let faith override common sense. He made her promise that if she or her sons ever thought she might be ill, they would call a doctor immediately. Then pray.

The good people at Lourdes handled the funeral arrangements at minimal cost. Mr. Krebs was very kind to her, and took special care with Bartholomew, who moved about in a daze.

Simpson did not cry at the black-draped funeral service amid the oppressive lilies and white roses, or at St. Perpetua's when Gasper's ashes were interred in a concrete vault. It was not until he was back in his parents' bedroom, clearing out his father's chest of drawers by Mother's request, and pulled open a drawer and saw the leopard spot underwear. Before he knew what was happening he had broken down and was sobbing, blubbering and gagging like he was drowning or losing his mind. The wildcat underwear set had been one of his most inspired presents to his father: a package of three jockey shorts printed with the bright spots and stripes of the tiger, the leopard, and the bold-colored cheetah. A master stroke of gift-giving that had ranked high on his self-satisfaction scale. Gasper wore those big-cat briefs threadbare.

Simpson was crying because he could not honestly recall whether he had chosen the gift sincerely or ironically. Had he given the underwear open-handedly or by cynical sleight-of-hand? Was it like some of the presents he'd carelessly given his mother, just to be giving something, such as the I'D RATHER BE BOWLING license plate frame? It's the thought that counts. Of course it had been a trick: he had given his father the ugly briefs because he knew Gasper was silly enough to actually wear them. At the time, when he'd thought he was being so clever, he had not considered how the gift might look from the other side of his father's grave.

For more than a month after the funeral, Bartholomew sat on the sofa, staring straight ahead, absently stroking his stuffed green turtle and making low moaning sounds.

"Are you okay, Barto?" Simpson asked gently, leaning toward him. "Can I get you anything?"

He did not answer, did not move his frozen gaze. He kept making the same moaning sound in his throat and chest, as though the song he usually sang every day on the front porch swing had retreated, taken refuge.

Simpson turned to his mother. "Has he said anything?"

She shook her head. "I'm sure he'll be all right. He's just kind of upset right now."

"You think so?" he snapped. "His father's just *died*. You really think he might be upset?"

Melba started crying again, and Simpson moved closer and put his arm around her. "I'm sorry, I didn't mean that." Why did he have to be so cold and mean?

Bartholomew gazed blankly at the portrait of Jesus on the wall behind the black-draped television set. He stared at the walls and the warm receiving and penetrating eyes of the Lord for days, days that became weeks, months. He was waiting. For it is written that He will come again. Time did not pass, but hung there in the room like stale air, like a motionless pool of water up to his waist, surrounding him, holding still. The sounds of birds outside made him think of the pine trees at the camp at Audubon State Park near St. Francisville where the family had gone several times for summer vacation when the boys were young. They would go walking in the woods along the sloping dirt trails through the piney woods. He loved the smell of the trees warmed by the sun and the cool damp of pine straw in the shadows under the logs and fallen branches. Father pointed to a rabbit as it sprung quickly away, and Simpson found a box turtle in a crevice beneath a log. Mother sat on a wooden footbridge and dangled her toes in the stream and pointed to the sunlight flashing on the water and the smooth round gray and copper-colored stones in the streambed. The wind blew high in the whispering pines, and the sun came down from the bright blue sky through the glowing tops of the trees that waved in the breeze and the light warmed the red dirt paths through the woods.

Still Bartholomew sat there, his eyes on Jesus.

Melba brought him bowls of sliced oranges and bananas and apples, putting the fruit slices one by one into his mouth. "Eat, honey," she nudged him. His blank face made her think of her Big Mama and Old Paw's tales of soldier boys limping back from the Great War shell-shocked, all scrambled and disconnected inside.

"Chew, baby," she said. "You'll feel better."

Those sunlit trees were still there, Bartholomew thought as he hugged his turtle and stared into the eyes of Jesus. The trees at the state park were still waving in the breezes, shining in the sun. Everything is still the same there. *The trees don't know he's gone.* All this time away, those pines are still there, taller. They've been growing all this time, waving back and forth, and they make a whispery sound when the wind blows. That's where Father is. And he will come again.

A woman's tears is her own, Mama always said. Nobody else wants none of it. Put your sorrow to work for others. How did she do it? Melba wished she were here now to smack some sense into her. But she would never be as strong as her mother. Verna Flora was the kind to hold it in and keep it to herself. She would neither burden others nor let anyone try to comfort her, for none was needed. People are such crybabies, she said, always feeling sorry for themselves, thinking they got problems.

As Melba lay on her bed, still sobbing, nibbling on chocolates a month, two months after Gasper's urn was placed in the vault, she could feel her mother's eyes bearing down hard on her weakness. *Imagine, a daughter of mine behavin' like that.* Oughta dry her eyes and get her butt up out of bed. Go scrub the kitchen floor. Volunteer at the hospital. Anything.

She had always known he would go before her, and one day she would be left alone. A woman knows this, just as she knows when she looks down at the babe in her arms, eyes closed and suckling with avid contentment, this child will grow up and leave me and break my heart. Till death do us part. Diamonds are forever, men till they're sixty-five. In her mind she accepted the idea of surviving her husband, but her heart had never let it in, that it would happen to her just like everyone else, that the sun would rise one day and glare in through the window, shining indifferently into her eyes and onto the bed that he would never warm again.

It was comforting to think, though, that each time he fell, he was a little closer to heaven.

"Your daddy was always so good to me," she recalled fondly. "When he was courtin' me he used to bring me a nice beaucoup of flowers every Friday. The first year we was married he was so sweet I coulda ate him up. The second year I wished I had."

The years passed, and Simpson would remember Dad in odd moments, as when stuck in traffic near a parking lot or a concrete overpass, or when he heard the phrase

4-F. He was irked at the seemingly inappropriate occasions, too often bleak and empty. The involuntary associations—happening to think of Gasper when he smelled a dime store or passed a crumbling brick warehouse—affronted his sense of propriety and detracted from the dignity he wanted for his father. You never know what's going to remind you of a dead parent.

I wish he was still alive so I could tell him I know I'm a failure. But he knows I haven't given up yet.

It wasn't up for viewing in any museum of art, but there was an installation, a three-dimensional tableau displayed in an interior gallery of Simpson's imagination. The first time he saw the room was in a dream during a nap one weekend afternoon, a deep plummeting sleep from which he awoke feeling turned around and vacuumed out, with a sense that massive currents of time had passed. He sat up, rubbed his eyes, still seeing an old man, his father but not his father, bald and gray in a sleeveless undershirt, loosened suspender straps limp beside him on the small bed or cot where he sits in a small, sparsely furnished cell in a single room occupancy hotel, gazing out the grimy, pigeon-shit-flecked window across littered blacktop tenement roofs and TV antennas toward an orange sun low in the western sky. Was this old man someone his father might have been, in a city where he might have lived? It felt like him, but it could be anyone's father, or perhaps someone who had never had a family and lived to be an old man in a city where the sun is setting and no one knows he's alive.

8

It's Never Too Late to
Have a Happy Childhood

ONCE THERE WAS A FRIEND. But where are they when
you need them? They always let you down, leave you for
cooler kids, for girls, forgetting how you listened when
no one else would talk with them. The sensitive secrets
you once confided, they turn and use against you, or flush
them. Or they just walk away and go it alone, as solitary
as you.

Get used to it. Big boys don't cry.

But what kind of friend is it who runs when you need
a comrade, then never looks you in the eye again? What
becomes of all the talks you used to have, the shared
understanding? File under "lost friend." Then lose the
folder. Burn it. Ten, twenty, thirty years pass and if you're
lucky you forget he ever existed.

I have no need of friendship; friendship causes pain . . .

As the years passed, Simpson tended not to think
much about that time in his life, so on the rare occasions
when he happened to recall his former friend it came
as a surprise that they'd ever known each other. It was
not that he deliberately repressed the memory, but that
whole period around seventh grade was like a hazardous

243

waste site where nothing could ever grow again, at best an abandoned street where no one lived anymore. What few recollections occurred to him were usually prompted by some fleeting sensory impression—a sound or color, a scent on a breeze—or sometimes by seeing S. Peters on a street sign in the Quarter.

"I'm sorry about your little friend, honey," said Mother, "but you still have me and Daddy." She touched under his chin. "You still have Bartholomew."

He was stunned. Was she serious?

She added helpfully, "At the end of the day, family's all you can really count on."

He had heard this line before, but he had never thought of it as applying to his own. He nodded with a bitter sense of resignation that he would never find another friend to replace the one whose name he was already forgetting. Was it even worth looking?

Avoiding her eyes, he muttered "yeah" just to make her stop talking. Every adolescent knows parents don't understand. How could they?

When you're eleven, twelve, thirteen, you need someone outside your immediate nuclear unit you can open up to, a trusted friend who won't laugh when you let down your guard and talk about troubles, worries, or things you'd like to do someday.

As he thought about it later, Simpson figured he had had about a year of friendship with Steve, a kind of brotherhood of his own choosing, sharing private thoughts, secrets now lost, forgotten. He might have talked about wanting to be a writer someday . . . or maybe that all came afterward.

He was drawn to Steven Peters because he was talented, different. He could draw anything: cool rockets and flying saucers, robots, fantastic, otherworldly trees with intricately detailed branches above and below ground. As Simpson pored with admiration over his friend's portfolio, he could see Steve one day being a draftsman for General Motors or an aerospace firm, or an illustrator for science books or *National Geographic*. Without quite articulating it in these terms, he could sense, with one lonely child's understanding of another, that only someone who had spent a lot of time by himself could have developed his talent to such a refined degree at this young age.

Some of the other guys at school were less impressed. Simpson once defended Steve when a big seventh-grader called him a Tinker Bell. "That's not true," he said at once. The boy pushed him back against the locker and his head struck the hard steel doors. "Let your pussy friend take up for himself, if he's man enough." Some months later, a classmate said it was just as well Simpson wasn't spending time anymore with "that artsy little fairy." Some of the guys had suspected they were a couple and hinted that Simpson probably missed Stevie's little peter.

That was nonsense. They were just friends like any other normal seventh-graders. They talked while making model cars and airplanes together. They had sleepovers a few times on Friday nights, until Melba put an end to it. She could not rest easy knowing that the clock was striking midnight with her child under someone else's roof, even though the friend lived only five blocks away and she had Mrs. Peters's phone number in case of emergency. Melba phoned around 8:30 P.M. and asked if everything was all right. Everything's fine. Simpson wasn't homesick, was he? Did he eat his dinner? Mrs. Peters assured her all was well. "He's perfectly happy. He ate every bite, and now they're in there watching *Lost in Space* and *Twilight Zone* reruns." When Simpson came home the next day he sensed he must have hurt his mother's feelings by wanting to stay at a friend's house and not being homesick. He felt strangely guilty, but what had he done wrong? Did she perceive with a mother's intuition that he wished the Peterses would adopt him? They had a color TV and better air conditioners, and Steve had his own bedroom with a little corner studio with a good drawing table and lamp. "Yeah," said Steve, "but your mom's chocolate chip cookies are better." When Simpson was invited to stay over again a few weeks later, Melba said she didn't think these sleepovers were really such a good idea. Steve was welcome to stay at their house, though, if he wanted. She worried about Simpson being away in case of an emergency. What kind of emergency? he asked, picturing a yellow and black fallout shelter sign. Anyway, she claimed, Bartholomew had cried all night because he missed his big brother. When Simpson checked on this, little brother said he should go to Steve's more often; he liked having his parents all to himself.

"Call if you get lost." Her callous words chafed his sensitive ears. What if he called without getting lost? What if he got lost but didn't call? The day was bright and clear, a little cooler than the last time she sent him out job-hunting. High in the sky the white cumulonimbus cloud stacks glowed like the battlements of heaven, a mighty fortress. If Bartholomew had actually wanted to find a job, he might have taken the clouds' brilliance and majesty as a positive sign. Instead he grumbled impatiently and rocked from foot to foot, partly wishing the bus would hurry but mostly hoping it would never come.

When at last a city bus wheezed to a stop, he climbed aboard and with a dramatic sigh seated himself across two front seats reserved for handicapped and elderly passengers. The drivers allowed Bartholomew to sit in those seats because of his size; even when the bus was crowded, passengers never objected, for they assumed at a glance that he must be handicapped in some way.

He pulled Mother's job-search list from his shirt pocket and scowled at his prospects—usually he liked going to the public library—then looked out the window as the bus passed the old two-story wooden houses along Elysian Fields that were either filled with several families or boarded up and home to no one. Built in the last century for prosperous families long since departed, they appeared occupied mainly by children playing in the dirt front yards in the shade of the oaks and by adults sitting on front-porch chairs and sofas. The houses looked unpainted since the original coat, and the inside rooms' wallpapers were torn, scorched, rain-stained. But he was only imagining, based on the outsides: he had never set foot in any of these homes and never would. The city was largely unknown to him, all the backstreets behind the main avenues, the houses and people and trees and corner shops. Was heaven like this, too, full of untraveled neighborhoods? At a stoplight, he observed two boys about ten years old sitting at a card table in a front yard shaded by a live oak, working intently on some electronic model or radio set while loud music throbbed from a car parked nearby. The hood was up, and from underneath the engine protruded a man's legs beside an open toolbox.

He had to change buses downtown, then stepped off for the New Orleans Public Library at the broad, busy corner of Loyola and Tulane. He watched a man at a stoplight walking from car to car with a begging cup and a broken-off rearview mirror, turning the glass so the drivers could see their reflections as they said yes or no. As the bus drove away, Bartholomew straightened his shirt and brushed down his hair as though to calm his nerves, agitated by the city's noise and commotion. He pushed through the library's glass doors past the security guard and the firearms detector and walked up to the front desk.

"Where do I go to get a job?" He was breathing heavy.

A thin elderly woman behind the checkout desk positioned her eyeglasses to get a better look at him. His sweaty blond hair was wet against his forehead, his shirt was untucked in back and tight across his belly above the off-center belt buckle, and his brown pants had slipped a bit down his hips. The cuffs drooped over his large black shoes, the edges soiled and stepped on.

"Just go up to Personnel on the third floor and fill out an application. You can take the elevator right there, baby."

"Thank you," he said earnestly. "I need a job because my mother's sick and—"

"Good luck. The door's open," she pointed to the elevator. "Third floor."

Bartholomew approached the Personnel office looking like he'd walked a long way through many rain puddles to get there. He stood straight at attention and announced, in a loud voice that made his intended politeness sound imperious, "I would like to apply for a job."

A tall red-haired librarian smiled up at him and inquired calmly, "As a page? Shelving books, that kind of thing?"

Bartholomew sighed gratefully and relaxed a little. "Yes ma'am, thank you." He didn't know what kind of position to ask for. "I'm a good reader, you know. When I start a book I finish it."

She gave him an application and a sharpened pencil and led him out to one of the tables in the reading room. Bartholomew huffed and sweated over the form, unself-consciously making noises of annoyance and perturbation—"Some of these questions!" he exclaimed more than once—and the readers sitting near him raised eyebrows at each other.

The librarian accepted his rough-scrawled application, noting several places where his hard pressure on the pencil had punctured the form, and said with regrets that the library was not hiring for paid positions at the moment, "but in the meantime you know we can always use volunteers—"

"Oh, no ma'am," he objected, backing away. "I have to be paid money. I need—" He was still backing up when he tripped over a footstool and crashed back against a tall gray bookcase. The force of his weight propelled it against the next row and the next with terrible thundering clashes of steel on steel, and soon a half dozen heavy bookcases loaded with thousands of volumes were toppling like dominoes, possibly squashing innocent lives. The loud crashing set off alarms and sirens that clanged and wailed. The room was in a panic as mothers screamed and librarians rushed to see whether any patrons were crushed under the tons of books.

"Oh mercy!" cried Bartholomew, picking himself up off the floor. He patted his chest and wiped his face, all in a flutter. "Oh, chaos and catastrophe! Pandemonium!"

"You have to go," said the librarian.

Staff members were appearing from all corners of the library, expecting the worst.

"Please." The librarian pressed her palm on Bartholomew's back. *"Just go."*

Then he was standing on the sidewalk at Loyola and Tulane, scratching his head. Mother would say go on to the next place, but he wasn't going to press his luck. Know when to fold 'em, Father always said. He turned back toward Canal Street and Decatur to catch the 55 Elysian Fields.

He was just nearing the corner of Baronne and Common when he almost collided with his brother darting out of a travel agency onto the sidewalk.

"Bartholomew!"

"Simpson!"

"What brings you here?"

"What were you doing in there? Going somewhere?"

"Nowhere, just fantasizing." Simpson slipped the ticket in his back pocket. "What a surprise seeing you on Baronne Street. Have you ever been here before in your life?"

"I was applying for a job. At the New Orleans Public Library." He pronounced each word with reverent precision in his radio voice. "Don't be surprised if I get it."

"That's great! Good luck. What position?"

Bartholomew blinked quickly and his lips moved. His eyes flashed from side to side. "As a page. Shelving books."

He leaned around Simpson and looked at the ticket in his pocket. "Why aren't you at work?"

"You've never seen where I work, have you? Come on, I'll show you. It's just down the block. Tell me about the library. That sounds great."

"I made a little mistake, though. I knocked over some books."

"Well, that can't be too bad, can it? Knocking over some books? I'm sure it happens all the time."

Scanning the sidewalk ahead with nervous watchful eyes, Bartholomew tugged at Simpson's arm to make him walk slower. Such commotion! So many people! This was why he never came downtown.

Even as he slowed his pace, Simpson noticed, Bartholomew continued to hold on to his elbow like a handrail.

"This is it?"

"This is CopyQwik. Want to come in?"

"No." He shrank back, then came forward to shade his eyes and peer in through the window. "Isn't it frightfully loud?"

"Sometimes, in the back, runnin' the big boys, but the computers are very quiet. They whisper. Come see."

Bartholomew looked down at his hands fidgeting in front of his belly. "Okay, just a quick peek. Mother says this place is being bought out."

"Looks that way. Some accountant-types were in here yesterday looking at the books."

Simpson opened the door and let his brother go first.

No sooner had he entered than he was surprised by his financial adviser smiling and reaching for his hand. "Hey, big spender! Haven't seen you in a dog's age. Where you been, O.J., out spendin' all your mama's money?" He laughed and slapped Simpson's arm. "Just kidding!"

Simpson gasped and gave a weak, queasy smile.

"Hi. Bill Price," said the man, reaching to shake hands.

"Bartholomew Weems," he said, not deigning to look at him, and pronouncing his name with a dignified air, as though he were Bartholomew, Lord Weems.

"My brother," Simpson explained. Somehow it was hard to get the words out.

While he talked to Bill Price, with his back turned and arms folded across his chest, Bartholomew with light fingers slipped the ticket out of his back pocket and read the destination and the date.

"Well, look, y'all," said Simpson, "I really should get back to work."

When Bill Price was gone, Bartholomew asked, "What did he mean about Mother's money?"

"Oh, he's such a joker. It's just that he's not always in the office when I bring by a deposit."

Bartholomew pretended to understand what Simpson meant.

"I have to go," he said. "Here, this fell out of your pocket."

"Jesus, Barto!" Simpson snatched the ticket with alarm. "Did you look at it?"

"At what?"

"It's just a possible itinerary, anyway." He fanned himself with the ticket and assumed a cool, nonchalant pose. "You know how to get home okay?"

"Fifty-five Elysian Fields at Decatur Street. I know. I know."

"Call if you get lost."

Bartholomew stepped out to the sidewalk and immediately the fumes in the air and the sounds of a car alarm set off by a rumbling delivery truck and two taxis honking at each other assailed his senses and threw him into a panic.

"It's too much noise!" he wailed, backing up and waving his arms wildly. "There weren't this many cars and trucks before. I can't—." He screamed, "I don't know where I am!"

"Ssshhh, it's okay, Barto." Simpson patted his back reassuringly. "Come on back inside. I'll call you a taxi. Calm, now. Take deep breaths—that's what I do."

He phoned United Cab, and paid the driver in advance with a generous tip to take Bartholomew straight home. It did not occur to him to ask his brother to pay his own fare.

Ten minutes later his nerves were still jittery.

If he tells Mom about that ticket I'll tear his tongue out.

On the Sunday after the surprise run-in on Baronne Street, Simpson was leaning against the kitchen counter with a glass of iced tea, supervising as his mother separated his laundry into two piles. He clucked his tongue as she tossed a beige shirt among the whites. He picked it up and tossed it onto the correct pile.

"Aren't you particular," she said.

"Where's Tiny?"

"Out back at Puppy's grave. You know it's the anniversary." She pulled off her glasses and wiped her face with one of Simpson's socks.

"Of course. How could I forget?"

He had more important things to keep track of than the death date of a stray mutt buried decades ago. It was beyond his comprehension how Barto could fixate on and memorialize in perpetuity such brief moments in his distant past. He gets stuck in these little air pockets of time.

Maybe it wasn't the past.

Puppy was a young brown and white terrier mix who appeared in the Weemses's yard one morning and lived with them for a few weeks until he died for no good reason. Bartholomew loved Puppy with all his heart. He used to carry him around on his shoulder and feed him chocolates from Mother's Valentine's candy box. Puppy slept with Bartholomew every night, cuddled up against his large warm master.

One morning Bartholomew awoke but Puppy lay still, his spotted little body cool and stiffening on the white sheets. He pulled a hat box from Mother's closet shelf. The closet smelled of cedar and mothballs, old and clean, like her dresses. He opened the hat box and put Puppy inside, curled up in the cardboard drum, and lay pink tissue paper over him. He went with the box and a shovel to the backyard.

A while later, he was sitting on the cast-iron bench beside Puppy's new grave near the plastic Kmart garden fountain.

Father stepped outside and closed the door behind him.

"What'chya doing, son?"

Gasper struck a match and held it up to the pipeful of moist fragrant Borkum Riff tobacco. He was dressed for the occasion in his faded yellow bathrobe and brown pom-pom–tasseled slippers. "Burying your old *TV Guide*s? Ashes of my paystubs?" It was an old joke.

Bartholomew turned around. His eyes were wet with tears. "Puppy's with Jesus now."

"Aw, I'm real sorry to hear that." Gasper didn't know what else to say. He waved his arms limply and shrugged. Gasper stood there on the porch for a long time, just smoking, looking up at the trees. Then he tamped out his pipe on a brick and went back inside.

He didn't sound sorry. He didn't even ask how it happened.

Bartholomew visited the grave every Sunday. He envisioned Puppy walking with the Lord in green pastures beside clear waters where Jesus tends his flock by day. He would be a good shepherd's dog. Bartholomew could see the Lord throwing a stick to fetch. The bright eager terrier eyes would sparkle as Puppy dashed and retrieved and kept coming back for more till Jesus' arm got tired. Okay, Puppy, that's enough. And Jesus might have to perform a miracle to make the stick disappear just so Puppy would stop.

Now Simpson closed the door behind him. The ice cubes clicking in his tea glass shattered Bartholomew's inner peace. He pulled the plugs from his ears and said, in as exasperated a tone as he could pinch out, "*What*?!"

Simpson shrugged indifferently, tilted back for a sip of tea, and eyed the gray clouds approaching from the northwest. Their shapes were familiar. Something was going to happen.

"Just sayin' hello. Thought I'd come outside and jangle your nerves while your Mommy does my clothes."

And see if you've forgotten about that plane ticket.

Bartholomew frowned suspiciously. Every word out of Simpson's mouth had to be carefully weighed for its sarcastic content. When his voice sounded friendly he was actually being mean, with code words. But sometimes when he said nasty things like "jangle your nerves" he actually meant it nice.

"Mom says you've been wearing earplugs since you came back from downtown."

No reply.

"Hey, I had an idea I thought you might like for your birthday. You've heard me mention Button Menendez, my artist friend from LSU?"

"No."

"Well, I saw her recently, and she mentioned she's teaching a watercolor class at Delgado in the afternoons. Small classes, casual atmosphere, and you can pretty much paint anything you like."

Bartholomew was picking at a scab on his elbow, pretending not to listen.

"You know I'm always thinking about you, Bartholomew, and I remembered those paper towel sketches you made with your colored pens. And, I thought you might like to get out and meet people, maybe make some friends."

Smoldering nerves. They were always trying to improve him or destroy him, same thing. Like that time at the doctor's office when the nurse acted like she had permission to try to help him off with his undershirt, and her hand accidentally touched his bare stomach. With a sudden involuntary reflex he popped her back across the examining table. He said he was sorry; she was more frightened than hurt. People and their help. They promised milk but it came out like rat poison.

Sweat was breaking out on Bartholomew's red face and forehead.

"You think I need therapy! What I need is peace and quiet. Rest and prayer."

Rest? Simpson thought. From what, eating ice cream?

"Don't blow your manhole cover, Barto. It's just an idea. Your birthday's coming up, and I thought—"

"But you're gonna be in San Francisco on my birthday."

"No, no," Simpson assured him with strained calm. "Like I said, that was just a possible itinerary, like, theoretically. I'm not going anywhere. Or the Fish Tank. You said you wanted to go to the Aquarium of the Americas sometime."

"I said that to Mother. Stop trying to improve me. You're the one who needs treatment, Simp. She and I talk about this all the time and she agrees."

"Right. Okay. Never mind."

Simpson waved him off in hopeless exasperation and turned toward the house.

"Wait, Simpson, were you really thinking about my birthday?"

Melba moved from the kitchen window where she had been rubbing Jergens moisturizing lotion on her hands while watching her sons interacting in the back-yard. Those two. What would become of them?

"Simpson, honey, I—"

Without even looking at her Simpson ghosted through the kitchen and back to his old bedroom and lay down on the single bed still covered with a blue rockets-and-astronauts bedspread. His eyes went blank on the same old ceiling he had gazed on for nearly forty years. The walls were hung with pictures of cowboys and Indians and race car drivers—oppressive pictographs of an archaic, vintage type of masculinity that had always felt childish and foreign to him. On a card table near the window was the empty aquarium where his lizards used to live. Dead gray gravel and a smooth piece of driftwood covered in dust. The only relics in his room worth keep-ing were a silver-framed, black-and-white portrait of his grandparents, Gramp and Verna Flora Cremiere, and his old spelling bee trophy. The trophy was of the kind given to winners in debate and oratory: a gold-painted plastic figure of an orator at a lectern, hand upraised. What was the word he had spelled correctly? And what was the quotable remark that had impressed Mimi?

Could the word have been "fratricide"?

If he tells her, I swear, I'll . . .

His earliest memory of contemplating fratricide was when he was about eight and Bartholomew five, one Saturday afternoon when the boys were brought along on a shopping trip to the old Krauss Department Store on Canal Street. Mother wanted to shop for curtains and curtain rods, and she wanted Father to look with her because he (or some neighbor whose help he obtained) would be installing them.

"Simpson, go take your brother to the pets department to see the bunny rabbits. Show him the puppies. We'll meet y'all there."

Reluctantly he took his brother's puffy hand and led him away.

"Look at the bunnies," he said sullenly. "Cute, huh?"

"I want to pet one," Bartholomew said, eyeing the beautiful soft fur. He had that look in his eyes. He would scream and roll around on the floor till he got his hands on a bunny. "I want to *pet* one!"

"Okay, okay. I'll try to find somebody. Just wait here for a minute."

Simpson walked up and down the aisles of fish tanks and bird cages, getting dizzy with the smells of Hartz processed pet food and cedar shavings, but he didn't see a store clerk. He turned a corner and saw an amazing sight: a large tank filled with weak coffee–colored water, murky as the Mississippi. Then he saw several grayish brown water snakes twisting and swimming with cool malevolence through the dark water.

"People in England eat them ugly things," said a man behind him in a loud, somewhat raw voice whose accent was not from the city. The man wore the familiar brown vest that identified him as a floor clerk. His eyes were pale gray and his mustache was black. "Yep, jellied eels. No wonder they talk about mad dogs and Englishmen. 'Cept these here are *electric* eels, from the Amazon. Know

260

your geography? What country's the Amazon River in? Quick." He snapped his fingers sharply.

"Uh, Brazil?"

"It's in *South America*," the man announced authoritatively. "Yep. They got all kind of bizarre water creatures down there. Like the bottom of the ocean, them strange fluorescent deep-sea fish nobody ever seen."

"Did you say electric? They can shock you?"

"Shock the hell out of you, boy. Fry you up good. Don't touch. Ought to take some of these Death Row sons of bitches up in Angola and plunk 'em right in."

A scream tore at them from several aisles away. Simpson and the clerk rushed over to find Bartholomew sitting fatly on the floor near the bunny cage, his meaty fists clenched and his thick lips poised to scream again.

"What in God's name?" the man said. "You okay, son?"

"It's just my brother. He wants to pet one of the bunnies. Is it okay?"

"If he don't scream about it he can. Sounds like he's bein' gutted."

"He screams all the time."

"Yeah? Somebody ought to pop some sense into that boy. I mean discipline. Where's y'all's mama 'n' daddy?"

"Over in curtains." Simpson pointed across the store.

The man looked at Bartholomew dubiously, then unlocked the rabbit cage and let him move in closer to touch the bunny's soft warm fur.

"Mmmm," the boy said, as though savoring an exquisite chocolate. "Mmmm."

The man frowned and stepped back.

"You like that fur, eh, kid?" he snickered.

Simpson edged away and returned to the eel tank. He watched the gray-brown voltage units slithering along the bottom of the tank. Would he be shocked if he touched the glass?

When Bartholomew was satisfied, the man put the bunny back with the others and Simpson led his brother by the hand to see the interesting eels.

Bartholomew was fascinated too. He pressed his face and palms against the glass.

"You can see 'em better from above," said Simpson. "Here, I'll lift you up so you can see."

He put his hands under his brother's arms and strained to lift him. He could only hold Bartholomew up for a few seconds: he weighed over a hundred pounds.

Simpson glanced around for a stool or ladder of some kind.

"Here, why don't you try to climb up when I lift you—"

"Oh, there you are," said Melba. "Gasper, they're over here. Whatch'yall looking at? Oooh, how frightful. Did you find the bunnies, Bartholomew?"

That was his chance. He had tried. Never quick or strong enough.

A golden shaft of sunlight glowed on the spelling bee trophy. What *was* the word he had spelled right? Any clue would help.

The eel tank at Krauss was only the earliest occasion when Simpson could recall scheming to eliminate his brother. In his mind, Bartholomew was at least partly to blame for their father's demise. Gasper's near-fatal fall from the toilet had happened only weeks after he became, by grace of the Louisiana Lottery, a man of wealth. The winnings were usually in the millions. The Weems family was not quite so fortunate as that, but they had no complaints when Gasper's take, after taxes, would be about a hundred thousand dollars. Melba was so astonished she couldn't speak for a whole day. Instead she cooked a big roast beef dinner to celebrate, humming to herself with great spirit, pausing only to call Simpson home from school double-quick. He was stunned; he'd always believed the comedian Fran Lebowitz had it right, that your chances of winning the lottery were the same whether you played or not. But lo, what a shrewd investor the old man turned out to be, laying down that wager at Sammy Tong's grocery down the street. Simpson instantly began to calculate the varieties of freedom now possible. He did not want things for himself, or not much, anyway; the principal benefit would be an interest-bearing savings account and investments to provide for Melba and Bartholomew after Gasper passed on. Then he would be at liberty to go to California guilt-free.

Bartholomew saw things differently. He listened with increasing suspicion and revulsion as his mother and father and brother chattered and congratulated each other on their good fortune. There was greed in their voices, greed and avarice as they huddled together over a yellow notepad at the breakfast bar and kept interrupting each other with new additions to the wish list. Their expectations were appalling. He would have to act quickly, before things got really out of hand.

It is written that thou shalt not gamble. He distinctly remembered having read that commandment some-where. Church teaching. It was sin money.

The first thing Gasper did was go straight to Doerr's Furniture and pick out a nice new sofa for Melba, broad-cushioned, upholstered in a rich pattern of brown and orange paisley. The delivery men, on their last deliv-ery of the day, found themselves helping the Weems family rearrange their house, as Bartholomew claimed the old sofa for his room, then decided that as long as they were shifting things around, he wanted the entire master bedroom too. While Gus and Larry ate choco-late cake at the breakfast bar, Bartholomew talked his parents into letting him have their bedroom. Mother and Father, elated by their good fortune, did not mind; anyway, they knew he wouldn't hesitate to throw a full-blown screamer in front of the nice delivery men, so they let him have his way. With the lottery check on the kitchen counter, not yet deposited, Gasper felt wealthy, and generously tipped the men a whole extra dollar each to move their bedroom furniture into Bartholomew's room and his into theirs. Bartholomew supervised the movers, standing in the hall with his hips brushing the walls and directing from the doorway. "Mommy, why don't you bake these nice movin' men another chocolate cake instead of just standing there? We're working hard."

After the rooms had been swapped and he was seated comfortably on the old sofa in his master bedroom—all the more at ease because Gus and Larry had also moved his ULTIMA-KOOL air conditioner into the room for him—Bartholomew remembered that the lottery check was still sin money, gotten without honest labor. It is written that thou shalt not gamble, nor profit grossly in disproportion to thy labors. That night, while his family slept, he stood at the stove and held the check over the blue gas flame. They would thank him for this.

"Thou shalt not gamble," he quoted the next morning as everyone stood in shock around the stovetop. A few charred bits of check paper remained among the ashes.

"Wait, where is that written?" Simpson demanded. "Show me the chapter and verse."

"It's in there. It's in there."

"Show me. Come on, you know your way around that book like it's your bedroom. Show me the words."

"What were we going to do?" Bartholomew burst out. "Were we going to welcome sin money into our house and rejoice in it with no mention of the Provider from whom all blessings flow?"

"But I said 'thank God' a thousand times," Melba protested.

"But you didn't mean it. You didn't *feel* it."

"I think we all felt something," said Gasper.

"The Lord is my shepherd," Bartholomew announced. "I shall not want."

Simpson cut him a look that could slit a throat, hating him for his gross stupidity and utter lack of any practical sense.

"Yeah, we'll see if you're still saying that twenty years from now—if you're still alive."

Bartholomew's eyes went wide.

Their car was in the repair shop getting a new transmission made possible by the lottery money, so Gasper brought Bartholomew along with him on a bus ride downtown to the lottery office to help him explain the situation to the authorities, who turned out to be a solitary customer service representative in a cramped, off-white room.

It was an accident, a simple misunderstanding.

Sweating with desperation, Gasper mopped at his neck and forehead with his handkerchief.

"Just tell the lady, son. Explain her what happened."

All Bartholomew had to say, once again, was the simple truth that the lottery check was sin money and it was his responsibility, *if no one else would take it*, he intoned provocatively, to reject it as unclean. " 'Burn away the impurities,' saith the Lord."

She nodded sympathetically. "Some would say there's truth in that."

"Yeah," Gasper pleaded, "but he don't mean it. Can't we have another chance? We won't burn it this time, I promise. Please?" His voice rose, or regressed, to the whine of a six-year-old.

Bartholomew glowered straight ahead at the dead pale wall.

The customer service representative explained that, regrettably, as a matter of fact, it was not possible to disburse a replacement in a case where the winner or a member of the winner's family deliberately destroyed or caused to be destroyed the original and only existing certificate of redemption.

"Certificate of redemption," Bartholomew echoed with loud contempt.

She smiled and folded her hands together. "We thank you for coming in to share your concerns with us, Mr. Weems, and again we want to stress that every care has been taken to assure your complete satisfaction."

She stood, smiling graciously, and extended her hand in a gesture of professional goodwill.

Gasper was too astonished to do anything but obey and rise to shake hands with her and be dismissed.

On the bus ride home he sat in a daze, absently wringing the sweat from his handkerchief.

He looked at his son. "What happened back there?"

Then, a minute later, "I don't understand. I don't understand."

Bartholomew stared out the window at the houses passing by. In every window, through every door, down all these streets, everyone was sinning, in one way or another. It was inescapable.

"Do we get to keep the sofa?"

Gasper burst into tears, sobbing and moaning in broad daylight on the 55 Elysian Fields.

The brief apparition of a hundred thousand dollars had promised to change everything, and the thought of all the good it could have provided, only to go up in flames . . . It really was too bad. And the policy, that incomprehensible fine print that obscured more than it explained why the check once destroyed was irredeemable and irreplaceable—the family was baffled. Even Simpson with his college education couldn't figure it out. As time passed, Gasper came to look upon the loss with a measure of stoicism and good-natured acceptance of life's surprising turns of fortune, but there were moments when he had to pray hard for forbearance in order not to burn with wrath and resentment. Forgive and try to forget. He had to remind himself that Bartholomew truly believed he was doing it for the Lord.

But that money, it sure could have helped out.

"The Lord helps them who help themselves," said Bartholomew with his mouth full. "Mother, pass the sweet potatoes."

"Did you ever stop to think, Bartholomew," she said, her voice shaking with anger, "that maybe the lottery check came *from* the Lord? Maybe He was blessin' us."

He took the bowl and heaped his plate, savoring the sweet fragrant steam.

"Negative," he stated flatly. "Because the money's cursed. No blessing but only misery comes from tainted coin. Thou shalt earn thy bread by the sweat of thy brow."

"I don't see no sweat on your brow."

That night she stood a long time at her dresser, reading and rereading the helpful hints. Shine with good cheer. Lay up riches for yourself in heaven, etc.

It was late afternoon, near dusk as Simpson was walking home with his basket of washed and folded laundry. The wind was blowing in from the northwest, cooling the air by ten degrees in just a few hours, and the sky was orange in the west. A feeling of winter. Most of the live oaks had now shed their leaves; unlike other trees, the great, wide-reaching giants held their covering through year's end, as though too dignified to go naked through the holidays, and only let their foliage fall in January and February when spring was near. He stopped mid-way across the wooden bridge from where he could see the fountain statue of the weeping maiden, a slender graceful long-robed Greek virgin with head tilted back in an attitude of grief, the back of her hand raised to her forehead, and in her left hand a vase tilted down, emptying an endless stream of tears into the fountain's cast-iron bowl. About thirty feet behind her stood the black tree of Dangers Park, austere and desolate against the evening sky, scorched stumps on a blackened trunk, the bare ruined oak lightning-blasted years ago. He stared at the gaunt silhouette against the orange-red sky, then down at its reflection in the fiery water beneath the bridge. His fingertips on the railing traced the letters of names and obscenities carved into the wood, some recent and others time-worn like the inscriptions on St. Perpetua's tombs.

This was where it happened one bright spring afternoon. At that time there were no slides or swings in

Dangers Park—those would come later—but every day on the way to school they used to pass through this oak and cypress park and cross the bayou bridge. For a long time after the incident, he had been unable to think about anything else, like an earthquake survivor still rattled by aftershocks for months, years. Periodically, unexpectedly, he would feel it all again, the sharp all-killing pain that had blasted like lightning between his legs.

All because of an innocent question he asked one day at school.

"Why does Cutter wear those ugly old boots?" he had asked a fellow seventh-grader at recess. "They're so . . . klunky."

He didn't necessarily expect an answer; he didn't even know the kid. It was only an idle observation, just something to say to a fellow outsider to pass the time. The black military boots looked utterly awkward and graceless, and he couldn't understand why anyone would voluntarily wear such heavy ugly things. Cutter Kline liked to swing around a pole near the stairwell at the end of a row of lockers and do a wild Tarzan yell, and it was hard to see how he could do this day after day while wearing those boots.

The next day after lunch Simpson and his friend Steve Peters were leaning against a wall in the shade, reading comic books, when suddenly his *Superman* was torn out of his hands. An iron claw gripped his throat and a knee pressed hard into his groin.

"You had a question about my boots?"

About a half dozen other boys gathered around him. Simpson did not notice, but it was at about this point that Steve slipped away.

He gulped and realized he was about to die.

Nick Kline, who liked to be called Cutter, was a tall and muscular seventh-grader who would have been in ninth grade had he not been held back. There was a malevolent voltage about him, and a terrifying reputation; even the teachers dared not cross him. An assistant principal who once tried to stop Cutter from doing his Tarzan wild-man swing around the pole later found his car tires deflated, the battery missing. Kline's sharp eyebrows and nose and jaw looked hard, steel-boned; his face looked like it could smash blocks of ice. His black hair was wavy and wet, or just oily, and roughly brushed back with a rake of his fingers, Elvis-style. In his back right pocket he kept a black leather glove. When he smiled, his teeth were perfect, though shreds of meat stuck in the spaces between. He was handsome in a brutal way, and his good looks made his famous temper all the more terrifying. What frightened everyone was not only Cutter Kline's physical power but the stories of his random violence and hair-trigger mean streak. They said he'd been expelled from another school for slicing off half of a kid's ear for looking at him wrong.

"You were asking about my boots? I'm *talking* to you, pussyboy."

His knee pressed harder. He said in a close, confidential tone, "If you had a question about my boots,

271

Wimpson Seems, why didn't you just come to me?" He sounded disappointed, possibly hurt, and now vindictive, too, that Simpson had not brought his question straight to the authority.

I'm gonna die.

"I'm sorry," Simpson creaked dryly.

Cutter turned to the others. "He's sorry."

They snickered. "A sorry specimen."

"I just wondered—"

"He *wondered*," Kline echoed indignantly. "Weems wondered."

Simpson's neck was tensed and tight as a fist, his eyes squeezed shut, and his heart was beating hard, up and down, back and forth and sideways. It was going to happen at any moment, and he couldn't watch.

"Oh, I feel bad," said Cutter. "Look, pussyboy's crying. Let's go, guys. I'll answer his question later. We can have a special lesson after school."

Simpson opened his eyes, expecting to see them walking away.

Kline was stroking his black leather glove. He pointed down to his boots. "You may kiss them now. The right, then the left. But do *not* let your tears fall on my leather or you will die an ugly death."

Simpson hesitated, not sure if he was serious.

The black glove whipped across his face.

His hand jerked to his cheek, but his spine locked and he couldn't bend.

All the kids on the playground were watching. If any teachers saw, they did not intervene.

"If you don't kiss my boots now, you may do it after school, but it'll hurt so much worse."

Simpson was blubbering now, his body quaking but paralyzed, arms across his thumping chest, hands over his eyes.

"Come on, guys."

They left him.

Everyone was staring.

Only later did he wonder where Stevie Peters had disappeared to.

Not that same afternoon, for that would have been predictable, nor the next day, but three days later, Cutter Kline intercepted him in Dangers Park. Simpson and Steve were coming home from school, walking ahead of Bartholomew, who always shuffled along, deliberately, petulantly slower, to hold his brother back.

"God rewards defenders of the weak," Mother had reminded him that morning, speaking of his brother, knowing nothing about Cutter. Since Bartholomew's earliest days in the cradle, she had taught Simpson that it was his honor and duty as older brother to keep the little one always in sight. Walk him to school, check on him at lunch, and make sure he gets home safely. In winter, before putting on his own coat, Simpson had to see that Bartholomew's was buttoned and his gloves were on. When it rained, he held both their umbrellas so Bartholomew could keep his hands in his raincoat pockets and not catch pneumonia. In the summer at Pontchartrain Beach Simpson had to stay in the shallow end of the pool to make sure Bartholomew didn't drown or lose his temper and get beaten up.

They were walking through the park to the Weemses's house to look at comic books or work on model ships and cars. Simpson had asked Steve to come home with him for the past several days in a row, luring him with offers of Melba's fresh chocolate chip cookies.

They were just approaching the bridge when he heard Bartholomew yelp.

He whirled around and saw Cutter and his boys emerging from the bushes and trees. A few more crawled out from under the bridge. There were nine of them.

"Hey Red!" shouted Kline, hot-faced, already furious. "Where the *fuck* you think you're goin'? Did I say you could cross this bridge, Carrot Top?"

"Huh, did he? Answer him!" shouted a kid with dirty blond hair and charcoal smudges on his cheeks. He looked like a chimney sweep whose head was used to clean ashtrays.

The others joined in, and soon they were all jeering and cussing, waving their arms, acting hyper, hysterical, hepped up on something. They smelled like beer and cigarette smoke.

"Don't talk to my brother like that!" Bartholomew shouted abruptly, surprising everyone. He glared at them all. "My father is a king, and he—"

The boys all howled and hooted with laughter.

Again, Steven Peters disappeared, almost unnoticed.

"A queen, maybe."

"False!" cried Bartholomew. "My father is a king, and he doesn't allow—"

"Someone shut that thing up," Cutter commanded.

Bartholomew screamed, shredding the air, and everyone looked startled.

"I said shut your fat mouth, you screwed-up pig, or I'll stuff a brick in it."

Four of the boys grabbed Bartholomew by the arms and hustled him over to the bridge railing. He weighed over two hundred pounds and was resisting with all his strength, flailing and hollering, so it took all four of them to hold him by the legs over the railing, upside down, while he kicked and shrieked and bellowed. They dropped him and watched him splash in the shallow water. "Beached whale! Ha ha!" He crawled to shore and lay half in, half out of the water, furiously hyperventilating with his face in the weeds, crying and slapping the mud indignantly.

Simpson, shaking with terror, was not in a position to help. He knew what was going to happen, and there was nothing he could do to stop it. He'd heard what Kline and his brethren did to Kip Kidd and Joey Brennan; each boy was out of school for at least a week.

"Tell us you're sorry for bein' such a fag. Hey, where'd his boyfriend go?"

"Wet his panties and ran off."

From behind one of the boys pushed Simpson down to his knees.

"Hey," said the blond chimney sweep, "wasn't it Weems's old lady we saw suckin' off that old Sambo in the alley?"

"Yeah, she was down on her knees givin' that old coon a wang job, waggin' her butt back and forth."

"His daddy was right in there, too, just lickin' his lips, waiting his turn."

"Naw, Gasper likes 'em young," said Slake, a dark-eyed gap-toothed boy. "That why you're so queer, Weems?"

Simpson was glaring up at the accuser, to his right, when Cutter grabbed his face and screamed, "Look at *me*!"

He seemed to be breathing heavier and shaking harder than Simpson. He cocked his foot back and demanded, "Beg me, redhead. *Beg* me not to kick you in the balls. If you even have any."

"I think he's got somethin' else in his panties."

Someone behind Simpson shoved him forward, but Kline snapped him back on his knees.

"You asked about my boots. I wear them because I am *against all fairies* and I stamp out every one I see. But I don't like to have to do that. Now, it's simple. All you do is, apologize for being a faggot. Say, 'I'm sorry I'm such a queer, Master Cutter. Please forgive me.' "

Simpson was shaking so hard he couldn't speak; his heart was pumping its way up into his throat. He couldn't say he was not a faggot, he wouldn't apologize, there was nothing to apologize for. He could not kneel up straight, either; his back and shoulders were rigid with dread and humiliation. He wiped his cheek with the back of his hand.

"Oh, you make me sick."

From behind, someone kicked Simpson in the rear.

"Wimpson," said Cutter, gripping his head in dramatic exaggeration, "you are *not* going to make me watch you cry like a baby."

"He's not a man like us."

"He's not even male."

Cutter pulled the black glove from his pocket and passed it like a tarantula under Simpson's nose.

"Pull down your pants." He said this calmly, disinterestedly, like a physician.

"Don't," Simpson whimpered.

The glove across his cheek stung like it was spiked with needles.

"Weems, your weeping . . ." said Kline in a weary voice. "Tears are for queers. Are you *trying* to make me angry?"

He turned, put his hands on his hips and looked up to the trees around them, sighed loudly, and turned back to his captive.

"Pull down his pants for him, Slake. He's forgotten how."

"His homo daddy usually does it for him."

"Like his mama wipes his butt."

Cutter's foot was swinging back and forth like a scorpion's tail. "You had a question about my klunky boots, and I promised to give you an answer."

Bartholomew had crawled up out of the bayou unnoticed and was sitting behind a bush, with wet mud all over him, clutching his books to his chest like a box of popcorn. It was like watching a movie of a boy kneeling with each elbow gripped by two thugs and another pulling his pants down.

There was a sharp cry, and then Bartholomew heard the impact of the kick between Simpson's legs, like the sound of a watermelon hitting concrete from a ten-foot drop. Simpson howled and doubled over, rolled around, then frightened everyone by fainting.

His eyes were closed, and dirt from the path stuck to his face.

Cutter looked at Slake. "You think he's all right?"

"S'pose he'll live."

"I hate it," said Kline in a voice that sounded like real regret. He put his glove back in his pocket. "I'm innocently walking home from school and some flamin' red-headed Tinker Bell like this tries to flirt and take advantage of me. It was self-defense. Come on, guys. Let's get out of here before he starts to smell."

Chilly and wet and muddy all over, Bartholomew, not knowing what else to do, sat weeping and moaning beside his still, silent brother.

When he came to a half hour later, Simpson felt like a hand grenade had exploded between his legs. The swelling had already started, and his pants felt tight. He limped home, with a hand on Bartholomew's shoulder, and collapsed on the sofa. Melba screamed at the sight of Bartholomew all muddy, then again when she heard what had happened to Simpson. She called Gasper at work, and all four of them drove to the emergency room.

As Simpson slept following surgery, the urologist explained to the parents that the right testicle had had to be removed because it had ruptured from the impact against the bone of the pelvic girdle. The left side was uninjured, so he would be able to have a normal reproductive life. "A shock to the system like this is definitely traumatic, but pretty soon he'll be all right and shouldn't have any lasting damage. Unilateral orchidectomy—that's the removal of a testicle—does not result in hormonal deficit or any crippling aftereffects. The surviving testis will compensate. You can still be grandparents. He's lucky. He could have lost both."

When he awoke hours later, Melba was there to cheer him up. "Honey? The doctor says you're lucky."

9

Already Homesick

AS THE DAY APPROACHED when he would board a plane to resume his exploration of San Francisco, Simpson was nagged by guilt that he had still not told his mother where he was going. The longer he delayed, the harder to explain the late notice. All he wanted was a little time away, a change of scenery—was it really so much to ask? And was he not a grown-up? He shouldn't have to clear his trip with Mommy. Yet no matter how many times he assured himself that he was a mature, independent adult, still the worries like termites gnawed at him that by not telling her beforehand ("not to decide is to decide") he might somehow cause a spell of illness, a hysterical over-reaction to the shocking discovery that her eldest son on whom she depended was more than two thousand miles away. She wasn't getting any younger, and these short-ness of breath episodes worried him—not only that they were happening but that she kept mentioning them, for she was not normally one to complain, and now she was thinking about a will. What if there was an emergency? All he wanted was to be in San Francisco for a week. Or forever. Did it have to be so difficult?

Gordon Krebs, the director of Lourdes Funeral Home, welcomed Simpson into his office and offered him a Coke from a little cooler housed in a coffin of polished mahogany. Even seated in his leather-upholstered executive chair, with a backdrop of wine-red curtains and framed certificates on the wood-paneled wall, dark-suited Mr. Krebs appeared eminently tall, like the statue of Lincoln at the memorial in Washington, with a long and craggy face of a ruddy complexion that resembled the bark of a redwood. His voice sounded deep and sepulchral, as though echoing in a hollow mausoleum of granite or marble. But although his demeanor was serious and formal, he spoke warmly of Melba, and expressed his regrets about the unfortunate, untimely passing of Gasper. Simpson was impressed that after more than a decade he still remembered the month and year of the funeral.

"I'm going to see Dad's old taxidermy partner later this afternoon to see if I can tickle his memory about Gasper. Next to Mom, he probably knew Dad better than anybody."

Simpson gestured to the coffin cooler with a curious expression.

"It was a promotional item from one of our vendors. You wouldn't believe some of the things they give out. Let's see, I believe the last time you and I saw each other was at your mother's retirement party."

Simpson smiled at the vision of Bartholomew with his cone-shaped party hat, tooting the little party horn in between servings of chocolate cake.

"Yes," he recalled. "Bartholomew kept complaining about the air-conditioning, whining 'It's burning up in here!' " Spots of perspiration darkened his Xtra-Xtra-large T-shirt printed with the legend NOT PERFECT, JUST FORGIVEN.

"And you said if he was really that uncomfortable, he could go down to the freezer in the morgue, and that cooled him off real quick."

They chuckled and sipped their soft drinks.

"He's got two air conditioners in his bedroom. I guess he has a lot of body surface area to cool. Now, seriously, Mr. Krebs, please don't repeat any of this if you happen to see my mother. She and Bartholomew are kind of in denial about this, but I'm going to be moving to California soon, I hope, and I just want to make sure everything's taken care of and there won't be any surprises about her pension and burial policy. Not that we're expecting to use it any time soon, of course, though she has complained once or twice lately about shortness of breath. But you know my mother: even if a cement truck hit her she'd say, 'Well, I don't want to put the doctors to any trouble'."

Krebs raised his eyebrows. "But her complaints aren't serious enough that you'd need to reconsider or reschedule?"

"Oh no, I don't think so, no." Simpson could have kicked himself for mentioning the shortness of breath. It just slipped out.

"Besides, I'm just going out there for a kind of exploratory look around. Seems the responsible way to approach it."

Krebs pulled out the policy and showed it to Simpson, assuring him that Melba would indeed be taken care of. "Her pension would continue even if we were bought out by a larger company. We'd put it in the conditions-of-sale agreement that all current and former employees would continue to get their full monthly pension payments and receive the burial benefits as promised at the time of their retirement."

"That's good to know, 'cause we can't afford any rude surprises."

Simpson scanned the document carefully, and Krebs asked his secretary to make a copy for him.

"Also, I don't suppose there might be any simple kind of jobs around here that my brother might be able to do for you? It would be such a relief to Mom. I know he can be sort of a nuisance sometimes, but we're pushing him to find some kind of extra income to help Mom around the house. You know, like, I don't know, folding sheets in the morgue, or Mom suggested maybe as a kind of prayer counselor to the grieving families, because he's very devout and real experienced at praying. You should hear him asking the blessing. Once a week he reads news stories for the blind over at Dillard's community service radio station, but that's pro bono."

"Hmmm . . ." Krebs tilted back in his chair, his fingertips pressed pensively at his closed lips.

"He's applied at the public library and places like that, and I thought you might know of something, since you've got a pretty steady business here. Or maybe if someone you know at another company needs help . . ."

"Let me think about that and see if we can't come up with something we could use him for."

As they were walking to the front of the office, Simpson was stopped by the sight of an old blue IBM Selectric with its cord wrapped and tied.

"What's this?"

"An office machine left over from an earlier age. We're all computerized now. Tried to give it to the public schools, but for all their budget problems they don't seem to need it, either."

Simpson smiled. "I think I know somebody who'd be real happy to see this again. Matter of fact, she may have used this very machine to fill out forms here. Her fingerprints are probably still on it."

"She's welcome to it. I can have Johnson drive it over this afternoon. Don't worry about your mother. We'll make sure she gets full-service care, though I hope that's many years away. Give her my best. She's a good lady. And we'll see if we can't find something part-time for your brother. No promises, but have him pay me a visit when he has some free time."

Although he had been meaning for years to visit his father's old business partner, Simpson was not sure exactly what questions he wanted to ask him. Maybe it would be best just to see what Roscoe had to say, if his memory was still good, and take it from there. What he knew for certain was that in years to come, if he had neglected to seek the old man's recollections, and then he passed away, Simpson would never forgive himself. Didn't he have enough regrets already? He had read somewhere that maturation into true adulthood was through living each day in a way that left one with as few regrets as possible. Good luck with that. And one of the surest ways of doing this was, in the words of one of his affirmation posters, by putting off procrastination till some other time.

Roscoe Rabineaux looked about the same as Simpson remembered him, with thick white hair and eyebrows and pink complexion, bright as a boiled shrimp. His eyes watered and he sniffled almost constantly as though afflicted by allergies, but he rarely blew his nose or sneezed, and dismissed any suggestions that he should. Because of the congested, "ruddy doze" sound of his speech, Simpson and Bartholomew used to call him Rothko Rabbit Toe.

"How nice to see you, son. Come on in."

Roscoe shook his hand with a warm but weakened grasp and, limping slightly and leaning on a cane, led him back to the kitchen. Except for the new refrigerator, the high-ceilinged, linoleum-tiled kitchen looked and felt unchanged since the 1950s. Simpson said part of the reason why he wanted to talk was that his mother, who loved her Gasper dearly, rarely talked about him, except to repeat familiar, superficial pleasantries: he had always been a good husband, and he meant well. "It's a bit late, but I want to try to know him better. Bartholomew and I visited the tomb recently, and I want to go there again soon."

"That's good to hear. You'll have to take him a rose from Clara's garden. Your mother prob'ly thinks about him more than she talks. I know I sure miss him. God doze, half our customers dropped off after he was buried."

"I'm going to be moving to California soon. My mother and brother don't believe me when I tell them this, but I'm going out to San Francisco to become a poet. And if a poet doesn't know who his father was, what good is he? What can he do?"

"Well, dat's a good question." Rabineaux sniffled and wiped his nose with his sleeve. "I guess I never thought of that. Let's see if maybe I can help."

He pulled out three glasses and poured most of his last can of beer into two of them, and a few sips into the third. "For the dead," he explained.

Roscoe led his guest to the front of the house and motioned for Simpson to have a seat in one of the rocking chairs of faded gray wood on the green-painted veranda that was elevated some twelve feet above ground level and reached by a concrete stairway in the middle. Simpson relaxed and admired the wide view of the avenue and the late afternoon sun shining sideways in the leaves of the cedars and magnolias close by the porch.

They clinked their glasses. "To Gasper."

The creaking wood of the rocker and the cold beer on his lips plus the sight of the sunlight on the leaves combined to give Simpson a familiar sense that he had been here in this moment before, or he was meant to be here now.

Many years had passed since Simpson's last visit to the old taxidermy shop, which was set in the cinder-block-walled bottom half of the Rabineauxs' two-story house on Elysian Fields near Gentilly Boulevard. First the shop was simply called Rabineaux's Taxidermy, then Rabineaux & Weems. Their wives called it Jaws & Claws. After Weems died, Rabineaux did not have the heart to remove his partner's name, and it would not have made good business sense, anyway, though most of his custom-ers eventually learned to their disappointment that the cheerful near-master taxidermist was no longer among the living, so instead their catch would be mounted by the taciturn, matter-of-fact original proprietor.

Rabineaux was still open for business—he kept his license current—but fewer sportsmen brought by their catches anymore, and sometimes entire weeks would pass with no ringing of the phone or doorbell. Both partners had been disappointed that none of their sons wanted to follow them into the business, but maybe it was just as well, Roscoe said, because the business seemed to be drying up just as the species were thinning out and the Gulf's salt water was edging closer.

Simpson agreed that it was unfortunate. He asked how Rabineaux & Weems started their partnership, and where they had first met, but all Roscoe seemed to want to talk about was the erosion of the coast and salt water incursion. He had recently gone fishing at an old favorite spot for the first time in several years and couldn't find his old landmarks. At least once a week he dreamed of waking up in a bed surrounded by water, the waves lapping at his elbows. He worried that someday a bad storm would rupture the nearby London Avenue canal connecting to Lake Pontchartrain and flood the neighborhood worse than Hurricane Betsy did in '65.

"A customer at work was asking about that the other day," said Simpson. "I told her not to worry, those outflow canals were built to last. Now, when Dad started with you, was it full-time, or—"

"Don't bet on it. You remember Georges back in September? Dat bad boy was headed straight up the Mississippi's ass till it veered east just in time. How would you like all that storm surge spillin' over the Moonwalk and pourin' in from the lake, comin' at us from both sides? You were too young to remember Betsy, but she flooded out here and other parts of town. Some eighty people died, prob'ly more. There's places even around this neighborhood where you can still see broken windows, signs bent by the wind, and floodwater stains on the walls. I heard about some guys takin' their boats out to rescue folks in the Lower Ninth, but first dey'd say how much you gonna pay? I heard dis from a man who was a boy at the time, sittin' up on the roof under the hot September sun with his pregnant mama, all surrounded by water. No cash, no ride. How's that for love thy neighbor? You're old enough to remember Camille in '69, over in Gulfport and Biloxi? She raised storm surges twenty-six feet high. How well d'you think the London Avenue's gonna hold up with water like dat? And the ground's lower now than it was then. We're about five or six feet under right here, below sea level."

Roscoe paused for a sip of beer, but before Simpson could ask what the customers used to say about Gasper after he died, the old outdoorsman resumed.

"I tell you, breaks your heart goin' out to the old fishin' spots anymore. Fewer good catches, and the trees we used to use as landmarks are dead, dyin', or blowed away. Used to be all around here was cypress forest, all the way down to the Gulf, just about, for miles and miles. Cypress and oaks. Dat's your buffer, absorbin' the storm surge like a big sponge. But the lumber companies cut 'em all down in the last hundred years. That wood's in your house and mine, most likely. Cypress plank floors and cabinets. Den they're drillin' for oil and cuttin' shipping channels through the marshes like the Gulf Intracoastal Waterway and the Mister Go, lettin' in salt water that kills the trees and swamp grass, and den when the storms come, they funnel the storm surge right in here. It's crazy. Crazier than crazy. Look at the map, how they're angled right at us. Almost like dey were *designed* to drown the city. Death by a thousand shortcuts. They savin' a little time on shipping but they're cuttin' the city's time way short. Can't have both."

Simpson was impressed. "I never knew you were such an environmentalist."

"I never knew all our wetlands was gonna be killed off. Your daddy understood all this. I'm surprised if he didn't teach you about it."

"I think he was mostly trying to look on the bright side. Mind if I see the old shop again?"

The smell of the workshop was almost as familiar as his mother's living room. Rabineaux hobbled around the dimly lighted front room (the hanging 60-watt bulbs were burned out, so the shop was lit only by the fluorescent tube lights) and pointed with his cane to some of his favorite mountings along the old cypress walls: green-headed mallards in flight, speckled trout, largemouth bass, and deer and boar heads beside framed, yellowed phone book advertisements ("Award-winning mounts. Specializing in Game Heads, Fish, Birds, Tanning") and a shelf of books on anatomy, wildlife of Louisiana, and birds of the southeastern United States. A dusty sheet of plastic covered a five-foot blue marlin whose needle nose Roscoe had repaired, now waiting to be picked up by its owner. "Dat dere's empty," he said, pointing to the big freezer where he had kept fish and other specimens until time for mounting, each tied in a plastic bag and labeled with a tag to identify species, owner, and date. Dust had settled on the boxes and drawers of extra teeth, claws, glass bobcat eyes, and the supplies of wire, foam mannequins, and other tools of the trade. Simpson recalled his father once saying that to really master the craft, a taxidermist had to spend time out in the wild, studying deer, ducks, fish, observing how they move and stand in order to know what kind of life he was representing, otherwise the models would be flat and dead.

Rabineaux said he and Gasper had often talked about going up to New York sometime to see the professional mountings at the American Museum of Natural History, but they'd never quite made it.

"Really? My father wanted to go to New York?"

"We talked about it."

"I would have gone with you."

Roscoe shrugged. "It was just a dream we had. Would've been interesting, though."

He opened the freezer and reached for a chilled bottle of vodka, then pulled two short glasses from a cabinet. He blew the dust off the glasses, then wiped them with his shirttail.

"Do you still have your old fishing camp down at Grand Isle? Y'all still go there?"

"Not much anymore. Here, have a sip."

"Cheers. Would you mind if I maybe go down there sometime? I used to love it when you and Dad and I went fishing."

"Yeah, good times. Sure, just let me know when. You'll need the padlock key."

"Dad was a patient fisherman. Even when he caught nothing, which was rare."

Roscoe sniffled and wiped his nose on his sleeve. Simpson knew better than to offer him a handkerchief, even a clean one. He would not use it.

"Gasper was patient, all right. The fuddiest case I remember we had to handle was this crazy old gal whose cat had died, Rusty was his name, an old tabby house cat, and she wanted Rusty to be preserved in perpetuity. She was a former singer or actress, or maybe just an over-the-hill stripper, but she had a very theatrical way about her and a high opinion of herself, so I guess her cat was special too. Her hair was about the color of his fur, come to think of it. She knew somebody dat owned an ice cream factory in Bywater, and she paid him a storage fee to keep Rusty in a commercial freezer till she was ready to have him mounted. She didn't say how long he was in there, just that it was longer dan she'd intended. She rode out here in a taxi, and the driver warned us by twirling his finger around his ear that she had a few pieces of furniture loose up in the attic. He said she'd been talking to the dead cat in its freezer box all the way over from the Quarter. We told her it would be a while till we could get to it—we usually had a six-month waiting list—and she said 'Fine, I heard y'all are the best, so however long it takes to do it right.' It wasn't long before she was calling to see if Rusty was ready to come home, she missed him so bad. She'd start out all sweet and gooey, kind of slurrin' her sugar-talk, but withid a few minutes her voice turned rough and she'd be cussin' like a shit-drunk sea-hag, just the filthiest kind of language you ever did hear. Your dad's so patient, he'd just try to pacify her like she was a rational creature, but she was wasting our time, and I'd just come over and hang up the phone on her. Then she'd call again a month later, same thing all over again. When we finally got to work on old Rusty, it turned out the cat's body had been freezer-burned after all dat time at the ice cream factory. When it thawed, the fur started falling out, and we couldn't do nothing with it. It was a mess. Nothing we could do but give her her deposit money back. That's when we found out she'd had it in storage for *seven years*. Well, that's the story of Rusty. But your dad, he's so sweet, he really wanted to make that gal happy and give her her cat back looking like he used to, and all her ugly talk and abuse didn't faze him none."

"That's . . . that's quite a story. I'm surprised Dad never brought that one home."

"Well, he took things as they come, and things that you or I might find strange, he'd just roll with it. Gasper was the patientest man I ever knew."

Simpson smiled.

"What happened to the body? The freezer-burned cat?"

"Shit, I don't know."

"You said earlier you and Dad wished your sons would join the business, but my father never directly asked me. I probably would have said no anyway, but still, he never asked."

"Sorry, son." Rabineaux sniffled and winced as though he were pulling a piece of glass out of his foot. "Some things it's hard for a father to put into words sometimes. Dere's things a man used to be able to take for granted, like his son following in his trade, and maybe devver learned how to say in so many words. I wouldn't hold it against him. He prob'ly saw that you already knew what you wanted to do."

Which is not the same as actually doing it, Simpson thought with chagrin.

He said, "Since he died, I've kind of resented him for never asking me to come in sometimes and help out, like on weekends. I shouldn't hold it against him, but . . . Maybe I resented him so I wouldn't feel guilty for not volunteering. Even back then I could feel he wished I'd show some interest in his work, but I never did."

A catch in his voice, a sensation in his eyes told him he'd better stop talking. How was a boy in his teens to understand a time would come when he grieved the loss of moments, so many moments, when he couldn't be bothered with some little thing that would have pleased his father? It would only have taken a few minutes, or an hour or two, and that time might have been molded into something still present.

"Well, that's all right," said Roscoe, tossing back the last drops of his vodka and giving Simpson a warm reassuring look. "He'd be happy to know you came by. He was awful proud of you, always braggin' on how smart you are, goin' to college and all, so when you go out to California you be sure and keep your daddy proud."

Simpson turned away slightly as he gave Roscoe his word. It was just as well he hadn't let him use the handkerchief to blow his nose.

Dear Simpson Weems —

I hope this reaches you before you take off. I just got your note. Sure, I can show you around some when you get here. I'm a word-processing temp, so my hours are kind of flexible.

Admire the Beats if you like, but if you're interested in the literature of the present, or the future, you could probably stay where you are. There's not much going on here that I can see. More energy seems to go into honoring the past, but maybe I'm just disgruntled. Subscribe to *Poetry Flash*, if you haven't already. Actually I guess there is a lot going on—just not with me. If you're going to dip into olde-tyme S.F. for inspiration—and why not?—then there are earlier periods worth looking into. You mentioned the San Francisco Poetry Renaissance. There's also the bohemians of the 1870s and fin-de-siècle like Gelett Burgess and Frank Norris. Jack London, Ambrose Bierce, Mark Twain . . . They're more interesting, I think; more original. Read Parry's *Garrets and Pretenders*. He talks about the original Bohemian Club's procession through the streets of old San Francisco in the 1870s to their new quarters with the club's mascot, Dick the pet owl, held aloft on a palanquin. Now that's my idea of style. What a time to live that must have been. As soon as they set the owl down in the new club quarters on Pine Street, "he" laid an egg. Most auspicious, and very San Francisco.

One of my favorites is Gelett Burgess (see his map of Bohemia, enclosed), kind of an American Edward Lear, and a friend of Frank Norris's. A bohemian par excellence. He used to go around in

capes of different colors—there's an old photo of
him standing outside his Russian Hill apartment in
a top hat and cape. He's best-known for his dumb
"purple cow" poem, but he was part of an avant-
garde group called Les Jeunes, and in the 1890s he
and Norris edited literary magazines like *The Wave*
and *The Lark* that they printed in odd sizes on yellow bamboo paper from Chinatown. If you want
I can show you where the Monkey Block used to
be, on Montgomery Street where the Transamerica
pyramid is now. It was a big old four-story building
with restaurants and newspaper offices, and tons
of writers and artists used to have studios there.
Kipling, Stevenson, even Sun Yat-sen. Used to be
near the shoreline before all the landfill extended
the real estate out into the Bay. The Monkey Block
stood for about a century, surviving the 1906 earthquake, till it was razed to make a parking lot. It was
in a steam bath in that building that Mark Twain
met a man named Tom Sawyer. Again, very San
Francisco. I can show you that and more when you
get here. Really, there's so much more besides the
Beat boys' club.

Man, you're making me hand-write a letter.
Don't you have e-mail? If you move out here you'll
have to get with the program.

Good luck, and bon voyage,

Foster DeBris

It may have seemed he was only wandering, and it was true that in the early years his excursions were more aimless than purposeful, mostly idle curiosity, but in this cool morning's walk along Elysian Fields and Claiborne he was working: thinking, composing lines and phrases in his head, gathering impressions from these time-worn neighborhoods whose spirits could still be felt near certain trees or street corners. Sometimes he felt the presences most intensely in places where no one lived anymore. The uprooted communities of neighbors who once lived in little wooden houses demolished and paved over—their lives, their spirits spoke to him; he could feel them still living and breathing. Lost settlements buried under layers of white shell, asphalt, and cement spread thick like desert sands. Here in this space beneath the elevated Claiborne Expressway was a neighborhood, a house, a bedroom. A woman's dressing table and mirror once stood where this stop sign is now. Over that burned patch of concrete where Simpson saw a homeless man crouching before a fire, pulling his blanket tighter around his shoulders in the chill morning air and warming his hands as he cooked a can of beans for breakfast, there a wife and husband's bed once lay, and there they loved and brought forth children whose descendants still live nearby.

Two men leaning against a concrete column, smoking, watched in silence as the figure in the trench coat paused to write something in a little pocket notebook.

All along North Claiborne, once known as "the Ne-
groes' St. Charles," or "black folks' Canal Street," the
great live oaks and pretty pink azaleas that grew in the
neutral ground along the formerly grand boulevard were
uprooted in the 1960s to make way for the Claiborne
Expressway part of Interstate 10. During Carnival and
St. Joseph's Day, neighbors used to set out their bar-
becue grills for the all-day party to watch the tribes of
Mardi Gras Indians parading down the street, with Spy
Boys and Flag Boys going ahead of the Big Chiefs in
their brilliant plumage and iridescent sequins, the yellow, red and turquoise feathers spanning as wide as the
Chiefs stood tall, the Ninth Ward Hunters or the Wild
Tchoupitoulas strutting to the drumbeats, tambourines,
and chants of "Iko-Iko . . . jock-a-mo fee na-né." Then
in the sixties some five hundred homes were cleared, and
many of those that survived were abandoned. The proud
tribes lived on, however, and now the cookout grills were
set up in the shadows of the overpass, but most of the
neighborhood's higher-quality clothing stores and the
music halls, bakeries, and barber shops gradually closed.
The Capital Theater and LaBranche's drug store, Two
Sisters restaurant, Moe's pie shop and Joe Sheep's sand-
wich place were long gone. About the only businesses
that survived or moved in to the deserted sites were car
repair shops and spare parts dealers, po-boy joints and
convenience stores. The gray spaces beneath the freeway
were littered with malt liquor bottles, cigarette butts, and
burned-out husks of abandoned cars, the wheels stripped

off, seats torn out. Here and there, pigeon feathers fluttered down from the trusses that held the concrete sections of elevated road where the traffic never stopped.

Across the Quarter from Elysian Fields, he was walking under the twin spans he still thought of as the GNO (Greater New Orleans), fondly remembering the Bay Bridge over the Embarcadero, when a white and blue NOPD squad car pulled up, blocking his path, and two officers stepped out. The star in the crescent. To protect and to serve.

He was only surprised he had never been stopped before.

"See your I.D., please," said the shorter officer. Spots of pink, melanin deficit blotches on his otherwise brown face and hands. The dim predawn twilight reflected in the mirrored lenses of his sunglasses.

"I hope I'm not doing something illegal."

As Simpson noted the name LOVE on his silver name-tag, the officer shone his flashlight on the license, then pointed the light at Simpson's face to compare with the photo I.D.

WEEMS, SIMPSON MANDEVILLE
797 Dormition Street, New Orleans, LA
SEX: M.   HEIGHT: 6-6.   WEIGHT: 180.   EYES: GRN
DATE OF BIRTH: 11-22-1962

"Kind of early to be out walking, isn't it? Or you just out late?"

"I—"

"Why are you walkin' around the entrance ramp of the bridge?" said the other, now adding his flashlight to the interrogation. "Why aren't you home, asleep, or at work?"

"Or in church?"

"For whatever reason, I feel drawn to this place," Simpson began, shading his eyes and watching his reflection in the lenses with a sense of unreality, heightened by the predawn mist and fog floating near the river, as though dreaming that he was looking into the hypnotizing mirror eyes of a short, pink-spotted black police officer named Love.

"I'm a poet, you see, but—"

"For whatever reason," the taller one echoed. "That's what we're tryin' to get at. You're a poet. So why don't you go to the park and write about the trees?"

"During business hours."

"Like I said, I can't really explain it, but—"

"Shouldn't do things you can't explain. Next thing we know, you'll be up on the bridge tellin' us you just wanted to see how it looks from the other side of the railing. Go on home, now. Don't make us have to stop you again."

"Yes sir."

They switched off their searchlights and gave back Simpson's license.

"You know, if you hadn't've been wearin' that trench coat . . ."

"That's why we checked on you. Need a ride somewhere?"

"No, thank you. I'll catch the bus."

"Do that."

As the squad car's taillights disappeared into the mist and fog, the sense of unreality slowly lifted. Shouldn't do things you can't explain. Right. What else is there? And which was more haunted, he wondered, the early-morning walker or Annunciation Street's old empty houses where he stepped slowly, reverently, pausing as though to listen not to echoes from a time before his birth but to voices speaking now? Here in the lower Irish Channel part of Faubourg St. Mary, where Annunciation was intersected by Terpsichore and the other muses, the formerly grand Greek Revival homes with columned galleries upstairs and down whose worn gray paintless boards were twisting away from the warped studs—these stately residences of the prosperous had been ghost houses since before the Depression, before the Great War, already gaunt tilting ruins when Clarence John Laughlin photographed them in the thirties and forties. The names of their former occupants were half-eroded from their tombs' inscription tablets at the Lafayette Cemetery over on Washington and Prytania. No air conditioners had ever been set in these windows that held only dusty, mildewed shards of glass, and flowering vines had been growing up the sun-bleached walls since the days when the cool air machines were a novel luxury in the moving picture houses on Canal Street.

Was he any less a ghost, or any more substantial? No need to make believe he was in the presence of other spirits—it was a plain fact. They were all around, the specters of decades and centuries hovering, passing through the air, through walls, up and down the allées of the cemeteries and the warehouse district and the Vieux Carré, retracing steps, seeking lost connections, the missing pieces they died without. Ghosts dwell in every town and city of a certain age, just as regrets haunt adulthood, but they crowd the air in an old port city, a crossroads of the world where so many have died suddenly, violently, often without time to pray or even make the sign of the cross. Drunken flatboatmen murdered by thieving prostitutes or brass-knuckled bouncers in the long-vanished hellholes of the Swamp on Girod or old Gallatin Street in the Quarter. Yellow fever, alcohol drownings and drug overdoses, slashed throats and wrists, infected gunshot wounds, dead men planted up to their ankles in concrete buckets and dumped in the river to feed the fish . . .

He walked on as dust motes hovered and settled in silent hallways of abandoned mansions where now only shadows, spirits, and spiders dwelled. At last he went home, as directed, his thoughts reaching forward, not back, to the neglected and forgotten places where life goes on, quiet as wisteria growing through broken window panes, simple as rain through the holes in an old slate roof.

10

Almost Bon Voyage

THE DAY BEFORE HE WAS TO FLY to San Francisco, Simpson stopped by his mother's house to see whether Lourdes had delivered the typewriter, though his secret purpose was to say good-bye without actually speaking the word. When he walked in she was sitting at the breakfast bar, smiling and humming as she cleaned the surface of her pretty blue Selectric with a damp cloth while Bartholomew on the sofa scanned the sports section with a magnifying glass, memorizing the weekend's basketball scores. Thirty years later he would still remember the score of the LSU–Auburn game, and Georgia vs. Ole Miss, and the teams' rankings in the Southeastern Conference, if he lived that long.

"Nice typewriter you got there, Mom."

Melba beamed, "Ain't she just a beauty?"

She looked happier than he had seen her in a long time, but when she didn't thank him for his part in making sure the Selectric came to her, he had to inform her that he had asked Gordon Krebs for it, though no sooner were the words out of his mouth than he realized he had blundered.

"Mr. Krebs? When did you see him?"

"Oh," Simpson cleared his throat, "when I went to Lourdes to check on your pension plan and benefits."

"You did what?" She frowned and put her hand to the middle of her chest. "Why would you do that? You plottin' something?"

"Don't you remember me saying I was going to check on the policy?"

"No, I don't believe so." She shook her head. "I'm quite sure I don't."

"After y'all shredded Dad's taxidermy collection looking for dollar bills, I thought we should probably check to make sure there wouldn't be any, you know, future financial surprises."

He watched her face relax as she processed this news.

"And," he added, feeling obligated to give her some glad tidings to make up for the information he was not sharing with her, "while I was there, Barto, I asked Mr. Krebs if he could be thinking of some kind of job you could do there to earn a little extra money."

"Oh, this pleases my heart to hear," Melba sighed. "Praise be. Isn't this welcome news, Bartholomew?"

"You talked to *Krebs* about me?!" Bartholomew burst out with hot indignation. He threw down the sports pages and sat there fuming and grinding his knuckles together. *He gnasheth upon me with his teeth; mine enemy sharpeneth his eyes upon me.*

"Barto, I thought Mom had a great idea about you maybe being a prayer-companion or something. So I mentioned the idea, and he says come by whenever you have some free time."

"You're all driving me coo coo for Cocoa Puffs!" He tried to heave himself up from the sofa, but sank deeper with each attempt. "Coo coo! Coo coo!"

"He's just trying to help, Bartholomew."

"Stop helping! I'm *already* looking for a job and the pressure's *killing* me!"

He slapped the sofa cushions and screamed, and Simpson and Melba put their fingers in their ears.

Vengeance is mine.

Slowly, quietly, Simpson was taking deep breaths.

Now Bartholomew gave him a look, a glare of evil intent, and Simpson's stomach twisted and sank.

"Bar—" He held out his hands to stop him.

"Simpson's planning to abandon us, Mommy. He'll be in San Francisco on *my birthday*. He already has a ticket. I saw it fall out of his pocket, just like I saw—"

Simpson stood between his brother and mother, waving his hands to deny and negate, but he could no more stop a storm.

"Barto, you absolutely kill me. You're just changing the subject from you getting a job and seeing a doctor like we talked about. As you *promised* to do."

"No! False! And you know what else—"

"Boys, boys—"

"Quiet, Mother!" they shouted.

"Mom, I told him the piece of paper he saw was only a possible itinerary. Of course I would talk to y'all first before making any plans. I just need a vacation. God, do I need a break."

"Mommy, he's—"

"All I want is to live where *I* want to live," Simpson nearly shouted, forgetting his deep breathing. "I've been stuck in this swamp, wasting my life away in this dead-end copy shop 'cause you made me promise to help you take care of him, but year after year goes by and you're both *strangling* me! How can I be a poet when I can't even breathe?"

"A poet?" they exclaimed.

"He wants to abandon us forever, Mother. He—"

"Hush, Bartholomew. Simpson, honey, you can go anywhere you want. You never said anything about this before. Poetry? Talk to us. I'm sure Bartholomew doesn't mind if you want to write some poems. And you work so hard, of course you need a vacation. Don't worry about us. You can visit San Francisco if it makes you happy. Just please don't stay gone too long."

"Really? Gee, Mom, I didn't realize you felt that way. I feel foolish. I feel—"

"You *are* foolish!" Bartholomew shouted. "You were gonna sneak away just like you did last time."

"I wasn't in San Francisco, I was in Austin, I told you."

"I never said you were. You just exposed yourself. O what a tangled web we weave."

"Bartholomew, I told you to hush," she said sharply.

"Look at his face. The truth is not in him. Admit it, Simpson. Tell her where you really were. I checked the map, and it doesn't take that long to drive from Austin, Texas. Who do you know there, anyway?"

"Bartholomew, stop tormenting your brother."

"Mother I can take care of myself."

"Quiet, both of you. Y'all givin' me the grandes douleurs. Sit down, Simpson, and—"

Suddenly she clutched at her chest and made a gasping sound.

"Melba!" Bartholomew pushed and heaved to raise himself from the sofa.

"It's okay," she wheezed, though her face had gone white and she looked faint.

"See what you've done?!"

"Where's your medicine?" Simpson asked. "Should I call Dr. Garcia?"

"I'll be okay. Just bring me a pill and some water. It's the little orange thing in the medicine cabinet."

While Simpson rushed to the bathroom, Bartholomew lumbered to the kitchen sink and ran cold water over a dish towel. He dabbed gently at his mother's cheeks and forehead, moaning with worry.

"Don't let your wig slip," he warned.

Simpson came back with a little white pill and a glass of water. He watched her take the medicine, then put his arm around her and led her over to Gasper's old La-Z-Boy. "There now."

"See what you do to her?" Bartholomew hissed. "Maybe you *should* go to California. Leave us alone. We don't need you."

"Ssshhh." Simpson raised his finger to his lips. "Let her rest."

He looked down at her, tilted back in the recliner.

He gritted his teeth. "Well, it was just a possible itinerary anyway, but I guess I'd better wait till this shortness-of-breath condition clears up."

She smiled and closed her eyes. "That's my boy."

He went to the yellow wall phone at the breakfast bar. He raised his hands to his head and sighed, then dialed the number on the smudged index card taped to the wall. "Dr. Garcia's office, please. Yes, I'd like to make an appointment for Mrs. Melba Weems as soon as he can see her. She's having chest pains, and—sure, yes, I can hold."

His voice caught on the word 'hold', and he had to turn his back to them as he squeezed his eyes shut.

After a moment he cleared his throat and said over his shoulder, "Don't worry, Mom, I'll pay for the checkup and any medications."

It was a bright clear February morning in 1997 when he slipped quietly out of town for that long-awaited journey of discovery. A quick cab ride to the airport and he was free, free to fly to San Francisco without telling his mother. He could not believe it was actually happening. *A dream comes true*, he kept thinking. *Bon voyage.* He was happy, yet the thrill felt muted, unequal to the magnitude of the event: he had been planning this trip for so many years that he felt a kind of poignant, anticlimactic letdown before he even landed. This visit should have happened years ago; was it already too late?

He slept much of the way across, tired from having stayed up late, meticulously packing and repacking, too excited to sleep. A few hours into the flight, several states west of the hot green swamps of home, he was looking down at the shadows of clouds passing across the bleached treeless expanses and dried veinlike streambeds of the Basin and Range. Something in the shapes was familiar. He had read that you can journey far and never leave home; he began to understand what that meant when somewhere over Nevada he awoke from a recurring dream that he feared might follow him to the ends of the earth.

Bartholomew is stalking furiously up the concrete incline of the Mississippi River bridge, and Simpson is skulking furtively behind him, peering around pillars, dodging behind columns whenever Bartholomew appears about to pause or look back. Then they are together at the midpoint of the bridge, no hiding now, standing side by side like brothers, their heads close, shoulders touching, looking out over the great brown waters far below where the riverboats and oil tankers and towboat-driven barges are passing up- and downriver. Bartholomew is fascinated by the boat traffic, their shapes and cargoes, watching their wakes spreading out behind them. The bridge's railing is orange red, and Bartholomew points down to the sailboats with pretty colors. "Is that Alcatraz over there? Where's Fisherman's Wharf?" Bartholomew is not supposed to be here! He leans farther over the railing for a closer look. Behind him, Simpson crouches down and grabs his feet and flips him up and over the railing. He sees the splash far below, but somehow it's not enough; it seems Bartholomew should make more of an impact than that tiny little "plink."

The taxi dropped him off at the Hotel Bohème on Columbus Avenue, where he left his suitcase in his small windowless room. He went around the corner for a cappuccino and pizza at Caffé Trieste on Grant and Vallejo, where a guidebook said the Beat poets used to frequent. Feeling their ghosts hovering still, the air vibrant with poetic energy, Simpson opened his notebook and, while Caruso and Pavarotti sang from the jukebox, he poured out a relaxed and rambling free-verse description of the interior and his excitement at being here. Here! At these very tables under the tall glass windows with a view of Coit Tower up on Telegraph Hill, here under the mural of Sicilian fishermen mending their nets, amid these framed photos and paintings along the Tuscan orange-red walls, Ferlinghetti and Corso and friends could still be seen writing, reading, drinking coffee or Chianti and talking about poetry, art, and probably sex and politics, too. The café felt powerfully familiar—surely he'd been here before; he'd always been here—and imbued with concentrated history and culture, rich as dark roast coffee. He glanced up to the pretty young woman behind the counter, comely with short dark hair and greenish blue eyes, high cheekbones. He sensed that she had been looking his way. She could tell he was a poet. A Romantic. The song on the jukebox was sung in Italian but maybe it was about their love, the *amore* that could grow between them. It was time to go to City Lights. On his way out the door he smiled and said hello to her with a friendly, see-you-soon wink as he dropped a few long-folded dollar bills in the tip jar. What a convenient location for breakfast tomorrow, just around the corner from his hotel. That half hour felt like a day, the dawn of a whole new life.

From the Trieste he walked over to City Lights Bookstore near the wide intersection of Columbus and Broadway. *This is it*, he thought: the epicenter. You are here. He inhaled hungrily to bring into himself the creative spirit, the sublime genius of the place. Standing on the sloping sidewalk where Kerouac and Ginsberg had passed so often, where Ferlinghetti might be upstairs working *at this very moment*, he gazed avidly, salivating at the sight of the little Pocket Poets editions in the window (*Becoming Visible, Pictures of the Gone World, Gasoline*), the anarchist manifestos and art and poetry journals he had never seen before. He decided to prolong the anticipation and savor this delicacy later. First he would go out to see the ocean—it felt important to begin by paying his respects to the great Pacific—and perhaps walk along the waterfront, then he would return to Telegraph Hill for a good Italian dinner in a North Beach restaurant—he could already taste the pure red Chianti—then maybe go hear some jazz later.

The air tasted refreshingly cooler and cleaner than the warm stagnant swamp-haze he was accustomed to. *You're in San Francisco now*, he congratulated himself with awe and amazement, as though he had already established residency. There, down the slope of Columbus Avenue, stood the great Transamerica pyramid. Was it actually happening, and was this the first of many days to come? For so many years he had anticipated being here that he now worried maybe something had hardened or gotten stuck between his eyes and the real San Francisco. How do you know when you're really in a place? If it doesn't feel as fresh and intense as you'd hoped, is that part of the authenticity? He pinched his arm and took in deep gulps of cool air, faintly scented with fumes of diesel and pungent aromas of Chinatown's fish and poultry markets wafting through Kerouac Alley.

He took a 30 Stockton bus down through Chinatown to Market Street. Along the way he stared at his transit map, perplexed. There must be a system to it all. Bus lines, cable cars, MUNI streetcars, BART trains . . . Someday he would understand the significance of all the numbers and colored lines.

He stepped off at Market and approached a young woman wearing geeky black-framed glasses and a wool cap, carrying a shopping bag with an architect's T-square leaning halfway out. She was walking slowly past a pair of rainbow-faced clowns juggling and pantomiming for a crowd of tourists.

"Excuse me, miss?" he said, unfolding his map. "I'm trying to get out to Ocean Beach."

"Sorry, what was that?"

He repeated the question.

"Oh, it's easy. Just go down to the Powell Street station here and take the N–Judah streetcar—not the big BART train at the lowest level, but midway down—take the N all the way out. You'll know when you're at the ocean. It's kind of self-explanatory."

She showed him on the map, though she stood at something of a distance and leaned to squint and point.

"Thank you so much. If the other people in San Francisco are half as nice as you—"

"Don't mention it." She waved the compliment aside and moved on.

As the N–Judah streetcar whirred along the underground rails, he smelled a curious fume, like diesel but not quite. Strings of lights in the black tunnel, then another station, a long fluorescent cave. The doors opened and many more people crowded on, dozens, hundreds on every platform, in every street and station, thousands of immigrants, apparently, from he knew not where. He gazed with fascination at the unfamiliar skin tones, facial structures, and body types. Wow, he thought: It really is an international world. All coming to discover America.

He was sitting by a window, feeling on his arm the light puff of a Chinese woman's green quilted jacket, sensing her body occasionally pressing him as the rail car rounded a curve. It was amazing, beautiful, otherworldly, the fabled city unreeling before his eyes, a moving picture show of shop fronts and dark evergreens and Victorian-style houses in shapes and colors all new to him. As the gray and yellow and beige two-story houses passed by, with the gray Pacific skies reflected in their bay windows, he thought, with a kind of poignant melancholy, It will never be quite this new for me again. He worried that he wasn't experiencing it for the first time in quite the right way.

Simpson, honey? His phone back home was ringing. Mother was trying to reach him, he could feel it. *When are you coming over?* Something was happening and she needed her eldest son.

A half hour later he was at the end of the line, end of the land. Across the Great Highway was Ocean Beach. He took off his shoes and socks to feel the sand as he strode across a wide strand toward the rolling sea. He stood on the long wide grayish brown beach, like Grand Isle more dirt than sand, looking out across the western horizon where the sun was a vague luminescence behind the thick blanket of cloud cover. The waves were coming in strong and regular, successive surges of gray blue water and sea foam. The soft roar soothed him, the splash and sizzle across the sands.

For the first time in his life he felt he could see forever; there was no limit to what he could envision if only he opened his eyes wide enough. So ready to bolt. I could just stay here and never go back. They'd never find me in a million years. The waves were strong, incessant, massive sheets of liquid thunder, and for a moment he felt the surging power of Poseidon the earth-shaker. He had seen salt water at the Gulf of Mexico, but this . . . knowing that the shores of Japan and China were halfway around the globe, and that somewhere out there the

Pacific reached depths of almost seven miles, impressed upon him with fresh force the potent magnitude of the all-encircling sea. How many people had come to this place before him, he wondered, and what emotions did they feel standing here, looking out to the west at sunset, hearing the seagulls *skreeking* overhead and the waves crashing and hissing across the cool gray sands? Feeling the distance from home, some of them. End-of-land sadness. So far from Lowell, from Paterson and Bleecker Street back East. Lovers came here holding hands, parents with their children and kites of many colors, painters with their easels, wet-suited surfers with their waxed boards, and all went away with the sea roaring in their ears, the salt in their blood.

He walked back across the Great Highway to the streetcar platform, the terminus of the N–Judah, but there was no car taking on passengers, and none approaching as far as he could see up the long straight slope from the sea. Unaware that he was only blocks away from Golden Gate Park, he strolled back toward town through the Outer Sunset district, taking his time, looking in the shop windows, passing by the stucco box houses of gray and yellow and bone white under the overcast sky. Like the beam from a distant, now extinct star, the flickering old neon of the Sunset Lounge shone with the light of a simpler time that he could almost remember. He could walk through the door and be in Temps Perdu. All his life and longer, this street had been here, looking exactly like this, and although he'd never seen pictures of this neighborhood it felt very familiar:

1940s-style beauty parlors, hardware stores, printing shops, dry cleaners, travel agencies with posters of cities and nations now called by different names. Cobwebs and dust on the window displays, cracks in the lettering painted on the glass, water stains on the sun-faded curtains. The street must have looked like this on the day of Hiroshima, and when Kennedy rode through Dallas. He imagined himself standing here fifty years ago, on this gray corner crisscrossed overhead by electric wires, under the bay windows, gazing up at the big Spanish mission–style church. And when I am gone, he thought, it will look just the same.

An hour later he was back downtown at rush hour, riding an escalator up from the platform in the Powell Street BART station, an extensive underground network of white tile and marble passageways, steel and glass surfaces, swelling with streams of people of every description, all dressed for cool weather. Many layers of dark clothing, much of it black, charcoal gray, touches of purple. Women in long pants, men in tailored suits and elegant, slipper-like Italian shoes. The men's fancy shoes annoyed him and he couldn't stop thinking about them. As he entered the great flow of humanity moving without interruption through the station it struck him that this precise combination of individuals had never existed in quite this arrangement before—everyone going their own way at their own speed, accelerating, turning, cutting across, striding briskly ahead—yet no one bumped into anyone else. The traffic could not have flowed this smoothly if it had been rehearsed.

From the station he walked east along Market Street to the Ferry Building at the water's edge. He crossed the wide street where a freeway had stood until destabilized by the 1989 earthquake—its outlines still showed on his multicolored map—and turned to walk north along the Embarcadero. He heard waves splashing against the pilings, sharp squawks of seagulls. It was dusk, a soft pigeon gray light in the sky as he walked northward past the piers, concrete docks, large gray warehouses of concrete, corrugated steel doors padlocked shut, past the open spaces between the wharves. The wind was blowing colder. Across most of North America it was already night.

It's late, and Mother must be wondering . . .

Between pier buildings he looked down at the dark water and foam splashing against the pilings. Sparkling San Francisco Bay, whose cold glittering waters have borne in boatloads from around the world, across whose great bridges have driven lost souls and seekers to mingle all through the hills and alleys of the city by the bay. All along the dark Embarcadero where the lights were flickering in the water and ships were passing through the Golden Gate toward the docks of the East Bay, and traffic streamed in and out on the upper and lower decks of the great span of the Bay Bridge arching over to Treasure Island and Yerba Buena and on across to the industrial flatlands of Oakland and the hills of Berkeley, and for miles north and south along the bay, a golden continuum of lights glittering like the star-jeweled belt of a galaxy.

Footsteps approached, two men walking. They passed on, their deep voices charged in some impassioned discussion. Soon another pedestrian out taking the night air passed by slowly, too slowly, staring with a provocative, penetrating directness. Come touch me. His blue jeans were tight over his muscular legs, black jacket shiny and hard.

Simpson frowned and looked away. Get your eyes off me.

Fog was moving in across the water, a white mist through the air thick with smells of fish on the decks and oil in the water, cigarette smoke from the shadows among the tin sheds beside the warehouses where shades of men awaited furtive encounters. Figures huddling, pressing close, smoldering love on the waterfront. Ghosts, maybe. The fog passed across the water and the concrete wharves and wooden timbers of the piers, surrounding all. Pale white lights flashed in the distance and foghorns tooted intermittently. Everything around him was years and years ago, before color was invented. The pavement and the pier were dissolving into the haze, and out across the water pale flashes of light pulsed through the mist and dispersed, absorbed in the fog billowing around him as in a scene from Victorian London along the Thames, with wharf rats and rotting wood, pipe smoke from a mustached Scotland Yard inspector, and a murderer crouching behind stacks of coiled rope. Then a tugboat sounded its horn and Simpson heard the traffic behind him on the Bay Bridge, the salt water slapping at the concrete piers.

He turned around and walked south toward the bridge, gazing up at its massive towers, the inbound traffic on the upper deck, outbound on the lower. A good place for infrastructure walks. As he moved on, feeling curiously at home here as in his strolls around the backstreets and drainage canals of New Orleans, it was some consolation to think that in his early days here his acquaintance with solitude would serve him well, until he made friends. *In restless dreams I walked alone* ... But meeting and befriending should be easy here, for this city was full of seekers and searchers like him. There were people here he was destined to meet, special people—he could feel it—and with their influence his poetry would flourish. Maybe it would begin tonight.

He returned to North Beach for a drink at the Vesuvio Café, thinking he might ask someone there to recommend a good Italian restaurant, and then afterward he could browse to his heart's content at City Lights.

All day, since the bridge dream of Bartholomew, he had been worrying that maybe he should call her and let her know where he was, or at least make sure everything was all right. But what if the shock of learning he was so far away caused heart palpitations, or something worse? And if everything was not all right? Was he going to turn around and hurry home?

For a while he sat at a small round-topped table along the windows upstairs at Vesuvio, sipping a cold Anchor Steam and watching the traffic and pedestrians passing by on the wide sloping intersection of Columbus and Broadway, colored by the flashing lights of Big Al's, the hungry i, and the Condor Club. Just fifteen feet away, across Jack Kerouac Alley, people were going in and out of City Lights, and he would soon be in there with them. He felt he was at a crossroads of the world where you might see anyone. Streams of humanity from around the globe. A classmate from years past, famous actors, musicians, Nobel Prize–winning poets or physicists. Nearby, two women were talking at a corner table beneath a striped awning and a hand-painted sign marking it as the Booth for Lady Psychiatrists. Talking about a spiritual center, he imagined, or maybe sharing memories of Esalen and Big Sur. Small tables like his were lined along a railing overlooking a large D-shaped opening on the second floor that allowed an open view down to the bar. The walls and tabletops were decorated with shellacked collages and portraits of French painters and symbolist poets. In this former Italian bookstore, a bar since the late forties, and across the street at Specs', artists and writers met to talk about their latest works, or friends they'd seen recently at the White Horse Tavern, while the tenor sax of Ben Webster and the folk tunes of Woody Guthrie lightened the air.

He was here. He was ready. Where was everybody else? The setting looked right, and yet somehow this was not quite how he had imagined it. For years, at least as far back as his college days with Button, his soul's true habitation was a private art-dream of San Francisco decades ago and in time to come. While physically he had resided in Louisiana and was listed in the New Orleans phone directory, whenever possible his thoughts had been disengaged from his everyday surroundings, outside of standard time, burrowed away in a cinema of his own imagining where his favorite old black-and-white movies played while the rest of the world carried on its business in the full light of the present day. Now he was here, but where were his fellow poets? At a big poetry reading he didn't know about? A happening, or a be-in? City Lights next door would surely have flyers and calendars of readings.

As though losing his radio's easy-listening signal to a stronger transmitter, his reveries were interrupted by harsh static, interference, and now all he could hear was Mother's importuning, Bartholomew's complaining. A second beer did not mute the voices. *Simpson, honey, where are you?* When he could put it off no longer, he went down to the pay phone beside the stairs outside the basement-level men's restroom. It wasn't that he needed to call home, and he was not a mama's boy: he was telephoning because he was responsible. Because he cared. It was a sign of his maturity and confidence. And if he didn't call, his whole vacation would be haunted by nightmares, static, and telepathic voices.

And who should answer but the very last voice he wanted to hear?

"Let me speak to Mom, Barto."

"She's in the hospital. Where are you? We tried calling you."

Simpson's stomach dropped. "Oh my God. Please tell me you're not serious."

"She was having chest pains. You need to come see her right now." Bartholomew began stomping his feet, rattling the pictures on the walls. "Right this minute!" he bellowed.

The sounds of Bartholomew's stamping combined with the closer sounds of flushing toilets and men's heavy footsteps crunching down the wooden stairs pounded in his head.

Simpson's pulse accelerated. "Easy, now, Barto. Are you okay? What did the doctor say?"

"Where are you, in a bus station? Sounds like long distance."

"She's really in the emergency room? At Charity?"

"Bring me home a *TV Guide* for my collection."

"What? What are the doctors saying?"

"You're calling long distance, I can hear it. Where are you when she needs you?"

Simpson's heart was pounding, his palms sweating.

"*Damn* it, Bartholomew, can't I take a vacation for even a day without you ruining it? Tell me about Mother."

"I told you. She's at Charity. Where else?"

"Take care of her till I get back."

"Of course. Don't boss me. And don't forget my *TV Guide*."

"Is that all you care about?"

He hung up before Simpson could say another word.

The trip was aborted, the carefully packed suitcase never opened. Au revoir, mon amour. Simpson's time on the ground there was not much longer than the combined flight times to and from San Francisco International Airport.

He returned to find, with a conflicted, head-splitting collision of relief and outrage, that in fact his mother had not gone anywhere near Charity Hospital—she hadn't even left Dangers Park. Her only health-related complaint was of some tension in her chest and neck after Bartholomew bellowed at her for buying only one super-size bag of chocolate chip cookies. Simpson berated himself for not having had sense or suspicion enough to phone Charity's coronary care unit to check on his mother, as any truly concerned son—as any clear-thinking adult—would have done. In his rush to get back to the airport it had not occurred to him. How could he have been so gullible as to take Barto's word for it? If he had only thought to make that one call, the spiteful, villainous falsehood would have been exposed. But even if he had confirmed her safety and continued his vacation, he told himself later, then some other catastrophe, possibly something worse, might have befallen her. When he got back to New Orleans and found Melba contentedly folding laundry and humming a happy tune, and Bartholomew occupying half the sofa as usual and engorging himself on a carton of chocolate ice cream, seeming to spread wider before their very eyes, he pretended nothing was amiss until he leaned close to his brother and hissed, "I thought you said she was at Charity!"

"Oh, no, you must have misheard me," said Bartholomew nonchalantly. "Long distance, bad connection. Must be your guilty conscience. What took you so long? Where's my *TV Guide*?"

"Bartholomew!"

Simpson's ensuing tension headaches began to sub-side only after several weeks of acupuncture treatments by Dr. Priscilla Gong.

Two years later, fortunately, he still had Dr. Gong's phone number.

But first he had to call the travel agent to cancel the trip.

He winced with each digit he pressed on the phone's keypad.

"Sorry about your mother," said the agent. "The airline will be happy to credit your account."

"What? I don't have an account, I have a credit card. Tell 'em to credit that."

"Sorry. They can apply the charge to your next trip."

He moaned, "But that could be—God knows how long—another year or two."

"They'll probably still be in business then," she said brightly.

When he'd phoned the doctor from his mother's house, he was told that Hector Garcia had retired years ago, which showed how long it had been since Melba had had a checkup. Apparently the office kept auto-matically renewing her prescriptions without requiring annual visits. A younger physician in Dr. Garcia's group had inherited most of his patients, so Simpson made an appointment with her. The next available time was three weeks away. He kept repeating "chest pains" and "difficulty breathing" until the office assistant promised to make an opening for Mrs. Weems within the next day or two.

Mother was too considerate to deliberately spoil his vacation, yet he had to wonder whether maybe subconsciously she had brought on an attack, or faked one, just to keep him grounded in Orleans Parish so help would be close at hand. It was possible that she had somehow intuited what he was planning. He prayed that the California savings account he had been building up all these years would not be depleted by catastrophic hospital bills. He hated to be so cold, yet the more she held him back, the less he wanted to help her. But although much else was disintegrating, California hadn't fallen off into the Pacific yet, so he supposed he could wait a while longer. How much longer? Like a certain prince waiting well into middle age, even into early old age, to inherit the throne from his superannuated but still healthy and unyielding mother, like that monarch-in-waiting who must wonder if each cough might presage a change of fortune, he worried that his best years would be behind him before he could set himself to the work he was born to perform.

It would take time for the healing waters of forgiveness to cool the rage and resentment. Perhaps in the raw wound of his crushed hopes—the cancellation was worse than a disappointment, he fumed; more like an abortion—in this hurting, bleeding tissue there might be material for some honest truthful writing.

And maybe if he worked it right, between now and his eventual liberation he might actually manage to complete a good poem or two. Anyway, he thought, if he truly wanted to honor his father's memory, he should man up and look after Melba, who, however clinging, had been so kind to him all these years. The realization came to him like a rotary saw blade in the chest that if he had been helping her with medical expenses instead of going to Lust Heaven all those times, she could have been seeing a specialist, and then maybe her condition would not have deteriorated to this degree. Then he would have been free to move to San Francisco. He could be there now.

But there was still the little brother problem. At one moment he was Simpson the merciful, then in the very next breath he was plotting fratricidal scenarios, some of which might work. He had proven skills in exacting revenge. But that was then. Yet the past is never dead. He could use his imagination for anti-Bartholomew intrigues or in the service of Literature. Torn between revenge and forgiveness, pushed and pulled by strong arguments for each. He was inclined to tolerate and forgive not just because it was the noble thing to do but because his long-delayed career as a poet could not endure any more impediments. He needed to do whatever would help him to write with a mind uncluttered by anger, resentment, recriminations.

Then, too, settling scores had a way of clearing the mind.

Revenge they say is a dish best served cold. At whatever temperature, it's pointless unless the avenger survives the delivery. Leave no fingerprints. No one needed to know about the attack in the park after school, nor about the plan taking shape in Simpson's mind. While he was at home convalescing he envisioned various cunning schemes with an array of weapons, poisons, viewing scenarios of retribution from every angle, as a mystery writer must survey her plot from all points of view, above and below, before and after. After much consideration, he arrived at a plan that could work. And it could do some damage.

Had Simpson needed documentation to excuse his absence, he had a note from the surgeon, but his teacher and classmates were told only that he was out sick for a week, and when he returned to school with a limp he simply said he had tripped and sprained his knee. Seeing his classmates' disappointment with that prosaic explanation, he improvised: he was kicked in the hip by a mule, a jackass . . . his fat brother couldn't see over his own belly and accidentally sat on him. Only the gang who were with Cutter that day in the park knew the real story, and they weren't talking.

It is said that someone who studies revenge keeps his own wounds green. But maybe not if you're quick about it. His aim was simple: self-respect. All he wanted was the private satisfaction of knowing that no one could wound or humiliate him with impunity. Simpson had been damaged in a place whose healing would take more than physical repair. Counsel about restoring self-respect would not have come from his all-forgiving Christian mother—she would have said turn the other cheek; pretend it never happened—and it did not come from his father. For many years he would resent Gasper's silence; he may as well have not even had a dad. Nor did it come from a pastor, priest, or any other adult, and didn't need to. It came from within, which felt like a higher authority: from the council hall of honor, the temple of conscience. He didn't need anyone to tell him what must be done; it was obvious.

Just one swift stroke of vengeance, then let it go. No brooding, no festering.

There would be no backlash against faithless little Steven Peters, who, if thought of now at all, was dismissed as Stevie Peters Out. Anyway, Simpson meant him no harm; he just didn't want to see him anymore. The companionship had been good while it lasted, and that was about all that needed to be said about it. Peters Out could slink away and shed his self-respect, if that was his idea of being alive. He could walk alone the rest of his days or befriend cowards as fickle as himself; it was of no concern to Simpson.

Cold, cold is the dish.

The plan was quite simple. Every day between fourth and fifth periods, Cutter Kline liked to swing himself around a steel pole near the stairwell by the second-floor lockers, making a Tarzan yell and showing how wild and free he was. His fireman-pole, some of the guys called it. *Man*-pole, said Cutter, and don't you forget it. He liked applause. "Good swing, Cutter!" "Wow, did you see that?" He had been doing this for as long as anyone could remember, and the teachers knew to look the other way. You could set your watch by it. If you heard a Tarzan yell, it was time to go to P.E. or science class.

From his locker nearby, Simpson quietly scouted the surroundings, noting the lighting dimmed by a burned-out bulb, the direction Cutter was coming from and how close he was to the stairwell when he grabbed his pole and swung, where his feet in their heavy klunky boots left the floor and where they landed, where other students usually were as they passed by on their way to class, and so on. For several weeks he took note, biding his time, quietly observing the conditions as Cutter swung round the man-pole. Unless the bully was skipping school, it was the same every day, as habitual and mechanical as the way he combed his hair or laced his boots.

Then came the day when the change between fourth and fifth periods went differently. All it took was a little Wesson cooking oil discreetly dripped on the dimly lit floor where Cutter took his leap, and the rest took care of itself. Simpson was innocently standing at his locker as a flash of motion and a cry of alarm was followed by the stomach-turning sound of a body tumbling down the hard concrete stairwell to the landing between the first and second floors and the gasps of alarm and quickly stifled laughter that turned to calls for help.

Simpson watched from the edge of the crowd as the school nurse told the students to stand back from the figure sprawled out as though he'd been dropped from the ceiling. His head was turned awry, nearly face-down, his knees and elbows bent awkwardly, in the wrong directions. Not much blood—the injuries were mostly internal—though his nose and jaw were scraped and bleeding. An ambulance was called and Cutter was taken away. When he returned to school three or four weeks later he was on crutches and didn't want to talk to anyone. He snarled at his old pals to stay clear. He moved awkwardly on his crutches, furious and humiliated, nervously wary that someone walking too close might cause him to trip. They said after that tumble down the stairs Cutter could barely concentrate in class, and his already poor grades dropped lower.

During the weeks Cutter Kline was out of school, a few of his followers asked Simpson if he knew anything. "I have no idea, but it looked terrible," he said with just enough concern and sympathy in his voice to sound credible. They asked if he thought maybe it was some classmate seeking revenge. "I doubt it. Everybody's too scared of him to dare such a thing." This seemed to satisfy them. To his surprise they did not look at him like they suspected he would have the guts to take revenge himself. "Maybe it was just an accident," he suggested, and stopped himself before adding, Then again, he's bullied so many kids, it could have been just about anyone.

The doctor says you're lucky.

It would not be accurate to call the Kick a gift that
kept on giving, but that attack had driven away his only
friend, and soon afterward Simpson began writing a
diary that evolved into a little series of poems. Not much
time had to pass before he could see that the poems
weren't any good, but even Keats and Shakespeare had to
start somewhere. Whether weeds or roses, they sprouted
because he felt all alone, pained by a terrible misery roiling inside him that needed to be released. It would have
helped if he had had some friend to talk to. He could
not play an instrument, and he couldn't draw like a kid
he used to know, but he knew how to spell, and since his
earliest childhood, farther back than he could remember,
the poetic language of the Scriptures was part of the air
he breathed, poured into him by his mother day after
day, bedtime after bedtime. Therefore he did the natural
thing: every day after school he sat at his cheap little
student desk of unfinished pine with his spiral notebook
and ballpoint pen from the dime store, the page lighted
and warmed by a 60-watt bulb, drilling deeper into his
own solitude to a level where there was no loneliness.
It was something he could do—it came so naturally he
hardly thought about it at first—and it made him feel
a little stronger to realize that this was one activity for
which he didn't need to ask for help from anyone.

11

Not Perfect, Just Forgiven

"MESSAGES OFTEN COME IN THREES," Simpson was once advised by a ten-buck fortune-teller in Jackson Square, before handing over ten dollars more than he thought the wisdom was worth. If you truly want to change, she said, ways will be shown to you. "Just like famous people die in groups of three sometimes. You never know who you're going to end up next to on the obituary page." He wasn't sure about the obituary part, though he did detect a threesome when he observed that Mr. Dumond's announcement about CopyQwik was preceded and followed by unsettling encounters that could be interpreted as clues sent to guide a seeker. First there was Cutter, then Mimi, and then . . .

He was ringing up a sale one slow afternoon when he noticed the customer's Wells Fargo bank card.

"Wow, cool. San Francisco?"

Her face brightened. "Yep. Moved here last month."

She looked familiar. She was about his age, wearing a crisp white blouse with a colorful Guatemalan vest and hand-crafted earrings of green and blue glass beads. Clear hazel eyes, no visible cosmetics.

"Wait, I remember you. You were asking about flooding. You moved *from* San Francisco *to* New Orleans? From the earthquakes to the hurricanes?"

"I guess so. You look surprised."

"Not surprised, really, just . . . stunned."

"Just take time to let it settle in. People move all the time. America is motion."

"I know, but . . ."

She smiled, watching his face as he struggled to process this information.

"Why move from there to here, you're wondering? I'm a painter. I love it here, and it's so much more affordable. And warmer. I kept coming here for visits, but after a while the visits weren't enough."

"I think I know the feeling."

"I like your busted timepiece there. I was in Dublin once, and all the public clocks told a different time of day. Who knows, maybe they were all true."

He studied the cracked crystal. Mixed emotions were welling up in him. For much of the day he had managed not to think about where he was supposed to be this week.

"I wish I'd met you before. We could have arranged some kind of apartment exchange. I've been wanting to move there forever, but family obligations . . ." His voice broke. "I was actually supposed to be there now, this week, but my mother, and then my brother—"

He stopped abruptly and touched the corners of his eyes. "Sorry. It's just so . . . I've been trying for years and I feel like I'll never get out of here. America may be motion, but I'm ... See, I've been trying to get started as a poet, but ..."

She nodded sympathetically. "I know. It's not easy. But if you're helping your family, that's a blessed thing, and you'll be rewarded, believe me. Don't give up."

"Thank you." He felt he didn't deserve such kind words.

"Time given to others is never time lost, don't you think?"

He nodded. He wanted to say something, but his voice would break and more tears would flow.

"When you do get out there, try to get a well-paying job if you can. Even in the cheaper neighborhoods like the Mission, the rents have just gone beyond insane."

"So I've heard." He nodded as he wrote his name on a CopyQwik business card.

At first she hesitated to reciprocate, then gave him her name and e-mail address.

"Wait, that wasn't the name on your bank card, was it?"

"So I have a new identity. Isn't that part of it?"

After she left, he dismissed the impulse to drop her contact info in the shredder. Normally, by habit, he shunned entanglements; he had places to go and didn't need more ties holding him back. But some kind of house share might be possible someday. And anyway, everything else was holding him back, so why not one more entanglement that happened also to be pretty, creative, and kind?

He moved through the rest of the day in a dream of bewilderment. It was hard to know what was real. She's an artist and *she chose to move here*, he kept telling himself, as though sheer repetition might help the fact sink in, but it could not be absorbed. He had never heard of such a thing. It all sounded backward and upside down. There was no reason why this stranger's move here should call his own plans into question, but the experience left him with a slippage of confidence, a growing suspicion that maybe all this time his California dream had been some kind of elaborate diversion fabricated to evade something else he should be doing instead. The same disquietude he had felt after seeing Mimi. Bewildered though he felt, however, at least this encounter gave him something to think about besides the aborted vacation.

Meanwhile, if there were any new developments with the potential buyout, Mr. Dumond was not sharing.

Chronically naive. Terminally misguided. Who but a fool would scheme for all these years to flee a place that inspired and attracted so many other artists? New Orleans had not been so bad for Tennessee Williams's career, and countless others likewise had come here and flourished. But Williams was from elsewhere; it's different if you're *from* here. Wherever he called home, though, there would be no poetry, no biographies, not even an obituary, if he didn't do something to restart his engines. Parroting George Eliot's "never too late" was no substitute for actually writing. The only way to avoid going to San Francisco only to crash and burn and despise himself forever as a permanently hopeless, one-balled failure and locked-in loser was to get some poetry flowing here and now.

As in *now*.

She shows me something . . .

That night after work he went home and ripped up the ridiculous desperate affirmation posters and incinerated them in his kitchen sink. He felt a certain grim satisfaction until the smoke set off the fire alarm. An electronic voice warned, "Fire! Fire!" but the batteries were low, so the warning sounded like a mortally wounded Confederate artillery captain ordering "fiyah . . ."

Then, energized by his decisive action, he sat down at the bare pine desk and pulled out a sheet of paper.

Just write something. Anything.

He patted his face and forehead with a paper towel.

He could see what would happen: He would move out to California and spend the rest of his life writing about the place he'd left behind. Or not writing at all. *If you move out here you'll have to get with the program.* He would fail there unless he practiced succeeding here, or at least succeeded in practicing. And wouldn't failure there be ten times worse than inertia here? Or better, because at least he would have gone there and tried?

He was tired, tired of overthinking, struggling to decide.

It's okay if I'm not a poet.

He gasped. He shocked himself. The very idea was radical, frightening in its implications. It's okay? Was everything he had thought about himself in the past twenty years, positive or negative, built upon sand, fabricated out of spit and fairy dust?

If so, it's all right.

He leaned back in the chair and looked around the room. What a strange thought. What a relief!

But still I feel I have the soul of an artist.

Then write something. Just a line, then another. It doesn't have to make sense. Rough, raw—just get it down.

He closed his eyes and breathed slowly, remembering a phrase that had echoed in his mind as he awoke that morning. Frightened of the distances. Frightened by distances. Everything so far away.

You're frightened by the distances
between that long dark narrow road through nowhere
and now, wherever you are,
wherever you think you're going—scared
because it's the distances that are growing,
not you.

There. Six lines, just like that. Maybe it was gibberish, but it was more than he'd had a minute ago. He put the page in the desk drawer and decided not to look at it until he had written ten or twenty more. A poem every morning before going to work, and then maybe more at night. It can be a few lines, or a few pages: just get something down that feels like a complete thing, simple and direct and honest. Produce now, critique later. He opened the drawer and looked at the page, not reading the words but seeing with soft focus the presence of ink on paper, multiple lines of verse in his own handwriting. Keep that image, he told himself. *You did that.* With a tight wry smile he turned the page facedown and closed the drawer.

He felt an unusual serenity.

Your daddy was awful proud of you.

It was possible—he had to admit this, and he had to really mean it—it was possible that he, Simpson Weems, had never been a poet and never would be. It was all right if he was not any kind of artist. And he felt calm. He could breathe. The biographers could write about someone else. They always do, anyway. Maybe all those stupid affirmations were but propaganda for a false idol, a juvenile ambition he should have outgrown already. Perhaps there was some other valuable kind of work he could have been doing for the past so many years, something he had never imagined because he was fixated on this one literary form. Steichen believed he was destined to be a painter until he met Stieglitz; then he realized photography was his medium. Changes of direction like this happened all the time. And it might help him to move to San Francisco, for there he might discover the art form he was meant to practice. Surely in the new century, the oncoming millennium, things would be possible that were as yet unimaginable. A bright new age of possibility, and he could play a part.

It's okay if I'm not a poet.

The darkening clouds had been building up for days, and thunder rumbled ominously, threatening rain, but not a drop would fall, and no lightning cracked to break the tension.

"This thunder is driving me crazy, Mother. Do something!"

Bartholomew bounced in his seat, slapping the sofa. "Crazy crazy crazy . . ."

Not looking up from her crossword puzzle, Melba licked her pencil and filled in 57 down.

"I'm gonna go make it stop," he said.

"Thunder don't take orders, lamb." She checked off 57.

"Maybe it's the voice of the Lord talkin' to us, ever think of that?" She looked at him over her silver-framed glasses.

His eyes went wide. The Coming.

"No! False! I'm not ready."

He heaved himself up from the sofa and stomped indignantly across the room. The floor trembled and the walls groaned, and for a moment the thunder was indoors.

Melba watched him bolt out the door.

He stalked into the yard, dark at midday, and screamed at the sky, "Cease! Right this instant! Enough!"

He came back inside and stood in the center of the living room with his arms folded awkwardly across his chest, heaving with excitement, not knowing what to do next.

"That oughta do the trick," she said, not looking up.

Bartholomew wiped his face but made no reply. His throat hurt from screaming.

He turned on the television. A commercial for weight reduction by liposuction. He switched off the TV abruptly.

"Honey, he was still talkin'. At least let him finish the sentence."

"This thunder needs to stop."

"What kind of birthday cake you want this year, hon'?"

"You know what I want. There's only one cake."

"I tried callin' Simpson, but he don't answer."

Bartholomew snorted. "Birthdays are happier without him."

"That's a bitter thing to say. Sweeten your tongue."

"Maybe he went to San Francisco anyway."

"Hush, now. He's your brother, and after I'm gone he's all you'll have left."

He clapped his hands to his ears, over his eyes, back and forth.

Melba watched his antics, feeling far away and indifferent, and turned back to her crossword. She felt tired, too heartsick to even sigh, and wished Simpson would at least make a brief appearance for his brother's birthday. It was so little to ask, and it would take some of the strain off her. He disliked singing the happy birthday song and refused to put so much as a crumb of the cake in his mouth. But really, it wouldn't kill him.

She had tried to make Bartholomew understand that the custom was to serve the special cake only on Jesus' birthday or in the days leading up to December 25;

it was not a movable feast. She should never have let the family tradition get this this deeply entrenched, but each attempt to let it lapse provoked a full-blown tantrum. Once he smashed her precious ceramic Sally & Peppy salt and pepper shakers, and another time he pulled all the food from the refrigerator onto the kitchen floor and left it for her to clean up. She no longer dared bypass even the smallest element of the ritual. He insisted on having the cake, which had to be called by its official name, the baby Jesus birthday cake, and singing happy birthday. She had to sing with him.

> *Happy birthday to you,*
> *Happy birthday to you,*
> *Happy birthday sweet Jesus,*
> *Happy birthday to you.*

Last year she did not risk any meltdowns, and, aside from her sorrow at Simpson's absence, everything had gone smoothly.

On his thirty-third birthday last year, Bartholomew clapped his hands with joy. "He really is happy, isn't he, Mommy? This is a special day. Were those really the only presents you got me? A gray sweater and a Bible stories bookmark? There must be something else. You're just trying to surprise me because you love me so much. Time's up. Where is it?"

"Hush your foolishness and show some gratitude. My word, the way you act, you'd think you were brung up in a toy store."

"There is one thing I'm grateful for."

"What's that?"

"Simpson's not here!"

"You're so mean. He never is, though. And you know why."

"He hates me, and he's never loved Jesus."

"Not true. I'd say he just doesn't understand you, you know, the way we wish he did. I really bet he'd be here if you didn't insist on the cake and the singin' every year."

"Maybe that's why I do it. I'm glad it's just you and me."

"Be nice to your brother, now, or when I'm gone you'll be on your own. I don't see Simpson bakin' you a cake of any kind."

Bartholomew could sing happy birthday to his own damn self. He couldn't seriously expect a gift after what he had done to Simpson's trip. How about the sharp end of a shovel, or a deep tank full of supercharged electric eels? He needed to be taught a lesson he'd never forget.

But really, even though he was able to memorize statistics and state birds like an idiot savant, could it be said that Bartholomew ever actually learned lessons?

Could it be said of me?

And who am I anyway to teach anyone a lesson?

While Melba had her church and Bartholomew his air-conditioned chamber of prayer and his old preacher friend, Simpson had no sanctuary for meditation and solace other than his long meditative walks. He used to like Bourbon Bath, but his favorite water-nymph had slipped away, so for a quiet, contemplative place he turned to his father's tomb at St. Perpetua's. Not quite the same.

He walked to the cemetery on an overcast Sunday afternoon under the canopy of his black umbrella because he was sure the rain was going to start falling at any moment. He would have been in San Francisco now. He couldn't bear to think about it, and yet, aside from the artist he'd met at CopyQwik, he could think of little else. His mind was being consumed by termites. He walked past the black tree of Dangers Park and the statue of the weeping maiden, over the wooden footbridge, and with the umbrella screening his face he moved in an almost furtive crouch to the cemetery's gate along Invalides Street. They could be watching from the front window. He did not want to have to explain why he had passed so close to their house without visiting. They should know why.

The white rose from Mrs. Rabineaux's garden had bent and wilted where he had placed it among the artificial flowers still duct-taped to the granite inscription tablet. The plastic orange and pink petals were already fading, sun-bleached. He sat down on a concrete bench across the white shell path from the long wall of tombs, four vaults high and many dozens wide. His father's inscription tablet like all the others was about two feet wide and thirty inches high, about the dimensions of a filing cabinet drawer. Behind the granite plate was a layer of red brick and mortar, and behind that the urn of ashes, the tomb dark and silent as outer space. A light breeze rustled the branches of the weeds and small young trees that had sprouted from cracks along the top of the brick-and-plaster wall of vaults, and mockingbirds sang in the cedars nearby.

Thirteen years. Imagine if someone else had been dead that long.

As much as he wanted to crack Bartholomew's thick skull, it was not normally like him to be vindictive, nor to holler and rampage like some people. Thus the tension headaches. He liked to think of his attitude as stoical realism, not passivity, but maybe he was more like his father than he wanted to admit, resigned with philosophical acceptance of things as they are—the serenity to accept the things I cannot change, without the serenity. Maybe he could trade in his potential career as a poet for a philosopher's robes. The unexamined life and all that. But really, what else could he do but bide his time and stay alert for an opportune moment, if one should arise? There were no magic eel tanks, and despite his mother's fears Bartholomew was not likely to run out in front of a city bus. She said of course you can take a vacation, but when was he ever actually able to extricate himself from their entanglements, even for a few days? Every time he reserved a flight, red emergency lights flashed. There was nothing to be done about it except to try with redoubled determination to concentrate and compose his lines; to apply his powers of visualization not in fantasies of fratricide but in *mentally* inhabiting his idealized North Beach apartment—to be there in his astral body, perhaps—and write and write as though he were actually there. Like Button said, be an artist wherever you are. That is what the great authors of yore would do: they found ways to turn obstacles into fuel, material for work. From the ancient Hebrew prophets to prisoners in Soviet gulags, even in harsh and brutal conditions it's possible to compose a few enduring lines. And was he any less a poet?

He came back to himself and found he was staring at sprigs of ferns growing between the bricks and cement where an inscription plate had fallen from its tomb. The green of spring. Hope. Liberation through stealth. There were certain steps that could be taken, and, if handled judiciously, no one would ever have to know.

What would Father do? What would he want Simpson to do?

It felt pointless to think in terms of *forgiving*—that would be a profound conversion that could take the rest of his life—but if he could just begin to try to *accept* Bartholomew, then the wounds might begin to heal. After all these years, wasn't it about time to try to make peace with the fact that Bartholomew existed, and that, however exasperating, he was his parents' child just as surely as Simpson himself was? Assuming, of course, that the *mariage blanc* "virgin birth" story was all in Melba's imagination.

Yes, he supposed he could try, though he could also do them all a favor by sprinkling odorless rat poison on Bartholomew's Cap'n Crunch breakfast cereal. There were so many ways he could make it look like an accident.

Easy, now. Not at Dad's tomb.

Think of it this way, he counseled himself as though he were an older, wiser writing instructor: You'll have more fertile experience for your work if you just try to accept him. One day at a time. Stop resisting the fact that he is what he is. Help him get situated with a job and the SSI. That will help Mom breathe easier.

Bartholomew's obstruction of Simpson's vacation was infuriating, but it was consistent with his burning the lottery check, or spray-painting JESUS JESUS and crosses all over Dad's Skylark. Gasper had had every right to chop the kid's head off, but he only shrugged and sighed, "Bartholomew will be Bartholomew." Simpson had often thought that if his father had had the courage of a minnow he'd have thrashed the corpulent brat within an inch of his life—think of all the taxidermy tools he could have used!—but Father and Mother had never been tough enough. Frightened of his volcanic tantrums, they had let the baby tyrant rule. Forgive and forget. Better yet, pretend it isn't happening.

So what would Gasper advise now? Simpson worried that he might be watching from his place in heaven, or wherever in the afterlife he was—perhaps rambling through celestial meadows with the souls of the animals whose skins he had mounted—and didn't want to cause him any more grief. Dad would want the same thing that Mother asked: Be patient with your brother. Suffer his little annoyances and try to love him as we have loved you.

Time was running out. His birthday was approaching. Bartholomew was a hard one to buy for; ordinary gifts left him cold—or hot-flustered and whining—but small oddities could please him to no end. Who cares? Just buy him a new NOT PERFECT, JUST FORGIVEN T-shirt to replace the old one that was chocolate-stained and threadbare from years of washing and stretching.

But he doesn't deserve a gift.

Now, now, he could hear his mother saying, it's not for you to decide who deserves what. And anyway, Simpson thought, maybe he doesn't have to deserve it— maybe that's not the point of giving—but you have to accept him or you'll be crippled inside. All right, then: the T-shirt. He had found the idea in one of the philosophers or mystical poets he read in lieu of going to church, something about forgiveness being the path to liberation, inner peace. It had to be worth a try, because a lifetime of resentment and blaming had only bound the barbed wire tighter around him.

The heart pain caused by Simpson's absence was not helping the tightness in her chest. She phoned the office of Dr. Garcia's young replacement but was not able to get through to an actual person, so she left another voicemail message.

Sometimes it helped to go out and get some fresh air. When she got back she would sit down at her new typewriter and start drafting a living will. Simpson said he would give her notes to an attorney he knew downtown to get it drawn up nice and official.

She needed to stock up on plastic babies for Bartholomew's cakes, anyway, so she took the bus down to

McKenzie's Pastry Shoppe on Elysian Fields near Gentilly where her old girlfriend Buzz was still behind the counter after all these years.

They had been best friends since they worked together in their early twenties. Buzz was always happy to see Melba come in alone, free from that big fat nuisance son of hers. Melba Flo was so sweet and kind, she didn't deserve to be cursed and afflicted with a baby-man like that, pouting and pulling on her and carrying on all the time. He couldn't let his mother have a minute's chat with an old friend without turning jealous and acting up. It didn't matter if two or twenty people were in the store. Everything was him him him. So it was a relief to see old Melba come in by herself because it meant she had a little time to herself which Lord knows a gal needs now and then. Buzz never could go by and visit with Melba at her house because *he* was always there, glaring and grumbling. She was surprised Melba had lived as long as she had with him demanding on her all day every day for thirty some years now. And that other son of hers didn't seem to be no help at all.

Buzz was plump like Melba, but despite all her years at the bakery, she wasn't as far gone as some of her customers, the ones who always had to have "two a dem and gimme six a doze." She wore thick black-framed eyeglasses and a pink uniform that made her look like a hotel maid, but she didn't mind. A job's a job.

"Melba Flo. How's life been treatin' you, girl?"

"Can't complain. Mardi Gras wiped y'all out?"

Buzz shrugged. "About like usual. Glad it's over for a while."

Melba leaned over the counter and gave her a kiss.

"How was your Christmas, Melba? Santy good to you?"

"My, I haven't seen you since then? Oh, it was all right. I got Bartholomew some cute new dinosaur pajamas, and he gave me a nice potholder. Simpson don't celebrate Christmas anymore, and won't even let me give him a present, so that kind of cuts down on the shopping. So what I do is I just send him a check in the mail, or stuff an envelope in his laundry basket."

"Don't celebrate Christmas? What, he gone and took up one of them foreign religions that don't even recognize the birth of Christ?" She raked her fingers back through her thick silver hair and frowned at the tray of gingerbread men.

"Well, sometimes he likes to help out at a church soup kitchen down on Rampart, so I guess that's his way of celebratin' the holidays. He just says Christmas is for children and he's all grown up and don't have his own kids so why mess with it."

Buzz shook her head. Some of these college types seemed to care more about the destitute than their own flesh and blood.

"But it would please his mother, wouldn't it?"

"I think it just depresses him, you know, bein' unmarried and all." Melba sighed, sadly eyeing the trays of sweets. She was surprised to hear herself admit it.

"Depresses him? Why, it's a time of cheer and joy. Your boys got some funny brains in their head, Melba Flo."

"He and Bartholomew both have charity in their hearts. Bartholomew does his readings for the blind. It doesn't bring in any money, but it's a service to those who need it."

Buzz nodded but said nothing to this.

"Well, I can't stay long. I just wanted to say hey, and pick me up my babies."

"Oh, yeah, I set some aside. Let's see where I put 'em."

She walked to the back room while Melba stood absently rubbing her chest, looking at a photograph slipping in its frame, an old black-and-white of Buzz and Melba and the other counter girls back in the 1950s.

"Here we go," said Buzz. "All we got left is the black babies, though. Can he do with that?"

"Reckon he'll have to. Jesus is Jesus."

"A dozen'll do you for a while?"

"Oh, yeah. He just likes 'em in his cake. You know how children get used to having things done a certain way."

"Yes. I know how children are."

"I was looking at your picture there," said Melba, putting the little bag in her purse. "You and the girls smilin' so fresh and pretty. Were we ever really that skinny?"

Buzz smiled. "You're in there too, ladybug, cute as a button." She straightened the tilted frame and dusted the glass with a napkin. "Yeah, I loved my girls. That was a good time. Jo Raye died just last year, you heard? Cancer, poor heart."

"God rest her."

Buzz smiled sadly. "I was thinkin' about you just the other day, what good care you took of Mama. You made her look so pretty. I love you."

Melba smiled and blinked hard. "I was happy to do it. She was a fine lady." She dabbed a Kleenex under her eyeglasses. "Well, I should be gettin' on home. He's expectin' me."

"Stay and talk to me a while. Ain't seen you since forever. Saw old Rabineaux last week. Poor thing. Nothin' to do now that he closed the shop. His boy didn't want nothin' to do with it."

"Simpson neither. He says Roscoe's still open, he just don't have any business, so it's like he closed it. Bartholomew worked there one day about ten years ago, but that was all. Roscoe said he couldn't take him talkin' about Gasper like he was still alive."

"Can't blame him. It's creepy as hell."

Melba said it might be unusual, or it might be normal, she wasn't sure anymore. "As long as he's happy."

"But he *ain't* happy, Melba. And you ain' neither."

"We're fine," Melba assured her. "Richly blessed. The Lord's good to us."

Buzz twisted her apron strings tight around her finger. It did no good to tell her otherwise. Melba was the uncomplaining type exactly as that son of hers was quick to air the slightest annoyance. It was the kind of situation you could do nothing about. It had to take its own course.

"Well, I'd better go."

"You okay? You keep rubbin' your chest. Heart pains?"

"Well, in a way, 'cause I really wish Simpson would come for his brother's birthday tomorrow, but he don't answer the phone. I don't know where he is."

"No, I mean—"

"Oh, it's just a little itch. Well, I better get on home and start bakin' his birthday joy."

Buzz looked at her sadly. With each visit it seemed they had less and less to talk about on account of Melba's insisting everything was fine.

"Well, here, take some of this king cake for yourself. It's experimental. I made it just this morning, tryin' out a new cream cheese. But like I said, we ran out of the little pink babies. Let me know how you like it."

Bartholomew knocked a second time and still there was no answer. His heart was sinking. It was too terrible to imagine there could come a day when he came to Rev. Bud's door and it was closed forever. As far as he knew, he was the only member from Rev's old church who still remembered him, except for the anonymous deliverer of the weekly food basket. Whoever brought the basket never bothered to knock, but only set it on the porch by the door. Once a week Rev would open the door and feel around for the wicker handle. Bartholomew felt the church basket should not be Rev's only food supply, so he sometimes brought a brown paper bag of apples or Plaquemines oranges from the neighborhood fruit vendor.

He knew people talked about Rev behind his back, though he didn't see what the fuss was about. Tales and rumors. His mother, who rarely uttered a word against anyone, tried to warn him away from the old man. But who else was he supposed to turn to? His own father was long dead, and no one else saw him for who he really was. *A blind man alone sees the real me.* He recalled a T-shirt he once made for himself with magic markers, after a bumper sticker he'd seen, that read DON'T SEE 'ME'—SEE JESUS! —GAL. 2:20.

But Father wasn't really dead. Bartholomew sometimes heard him speaking, and the sound was natural and immediate, a resonant presence, not an echo.

Father was still close by, but it was confusing sometimes the way a memory of him from long ago could feel closer than one more recent. Summer nights when they sat together in the backyard counting the fireflies felt more immediate than Gasper's burial.

He must not have explained it well, because the notion of slippery time had made no sense to Rev. "That's the craziest damn thing I ever heard of. You tellin' me that something that happened in '86 feels longer ago than '76, like? Can't help you with that one, son. You need to get your clock fixed."

And so he had asked Mother.

"Oh, I don't know, Pumpkin, you know things just kind of flit through my head like birds of a feather and I don't pay 'em much mind, but I'm sure I've prob'ly felt things close up and far away just like you say you have. I think it just means you're a normal healthy growing boy."

As ever, she had a way of putting his worries at ease.

Why was Rev not answering the door? He knocked a third time.

Lately it seemed that Rev. Bud was often irritable, on edge, just as Father had grown cranky in his last year. He hoped this didn't mean what he was afraid it meant. And Rev's thoughts were getting hard to follow, as though several streams of biblical and even pagan stories were mixing in his head and he couldn't remember what he had started out talking about.

Finally an object struck the door.

"Reverend Bud? It's me, Bartholomew. Are you okay? Are you mad at me for coming?"

"Not at all, boy, I'm always glad to see you. Come on in. I'm just mad. I'm just mad."

The old man's breathing sounded agitated, and shallower than usual.

"Here, I brought you some apples, fresh from J.J. the vegetable man. I came to read to you like you asked me to."

"Thank you. How thoughtful. Got your Bible?"

Bartholomew knelt and opened the holy book. With the help of a little pocket flashlight he read the passage Rev had requested, from the book of Ezekiel—the old man's favorite, after Lamentations—about the prophet's vision in the valley of dry bones.

Bud Rex was smiling, nodding his head, and his voice joined with Bartholomew's as he read, "*I will open your graves, and cause you to come up out of your graves, and bring you into the land of Israel.*"

"Thank you, son. You have a good voice. You are a comfort to an old man in his sorrows. Here, I have one for you:

"*If thou draw out thy soul to the hungry, and satisfy the afflicted soul; then shall thy light rise in obscurity, and thy darkness be as the noonday. And the Lord shall guide thee continually, and satisfy thy soul in drought, and make fat thy bones: and thou shalt be like a watered garden, and like a spring of water, whose waters fail not.*"

"Oooh, Isaiah," Bartholomew sighed contentedly. He was kneeling, his hands together in prayer.

"I stopped by that shrine on the way over here," he said. "I like that place, and the sound of the water in the fountain. A watered garden."

Rev. Bud smiled and nodded. "Poor old St. Roch. He was like St. Francis. Grew up a rich boy, gave it all away to help the poor. He was on a pilgrimage to Rome when he started finding all these poor souls dying of the plague. He healed people by making the sign of the cross over them, but then he got infected, himself, and developed these terrible sores. He went into a forest to die alone so he wouldn't infect anybody, but a dog befriended him, and every day the dog would bring him food. The Lord healed him. When Roch recovered he went back to his hometown, but he had gotten so wasted looking they didn't recognize him. They called him an impostor and threw him in jail. After he died, there was a miraculous sign of a cross on his chest called a stigmata. Then they knew he really was who he'd claimed to be. People here used to pray to St.

Roch in times of yellow fever. He's the one you call on for help in hopeless cases. You ever been over to the St. Roch cemetery, the Campo Santo?"

"No." Bartholomew shuddered. "Mother says she's heard it's creepy and scary. There's a glass case with a statue of a dead bloody crucified Christ lying down in it. She says I don't need to see that."

"In the paintings St. Roch is always shown with a wound on his leg and a dog with a loaf of bread in its mouth. In school we used to say it was french bread, a shrimp po-boy. They say if you want St. Roch to help you, you need to feed his dog. It means you got to do deeds of charity for the poor, because that's where he is found, always helping the destitute. Blessed are the poor in spirit. Feed St. Roch's dog."

"You really do like these saints and martyrs, don't you? I guess ever since your church pushed you out and you got mugged, you identify with the martyrs. Like you've gone Catholic or something."

Bud Rex shrugged, fluffed his long white hair about his shoulders, and stroked his beard thoughtfully.

"I identify with the martyrs, too," Bartholomew said. "I feel their pain."

Rev. Bud cleared his throat.

"Have you done what your mother was asking?"

Hearing no reply, he asked again.

"Yes sir, I've been looking." Bartholomew was beginning to sweat. "I applied at the library downtown, and I'm going to check at the funeral home, too. Can we begin the lesson now, Rev?"

"Good, I'm glad to hear it. And wasn't there something else, too?"

He should not have come. Should have turned around after the second knock. "I'm supposed to make an appointment to see a doctor. But do I *have* to?" he groaned. "Okay. But tomorrow's my birthday so *please* don't make me talk about this any more."

"Well, well, happy birthday, Bartholomew. May the Lord richly bless you. Your mama gonna bake you a nice cake? Bring me a piece. Now read me that part in Ezekiel again, about the parents eating their children."

In the dim stuffy room Bartholomew clicked his penlight and pointed to the dog-eared passage. The battery was low, the light dimming.

"*Therefore the fathers shall eat the sons in the midst of thee, and the sons shall eat their fathers; and I will execute judgments in thee, and the whole remnant of thee will I scatter into all the winds.*"

"That's enough, thank you. That'll get me started."

Bud Rex stroked his beard and pondered awhile.

"All men are savages," he began. "By nature, by instinct, any one of us . . ."

He was doing it again. Over the past year or so Bartholomew had watched helplessly as the Reverend went more and more often into long trances, as though a spell had been cast on him that gave voice to strange utterances or prophecies that were mystifying, sometimes frightening. Long intricate tales and legends that for all Bartholomew could tell bore no relation to the Scripture they were supposed to be discussing. Rev might begin with Genesis, but with an abrupt turn he would be telling about the four horsemen of the Apocalypse, or the children roasted in the sacrificial ovens of Moloch. Just as suddenly, he might start weeping for the lost little ones. "What lost little ones?" Bartholomew asked. "The burning children? The sons eaten by the fathers?" But the trance could not be broken.

"Rev," he said, "tell me again about the caves," but the elder heard him not.

"All men are killers . . ."

Bartholomew nodded faintly, and patted his forehead with his handkerchief. His stomach rumbled. He was uncomfortably warm, and felt he should go. There were no clocks in Rev's house, and if there were, they wouldn't tell the time, and even if they did, it would be too dark to see. Bartholomew wanted to stay and hear more wisdom, but he was drowsy and hungry. Something was telling him to go.

"Women too?"

"Women *are* men. I count women among men."

Bartholomew blinked and dabbed at his face.

"And then are men women, too?" It was hot and he was confused.

"It's the same thing," Rev said impatiently, sounding tired. "It don't matter. Yes, logically they would be. I just say 'men' 'cause that's what I'm used to sayin', but you could say it the other way and it's just as true."

Bartholomew echoed inwardly what he had heard the old man say, but it made no sense. He did not mean to be disrespectful, but remarks like these made him wonder whether the Reverend Bud Rex really understood what he was saying anymore. He really should be going.

Bartholomew was away when Melba got home. As soon as she put down her bags she took a bite of Buzz's experimental king cake. The first slice was exquisite: moist, creamy, just at the edge of too sweet. A taste of decadence. Buzz had really done it this time. The flavors spread out over her tongue in waves of pleasure and sweet satisfaction. She didn't know what came over her, but it was pulling at her. Irresistible. The second slice was even better. She had meant to save a piece for Bartholomew, but it was going fast. He'd better not stay gone too long or it would all be gone. Melba was just biting into the last slice when she heard him halfway down the block singing his song.

He would be furious if he discovered that she had had some McKenzie's king cake and hadn't saved any for him. Furious! Quickly she gobbled in a panic—so quickly she couldn't even taste the flavors—in big bites that she didn't even chew: she just swallowed huge gulps of the soft cake till suddenly a chunk of hard plastic caught in her throat and lodged there.

She could not breathe, couldn't cough it up. She staggered and fell to the floor, gripping her throat, kicking and flailing about. The last sound she heard, over her own gulping convulsions, was Bartholomew's happy tune, "I love my sweet Jesus . . ."

I see thee blessed soule, I see,
Walke in Elisian fieldes so free.

SPENSER, *The Shepheardes
Calender* (1579)

March 1999

MELBA HAD ONCE EXPLAINED to the boys that although some might think the Elysian Fields were some kind of ancient Greek or Roman athletic fields, like for the Olympics, what she had learned in school was that they were golden grassy sunlit islands at the ends of the earth where the happy spirits of the dead dwell in paradise forever and a day. Even as a child Simpson had immediately thought of the West, of California, while Bartholomew understood her to mean that Elysium was a place where people are glad they're dead.

Now, in his mother's semiprivate room on the thirteenth floor at Charity Hospital downtown, Simpson held her hand as she spoke in a soft whisper about going west, out to the islands of heaven. He nodded, not catching every word but envisioning sunlit meadows waving in the breeze, a land of asphodel and golden apples under celestial blue skies and eternal sunshine where hurricanes never blow.

He touched the corners of his eyes. "That's nice. That's good, Ma. Maybe I'll see you out West someday. We could, you know," he paused to swallow hard, "hang out together."

"I'll be all right, honey," she whispered. "Just catching my breath."

She smiled weakly and moved her hand across the bedsheets toward him, but couldn't quite raise her arm. The veins of her hand showed blue and purple through translucent skin. Hypodermic needle bruises up and down her arms.

The greatest shock, at first, was seeing her without her wig: her wisps of white hair were short and thin as a baby's. She looked small and thin, as though she had shrunk and aged years in only a few days, and her blue eyes were cloudy and sunken amid dark gray circles. Feeding tubes inserted through her left nostril were held in place by strips of translucent plastic surgical tape across her upper lip, and an intravenous tube was taped to her right forearm. The purple bruise around the insertion point was spreading like wine spilled on a tablecloth.

He stroked her thin tufts of hair with a soft-bristled baby brush and told her she looked pretty, but she had gone back to sleep. It struck him that before long someone at Lourdes would be brushing her hair and giving her face, cold and still, the touch-ups of powder and blush that it had once been her job to give to others.

All the mortuary cosmeticians who have gone before her.

A nurse had explained to him that his mother had choked on a plastic king cake baby ("it happens more than you'd expect") thickly clotted with cake and icing, and while unconscious Melba's heart and brain had suffered oxygen deprivation damage. Her condition was listed as critical but stable, the nurse said, though the only stability he could see was a steady decline. Mother's strength was diminishing as the shortness of breath was encroaching: with each shallow breath she felt a stabbing pain in her chest.

"White roses?" She squinted toward the window. "I ain't dead yet. Where's Bartholomew?"

When Simpson arrived, noticing that the other bed was now unoccupied, he had set the vase of roses on the windowsill where the light of day seemed to pour directly into the blossoms and brighten the room.

"He'll be over in a while." He had come early, without his brother, wanting to visit her alone for a while, in peace. "I think he's making an appointment with Dr. Finestein. I gave him some money so he can call a taxi."

"You take good care of your brother. Promise you'll make sure he's provided for."

I'll take care of him all right.

He cleared his throat. "I promise. Of course."

After a long silence she said, "He's been so sweet, sittin' here singin' to me."

Her eyes were closed. He could hardly hear her breathing.

Some time later she opened her eyes a crack and said, "All is forgiven."

"Forgive me? For what?" he whispered. "Mother, what are you talking about? San Francisco?" The mutual fund?

He felt a heavy sinking sensation of dread in his stomach, a kind of vertigo of guilt. Just a little less conscientiousness or paranoia and he would have been out there now, at this moment, blissfully oblivious, and he might not have known she was in the hospital at all until it was too late.

As her words echoed, he thought, Wait—*you* forgive *me*?

Each day she slept more than the day before. Critical but stable? She was only getting weaker, the sharp pains piercing deeper.

"Doctor, is there any chance she might turn around?" Simpson asked a young intern who came by each morning to check on her. The doctor frowned and tilted his head. If the EMT had been called right away—Simpson knew what he meant: had Bartholomew dialed 911 instead of sitting frozen on the sofa in a panicked state of denial, waiting for the Holy Spirit or his mother to revive herself—then her prognosis might be brighter. Thank God Mrs. Dupuy from next door had come over to borrow a cup of sugar. But even then, the organs had been damaged by prolonged oxygen deprivation.

"Her heart and lungs were weak before the choking," said the intern. "It looks like for a long time they were only getting about half the blood and oxygen they need, so she was already not in good shape. I'm sorry. I wish we could be more optimistic."

Now she was moaning. The nurses said it was pitiful. They and the doctors were having a hard time calibrating the pain medication, a morphine derivative administered through the IV tube in her arm. If the dosage was too low, she felt the stabbing pains when she inhaled, yet, if they gave her too much, it was harder to breathe.

Her pale, sweaty face twisted in pain and she squeezed Simpson's hand weakly, but though he expected a sharp intake of breath he heard only a faint, labored inhalation.

"Please." She spoke with effort. "If you loved me you'd pull the plug."

"Mom, honey," he reached for her hand and squeezed tenderly, "you know I love you, but there's nothing plugged in to you."

He gently pressed a cool washcloth to her cheek and forehead, then touched the cloth to the corner of his eye.

"It's up to you, the eldest son. Bartholomew can't do it. Remember, you promised."

She pushed a pillow toward him.

"Ssshhh. You don't mean that." He fluffed the pillow and propped it behind her head. "Get some sleep, now."

"That's what I'm axin' you for. I have prayed to the Lord for mercy. Now do as your mother tells you." With her eyes half open she drew her forefinger like a blade across her throat.

He did not know it yet, but these were the last words he would ever hear her speak because that afternoon the doctors raised the dosage of the morphine and inserted a ventilator tube down her throat to help her breathe. The pain medication also helped her get the rest her body needed, though she was still hurting because at times she moaned or whimpered in her sleep. After this point it was rare that the brothers saw her eyes open.

Their mother's last days in the hospital would have been less contentious, and Simpson's tension headaches might have throbbed less violently, had Bartholomew agreed to cosign the consent form, and had there been a living will to refer to. Simpson had told her he would help her get it drawn up if she would get a rough draft down on paper. He distinctly remembered that at least twice in recent months, and as recently as several weeks ago, she had told him that if she were ever deathly ill she would not want to be kept alive by artificial means. But did she ever tell her other son?

"When the time comes, let nature take its course."

"Okay, Ma," Simpson said. "That's fine. I understand."

"When the Lord calls me, I am His."

He had gone down the hall and knocked on his brother's locked bedroom door. "Please, Barto, Mom needs you to come hear this." Bartholomew ignored him, so Simpson stood outside, reciting her wishes: no life support, no extraordinary measures, etc. As he repeated the main points for good measure, his voice echoing in the hallway where their father had fallen while changing a lightbulb, where minute splinters and glass dust from the shattered 75-watt Sylvania probably still lay in crevices along the molding, he could picture Bartholomew in there on his sofa between two humming air conditioners with his eyes closed and his fingers in his ears, frowning, sweating.

Now, as the brothers sat on either side of their mother's bed, Simpson said, "Do you know if Mom ever got around to typing up a living will? She said she was going to, but I can't find it anywhere."

Wedged into a visitor's chair with his arms folded and resting on his belly, Bartholomew frowned and shook his head. She had to come back. She was a mother with responsibilities. He was still angry at his father for getting away. Coward.

He seldom left this room anymore. Frightened that she would slip away if he went home, he kept a vigil as though guarding an eternal flame, an occupation that annoyed the nurses who had to step over and around him. They did not like the look or the smell of him, or the way he littered the floor with empty bags and cups from local fast food franchises. They pleaded, bossed and bullied, but the loyal son would not budge until his mother recovered. A doctor quietly directed the nurses to let him stay as long as he didn't disturb other patients. "But, Doctor, he smells, and he ain't showered." The doctor shrugged, prescribed toleration. He knew it was against regulations, but it would hardly be the first time, and anyway the vigil would likely not last much longer.

With Bartholomew now occupying the room at all hours, Simpson had to negotiate for some occasional moments of private time with his mother. After numerous diplomatic entreaties, he managed a few times to persuade Bartholomew to leave the room briefly, begrudgingly, to roam the halls, grumbling with displeasure at his brother's intrusion and complaining to the indifferent nurses.

In those few quiet, peaceful interludes alone with his mother, Simpson talked to her about what he had been thinking in his recent visits to the cemetery, about his father, his brother, and his hopes of California. Even though she was no longer conversant, apparently no longer conscious, he felt that somehow, heart to heart, she was still listening.

The respirator machine and monitors were beeping on a regular rhythm, their red and green lights and numbers pulsing.

Simpson had asked for a nurse or doctor some time ago. Was her condition still stable, or only critical? Someone should have come by now.

Even if there had been a written will, he realized, Bartholomew would simply deny it was real.

Then it struck him: *He's scared shitless.* His mother's dying and he doesn't know what he's going to do. For a moment Simpson saw Bartholomew not as his brother, not in relation to himself, but as a frightened child.

Who would bake his baby Jesus cake?

He sensed they were probably equally frightened. Seriously, what were they going to do without her? Grievances between brothers were irrelevant. Right now she needed prayers, mercy, calm. She needed love.

If you really want to be a grown-up, he told himself, now would be a good time. You're only as big as your capacity to forgive.

A brief flame of compassion warming his heart was chilled and extinguished as he remembered it was because of Bartholomew—his all-demanding neediness and his sheer exhausting intensity—that Mother was here at all. And he had worn Father down to death.

"Christ, Barto, sign off on the consent form already, will you? We have to let her go. It's the only humane thing to do. She never wanted this."

"No. Respect life."

"That's what I'm talking about."

Bartholomew leaned forward with his elbows on his knees and stared hard at the floor. He was not going to tolerate much more of this foolishness. Simpson had a weakness for overdramatizing, especially to vex others.

"Respect life. Respect life," he intoned with machine-like repetitiveness. The sweat dripping off his nose and chin to the linoleum floor formed a reflecting pool between his feet.

A piteous sound in her throat tore at Simpson's heart.

"For God's sake, Bartholomew, can't you hear she's in pain? I'm signing the goddamn form without you."

"I'm sorry, Simpson," he replied in a voice that sounded eerily calm, robotic, otherworldly. "We can't allow you to do that." He wiped the sweat from his face with one of their father's old monogrammed handkerchiefs.

" 'We' ?"

Was he deliberately channeling the voice of Hal 9000, the master computer in *2001: A Space Odyssey*?

"She's fine," Bartholomew said. "She'll be back."

"Right. Just like Dad."

"Well, didn't he? Isn't he with us?"

"Barto, you have to stop talking about Dad as if he's still alive. Accept reality. We went to his tomb, remember?"

"Accept reality," Bartholomew snorted. "What's the matter, am I confusing you? Anyway, you just want her out of the way so you can abandon me."

Don't take the bait.

"Look, she's not going to come back like Dad did those times. That was weird. I'm not sure what happened there. You hear her moaning. Doesn't it break your heart?"

"O ye of little faith. It's ecstasy. She feels the Lord's embrace."

"You're not just crazy—you're cruel! Where's the god-damn doctor? Where's the nurse? We called for them twenty minutes ago."

"I canceled the order while you were in the bathroom, doing whatever you were doing in there that took you so long."

"You what?! I thought it was safe to go. Usually they don't come for at least ten minutes anyway. You didn't really."

"*Someone* has to be the responsible grown-up here."

As it was today, and yesterday, so it would be again tomorrow, the brothers arguing in circles as their mother's strength ebbed away.

What was he even doing here when he should be at his desk in North Beach, or writing at Caffé Trieste as the pretty barista glances at him while steam-pressing cappuccinos and Caruso sings "O Sole Mio" from the jukebox . . . ?

Bartholomew was standing over their mother, on the other side of the bed, saying something about how peaceful she looked.

Had she died while he was daydreaming of North Beach?

Alarmed, Simpson checked the monitors, then touched his mother's wrist. A feeble pulse.

"The maid is not dead, but sleepeth."

These were Bartholomew's words, said Thelma Dupuy, when she first let herself in and saw Melba unconscious on the floor. "I knew she was home, and thought it was strange when she didn't answer the door. No tellin' how long he would've just sat there, maybe waitin' for her to resurrect herself like they said your daddy did."

After taking some deep breaths to slow his panicked heartbeat, Simpson spoke in as controlled a voice as he could muster, though his vocal cords felt taut as overstretched violin strings.

"Remember when I asked you to come listen to Mom saying she didn't want to be kept alive by artificial life support?"

"I'm sorry, Simpson." The Hal voice again.

In the same placid voice he suggested, "Why don't we pray together? The Lord is with us."

"Bartholomew . . ."

Well, it couldn't hurt to try. Wasn't this something she would want?

"Okay. Maybe you're right. Why don't you start us off?"

Bartholomew reached across the bed, and they joined hands, like a bridge over still waters. Sensing the damp warmth of his brother's fingers, Simpson waited.

Would it be the voice of Hal? How was this supposed to work?

He was just beginning to string some words together to say a silent prayer himself when Bartholomew said aloud, as though beginning one of his interminable blessings at the dinner table, "O Lord, guide her safely back, and let her not be troubled by brotherly strife and petty differences, most of which are Simpson's petty differences, and—"

Simpson jerked his hands away. "You call this a prayer?"

Bartholomew smiled tolerantly, benignly, as if to say, Come, now, my brother, let peace prevail, and reached his hands forth again.

"Where there is pain, give comfort. And give my brother self-control to refrain from his unbrotherly selfishness—"

Simpson again pulled his hands away and glared with disgust at his brother who kept talking with eyes closed.

"I thought we were praying for Mom."

If he were a total unbeliever rather than a semi-agnostic, if he had only been indulging his brother's fantasies, he would quit the charade. But there was a chance Bartholomew had the right idea, and a sincere prayer, an authentic prayer, really might help her. Anything that could help was worth trying.

"Let's try again and do it right this time."

Bartholomew was still praying aloud, his eyes closed and palms upraised in the stance of a televangelist.

Without waiting for his brother to stop, Simpson began, at equal volume, "Lord, please spare her from suffering. . ."

Now they were both praying, their voices escalating in a contest as though the highest volume would reach heaven first and the Almighty would grant the prayer of the loudest.

". . . And comfort her. If this is the end, let her not be in pain—"

"Wait!" cried Bartholomew.

"Ssshhh. Help us know what's best for her, and agree to do what would give our parents peace of mind—"

Before Simpson could say another word Bartholomew erupted.

"Euthanasia!" he bellowed. "You want her to *die* so you can go to California!"

Simpson raised his hands to his head and raked his fingers back through his hair, massaging his skull and the weary brain throbbing within. The extra-strength aspirins weren't working. Hadn't worked all week.

"You want her dead!"

"No. You keep saying that, Bartholomew. Maybe *you* want her—"

"Silence!"

"Maybe that's why you just sat there on your fat ass while she was lying on the floor unconscious! It's because of you she's here at all. You wore her down, and you still haven't got a job or gotten on SSI. You—."

Then he remembered his mother. Their mother. Simpson looked at her lying there between them.

He leaned in close, trying to listen for her breathing, but all he could hear over Bartholomew's hollering was the rhythmic beeping of the heart rate monitor.

It was pointless to argue anymore.

It's up to you, the eldest son.

Mother, I'm sorry. I tried. It's only getting worse.

He gently withdrew the respirator tube from her mouth, then pulled one of the pillows from beneath her head.

Not registering at first what he was seeing, then too shocked to react, Bartholomew watched him lay the pillow over her face and press down slowly, firmly. At last he cried "No!" and frantically clutched at the pillow to pull it away.

He pounded on Simpson's back and shoulders, screaming, "Help! Stop him! He's killing my mother!"

Simpson pulled back and sat down in the guest chair with the pillow behind him.

That is where he was sitting, looking calm and innocent when a stout, thick-armed nurse opened the door, a glaring no-nonsense disciplinarian.

"*What* is goin' on here? Oh, it's you again."

"He's trying to suffocate my mother!"

"Yeah, it's always somethin', ain't it?"

"Sorry to trouble you, nurse," said Simpson, discreetly twirling a finger around his ear. "He'll be okay. He's just kind of in denial right now."

"He had the pillow over her face and was trying to smother her!"

"Oh, please." The nurse waved Bartholomew aside and replaced the respirator mouthpiece and checked the tubes and monitors.

"Visiting hours over for today, y'all. Gather up your things. Any more outbursts and y'all on probation. We don't have the staff to be babysittin' the babysitters."

She said to Simpson, "Why don't you take him out for some fresh air?"

"And a good shower," added a second nurse, frowning from the doorway.

"Some fresh air far away. Like, Grand Isle or something."

That is when an idea occurred to Simpson.

Alone in his apartment that night, he pondered for a long time about what had to be done. He even prayed. One step at a time. It did not take long to think it through; he had only to decide that he would do what was necessary, and to pray for a blessing upon his decision. He would probably never know for sure whether any blessing was given from above—he would have to have faith—but Mother had given permission when she kept pushing the pillow into his hands. That pillow had become a hard and heavy thing, like marble. She was already dying, in pain despite the morphine, but in her final days Bartholomew was only aggravating her suffering. He who oppresses the weak shall face his own reckoning.

The next day he came early. Bartholomew, a heavy sleeper, was snoring in the reclining guest chair. Simpson stood beside her bed, praying for peace for her spirit, and forgiveness for all the times he was cold and mean to her, even though she had already said all is forgiven. So many times he had let her down. Rare is the son who is truly worthy of his mother's selfless kindness. He hoped with all his heart that he was doing the right thing. This was a way of giving back. What else could he do? The doctors and nurses were not going to give her the one thing she wanted. It's up to you, the eldest son. Someone has to be the responsible grown-up here. Finally, with the door closed, he did as he'd been told.

"I'm sorry," he said, and his tears were absorbed as they fell onto the white cotton pillowcase. "I'm so sorry."

To Simpson's surprise, after the high emotions in the hospital room, at the funeral Bartholomew was more composed than he was. Because he didn't feel as guilty as he should, thought Simpson, heavy with remorse. The services were provided at no charge, just as Gordon

Krebs had promised. Lourdes handled all the arrangements, and although Mr. Krebs was perfectly professional, gracious and consoling and asking no questions, what may have been a sidelong glance at one point caused Simpson to worry whether the undertaker suspected anything. Checking on the burial insurance policy just weeks before a death? But maybe he misread the man's expression; after all, Simpson had told him about his mother's shortness of breath.

Another surprise was that although Bartholomew wept enough to soak several handkerchiefs, his tears flowed quietly—except when Mr. Krebs suggested he come see him if he was still looking for work—while it was Simpson who cried with loud sobs and snorts. The older brother did not often shed tears, but when he did, everyone knew it. He couldn't help it. Bartholomew was mourning a death, but Simpson wept for more than one. She said take care of your brother, and he had given his word.

Simpson blinked and looked around, feeling the hot sun on his arms, his head pounding. It took a few moments to gather his senses and recognize where he was. It felt like a long time had passed since his eyes were open. Someone was calling him. He pulled his leg out from under the cabin door that had crashed down on him when Bartholomew broke free. With a groan, he sat up, disoriented; for a moment it was as though he had forgotten how to sit up straight. His hands were splintered, his upper lip was cut and swollen, and a knot was forming on the back of his head. The harsh sunlight glared from fragments of his broken mirror sunglasses scattered around the pier.

"Let's go. Now! I'm burning up!"

Bartholomew was standing near the rental car parked at the edge of the pier, wild-eyed and drenched with sweat, waving his arms in agitation. "Come on, unlock the car. Take me home!" He pounded on the roof for emphasis.

"Oh hush, it's not that hot."

As he rose to his feet with a groan, still dizzy, Simpson's left ankle felt sprained. Cuts and scrapes on his knees had bled through his trouser legs.

He limped away from the pier to join his brother. As he unlocked the car, he glimpsed the red gas can by the cabin. At first he considered leaving it. Was I really going to—? Was I insane?

As he poured out the gasoline on the white shell road, he recalled again a memory that had come to him while pondering his options at the motel: Bartholomew's bedside vigil in the weeks after the rupture and surgery, reading to him every day after school, humming Sunday school tunes, or simply sitting with him. Somehow, for many long years, Simpson had forgotten that part.

All this time.

I always thought it was *him* I resented; thought it was him I needed to forgive.

The motel room looked much smaller now with Bartholomew in it. Simpson opened the curtains to let light onto the cinderblock walls painted the pale institutional green of an old morgue or mental hospital. Now it felt less like a suicide's room and more a place to recover from electroshock therapy. Bartholomew sat on the edge of the bed, which under his bulk resembled a cot or a footstool, pressing cool washcloths to his face as they were handed to him. He fanned and fluttered his hands before his face, saying "Mercy" and "Lordy," expressions Simpson had previously heard spoken only by their mother. *O my God, he's becoming Melba.* No, please. Then I really am leaving.

Simpson dragged a wooden chair closer to the bed, the legs scraping harshly across the grains of beach sand on the linoleum floor. With the tweezers in his Swiss Army knife he pulled a few splinters from his palms.

"Bartholomew," he began gently.

He reached over to touch his brother's elbow. "Look, I'm sorry. I kept you out there in the cabin 'cause I needed time alone to figure out what to do."

"Thanks a *lot*. I thought I was going to die."

The drugs were wearing off, and his mind was clearing.

"I'm sorry. I wanted to teach you a lesson. I wanted to say, 'This is what it's like to be locked up, you big fat freak. This is what can happen to you if you don't shape up and get your ass on SSI.' Sorry about the harsh methods."

Bartholomew shot him a sharp glare. "You think *I* don't know what it's like to be locked up? You could have *killed* me!"

"I'm sorry. Can you forgive—"

"Why do *I* always have to do the forgiving?" He stomped the hard floor.

This came as a surprise. He thinks he forgives?

"Bartholomew, please . . ."

He was surprised again as he found himself on one knee—*ouch*: kneeling on a scrape or cut pressed the pain into him—and looking up at his brother.

"I'm sorry. And look, once or twice, some of the money I was supposed to put in Mom's mutual fund, I used for myself. Some I put in my own California savings account."

Bartholomew gasped.

"But I paid it all back," he said quickly, "with that money I brought by last month. But I never confessed to her what I'd done. I'm asking you to forgive me, please—for Mom—if you can."

He waited. "Isn't that what Jesus says? 'Forgive us our trespasses' and 'Do unto others'?"

"I can't do his forgiving for him," Bartholomew said irritably, but after a quick glance at his brother's face, beseeching, sincere in his remorse, he conceded, "Okay. We forgive you."

"I'm trying to do some forgiving myself. Bro', why didn't you call me when you found her? You just sat there. From now on, if there's ever an emergency, call 911 right away. Got that? First call 911, then you can pray. Don't just sit there."

Bartholomew was crying. "I didn't know what to do!" He pulled the bedspread to his face and wailed.

Simpson frowned as he watched him bawling.

Bitter though he was, justified as he might be in blaming Bartholomew and harboring a colossal grudge for the rest of his life, he knew that only forgiveness would open the way to healing. One day at a time, moment by moment: drips and drops that form a pool, the cooling waters of forgiveness. He had thought about this many times over the past month. It wasn't enough to daydream his way out to California. First he would have to help Bartholomew get situated—if he didn't rat-poison him first. If he left too soon, everything would go wrong. The monumental grudge would block the light; the weight could crush him. Fifty-five-gallon drums of toxic resentment. Let it dissolve in the cooling waters. If he abandoned his brother, which would amount to deserting his parents, too, then he could spend the rest of his life on the West Coast writing about (or trying to forget) his mortifying guilt at having left behind the only family he had. How rich would that be?

Don't hold it against him.

He means well.

Bartholomew moaned with large undersea whale sounds.

"It's okay, Barto." Simpson put his hand on his back and rubbed him consolingly. "You'll be okay."

He went to the bathroom sink, then handed him another cool washcloth.

"Okay, look up. Dry your eyes. Look at me, Bartholomew. Listen, I promise I'll never do anything to hurt you like that again. That was very wrong of me. I just wanted to teach you a lesson. Now look, Mom's gonna need us to help each other. I've been planning to move you-know-where—and I will eventually, by God I will— but we need to get some things settled first. Now that they're both in heaven, we're going to have to do things different, aren't we, the way Mom and Dad would want us to?"

He touched his brother's arm. "Okay?"

"All right. If you don't *lord* over me. Are you going to move in?"

"God no," Simpson blurted instantly. "Sorry. No, you'll do fine there by yourself. Our plan is to make you more independent. That means we'll need you to get a steady job somewhere, even if it's just part-time. You'll go see Mr. Krebs, and talk to Mr. Levine. They like you, and they want to help. And you have an appointment with Dr. Finestein, right? I can go with you if you want. He'll help us get things set up. I can call him and explain things if you want me to."

"All *right*," Bartholomew said with a familiar tone of aggrieved irritation that was welcome to his brother's ears.

Simpson handed him another washcloth, but Bartholomew pushed it away. "Let's go. I'm cold."

"Oh, with everything happening with Mom I forgot all about your birthday. We can go by McKenzie's and get you a cake if you want. An after-the-fact cake."

"I think we've had enough McKenzie's."

Simpson laughed, and Bartholomew shivered and clasped his arms around himself. "It's cold in here! This air conditioner's *freezing*. Let's go. I'm hungry."

After checking out at the front desk, Simpson drove a short distance, then pulled the car over to the side of Highway 1. He got out and motioned for Bartholomew to come along. Limping on his sprained ankle, he led the way across the scrub grass and dirty sand.

They stood together on the shore and looked out at the brownish waves of the Gulf of Mexico sliding in with a flat and tired listlessness. No Coke bottle–green waves or pristine, sugar-white sands like Pensacola's. Here the beach was a muddy sand, darkened by silt from the Mississippi and Atchafalaya rivers over many millennia and now by occasional globs of crude oil from the offshore drilling platforms. Down toward the state park on the east end was a long wooden pier where several fishermen had cast their lines and seagulls perched along the railings, all facing the Gulf. Closer by, a family had set up a blue and white striped beach umbrella and towels and a little cooler.

A century earlier this barrier island had been a luxurious Creole Riviera for the elites of New Orleans, with fine restaurants and opulent hotels like the Oleander, a resort where Kate Chopin and Lafcadio Hearn came to relax and write and socialize with others of their milieu. In the early 1800s the island was one of Jean Lafitte and his pirates' hideouts, mostly on the landward side among the groves of live oaks bent by the wind toward the mainland. It was said that even today some of the Baratarians' descendants still ran the bait shops and marinas and the famous annual Tarpon Rodeo fishing tournament, though the buildings that had survived through decades of storms gave little indication of the isle's former grandeur.

Simpson looked out over the brown surf out into which Edna Pontellier walked and walked and kept on walking, like Virginia Woolf with her pockets full of stones. There was no need to take that kind of walk, deeper into the ooze. No need for an eel tank, either. He would endure till one clear day he could stand again at Ocean Beach and behold the great Pacific, same as it ever was.

"Hurricane season will be coming," said Bartholomew, shading his eyes as he scanned the horizon. "We need to be ready."

"Right. Let's draw up a list and we can go get the supplies. Candles, batteries."

It was not until later that Simpson would notice that he had not automatically recoiled from his brother's use of the word "we."

They would leave soon. He only wanted to stand here a moment or two, together with his brother, in this place where they used to come as children. It felt like something their parents would be pleased to see, the boys standing side by side like brothers and watching the waves come in.

Part of the reason why he had wanted to come here, and why he lingered now even though the sun was almost overpowering and his hungry brother was anxious to go, was that he worried that if he ever came here again, with Bartholomew or without him, he might find the ground they were standing on washed away, under water.

Be here now. Take a picture you'll remember.

A light sea breeze blew across their faces, and their hair waved in the wind. Slowly, subtly, lest he make him self-conscious, Simpson turned ever so gradually to look at his brother. In the bright sun his strawberry blond hair showed a reddish cast; this color and the shape of his eyebrows and the set of his mouth made him look more like Gasper than Simpson had ever seen before. Once he noticed the likeness he couldn't stop looking at him. Had he ever really looked at his brother before?

"What?" Bartholomew said irritably.

"Nothing. Just thinking. Remember the last time we came here?"

"The summer before Gasper died. Fourteen years ago."

Simpson nodded, holding his hand up to shade his eyes as he scanned the horizon.

As terns and seagulls glided overhead and a pair of shrimp boats cruised westward, someone in a car passing by on Highway 1 might have noticed two figures, one tall and thin and the other tall and rounded, standing side by side near the water's edge, and far out on the hazy horizon the dark shapes of oil drilling platforms. Viewed from an oblique angle, the two figures might be seen as one.

"Barto, I apologize about earlier. That won't happen again."

"All is forgiven. Let's go already. I'm starving and now because of you I'm gonna be sunburned pink."

The white shell crunched under the wheels as Simpson turned the car around to leave the island.

391

"What is *wrong* with this air conditioner?" Bartholomew wiped the sweat from his face and grumbled that it was going to be a long drive home.

Before they had gone a quarter mile, he pointed to a restaurant. "Food! Turn in there!" he drummed urgently on the dashboard. "Mmmm, fried shrimp." He was already salivating. "And crab cakes. Soon our troubles will be over."

"Troubles? What troubles?" Simpson smiled as he turned the wheel. "Either that, or they're just beginning."

ACKNOWLEDGMENTS

The author would like to thank the following professionals, mostly based in New Orleans, who generously shared their expertise: Richard Campanella, Tulane University; Dr. Martin J. Drell, New Orleans Adolescent Hospital; Michael R. Byers, M.D.; Jay Kayser, M.D.; John T. Magill, Williams Research Center, Historic New Orleans Collection; Wayne Spencer, Spencer's Taxidermy Services, Metairie; Jerry Tymphony, Tharp-Sontheimer Funeral Home; and urologists Donald P. Bell, Walter Levy, and Charles Secrest, M.D.

For their helpful readings of the manuscript, in part or entire, and their encouragements, sincere thanks to Christine Wiltz, Christopher Verdesi, Carole McCurdy, Coslough Johnson, Mary Jane Johnson, Caroline Upcher, and, many many times over, to Janet Cameron.

Special thanks to Jacques Barzun for his translation of the epigraph by Pascal, and to Stephen Mitchell for kind permission to quote from his translation of Rilke's "Autumn Day."

SOURCE NOTES TO VERSE AND SCRIPTURE

89   *O Poesy! for thee I hold my pen.* John Keats,
      "Sleep and Poetry" (1817).

102   *Whoever has no house now, will never have one.*
      Rainer Maria Rilke, "Autumn Day," translated
      by Stephen Mitchell, from *The Selected Poetry of
      Rainer Maria Rilke*. New York: Vintage Books,
      1989. Used by kind permission of Stephen
      Mitchell.

105   *O me! O life! of the questions of these recurring . . .*
      Walt Whitman, "O Me! O Life!" from *Leaves
      of Grass* (1892 edition). New York: Boni and
      Liveright, Modern Library, 1921.

106   *The lyf so short, the craft so long to lerne.* Geoffrey
      Chaucer, proem to "The Parlement of Foules"
      (ca. 1382).

122   *Hold yourself ready, therefore, because the Son of
      Man . . .* Matthew 24:44.

130ff. *I am the man that hath seen affliction*, etc.
      Lamentations ch. 3. ¶ *My son, despise not the
      chastening of the Lord . . .* Proverbs 3:11. ¶ *Let
      not your heart be troubled . . .* John 14:2.

176   *Let us be lovers, we'll marry our fortunes together.* Simon & Garfunkel, "America" (*Bookends*, 1966).

189   *West of the fields, west of the fields.* R.E.M., "West of the Fields" (*Murmur*, 1983).

199   Proclamation by the King of the Carnival, 1934 (epigraph to Interlude): from *Mardi Gras: New Orleans*, by Henri Schindler (Flammarion, 1997).

243   *I have no need of friendship; friendship causes pain.* Simon & Garfunkel, "I Am a Rock" (*Sounds of Silence*, 1968).

306   *He gnasheth upon me with his teeth; mine enemy sharpeneth his eyes upon me.* Job 16:9.

357   *I will open your graves.* Ezekiel 37:12.

358   *If thou draw out thy soul to the hungry.* Isaiah 58:10.

360   *The fathers shall eat the sons in the midst of thee.* Ezekiel 5:10.

377   *The maid is not dead, but sleepeth.* Matthew 8:18–24.

ABOUT THE AUTHOR

Mark LaFlaur grew up in the South, mostly in Louisiana. He earned an MFA degree at Louisiana State University, where he worked on the literary magazine *Exquisite Corpse*. His writings have been published in the *Village Voice*, *San Francisco Chronicle*, *Los Angeles Times Book Review*, and *Boston Review*, and about a hundred articles have appeared in encyclopedias and trade books published by Macmillan, Oxford University Press, etc. He has worked in book publishing in New York and San Francisco and as a freelance writer and editor in New Orleans, where he wrote *Elysian Fields*. He moved to New York in 2001. After Hurricane Katrina in 2005 he founded *Levees Not War*, a New York–based, New Orleans–dedicated blog focusing on infrastructure, the environment, and progressive politics. He and his wife, Janet, live in Kew Gardens, New York, where he is at work on a new novel.

CPSIA information can be obtained
at www.ICGtesting.com
Printed in the USA
LVOW12s1324201017
553165LV00001B/1/P